Mull
Mull, Brandon,
ablehaven. Grip of the shadow plague

19.99

FABLEHAVEN
GRIP OF THE SHADOW PLAGUE

THE PENDULUM SWINGS BETWEEN
LIGHT AND DARKNESS

FABLEHAVEN

GRIP OF THE SHADOW PLAGUE

BRANDON MULL

ILLUSTRATED BY
BRANDON DORMAN

SHADOW
MOUNTAIN

✻ ✻ ✻

*For Cy, Marge, John, and Gladys, who prove that
grandparents can be friends and heroes.*

© 2008 Creative Concepts, LC

Visit us at ShadowMountain.com

Library of Congress Cataloging-in-Publication Data
Mull, Brandon, 1974–
  Fablehaven : Grip of the Shadow Plague / Brandon Mull.
    p. cm.
  Summary: When Kendra and Seth go to stay at their grandparents' estate, they discover that it is a sanctuary for magical creatures and that a battle between good and evil is looming.
  ISBN-13 978-1-59038-898-3 (hardbound : alk. paper)
  [1. Magic—Fiction.   2. Grandparents—Fiction.   3. Brothers and sisters—Fiction.]   I. Title.
PZ7.M9112Fa   2006
[Fic]—dc22   2006000911

Printed in the United States of America
Publishers Printing

10   9   8

Contents

CHAPTER ONE

Nipsies

O n a muggy August day, Seth hurried along a faint path, eyes scanning the lush foliage to his left. Tall, mossy trees overshadowed a verdant sea of bushes and ferns. He felt damp all over—the humidity refused to let his sweat dry. Seth checked over his shoulder periodically and started at any sound in the undergrowth. Not only was Fablehaven a dangerous place to roam alone, he was terrified of getting spotted so far from the yard.

His skill at sneaking into the woods had improved over the long summer. The excursions with Coulter were fun, but not frequent enough to satisfy his appetite for adventure. There was something special about venturing out onto the preserve alone. He had become familiar with the woods surrounding the main house, and despite the concerns of his grandparents, he had proven to himself that he could explore safely. In order to avoid deadly situations, he rarely strayed far from the yard, and he avoided the areas he knew to be most perilous.

Today was an exception.

Today he was following directions to a secret meeting.

Although Seth felt certain he had interpreted the instructions correctly, he was beginning to fret that he had somehow overlooked the final marker. The trail he currently trod was one he had never roamed before, quite a distance from the main house. He remained intent on the shrubs along the left side of the path.

Many people had come and gone from Fablehaven over the summer. At breakfast, Grandpa Sorenson had notified Seth, Kendra, Coulter, and Dale that Warren and Tanu would be returning home that evening. Seth was excited for a reunion with his friends, but knew that the more people who were at the house, the more eyes would be watching to impede his unauthorized expeditions. Today was probably the last time he would be able to slip out on his own for a while.

Just as he was losing faith, Seth observed a stick topped by a large pinecone planted in the ground not far from the path. He should not have worried about missing it—the tall marker was unmistakable. Standing beside the stick, Seth took his compass from his emergency kit, found northeast, and set off on a heading not quite perpendicular to the meager trail.

The ground sloped mildly upward. He swerved to avoid

some thorny, flowering plants. Birds twittered in the leafy branches overhead. A butterfly with wide, vibrant wings bobbed on the breezeless air. Because of the milk he had drunk that morning, Seth knew it was actually a butterfly. Had it been a fairy, he would have recognized it as such.

"Pssst," a voice hissed from the bushes off to one side, "over here."

Seth swiveled and saw Doren, the satyr, peering over a glossy shrub with broad leaves. The satyr motioned him over.

"Hey, Doren," Seth said in a low voice, trotting over to where the satyr crouched. He found Newel hiding there as well, his horns somewhat longer, his skin slightly more freckled, and his hair a bit redder than Doren's.

"What about the brute?" Newel asked.

"He promised to meet me here," Seth assured them. "Mendigo is covering his chores at the stables."

"If he doesn't show, the deal is off," Newel threatened.

"He'll be here," Seth said.

"Did you bring the merchandise?" Doren asked, trying to sound casual, but unable to hide the desperation in his gaze.

"Forty-eight size C batteries," Seth said. He unzipped a duffel bag and let the satyrs inspect the contents. Earlier in the summer, Seth had given the pair dozens of batteries as a reward for helping him and his sister sneak into his grandfather's home under dire circumstances. The satyrs had already depleted their bounty watching their portable television.

"Look at them, Doren," Newel breathed.

"Hours upon hours of entertainment," Doren muttered reverently.

"The sports alone!" Newel cried.

"Dramas, sitcoms, cartoons, soap operas, talk shows, game shows, reality shows," Doren listed lovingly.

"So many lovely ladies," Newel purred.

"Even the commercials are amazing," Doren enthused. "So many technological marvels!"

"Stan would flip out if he knew," Newel murmured gleefully.

Seth understood that Newel was right. His Grandpa Sorenson worked hard to limit the amount of technology on the preserve. He wanted to keep the magical creatures of Fablehaven unspoiled by modern influences. He did not even have a television in his own home.

"So where is the gold?" Seth asked.

"Not far ahead," Newel said.

"Gold has become harder to find since Nero moved his hoard," Doren apologized.

"Accessible gold," Newel amended. "We know about plenty of treasure hidden around Fablehaven."

"Most of it is cursed or guarded," Doren explained. "For example, we know a wonderful nest of jewels stowed in a pit under a boulder, if you don't mind chronic flesh-eating infections."

"And a priceless collection of gilded weapons in an armory protected by a vengeful family of ogres," Newel added.

"But up ahead there's lots of gold with almost no strings attached," Doren promised.

"I still think I should get paid extra since you need my help collecting it," Seth complained.

"Now, Seth, don't be ungrateful," Newel chided. "We set a price. You agreed. Fair is fair. You don't have to help us retrieve the gold. We can just call the whole thing off."

Seth looked from one goatman to the other. Sighing, he zipped up the duffel bag. "Maybe you're right. This feels too risky."

"Or we could up your commission by twenty percent," Newel blurted, placing a hairy hand on the bag.

"Thirty," Seth said flatly.

"Twenty-five," Newel countered.

Seth unzipped the bag again.

Doren clapped his hands and stamped his hooves. "I love happy endings."

"It isn't over until I have the gold," Seth reminded them. "You're sure this treasure will truly be mine? No angry trolls will come to claim it?"

"No curses," Newel said.

"No powerful beings seeking retribution," Doren asserted.

Seth folded his arms. "Then why do you need my help?"

"This stash used to be free money," Newel said. "The easiest payday at Fablehaven. With the help of your over-sized bodyguard, it can be a bargain again."

"Hugo won't have to hurt anybody," Seth confirmed.

"Relax," Newel said. "We've been over this. The golem won't need to harm a fly."

Doren held up a hand. "I hear somebody coming." Seth heard nothing. Newel sniffed the air.

"It's the golem," Newel reported.

Several moments later, Seth detected the heavy footfalls of Hugo's approach. Before long, the golem crashed into view, crunching through the undergrowth. An apelike figure fashioned out of soil, clay, and stone, Hugo had a thick build and disproportionately large hands and feet. Currently one arm was somewhat smaller than the other. Hugo had lost an arm in a battle with Olloch the Glutton, and despite frequent mud baths, the limb had not quite finished re-forming.

The golem came to a stop towering above Seth and the satyrs, who barely reached his massive chest. "Set," the golem intoned in a deep voice that sounded like huge stones grinding together.

"Hi, Hugo," Seth replied. The golem had only recently begun attempting simple words. He understood everything anyone told him, but rarely sought to express himself verbally.

"Good to see you, big guy," Doren said brightly with a wave and a broad smile.

"Will he cooperate?" Newel asked out the side of his mouth.

"Hugo doesn't have to obey me," Seth said. "I don't officially control him like Grandma and Grandpa do. But he's learning to make his own decisions. We've done some private adventuring together over the summer. He'll usually go along with whatever I suggest."

"Fair enough," Doren said. He clapped his hands together and rubbed them briskly. "Newel, my fellow gold digger, we may be back in business."

"Will you finally explain what we're doing?" Seth begged.

"Have you ever heard of the nipsies?" Newel asked.

Seth shook his head.

"Tiny little critters," Doren elaborated, "smallest of the fairy folk." The satyrs watched Seth expectantly.

Seth shook his head again.

"They're most closely related to brownies, but stand at only a fraction of the height," Newel said. "As you know, brownies are experts at mending, salvaging, and inventively recycling. Nipsies are also master artisans, but they tend to start from scratch, tapping into natural resources to acquire raw materials."

Doren leaned close to Seth and spoke confidentially. "Nipsies have a fascination with shiny metals and stones, and a knack for finding them."

Newel winked.

Seth crossed his arms. "What will stop them from taking their treasure back?"

Newel and Doren burst out laughing. Seth frowned. Newel placed a hand on his shoulder. "Seth, a nipsie is about this big." Newel held his thumb and forefinger half an inch apart. Doren snorted as he tried to resist further laughter. "They can't fly, and they have no magic to attack or harm."

"In that case, I still don't see why you need my help getting the gold," Seth maintained.

The chuckling subsided. "What nipsies *can* do is prepare traps and plant dangerous vegetation," Doren said. "The little nippers apparently took umbrage at the tributes Newel and I demanded, so they erected defenses to keep us away. Hugo here should have no trouble getting us into their domain."

Seth narrowed his eyes. "Why don't the nipsies get help from Grandpa?"

"No offense," Newel said, "but many creatures at Fablehaven would endure considerable hardship to avoid human interference. Don't worry about the pipsqueaks appealing to Stan—he won't hear about this from them. What do you say? Shall we grab some easy gold?"

"Lead the way," Seth said. He turned to the golem. "Hugo, are you willing to help us visit the nipsies?"

Hugo held up an earthen hand, the thumb and forefinger almost touching. He gave a slight nod.

They tramped forward through the undergrowth until Newel raised a cautionary fist. From the edge of a clearing, Seth saw a wide meadow with a grassy hill in the middle. The sides of the hill were steep, but ended abruptly about twenty feet above the ground, as if the top were flat. "We'll need Hugo to get us into the hill," Newel whispered.

"Would you?" Seth asked the golem.

Hugo effortlessly placed Newel on one shoulder, Doren on the other, and cradled Seth in his larger arm. The golem set off across the meadow, crossing to the hill with long strides. Near the base of the hill, the weeds at Hugo's feet began to writhe and snap. Seth saw thorny vines curling around the golem's ankles, and the green heads of carnivorous plants striking at his shins.

"Part of the problem right there," Doren pointed out. "The little nippers cultivated all sorts of venomous plants around the outskirts of their territory."

"Underhanded vermin," Newel grumbled. "I was limping for a week."

"We were lucky to get away with our skins," Doren said. "We need to reach the other side of the hill."

"The slopes of the hill are full of traps," Newel explained. "A sealed entrance awaits on the far side."

"Take us around the hill, Hugo," Seth said.

The aggressive plants continued lashing and squirming and biting, but Hugo strode forward heedless of the onslaught. On the far side of the hill, they found an irregular boulder as tall as a man embedded at the base of the slope. A gooey mass of yellow slime pooled around the stone.

"Have Hugo shove the stone aside," Doren suggested.

"You heard him," Seth said.

Hugo stepped onto the slick slime, which slurped against his huge feet. With his free hand, Hugo thrust the boulder aside as if it were made of papier-mâché, revealing the mouth of a tunnel.

"Put us down in the entrance," Newel said.

"And then keep the slime at bay," Doren added.

"Do it, please," Seth implored.

Hugo placed Seth at the entrance to the tunnel, then

set the satyrs beside him. The golem turned and began kicking away the slime, which splashed through the air in sticky globs and strands.

"He comes in handy," Newel acknowledged, nodding toward Hugo.

"We need to get one for ourselves," Doren agreed.

Seth stared at the walls of the tunnel. They were made of polished white stone with veins of blue and green. Intricate carvings etched the entire surface from floor to ceiling. Seth traced a finger over the elaborate designs.

"Not too shabby," Newel commented.

Seth stepped back from the wall. "I can't believe all the detail."

"Wait until you see the Seven Kingdoms," Doren said.

The three of them proceeded along the short tunnel. The roof was just high enough that none of them needed to crouch.

"Watch your step," Newel said. "Take care not to crush a nipsie. Their lives are just as real and valuable as anyone's. If you accidentally kill a nipsie, the protections of the foundational treaty of Fablehaven will no longer be yours."

"He's just saying that because of the time he stepped on a supply wagon and knocked the driver senseless," Doren confided.

"He made a full recovery," Newel replied stiffly.

"I don't see any nipsies here in the tunnel," Doren reported after bending down to study the smooth marble floor.

"Then tread lightly at the far side," Newel recommended.

When Seth emerged from the far end of the tunnel, he unexpectedly stepped out into the sunlight. There was no top to the hill—the entire center had been excavated, leaving the slopes to form a circular wall around a unique community. "Look at that," Seth mumbled.

The entire area inside the hill was landscaped in miniature, bristling with tiny castles, mansions, factories, warehouses, shops, mills, theaters, arenas, and bridges. The architecture was complex and varied, incorporating soaring spires, swooping rooftops, spiraling towers, fragile arches, cartoonish chimneys, colorful canopies, columned walkways, multi-tiered gardens, and glistening domes. The nipsies constructed with the finest wood and stone, adding a gleam to many of their fanciful structures with precious metals and gemstones. Radiating out from a central pond, an elaborate irrigation system comprised of canals, aqueducts, ponds, and dams connected seven sprawling communities of dense habitations.

"Feast your eyes on the Seven Kingdoms of the nipsies," Newel said.

"See that squarish building there?" Doren asked, pointing. "The one with the pillars and the statues out front? That's the royal treasury of the Third Kingdom. Not a bad place to begin if they fail to cooperate."

Among the splendid edifices of the Seven Kingdoms, the tallest of which barely reached the height of Seth's knees, scurried thousands of minuscule people. At first glance they looked like insects. After rummaging through his emergency kit, Seth crouched near the mouth of the engraved tunnel where a crew of nipsies had been digging and peered at the undersized workers through a magnifying glass. They wore dapper clothing and, despite falling short of half an inch, looked just like humans. The group Seth was watching made animated gestures in his direction as they scurried away. Tiny bells started ringing, and many of the nipsies began to flee indoors or into holes in the ground.

"They're scared of us," Seth said.

"They'd better be," Newel blustered. "We're their supreme gigantic overlords, and they tried to lock us out with predatory plants and carnivorous slime."

"Look there, by the reflecting pool," Doren mourned, extending a hand. "They tore down our statues!"

Remarkable likenesses of Newel and Doren, each over a foot tall, lay toppled and defaced near vacant grandstands.

"Somebody has gotten much too big for their britches," Newel growled. "Who has desecrated the Monument to the Overlords?"

Pandemonium continued in the bustling streets. Frantic crowds pressed to get indoors. Dozens of nipsies recklessly descended the scaffolding of a building under construction. Nipsies armed with diminutive weapons congregated on the roof of the royal treasury.

"I see a delegation gathering around the horn," Doren said, motioning at an eighteen-inch tower topped by a large, pearl-colored megaphone.

Newel winked at Seth. "Time to open negotiations."

"Are you sure this is right?" Seth asked. "Taking from these little guys?"

Doren slapped Seth on the back. "Nipsies live to sniff out pockets of ore. Our taking some of their stored wealth gives them something to do!"

"Hail, Newel and Doren," a tiny voice chimed. Even magnified by the megaphone, it was squeaky and hard to hear. Stepping carefully, Seth and the satyrs leaned in closer. "We, the nipsies of the Third Kingdom, are overjoyed at your long-awaited return."

"Overjoyed, are you?" Newel said. "Poisonous plants were not exactly the welcome we expected."

The nipsies on the tower conferred together before answering. "We regret if the defenses we erected of late have proven problematic. We felt an increase in security was warranted due to the unsavory character of certain potential pillagers."

"Little nipper almost makes it sound like he's not talking about us," Doren murmured.

"They're none too shabby when it comes to diplomacy," Newel agreed. He raised his voice. "I noticed that our monuments have fallen into disrepair. Our tribute is long overdue."

Again the delegation on the tower huddled before responding. "We regret any lack of appreciation you may perceive," a voice squeaked. "You arrive in a desperate season. As you know, since time out of mind, the Seven Kingdoms of the nipsies have dwelt in peace and prosperity, interrupted only by the abusive solicitations of certain gigantic outlanders. But dark times have befallen us of late. The Sixth and Seventh Kingdoms have united in war against the rest of us. They recently decimated the Fourth Kingdom. We and the Second Kingdom are harboring thousands of refugees. The Fifth Kingdom is under siege. In the First Kingdom there is talk of retreat, a mass exodus to a new homeland.

"As you are aware, we nipsies have never been a warlike people. It is plain that a sinister influence has overcome the citizens of the Sixth and Seventh Kingdoms. We fear they will not be satisfied until they have conquered us all. As we speak, their navy sails toward our shores. If you simultaneously attack our community from the rear, I fear the Seven Kingdoms may fall into darkness. However, if you lend us aid in this tragic hour, we will gladly reward you handsomely."

"Allow us a moment to deliberate," Newel said, pulling Doren and Seth in close. "You think this is a trick? What the nipsies lack in size, they often make up for in guile."

"I see a large fleet of black ships, there in the central pool," Doren said. Although the biggest ships were no larger than Seth's shoes, there were dozens of them approaching.

"Aye," Newel said. "And look off to the left. The Fourth Kingdom does appear to be in ruins."

"But who ever heard of nipsies at war?" Doren questioned.

"We'd better have a chat with the Seventh Kingdom," Newel resolved. "Hear their version of things."

"We will return," Doren declared to the nipsies on the tower. He and Newel began walking away.

"Who are you?" the voice chirped from the megaphone. "The one without horns."

"Me?" Seth asked, placing a hand against his chest. "I'm Seth."

"O wise and prudent Seth," the voice resumed, "please prevail on the goat giants to come to our aid. Do not allow the wicked elders of the traitorous kingdoms to seduce them."

"I'll see what I can do," Seth said, hurrying after Newel and Doren, watching the ground carefully to avoid flattening any nipsies. He caught up to the satyrs outside of a walled kingdom built of black stone and flying sable banners. The streets of the kingdom were virtually empty. Many of the nipsies in view wore armor and bore weapons. This kingdom had a tower with a megaphone as well.

"The wall is new," Doren remarked.

"And I don't recall everything looking so black," Newel said.

"They really do appear more warlike," Doren conceded.

"Here they come up the tower," Newel observed, nodding toward the black megaphone.

"Greetings, worthy overlords," a voice squealed. "You have returned in time to witness the culmination of our labors and to share in the spoils."

"Why are you waging war with the other kingdoms?" Newel asked.

"You have yourselves to thank," the speaker answered. "The Seven Kingdoms sent out many parties in search of methods for preventing your return. No party ventured farther than mine. We learned much. Our vision expanded. While the other kingdoms constructed defenses, we quietly rallied support within the Sixth and Seventh Kingdoms and developed engines of war. After all, as you have long known, why *make* when you can *take?*"

Newel and Doren shared an uneasy glance.

"What would you have us do?" Doren asked.

"Victory is already inevitable, but if you help hasten our hour of triumph, we will reward you far more generously than any of the other kingdoms. Most of our riches are below ground, a secret they would never share. Surely the others have solicited your aid in stopping us. Such action would prove disastrous to you. We are in allegiance with a new master who will one day rule all. Stand against us, and you stand against him. All who defy him must perish. Join us. Avoid the wrath of our master, and reap the handsomest reward."

"Can I borrow your lens?" Doren asked.

Seth handed the satyr his magnifying glass. Doren stepped over the city wall into a vacant square, squatted, and examined the figures on the tower. "You two will want to have a look," he advised soberly.

Doren moved out of the way, and Newel took a long look through the magnifying glass, followed by Seth. The tiny men on the tower looked different from the others Seth had seen. Their skin was gray, their eyes bloodred, and their mouths fanged.

"What has happened to your countenances?" Newel asked.

"Our true form revealed," the voice responded from the megaphone. "This is how we look with all illusion stripped away."

"They've been corrupted somehow," Doren hissed.

"You won't actually help them?" Seth said.

Newel shook his head. "No. But it may not be wise to resist them either. Perhaps we should avoid involvement." He looked to Doren. "We do have an appointment elsewhere shortly."

"That's right," Doren said, "I had almost forgotten our other engagement. We don't want to disappoint the, uh, hamadryads. Can't afford to get behind schedule. We'd better head out."

"You don't have an appointment," Seth accused. "We can't just abandon the good nipsies to be destroyed."

"If you're so big on heroism," Newel said, "you go stop the navy."

"My job was to get us in here," Seth replied. "If you want batteries, you need to earn the gold yourself."

"He has a point," Doren admitted.

"We don't need to earn anything," Newel asserted. "We can go take what we need from the Third Kingdom treasury and be gone."

"No way," Seth said, shaking an upraised hand. "I won't accept stolen payment. Not after what happened with Nero. The Third Kingdom offered an honest reward if you help them. You were the one telling me the nipsies can't harm us. Is that any different just because some turned evil? Tell you what, I'll even waive my extra twenty-five percent."

"Hmmm." Newel rubbed his chin.

"Think of all the shows," Doren urged.

"Very well," Newel said. "I'd hate to see this little civilization ruined. But don't blame me if the eerie nipsies and their nefarious masters come hunting us down."

"You'll regret this," the hostile nipsies cried through the megaphone.

"Will I?" Newel asked, kicking a hoof through the city wall. He ripped the megaphone off the tower and threw it over the side of the excavated hill.

"I'll go stop the siege of the Fifth Kingdom," Doren offered.

"You stay put," Newel ordered. "No need to give them a score to settle with both of us."

"They really got under your skin," Doren chuckled. "What are they going to do?"

"There is a dark influence at work here," Newel said grimly. "But if I'm going to defy them at all, I may as well finish the job." He tore up the roof of a solid-looking building and scooped out a handful of minute gold ingots, dumping them into a pouch he wore at his waist. "Here's a lesson for you," Newel said, reaching into the treasure house a second time. "Don't try to threaten the supreme gigantic overlords. We do as we please."

Newel strode off into the pond, which was never any deeper than his furry shins. He rounded up the flotilla of ships and began carrying them back to the Seventh Kingdom, snapping off the masts and scattering the vessels around the city.

"Careful not to kill any of them," Doren cautioned.

"I'm being careful," Newel replied, sloshing through the pond, sending ripples of water crashing into the fragile docks. When he had dumped the final ships in an empty marketplace, Newel crossed to the Fifth Kingdom and began smashing the little siege engines and catapults that were attacking fortified locations around the city, including the principal castle.

Seth watched the proceedings with undivided interest. In a way, it was like witnessing a spoiled child destroying his toys. And yet when he looked more closely, he beheld the numerous lives the satyr's actions were affecting. From the perspective of the nipsies, a thousand-foot giant was thundering through their world, changing the course of a desperate war in a matter of minutes.

Newel scooped hundreds of attacking troops out of the Fifth Kingdom and placed them in the Seventh. Then he demolished several of the bridges that gave the Sixth Kingdom access to the Fifth. He stole several golden decorations from the proud towers in the Sixth Kingdom and systematically tore down their defenses. In the end, Newel returned to the tower of the Seventh Kingdom where the megaphone had been.

"Be warned—cease to make war, or I will return. Next time I will not leave so much of your kingdoms intact." Newel turned to face Doren and Seth. "Come on."

The three of them walked over to the Third Kingdom, near the engraved tunnel that led back to Hugo. "We have done what we can to halt your war," Newel declared.

"All hail the supreme gigantic overlords!" a small voice called through the pearly megaphone. "Today will ever be a holiday to honor your gallantry. We will raise and refurbish your monuments to unsurpassed splendor. Please take what you wish from the royal treasury."

"Don't mind if I do," Newel said, prying open the wall and scooping out infinitesimal gold, silver, and platinum coins along with some relatively large gemstones. "You nipsies keep your guard up. Something is grievously wrong with your cohorts over in Kingdoms Six and Seven."

"Long live Newel!" the squeaky voice approved. "Long live Doren! Long live Seth! Wise counsel from our heroic protectors!"

"Looks like we're done here for now," Doren said.

"Nice job," Seth said, clapping Newel on the back.

"Not a bad day's work," Newel sniffed, patting his bulging pouches. "Several kingdoms saved, a couple of kingdoms humbled, and a treasure won. Let's go weigh our loot. We've got shows to catch."

CHAPTER TWO

Reunion

F or Kendra Sorenson, there was no such thing as total
darkness anymore. She sat in a chilly hall in the dungeon underneath the main house at Fablehaven, her back
to a stone wall, her knees drawn up to her chest. She was
facing a large cabinet with gold trim, the sort of cabinet a
magician would use to make an assistant disappear. Despite
the absence of light, she could make out the contours of the
Quiet Box without difficulty. The hall was dim, the colors
muted, but unlike even the goblin wardens who patrolled
the dungeon, she needed no candle or torch to navigate the
gloomy corridors. Her heightened vision was one of many
consequences of her having become fairykind the previous
summer.

Kendra knew that Vanessa Santoro waited inside the

box. Part of Kendra desperately wanted to speak with her former friend, even though Vanessa had betrayed the family and almost gotten them killed. Her desire to communicate with Vanessa had little to do with nostalgic feelings about the conversations they had shared. Kendra yearned for clarifications about the final note Vanessa had scribbled on the floor of her cell prior to being sentenced to the Quiet Box.

Upon discovering the note Vanessa had left, Kendra had immediately shared it with her grandparents. Grandpa Sorenson had scowled down at the glowing letters by the ghostly light of an umite candle for several minutes, weighing the unsettling accusations left by a desperate traitor. Kendra still recalled his initial verdict:

"This is either the most disturbing truth I have ever encountered, or the most brilliant lie."

Nearly two months later, they were no closer to either verifying or disproving the message. If the message were true, the Sphinx, the greatest ally of the caretakers, was actually their archenemy in disguise. The message accused him of using his intimate association with the protectors of the magical preserves to further the sinister schemes of the Society of the Evening Star.

Alternatively, if the message were false, Vanessa was vilifying the most powerful friend of the caretakers in order to create internal dissension and provide a reason for her captors to release her from her imprisonment in the Quiet Box. Without outside assistance, she would remain trapped inside the Quiet Box in a suspended state until someone else took her place. Potentially, she could wait there standing upright in black silence for centuries.

Kendra rubbed her shins. Without another person to take Vanessa's place temporarily, releasing her one-time friend from the Quiet Box for a brief conversation would be impossible. Not to mention the concern that Vanessa was a narcoblix. Over the summer, before she was unmasked, Vanessa had bitten nearly everybody at Fablehaven. As a result, once outside of the Quiet Box, she could control any of them whenever they were asleep.

Kendra would have to wait for a chat with Vanessa until everyone else agreed. Who knew how long that might take! The last time they had discussed the subject, nobody had been in favor of giving Vanessa a chance to further explain herself. Under a strict vow of secrecy, Grandpa and Grandma had shared the troubling message with Warren, Tanu, Coulter, Dale, and Seth. They had all taken measures to investigate the truthfulness of the note on the floor. Hopefully tonight, with Tanu and Warren returning from missions, they would have better information. If not, might the others finally conclude that the time had come to hear what else Vanessa had to say? The narcoblix had tantalized them by hinting that she knew more than she had revealed in her note. Kendra felt convinced that Vanessa could shed more light on the subject. She resolved that once again she would argue in favor of hearing more from Vanessa.

A flickering light danced at the end of the hall. Slaggo rounded a corner. The creepy goblin carried a crusty bucket in one hand while clutching a guttering torch in the other.

"Skulking in the dungeon again?" he called to Kendra, paus-ing. "We can put you to work. The pay is unbeatable. You like raw hen flesh?"

"I'd hate to barge in on your fun," Kendra snapped. She had not been very polite to Slaggo or Voorsh ever since they had almost fed her to her captive grandparents.

Slaggo leered. "You'd think they locked your favorite pet in the Box, the way you sulk."

"I'm not pining for her," Kendra corrected. "I'm think-ing."

He took a deep breath, surveying the hall smugly. "Hard to picture more inspiring surroundings," he admitted. "Nothing like the futile moans of the condemned to set your wheels turning."

The goblin proceeded forward, licking his lips. He was short, bony, and greenish, with beady eyes and bat-wing ears. He had looked much more fearsome when Kendra was temporarily seven inches tall.

Instead of passing her, he halted again, this time gaz-ing at the Quiet Box. "I'd like to know who was in there before," he murmured, almost to himself. "I've wondered every day for decades . . . now I'll never know."

The Quiet Box had contained the same secret prisoner ever since it had been brought to Fablehaven, until the Sphinx had swapped Vanessa for the mysterious occupant. The Sphinx had insisted that only in the Quiet Box would Vanessa be unable to use her ability to control others in their sleep. If Vanessa's final message were true, and the Sphinx was evil, he had probably released an ancient and powerful collaborator. If the message were false, the Sphinx was merely relocating the prisoner to a new place of confinement. None of them had seen the identity of the secret captive, only a chained figure whose head was hidden by a coarse burlap sack.

"I wouldn't mind knowing his identity either," Kendra said.

"I got a whiff of him, you know," Slaggo said casually, giving Kendra a sidelong glance. "I lay low in the shadows as the Sphinx walked him by." He was clearly proud of the fact.

"Could you tell anything about him?" Kendra asked, taking the bait.

"I've always had a reliable sniffer," Slaggo said, wiping his nostrils with his forearm and rocking back on his heels. "Definitely a male. Something odd about the scent, uncommon, hard to place. Not entirely human, if I were to guess."

"Interesting," Kendra said.

"Wish I could have gotten a closer smell," Slaggo lamented. "I would have tried, but the Sphinx is not a man to trifle with."

"What do you know about the Sphinx?"

Slaggo shrugged. "Same as anyone. He's supposed to be wise and powerful. He smells exactly like a man. If he's something else, he hides it perfectly. Man or not, he's very old. He carries the scent of another age."

Slaggo of course knew nothing about the note. "He seems like a good person," Kendra said.

Slaggo shrugged. "Can I offer you some glop?" He swung the bucket in front of her.

"I'll pass," Kendra said, trying not to inhale the putrid stench.

"Fresh off the fire," he said. She shook her head, and he strolled away. "Enjoy the darkness."

Kendra almost smiled. Slaggo had no idea how well she could see without light. He probably thought she adored sitting alone in the dark. Which meant he thought she was his kind of girl. Of course, she *had* made a habit of spending time alone in a dungeon, so maybe he wasn't far off.

When the goblin was out of sight and the orange flicker of his torch had dwindled, Kendra arose and placed a palm against the smooth wood of the Quiet Box. Despite the fact that Vanessa had betrayed them, despite the reality that she was a proven liar, despite her obvious motivation for pretending to possess valuable information, Kendra believed the message on the floor, and she longed to know more.

※ ※ ※

Seth arrived at the dinner table wearing his best poker face. Coulter, the magical relics expert, had cooked meat loaf, with baked potatoes, broccoli, and fresh rolls on the side. Everyone was already seated—Grandpa, Grandma, Dale, Coulter, and Kendra.

"Tanu and Warren haven't shown up yet?" Seth asked.

"They called a few minutes ago," Grandpa said, holding up his new cell phone. "Tanu's plane got in late. They're grabbing food on the road. They should arrive in about an hour."

Seth nodded. The afternoon had ended profitably. He had already tucked away his share of the gold in the attic bedroom he shared with Kendra, the leather pouch containing the treasure bundled in a pair of athletic shorts at the bottom of one of his drawers. He still found it hard to believe he had stashed the gold before anybody could sabotage his success. All he had to do now was play it cool.

He wondered how much the gold was worth. Probably a few hundred thousand at least. Not bad for a not-yet-thirteen-year-old.

The one complication was the nipsies. Surely, as caretaker, Grandpa Sorenson knew of their existence. Seth was pretty sure Grandpa Sorenson would want an update on what had happened to them so he could investigate further. Who was the evil master the warlike nipsies had mentioned? Could it be the Sphinx? There were any number of shady candidates at Fablehaven. Despite the action Newel had taken to prevent the scary nipsies from defeating the nice ones, Seth felt certain that the conflict was not over. If he did nothing, the good nipsies could be wiped out.

Still, Seth hesitated. If he spilled what he had learned about the nipsies, Grandpa would know he had been venturing into prohibited areas of Fablehaven. Not only would he get privileges revoked, he would almost certainly have to return the gold. It made Seth shrivel inside to think of how disappointed everyone would be in him.

There was a chance Grandpa would discover what was

wrong with the nipsies as part of his routine duties watching over the preserve. But considering the defenses the nipsies had erected, Grandpa might not have any plans to visit them in the near future. Would he find out what was going on in time to prevent a tragedy? Ever since Kendra had discovered the final note from Vanessa, everyone had been so preoccupied by events outside of Fablehaven that Seth doubted whether anyone would check up on the nipsies for a long while. There was even a chance that Grandpa knew nothing about them.

"We'll still meet tonight to discuss what Tanu and Warren have discovered, right?" Kendra sounded concerned.

"Of course," Grandma said, spooning broccoli onto her plate.

"Do we know if they had much success?" Kendra asked.

"All I know is that Tanu failed to find Maddox," Grandpa said, referring to the fairy dealer who had ventured onto the fallen Brazilian preserve. "And Warren has done some serious traveling. I refuse to risk talking about the details of our secret concern on the telephone."

Seth added some ketchup to his meat loaf and took a bite. It was almost too hot, but tasted great. "What about my folks?" Seth asked. "Are they still pressuring you to send us home?"

"We're running out of excuses to stretch your stay much longer," Grandma said, giving Grandpa a worried glance. "School begins in just a couple of weeks."

"We can't go home!" Kendra exclaimed. "Especially not until we prove whether the Sphinx is innocent. The Society knows where we live, and they're not afraid to approach us there."

"I wholeheartedly agree," Grandpa said. "The problem remains how to persuade your parents."

Kendra and Seth had been at Fablehaven the entire summer under the pretense of helping to care for their injured grandfather. He really had been injured when they had first arrived, but the artifact they had collected from the inverted tower had healed him. The original plan had been for Kendra and Seth to stay for a couple of weeks. Grandma and Grandpa had managed to extend that to over a month through telephone conversations—Kendra and Seth kept reporting how much fun they were having, and Grandma and Grandpa emphasized how helpful they were being.

After a month, Grandpa could tell that his son and daughter-in-law were truly getting impatient, so he invited them to visit for a week. Grandma and Grandpa had decided that the best solution would be to help them discover the truth about Fablehaven, so they could all openly discuss the danger that Kendra and Seth were in. But no matter how many clues they left or hints they offered, Scott and Marla refused to catch on. In the end, Tanu had fixed them a tea that left them open to suggestion, and Grandpa, wearing a phony cast, had secured another month for the kids to visit. Yet once again, their time was almost up.

"Tanu is coming back," Seth reminded them. "Maybe he can slip Dad some more of that tea."

"We need to get beyond temporary remedies," Grandma said. "The current threats could persist for years. Perhaps the Society of the Evening Star has lost interest in you now that the artifact is no longer at Fablehaven. But my instincts tell me otherwise."

"As do mine," Grandpa agreed, giving Kendra a significant stare.

"Can we force Mom and Dad to see through the illusion hiding the creatures here?" Kendra asked. "Just give them milk and point them toward the fairies? Take them into the barn to see Viola?"

Grandpa shook his head. "I'm not sure. Total unbelief is a powerful inhibitor. It can blind an individual to obvious truths, no matter what others do or say."

"The milk wouldn't work on them?" Seth asked.

"It might not," Grandpa said. "That is part of the reason I let people discover the secrets of Fablehaven through finding clues. First off, it gives them a choice about whether or not they want to know the truth about this place. And secondly, the curiosity wears down their unbelief. It doesn't require much belief for the milk to work, but complete unbelief can be tough to overcome."

"And you think Mom and Dad have no belief in them?" Kendra asked.

"As to the possibility of mythical creatures actually existing, they appear to have none at all," Grandpa said. "I left them much more obvious clues than I provided for you and Seth."

"I even had a conversation with them where I all but told them the truth about Fablehaven and my role here,"

Grandma said. "I stopped once I could see they were gawking at me like I belonged in an asylum."

"In some ways their unbelief is good for their safety," Grandpa said. "It can be a protection from the influence of dark magic."

Seth scowled. "Are you saying that magical creatures only exist if we believe in them?"

Grandpa dabbed at his lips with a napkin. "No. They exist independent of our belief. But usually some belief is necessary in order for us to interact with them. Furthermore, most magical creatures dislike unbelief enough to steer clear of it, in much the same way you or I might avoid an offensive odor. Unbelief is part of the reason many creatures chose to flee to these preserves."

"Would it be possible for any of us to stop believing in magical creatures?" Kendra wondered.

"Don't bother," Coulter huffed. "Nobody could try harder than I have. Most of us just make the best of it."

"Gets pretty hard to doubt once you've interacted with them," Dale agreed. "Belief hardens into knowledge."

"There are some who learn of this life and then flee it," Grandma said. "They avoid the preserves and substances like Viola's milk that can open their eyes. By turning their backs on all things magical, they let their knowledge lie dormant."

"Sounds like good sense to me," Coulter muttered.

"Your Grandma and Grandpa Larsen retired prematurely from their involvement with our secret society," Grandpa said.

"Grandma and Grandpa Larsen knew about magical creatures?" Seth exclaimed.

"As much as we do or more," Grandma said. "They ended their involvement around the time Seth was born. We all had such high hopes for your parents. We introduced them to one another and quietly encouraged their courtship. When Scott and Marla refused to show interest in our secret, your Grandma and Grandpa Larsen seemed to lose their commitment."

"We had been friends with the Larsens since your parents were children," Grandpa mentioned.

"Wait a minute," Kendra said. "Did Grandma and Grandpa Larsen really die accidentally?"

"As far as we have ever been able to tell, yes," Grandma said.

"They had retired from our community ten years prior," Grandpa said. "It was simply a tragic mishap."

"I never guessed that they would have known about the secret preserves," Seth said. "They didn't seem like the type."

"They were very much the type," Grandma assured them. "But they were good at keeping secrets, and at playing roles. They did a fair amount of spying for our cause back in the day. Both were involved with the Knights of the Dawn."

Kendra had never considered the possibility that her deceased grandparents might have shared the secret knowledge held by the Sorensons. It made her miss them more than ever. It would have been so nice to share this amazing secret with them! Strange how two couples who knew the secret both had kids who refused to believe. "How will we ever convince Mom and Dad to let us stay here?" Kendra asked.

"Let your Grandpa and me keep working on that," Grandma promised with a wink. "We still have another week or so."

They finished the meal in silence. Everyone thanked Coulter for the meat loaf as they cleared the table together.

Grandpa led the way into the living room, where each of them found a seat. Kendra thumbed through an antique book of fairy tales. Before long, a key rattled and the front door opened. Tanu entered, a tall Samoan with heavy, sloping shoulders. One of his thickly muscled arms hung bandaged in a sling. A satchel bulging with odd shapes dangled from the potion master's opposite shoulder. Behind him came Warren, wearing a leather jacket, his chin stubbly with three-day whiskers.

"Tanu!" Seth ran up to the big Samoan. "What happened?"

"This?" Tanu asked, indicating the injured arm.

"Yeah."

"Botched manicure," he said, dark eyes twinkling.

"I'm back too," Warren hinted.

"Sure, but you weren't sneaking onto a fallen preserve in South America," Seth told him dismissively.

"I had some close calls of my own," Warren mumbled. "Cool ones."

"We're glad you both made it back safely," Grandma said.

Warren scanned the living room and leaned toward Tanu. "Looks like we arrived late for a meeting."

"We're dying to hear what you found out," Kendra said.

"How about a drink of water?" Warren sniffed. "A little help with our bags? A warm handshake? A guy could get the feeling you only want him for his information."

"Cut the theatrics and have a seat," Dale said. Warren scowled at his older brother.

Tanu and Seth entered the room and took seats next to each other. Warren plopped down on the sofa beside Kendra.

"I'm glad we're all here," Grandpa said. "We in this room represent the only persons aware of the accusation that the Sphinx may be a traitor. It is imperative that we keep it that way. Should the accusation prove true, his vast network of deliberate and inadvertent spies are everywhere. Should the accusation prove false, this is hardly the time to spread rumors that could provoke dissension. Given all we have been through together, I feel sure we can confide in one another."

"What new information have you uncovered?" Grandma asked.

"Not much," Tanu said. "I got onto the Brazilian preserve. Things are a mess there. A reptilian demon named Lycerna has overthrown all order. If Maddox found a good place to hole up, he may be all right, but I wasn't able to locate him. I did deliver the tub, and I placed some coded messages as to where I hid it. He knows how to use it."

"Good man," Coulter approved.

"What tub?" Seth asked.

Coulter looked at Grandpa, who nodded. "An oversized, old-fashioned tin bathtub that happens to contain a shared transdimensional space linked to an identical tub in the attic."

"That meant nothing to me," Seth said.

"One moment," Coulter said, rising and going into the other room. He returned with a battered leather satchel. After rummaging in the satchel for a moment, he retrieved a pair of tin cans. "These function the same way as the tubs, on a smaller scale. I have used them to send messages. Take this one, have a look inside." He handed one of the tin cans to Seth.

"Empty," Seth reported after glancing into it.

"Correct," Coulter said. He removed a coin from his pocket and dropped it into the can he had retained. "Check again."

Seth looked into the can and saw a quarter resting on the bottom. "There's a quarter in here!" he exclaimed.

"Same quarter as I have in mine," Coulter explained. "The cans are linked. They share the same space."

"So now we have two quarters?" Seth asked.

"Only one quarter," Coulter corrected. "Take it out."

Seth dumped the quarter into his palm. Coulter held up his can. "See, my quarter is gone. You took it out of your can."

"Awesome," Seth breathed.

"Maddox can use the tub to get home, if he can find it," Coulter said. "The only catch is that somebody has to be on our end to pull him out. Without outside help, he can emerge only from the tub he enters."

"So if somebody was on the other end to help us out, we could get to the Brazilian preserve through an old bathtub in the attic?" Seth said.

Grandma raised her eyebrows. "If you wanted to risk getting devoured by a gargantuan serpentine demon, yes."

"Wait," Kendra said. "Why didn't Tanu just come home through the tub?"

Tanu chuckled. "The plan was for me to use the tub after I delivered it, but I was also trying to ascertain whether the artifact had been removed from the Brazilian preserve. Sadly, I failed to find where the artifact was hidden. Lycerna cut off my escape route to the tub. I was lucky to make it out over the wall."

"We're talking about your side of the attic, right?" Seth asked. "The secret side—not where we're sleeping."

"Safe guess," Grandma said.

"How'd you bust your arm?" Seth wondered.

"Honestly?" Tanu said sheepishly. "Dropping from the top of the wall to the ground."

"I thought maybe the demon chomped you," Seth sighed, looking a little disappointed.

Tanu gave a rueful smile. "I wouldn't be here if she had."

"Any evidence that could implicate the Sphinx as a cause for the fall of the Brazilian preserve?" Grandpa asked.

"I found nothing to indict him at the preserve," Tanu said. "He was in the area soon after the trouble started, but he always shows up when things go wrong. Whether he was there to help or hinder, I have no idea."

"How have you fared, Warren?" Grandpa asked. "Any news of the fifth secret preserve?"

"Still nothing. I keep hearing about the same four, the ones we already knew about. Australia. Brazil. Arizona. Connecticut. Nobody can give me a location for the fifth."

Grandpa nodded, appearing mildly disappointed but unsurprised. "What of the other matter?"

"The Sphinx knows how to cover his tracks," Warren said, his demeanor growing serious. "And he is not the sort of figure you ask questions about openly. Trying to discover his origin has felt like wandering through a maze full of dead ends. Every time I take a few steps in a new direction, I hit a new wall. I've been to New Zealand, Fiji, Ghana, Morocco, Greece, Iceland—the Sphinx has lived all over, and everywhere there are different theories about who he is and where he came from. Some say he is the avatar of a forgotten Egyptian god, some say he is a sea serpent cursed to roam dry land, some say he is an Arabian prince who won immortality by cheating the devil—every account is different, each more farfetched than the last. I've talked to caretakers, magical beings, historians, criminals, you name it. The guy is a ghost. The stories I've heard are too diverse. If you ask me, I'd say he started all the rumors himself to confuse the exact sort of investigation I've been trying to conduct."

"The Sphinx has always shrouded himself in secrecy, which leaves him vulnerable to the sort of accusation Vanessa made," Grandpa said.

"Which Vanessa knew," Coulter pointed out. "He's an easy target for slander. It isn't the first time."

"Yes, but usually the accusations are the baseless ranting of the fearful," Grandma said. "This time, the circumstantial evidence is terrifying. Her explanation fit the events perfectly."

"There is a reason we don't convict people based on circumstantial evidence," Tanu said. "We know firsthand how devious Vanessa can be. She could easily have used the facts of the circumstances to weave a convincing lie."

"I have other news," Warren announced. "The Knights of the Dawn are having their first united gathering in over ten years. All Knights are required to attend."

Coulter sighed. "Never a good sign. The last united gathering I attended was when hard evidence came to light that the Society of the Evening Star was resurfacing."

"You're a Knight too?" Seth asked Coulter.

"Semi-retired. We're not generally supposed to reveal ourselves, but I figure if I can't trust you all, I can't trust anyone. Besides, I'll be in a grave before too long."

"There's more," Warren continued. "The Captain wants me to bring Kendra to the event."

"What?" Grandpa exclaimed. "Outrageous!"

"Only Knights are invited to the assemblies," Grandma said.

"I know, I know, don't shoot the messenger," Warren said. "They want to induct her."

"At her age!" Grandpa cried, his face reddening. "Are they recruiting at maternity wards these days?"

"And we all know who the Captain is," Warren said, "though he never openly reveals himself."

"The Sphinx?" Kendra guessed.

Grandpa nodded thoughtfully, pinching his lower lip. "Have they offered a reason?"

"The Captain suggested that she has talents essential to us in weathering the coming storm," Warren said.

Grandpa buried his face in his hands. "What have I done?" he moaned. "It was my choice to introduce her to the Sphinx in the first place. Now, good or evil, he wants to exploit her abilities."

"We can't let her go," Grandma said adamantly. "If the Sphinx is also the leader of the Society, this is undoubtedly a trap. Who knows how many other Knights may be corrupt!"

"I have worked with many of the Knights," Tanu said. "I've seen lives risked and sacrificed. I would vouch that most are true protectors of the preserves. If the Knights are harming our cause, it's because they've been duped."

"You're a Knight too?" Seth asked.

"Like Warren, Tanu, Coulter, and Vanessa are all Knights of the Dawn," Grandpa said.

"Vanessa didn't turn out very well," Seth reminded them.

"Which is another good point," Grandma said. "Even if the Sphinx is honorable, Vanessa proves that the Knights have at least some traitors among them. A meeting where all the Knights are gathered could prove perilous for Kendra."

"Where will it be?" Grandpa asked.

Warren scratched the side of his head. "I'm not supposed

to say, but half of us will have formal invitations by tomorrow, and the others have a right to know. Outside Atlanta, in the home of Wesley and Marion Fairbanks."

"Who are they?" Seth asked.

"Billionaire fairy enthusiasts," Grandma said. "They have a private collection of fairies and whirligigs."

"For which they paid handsomely," Grandpa added. "The Fairbankses have no idea of the extent of our community. They've never seen a preserve. They're outsiders, useful for funds and connections."

"And they have a big mansion ideal for gatherings," Coulter said.

"But there hasn't been a gathering for ten years?" Kendra asked.

"No united gathering," Tanu said. "A united gathering means everybody is supposed to come, no excuses. Secrecy is important to the Knights, so such gatherings are rare. Normally we assemble in smaller groups. When we do meet in a large body, we wear disguises. Only the Captain knows the identity of all the members of the brotherhood."

"And he might be a traitor," Kendra said.

"Right," Warren agreed. "But I don't see how we can deny the request."

Grandpa stared at him, eyebrows raised. He motioned for Warren to explain further.

"The last thing we can afford to do, in case the Sphinx is actually an enemy, is show we are suspicious of him. Based on Vanessa's assertion, if he is evil, there can be no question of how he would retaliate if he knew we had uncovered his secret."

Grandpa nodded reluctantly. "If he were going to make a move against Kendra, it would probably not be when she is supposed to be under his protection. He knows that many assume he is the Captain of the Knights. I wonder why he is requesting her presence?"

"Perhaps he has a talisman that needs charging," Grandma proposed. "Her ability to recharge magical objects through touch is unique."

"Might even be the Brazilian artifact," Tanu murmured.

The implications made the room go silent.

"Or the Sphinx may be on our side," Coulter reminded everyone.

"When is the united gathering?" Grandpa asked.

"Three days," Warren said. "You know how they never tell anyone until the last minute, to help prevent sabotage."

"Are you a Knight too?" Seth asked Grandpa.

"I was," Grandpa said. "None of the caretakers are in the brotherhood."

"Will you be going?" Kendra asked him.

"The gatherings of the brotherhood are only for current members."

"Tanu, Warren, and I will be there," Coulter said. "I agree, regardless of the true intentions of the Sphinx, Kendra should attend. We'll stay at her side."

"Could we devise a plausible excuse for her absence?" Grandma asked.

Grandpa shook his head slowly. "If we had no doubts

about the Sphinx, we would go out of our way to fulfill his request. Any excuse we offer might raise suspicion." He turned to Kendra. "What do you say?"

"Sounds like I'd better go," she said. "I've walked into more dangerous situations than this. The Sphinx would have to risk revealing himself in order to harm me. Besides, hopefully Vanessa is wrong. Do you think it might help to speak with her?"

"Help add to our confusion maybe," Coulter spat. "How can any of us trust a word she says? She's too dangerous. From my point of view, if we let her breathe fresh air, we'll be playing right into her hands. Whether the note is true or false, escaping the Quiet Box was surely her only goal in leaving it."

"I have to agree," Grandma said. "I think if she could have added further proof to her accusation, she would have done so in the message. It was plenty long."

"If her accusation proves valid, Vanessa may still be of great use," Grandpa said. "There may be others in her organization whom she could reveal. Once we offer her the opportunity, we can count on her trying to use such information as leverage to avoid returning to the Quiet Box, which is not a headache I care to endure at the moment. For now, I would rather seek out more evidence on our own. Perhaps the four of you can learn more at the united gathering."

"Then I'm going?" Kendra asked.

The adults in the room exchanged tacit glances before nodding.

"Then we only have one problem left to discuss," Seth said.

Everyone turned to him.

"How do I get invited?"

CHAPTER THREE

Sharing Discoveries

K endra lay on her bed, perched on her elbows above an oversized journal, reading strong, slanted handwriting that looked like it belonged on the Declaration of Independence. The author of the journal was Patton Burgess, the former caretaker of Fablehaven, the man who had lured Lena the naiad out of her pond more than a hundred years ago. As she had scoured Patton's journals over the summer, Kendra had become more fascinated than ever by Lena's story.

Even though leaving the water had transformed the nymph to a mortal state, she had aged much more slowly than Patton. After Patton had succumbed to his years, Lena had traveled the world, eventually returning to Fablehaven to work with Kendra's grandparents. Kendra had met Lena the previous summer, and they had become fast friends. All of that had ended when Kendra had gotten help from the Fairy Queen to summon an army of giant fairies to stop a witch named Muriel and the demon she had freed. The fairies had defeated the demon, Bahumat, and imprisoned Muriel with him. Afterwards, they had repaired much of the hurt the witch had caused. They had changed Grandpa, Grandma, Seth, and Dale back from altered states, and rebuilt Hugo from scratch. They had also restored an unwilling Lena to her state as a naiad. Once back in the water, Lena had reverted to her former ways, and she had not seemed eager to return to dry land when Kendra had tried to offer help.

Kendra had good reason to study the journal entries. During her stay at Fablehaven, Vanessa had spent much of her time perusing the records of former caretakers. If, as a traitor, Vanessa had been so intent on examining the history contained in the journals, Kendra had decided the information must be valuable. No caretaker had kept a tenth as many records as Patton, and so Kendra had mostly found herself poring over his writings.

He was an intriguing man. He oversaw the construction of the new house and barn at Fablehaven, along with the stables, all still in use. He prevented the ogres from eradicating themselves by negotiating the end of an ancient feud. He helped erect the glass observation domes that served as safe rooms around the preserve. He mastered six of the languages spoken by magical beings, and used the knowledge to establish relationships with many of the most fearsome and elusive inhabitants of the preserve.

His interests were not limited to the upkeep and improvement of Fablehaven. Rather than staying rooted to the preserve, Patton traveled extensively in an era before airplanes made the globe feel small. Sometimes he was open about his visits to exotic locations like foreign preserves. Other times he omitted the destinations of his excursions. He was playfully boastful about his journeys, often referring to himself as the world's greatest adventurer.

In his writings, Patton was shameless about his ambition to woo Lena to be his bride. He detailed the gradual progress he made, playing music for her on his violin, writing her poems, beguiling her with stories, engaging her in conversation. It was clear that he obsessed over her. He knew what he wanted and never relented until she was his. Kendra was currently rereading the culminating entry of the romantic account:

Success! Victory! Jubilation! I should no longer be alive, though I have never felt more so! After the tiresome months, nay, years of waiting, of hoping, of striving, she reposes in a room in my home as I pen these exultant words. The truth of it refuses to settle in my mind. Never has a fairer maiden walked on dry land than my precious Lena. Never has a human heart felt more satisfied than mine.

I unwittingly put her affection to the test today. It shames me to confess my folly, but the disgrace is eclipsed by my elation. While adrift on the pond, I leaned too close to my love, and her wretched sisters promptly took advantage of my laxity and hauled me overboard. Tonight I should be slumbering in an aquatic grave. I was insignificant compared to them in the water. But my love swam to my rescue. Lena was magnificent! She bettered no fewer than eight of the watery maids in order to wrest me from their clutches and deliver me to the shore. To complete the miracle, she joined me on land, at long last accepting my invitation and renouncing her claim on immortality.

After all, what is immortality when confined to a sad little pond with such petty companions? I will unveil wonders to her that others of her kind have never imagined. She shall be my queen, and I her most ardent admirer and protector.

I suppose I should thank her spiteful sisters for endeavoring to steal my life. Had such a dire situation failed to arise, I might never have inspired Lena to action!

It has not eluded my attention that many around me have elected to mock and deride my adoration behind my back. They anticipate a recurrence of the calamitous escapade that ruined my uncle. If only they could somehow sample the authenticity of my affection! This is no paltry dalliance with a dryad, no trifling indiscretion swollen out of proportion. History will not be imitated; rather, a new standard of love shall be established for the ages. Time will certify my devotion! On this I would gladly stake my very soul!

No matter how many times Kendra read those words, they never failed to thrill her. She could not help wondering if one day a person might experience such strong feelings for her. Having already heard Lena's side of the story, Kendra knew that the adoration expressed by Patton had been reciprocated over a lifelong romance. She tried to prevent her thoughts from wandering to Warren. Sure, he was nice-looking, and brave, and funny. But he was also way too old, and her distant cousin on top of it!

Kendra thumbed through the pages of the journal, enjoying the smell of the old paper, unable to avoid hoping that one day she would find someone like Patton Burgess.

An umite candle rested on the nightstand beside her bed. Vanessa had introduced Kendra to umite wax, a substance made by South American fairies dwelling in hivelike communities. When you wrote with an umite wax crayon, the words were invisible unless you read them by the light of a candle made from the same substance. Vanessa had used umite wax to scrawl her final message on the floor of her cell. And Kendra had discovered that Vanessa had taken notes using umite wax in the journals she had studied.

Whenever Kendra lit the candle, she found herself guided to key pieces of underlined information, accompanied by occasional notes scrawled in the margins. She had identified the notes that Vanessa had left while deducing that the grove with the revenant was the hiding place for the inverted tower. She also found several false trails Vanessa had followed referencing other dangerous areas of Fablehaven, including a haunted tar pit, a poisonous bog, and the lair of a demon named Graulas. Kendra could not make sense of all the observations Vanessa had jotted—some were in an indecipherable shorthand.

Kendra sat up and opened a drawer, planning to light a match and use the candle to scour more pages. She had to do something to keep her mind off of her impending trip to Atlanta!

"Are you missing the library again?" Seth asked, startling her as he walked into the room.

Kendra turned to face her brother. "You caught me," she congratulated him. "I'm reading."

"I bet the librarians back home are panicking. Summer vacation, and no Kendra Sorenson to keep them in business. Have they been sending you letters?"

"Might not hurt you to pick up a book, just as an experiment."

"Whatever. I looked up the definition for *nerd* in the dictionary. Know what it said?"

"I bet you'll tell me."

"'If you're reading this, you are one.'"

"You're a riot." Kendra turned back to the journal, flipping to a random page.

Seth took a seat on his bed across from her. "Kendra, seriously, I can sort of see reading a cool book for fun, but dusty old journals? Really? Has anybody told you there are magical creatures out there?" He pointed at the window.

"Has anybody told you some of those creatures can eat you?" Kendra responded. "I'm not reading these just for fun. They have good info."

"Like what? Patton and Lena smooching?"

Kendra rolled her eyes. "I'm not telling. You'll end up drowning in a tar pit."

"There's a tar pit?" he said, perking up. "Where?"

"You're welcome to look it up yourself." She gestured at the huge stack of journals beside her bed.

"I'd rather drown," Seth admitted. "Smarter people than you have tried to trick me into reading." He sat still, staring at her.

"What's going on?" she asked. "Are you bored?"

"Not compared to you."

"I'm not bored," Kendra said smugly. "I'm going to Atlanta."

"That's below the belt!" Seth protested. "I can't believe they're making you a Knight and not me. How many revenants have *you* destroyed?"

"None. But I did help take down a demon, a witch, and a huge, winged, acid-breathing, three-headed panther."

"I'm still mad I missed seeing the panther," Seth muttered sourly. "Tanu and Coulter got their invitations today. Sounds like you guys are leaving tomorrow."

"I'd let you go in my place if I could," Kendra said. "I don't trust the Sphinx."

"You shouldn't," Seth said. "He let you win at Foosball. He pretty much told me. The guy is a pro."

"You're just saying that because he creamed you."

Seth shrugged. "Guess what? I have a secret."

"Not for long, now that you've said that much."

"You're never getting it out of me."

"Then I'll die unfulfilled," she said dryly, grabbing a new journal from the stack and opening it. She could feel Seth watching her as she pretended to read.

"Have you ever heard of nipsies?" Seth finally asked.

"Nope."

"They're the smallest fairy people," Seth informed her. "They build little cities and stuff. They're about half an inch tall. The size of tiny bugs."

"Cool," Kendra said. She continued to feign disinterest, eyes scanning the shapes of words. It rarely took Seth long to crack.

"If you knew something that might be dangerous, but telling people about it could get you in trouble and make you lose a lot of money, would you tell anyone?"

"Grandpa!" Kendra called. "Seth has a secret to tell you about the nipsies!"

"You're a traitor," Seth grumbled.

"I'm just helping Smart Seth defeat Idiot Seth."

"I guess Smart Seth is glad," he said reluctantly. "But be careful. Idiot Seth is the guy to watch out for."

※ ※ ※

"So," Grandpa said, taking a seat behind the desk in his office, "how is it you know about the nipsies, Seth?"

"Common knowledge?" He felt uncomfortable in the large armchair. He silently vowed to make Kendra pay for this.

"Not very common," Grandpa said. "I keep quiet about them. The nipsies are abnormally vulnerable. And they live very far from the yard. Do you know a secret about them?"

"Maybe," Seth hedged. "If I tell you, will you promise I won't get in trouble?"

"No," Grandpa said, folding his hands on the desk expectantly.

"Then I'm not saying another word until I consult an attorney."

"You're just digging yourself in deeper," Grandpa warned. "I don't negotiate with delinquents. On the other hand, I have been known to show mercy for forthrightness."

"The satyrs told me the nipsies are at war with each other," Seth blurted.

"At war? The satyrs must be mistaken. I don't know of a more peaceful society in all of Fablehaven, except perhaps the brownies."

"It's true," Seth insisted. "Newel and Doren saw it. The Sixth and Seventh Kingdoms were attacking the others. The bad nipsies say they have a new master. They look different from the others, with gray skin and red eyes."

"The satyrs were very descriptive," Grandpa noted suspiciously.

"They might have shown me," Seth admitted grudgingly.

"Your grandmother would go through the roof if she knew you were spending time with Newel and Doren," Grandpa said. "I can't say I disagree. It would be hard to think of a worse influence on a twelve-year-old boy than a pair of satyrs. Follow their lead, and you'll grow up to be a hobo. Wait a minute. Were the satyrs stealing from the nipsies again?"

Seth tried to keep his expression composed. "I don't know."

"I've spoken with Newel and Doren before about taking

from the nipsies. I had been apprised that the nipsies had managed to remedy the situation. Let me guess. You've been selling the satyrs more batteries, against my wishes, which compelled them to find a way to reenter the Seven Kingdoms?"

Seth held up a finger. "If they hadn't, we would not know the nipsies were at war, and they might have gone extinct."

Grandpa stared at him. "We've spoken before about stolen gold. Around here, it has a way of causing more trouble than it's worth."

"Technically, it wasn't stolen," Seth said. "The nipsies gave it to Newel for fending off the Sixth and Seventh Kingdoms."

Grandpa's lips pressed together into a thin line. "I'm grateful that you shared this with Kendra, and that she helped you bring it to me. I'm grateful to learn that there is an unusual situation with the nipsies. However, I'm disappointed that you went behind my back to sell batteries to those eternal adolescents, that you accepted dubiously acquired gold as payment, and especially that you strayed so far from the yard without permission. You will not be permitted out of this house unaccompanied for the duration of the summer. And you will not go on chaperoned excursions for three days, which means you will miss joining Tanu and Coulter to check up on the nipsies this afternoon. Furthermore, you will return the gold to me, so I can restore it to the nipsies."

Seth lowered his eyes, gazing into his lap. "I knew I

should have kept my mouth shut," he mumbled miserably. "I was just worried . . ."

"Seth, telling me was the right choice. You did the wrong thing in disobeying the rules. You should know by now how disastrous that can be."

"I'm not a moron," Seth said, looking up fiercely. "I made it back just fine, and with useful information. I was careful. I stayed on paths. I had the satyrs with me. Sure, I made some mistakes before I knew much about this place. Terrible ones. I'm sorry for that. But I've also done some things right. Lately, I roam around here all the time on my own without telling anybody. I stick to places I know. Nothing bad ever happens."

Grandpa picked up a knickknack from his desk, a tiny, humanlike skull encased in a crystal hemisphere, and absently passed it back and forth between his hands. "I know you've learned a lot from Coulter and the others. You are more capable than you once were to safely negotiate certain areas of Fablehaven. I can understand why that would increase the temptation to ignore boundaries. But these are dangerous times, and there are many perils within these gated woods. Journeying as far from the yard as you did, to an unfamiliar location, relying on the judgment of Newel and Doren, shows a disturbing lack of common sense on your part.

"If I ever choose to expand the areas of Fablehaven where you're allowed to venture alone, I'll have to make you aware of many forbidden but intriguing regions that must be avoided. Seth, how can I ever trust you to keep the more complicated rules if you stubbornly refuse to follow the simple ones? Your repeated failure to keep the basic rules is the main reason I haven't given you more freedom to explore the preserve on your own."

"Oh," Seth said awkwardly. "I guess that makes sense. Why didn't you tell me staying in the yard was a test?"

"For one thing, it might have made the rule seem even less important." Grandpa set down the flat-bottomed crystal with the skull inside. "None of this is a game. I created the rule for a reason. Bad things really can happen if you wander the woods unaccompanied, even when you think you know what you're doing. Seth, you sometimes act as if you think growing up means the rules don't apply anymore. On the contrary—a big part of growing up is learning self-control. You work on that, and then we can talk about expanding your privileges."

"Can I earn time off for good behavior?"

Grandpa shrugged. "You never know what might happen if that miracle occurs."

※ ※ ※

A petite fairy with short hair as red as a ripe strawberry alighted on the edge of a marble birdbath and peered into the water, her translucent dragonfly wings almost invisible in the sunlight. Her crimson slip of a dress shone like rubies. She twirled and peered over her shoulder at her reflection, pouting her lips and tilting her head at different angles.

A yellow fairy with black highlights marking her dazzling butterfly wings stood preening nearby. She had pale skin and long, honey-blonde tresses. The yellow fairy tittered, a sound like miniscule bells tinkling.

"Am I missing something?" the red fairy asked with false innocence.

"I was trying to imagine my reflection with ugly, colorless wings," the yellow fairy replied.

"Funny coincidence," the red fairy remarked, smoothing a hand over her hair. "I was just picturing myself with big, gaudy wings that distracted from my beauty."

The yellow fairy arched an eyebrow. "Why not pretend you have wide, elegant wings that augment rather than detract?"

"I tried, but all that came to mind was a horrid backdrop of clumsy yellow curtains."

Kendra could not resist smiling.

She had developed a new habit of pretending to take a nap outside near a birdbath or a flower bed and listening to the fairies gossip. The fairies did not often speak to her if she tried to initiate a conversation. After leading the fairies into battle and becoming fairykind, Kendra had grown too popular for her own good. All of the fairies were jealous.

Among the happy consequences of the gift the fairies had bestowed was Kendra's ability to understand the language they spoke, along with several other related magical tongues. They all effortlessly sounded like English to her. She enjoyed using the talent to eavesdrop.

"Look at Kendra sprawling on that bench," the yellow fairy muttered in a confidential tone, "lounging around like she owns the yard."

Kendra fought back laughter. She loved when the fairies discussed her. The only conversations she liked more were when they bad-mouthed Seth.

"I have no problem with her," the redhead chimed in her tiny voice. "In fact, she made me this bracelet." She held up her arm to display the trinket, thin as a spider's thread.

"It's too small for her awkward fingers to have made it," the yellow fairy objected.

Kendra knew the yellow fairy was right. She had never made a bracelet, let alone for a fairy. It was funny—even though the fairies rarely spoke to Kendra, they often debated over whom she favored the most.

"She has many special talents," the red fairy insisted. "You'd be astonished by the gifts Kendra offers to her closest friends. Those of us who fought alongside her to imprison Bahumat share a special bond. Do you recall that day? I believe you were an imp at the time."

The yellow fairy kicked water at the red fairy and stuck out her tongue.

"Please, darling," the red fairy said, "let's not stoop to impish behavior."

"We who spent time as imps know secrets that you don't," the yellow fairy said slyly.

"I'm sure you're an expert about warts and crooked limbs," the red fairy agreed.

"Darkness affords different opportunities than light."

"Like a ghastly reflection?"

"What if we could be dark *and* beautiful?" the yellow fairy whispered. Kendra had to strain to hear.

"I pay no heed to such rumors," the red fairy replied haughtily, flitting away.

Kendra held very still until, through her cracked eyelids, she saw the yellow fairy take flight. The exchange had ended on a strange note. The restored fairies did not often refer to their time as imps. Those who had been imps normally seemed ashamed. The red fairy had dealt the other a low blow. What had the yellow fairy meant about being dark and beautiful, and why had the red fairy ended the conversation so abruptly?

Kendra arose and walked toward the house. The sun was plunging toward the horizon. Upstairs, her suitcase was packed. Tomorrow she would be driven to Hartford, and then fly to New York to meet a connecting flight to Atlanta.

The thought of meeting with the Knights of the Dawn filled her with worry. It all seemed so mysterious. Even without the threat of traitors, it did not sound like a place where she belonged. Her chief comfort was remembering that Warren, Coulter, and Tanu would be there as well. Nothing too terrible would happen with them around.

As Kendra walked up the steps to the covered porch, she saw Tanu and Coulter reach the yard in a cart pulled by Hugo. When the golem came to a stop, Tanu and Coulter sprang to the ground and started toward the house. They both wore serious expressions and walked purposefully. There was no panic in their movements, but it looked like they had bad news.

"How'd it go?" Kendra called.

"Something very strange is going on," Tanu replied. "Go tell Stan we need to talk."

Kendra ran into the house. "Grandpa! Tanu and Coulter found something!"

Her cry brought not only her grandfather but Grandma, Warren, and Seth as well. "Are the nipsies still at it?" Seth asked.

"I don't know," Kendra answered, turning to face the back door as Tanu and Coulter entered.

"What is it?" Grandpa asked.

"When we approached the meadow of the Seven Kingdoms, a shadowy figure fled," Tanu said. "We gave chase, but the scoundrel was too quick."

"It wasn't quite like anything we'd ever seen," Coulter said. "Maybe three feet tall, it wore a dark cloak and ran low to the ground, in a crouch." As he used his hands expressively, Kendra was reminded that Coulter was missing a pinky and part of the neighboring ring finger.

"A hermit troll?" Grandpa asked.

Tanu shook his head. "A hermit troll could not have entered the meadow. And this did not quite fit the description."

"We have a theory," Coulter affirmed. "We'll get to that in a second."

"What's a hermit troll?" Seth asked.

"The smallest of the trolls," Warren said. "They never stay in one place long, setting up temporary lairs anywhere from a quiet attic, to under a bridge, to inside a barrel."

"Go on," Grandpa encouraged Tanu.

"We got inside the hill and found the Sixth and Seventh Kingdoms gearing up for war again, in spite of the extensive damage Newel had caused."

"Stan," Coulter said, "you wouldn't have believed it. The Sixth and Seventh Kingdoms are draped in black, with most of the citizens bearing arms. The nipsies in those kingdoms were as Seth described, with gray skin, dark hair, and red eyes. They tried to bribe Tanu and me to assist them, and issued threats when we refused. If I didn't know better, I would say they had fallen."

"But nipsies don't have a fallen state," Grandma said. "At least nothing documented. Fairies can turn to imps, nymphs can become mortal, but who ever heard of a nipsie being transfigured?"

"Nobody," Tanu said. "But there they were. Which leads me to my theory. I think the creature we were chasing was some species of fallen dwarf."

"Dwarfs don't fall either!" Grandpa huffed, clearly perturbed.

"Tell that to this one," Coulter muttered.

"It's our best guess," Tanu said. "We interrogated the nipsies to see how all of this originated. Evidently it began when they were exploring the preserve, looking for ways to keep the satyrs out. That was how the dark ones met their new master."

"When we started fishing for specifics, they clammed up," Coulter said.

"What could make a nipsie fall?" Grandpa mused, as if speaking to himself.

"I've never seen anything like it," Coulter said.

"Nor heard of anything like it," Tanu added.

"Nor I," Grandpa sighed. "Normally, my first call would be to the Sphinx. Maybe it still should be. Friend or foe, he has always given sound advice, and none can match his knowledge of lore. Does the condition appear to be spreading?"

Tanu noisily cracked his knuckles. "According to some of the normal nipsies, after the Fifth Kingdom was invaded, a good portion of those nipsies were carried off and became like the others."

"Do you want Tanu and me to skip meeting with the Knights?" Coulter offered.

"No, you should attend," Grandpa said. "I want all three of you watching over Kendra and learning what you can."

"I overheard the fairies saying something strange today," Kendra said. "It might be related. They were talking about a way to be dark like imps, but beautiful. One fairy seemed enamored by the idea. The other flew away immediately."

"Strange things are certainly afoot at Fablehaven," Grandpa said. "I had better go make some calls."

Grandpa, Grandma, and Warren left the room.

"Seth, a word, if I may," Tanu said. Seth crossed to the hulking Samoan, who shepherded him into the corner. Kendra lingered to hear. Tanu glanced at her and went on.

"I noticed some interesting tracks in the meadow of the Seven Kingdoms," Tanu said casually. "Looked like the satyrs had some help gaining entry."

"Don't tell Grandpa," Seth pleaded.

"If we were going to tell him, we already would have," Tanu said. "Coulter and I figured you were in enough hot water already. Just keep in mind, Hugo is not a toy for helping satyrs steal."

"Gotcha," Seth said with a relieved smile.

Tanu looked at Kendra. "Can you keep this one under your hat?" His eyes demanded a yes.

"Sure," she said. "I've filled my daily quota for ratting on Seth."

CHAPTER FOUR

New Knights

When the baggage carousel jolted to life, passengers from Kendra's flight pressed to be closest to the opening from which their belongings would emerge. A parade of suitcases commenced, many of them black and about the same size. Several had ribbons tied around the handles to help the owners differentiate between them. Kendra had placed smiley-face stickers on hers.

It was peculiar hanging out with Tanu, Coulter, and Warren at the baggage claim. She associated them with magical potions, enchanted relics, and supernatural creatures. This setting seemed much too common. Tanu dipped a pretzel into a small plastic container of molten cheese. Warren turned to the final page of his paperback. Coulter penned an answer on the crossword from the in-flight magazine. Around them waited a random assortment of passengers. A pair of business travelers stood nearest, wearing slightly rumpled suits and expensive wristwatches.

Kendra lunged forward when her suitcase appeared, darting between a nun and a grungy guy in a tie-dyed shirt and sandals. Tanu accepted the bag after she yanked it off the carousel. Their other luggage followed soon after.

Tanu wadded his napkins into his cheese cup and chucked it into a garbage can, then collected his baggage. Coulter threw out the magazine.

"Anybody want to read about a genetically enhanced superspy?" Warren asked, waving his paperback. "It's a bestseller. Lots of action. Twist ending." He held it toward the trash receptacle.

"I might check it out," Kendra said, uneasy about the thought of discarding an undamaged book. She zipped the rescued paperback into her suitcase, then extended the handle so she could wheel the bag around.

The four of them headed away from the baggage claim toward a set of automatic doors. A man in a suit and a black cap was holding a sign with the name *Tanugatoa* printed in marker.

"We have a chauffeur?" Kendra asked, impressed.

"For going out of the city, a limousine cost only a little more than a taxi," Tanu explained.

"Why isn't my name on the sign?" Warren complained.

"My name is the rarest," Tanu said with a smile. He greeted the man with the sign and waved him off from trying to help carry bags. They followed the man out to the curb and along a sidewalk to where a black limousine with tinted windows idled. The driver, a well-dressed Middle Eastern man, loaded their suitcases into the trunk and then held the door as they entered the vehicle. Warren kept his smaller suitcase.

"I've never ridden in a limo before," Kendra confided to Coulter.

"It's been a while for me too," Coulter said.

She and Coulter sat on one side, facing Tanu and Warren on the other, with plenty of room between. Kendra ran a hand over the plush upholstery. The air smelled like pine, with a faint undercurrent of cigarette smoke.

After Tanu confirmed the address with the driver, the limousine nosed out into a clogged lane. They made small talk as the driver found the highway.

"How long is the trip?" Kendra asked.

"About an hour," Coulter said.

"Any last-minute tips?" Kendra asked.

"Don't reveal your name to anyone," Coulter said. "Don't mention Fablehaven, your grandparents, or where you come from. Don't tell your age. Don't show your face. Don't allude to any of your abilities. Don't mention the Sphinx. Don't speak unless you must. Most of the Knights eagerly gather information. Goes with the territory. Whether they're good or bad, I say the less they know the better."

"So what *can* I do?" Kendra asked. "Maybe I should just wear the invisibility glove and hide in a corner!"

"Let me qualify Coulter's recommendation not to speak," Tanu said. "Feel free to ask questions of your own. Get to know people. The fact that you're new gives you a valid excuse to solicit information. Just try not to reveal much. Gather info, don't dispense it. Be wary of any stranger who takes too much interest in you. Don't go anywhere alone with anyone."

"We'll stay close, but not too close," Warren said. "We all know other Knights, a few of them rather well. They will be able to spot us. We don't want to make it too easy for others to associate you with us."

"Do we have you wound up yet?" Coulter asked.

"I'm pretty nervous," Kendra confessed.

"Relax, have fun!" Warren encouraged.

"Right, while I try to follow all of my instructions and avoid getting abducted," Kendra moaned.

"That's the spirit!" Warren cheered.

Other cars on the highway had their lights on as dusk approached. Kendra settled back in her seat. The others had warned her it might be a late night. She had tried to sleep on the plane, but had felt too anxious, and the seat had not reclined enough. Instead she had used headphones to listen to the flight's different audio channels, including hit-and-miss selections of stand-up comedy and pop music.

Now, in the dim limo, she had a little more room, and drowsiness caught up to her. She decided not to fight it. Her eyelids drooped and she spent a few minutes on the edge of sleep, hearing the others make occasional comments as if from underwater.

In her restless dream, Kendra found herself roaming a carnival holding a blue cloud of cotton candy on a disposable white stick. At the age of four, Kendra had gotten separated from her family at a fairground for almost half an hour, and the scene before her was quite similar. Calliope music hooted and shrilled. A nearby Ferris wheel ground round and round, elevating riders high into the evening sky before plunging them back down, the mechanism squealing and growling like the ride was about to collapse.

Kendra caught glimpses of family members in the crowd, but when she tried to shoulder through the throng to reach them, they were gone. On one such occasion, she thought she saw her mom walk behind a popcorn stand. When Kendra followed, she found herself confronted by a tall stranger with a gray afro. Smiling like he knew a secret, the man tore away a big piece of her cotton candy and stuck it in his mouth. Kendra held her treat away from him, glaring, and a fat woman wearing braces plucked at it from behind. Soon Kendra found herself pushing through the multitude, trying to get away from the many strangers devouring her cotton candy. But it was no use. The entire crowd was stealing from her, and soon all she retained in her grasp was a naked white stick.

When Coulter jostled her awake she felt relieved, although a lingering unsettled feeling persisted. She must be even more stressed about the evening than she realized to have such an obnoxious dream!

Warren had opened his bag and was dispersing robes and masks. The long robes were constructed of a thin, strong material, dark gray, with a slight shimmer. "We're almost there," Warren informed her.

Unfastening her seatbelt, Kendra pulled the robe over her head. Warren handed her a silver mask. Coulter put on his. All four masks looked identical. Smooth and shiny, the simple, grinning mask covered her entire face. It felt a little heavier than she liked.

Kendra tapped her knuckles against the metallic forehead. "Are these things bulletproof?"

"They're not flimsy," Tanu said.

"Use your hood," Coulter suggested, his voice somewhat muffled by his mask. His hood was up, leaving none of his head exposed. He could have been anyone.

Warren handed Kendra light, snug gloves that matched the cloak. She removed her shoes and stepped into gray slippers. Warren and Tanu put on their masks.

"How will I know you?" Kendra asked.

"Tanu will be easiest because of his size," Warren said. "But he isn't the only large Knight." Warren raised a hand and laid two fingers beside his temple. "This will be our sign. You need never make it. We'll keep you in view."

The limousine turned off the road and advanced through open gates along a smooth driveway flanked by white statues of maidens clad in togas, armored heroes, animals, mermaids, and centaurs. Up ahead the mansion came into view.

"A castle," Kendra gasped.

Illuminated by numerous lights in the yard and dozens of electric sconces, the fortress loomed bright in the dwindling twilight. Built entirely of yellowish stone blocks, the broad stronghold boasted multiple rounded towers of varying height, a lowered drawbridge, a raised portcullis, lancet windows, arrow loops, and battlements atop the walls. Liveried servants stood at attention at either side of the drawbridge, bearing lanterns.

Kendra turned to her masked companions. "I know you call yourselves Knights, but seriously?"

"Fairy collectors," Warren grunted. "They tend to be an eccentric crowd, but Wesley and Marion Fairbanks might take the prize."

The limousine pulled to a stop. The driver opened the door facing the drawbridge. They got out, and Tanu pulled the chauffeur aside, speaking softly and handing him some money.

A servant wearing a powdered wig and red knickers over white stockings approached and offered a dignified bow. "Welcome, honored guests. Please follow me."

Kendra saw a battered white van pulling up behind the limo. The driver was wearing a silver mask. Off to one side of the grounds a pair of helicopters sat on the lawn. In another area a few dozen cars were parked, ranging from luxury vehicles to junk-lot candidates.

The costumed servant escorted Kendra and her friends toward the drawbridge. Her robe reached her ankles, allowing her to take normal strides without feeling too billowy. The mask limited her peripheral vision, but otherwise she could see fine.

The group passed into a cobbled courtyard, lit by electric cressets. Swirls of insects orbited the light sources. A few clusters of robed figures in silver masks strolled the area conversing. Above them, banners and flags hung limply in the still night air. The servant led Kendra and the others across the courtyard to a heavy, ironbound door, opened it with a key, stepped aside, and bowed.

Warren led the way into an ornate antechamber at the mouth of a cavernous hallway. A desk sat off to one side of the antechamber, before a pair of curtained booths. A person in a silver mask sat at the desk. Behind stood four robed figures, their silver masks trimmed with gold.

A short woman wearing a mauve gown greeted them. "Welcome, travelers, to our humble retreat. May you find safe harbor here until duty whisks you elsewhere." She had an average build, and looked to be in her fifties. Her chestnut hair was plaited in an antiquated style. A ring on her left hand held an obscenely huge diamond.

"A pleasure to see you again, Mrs. Fairbanks," Warren said with a genteel air. "Our thanks for opening your home to us."

She flushed with pleasure. "Anytime. No invitation required!"

Behind her stood a jovial man in a powdered wig eating chicken and vegetables off of a skewer. "Quite so," he said, juice dribbling down his chin.

"A pleasure as always, Wesley," Warren acknowledged, inclining his head.

Biting into a mushroom, the man in the wig nodded back.

Warren turned to face the four masked figures in front of the booths. "North," he said, jerking a thumb at himself.

"West." He gestured at Tanu and Coulter. Then he indicated Kendra. "Novice."

"The novice is East," said the man seated at the desk.

Warren leaned in to Kendra. "These are the four Lieutenants. They verify who we are under the masks, as a security measure. Each oversees a certain group, named by the points of the compass. The Eastern Lieutenant will confirm your identity."

Warren went into a booth with one of the figures in a gold-trimmed mask. A different Lieutenant marshaled Tanu into the other booth. Warren emerged promptly, mask in place, and another Lieutenant, the tallest one, guided Kendra into the vacant booth.

"Remove your mask, please," said a gruff voice.

Kendra took off the mask.

The Lieutenant nodded. "Welcome. You may proceed. We'll speak more shortly."

Kendra replaced her mask and exited the booth at the same time as Coulter left the other one. Together they followed Warren and Tanu down the extravagant hall, treading on a long red carpet edged with intricate embroidery. Tapestries hung from the walls and full suits of gleaming armor flanked the corridor. Warren and Tanu passed through white double doors into a spacious salon dominated by a tremendous chandelier. Robed figures stood about, most of them conversing in groups of two or three. Sofas, chairs, and divans were spaced around the room to allow for many separate groups to sit and chat in comfort. The outside of the home might look like a fortress, but inside it was definitely a mansion.

Tanu and Warren split up after entering the room. Following their lead, Kendra wandered over to a corner on her own. A couple of masked figures nodded at her as she passed. She nodded back, terrified to say a word.

Finding a place where she could stand with her back to the wall, Kendra surveyed the crowd. She was a good height for her age, but in this room, she was on the short end of the spectrum. A few of the other Knights were unusually tall, a few were abnormally fat, several looked broad and burly, a decent number were obviously women, and one was small enough to be eight years old. All wore the same silver masks and similar robes. Kendra counted more than fifty Knights in total.

The nearest Knights were a group of three, talking and laughing. After a while, one of them turned and stared at Kendra. Kendra tilted her face away, but it was too late, the figure was already crossing to her. "And what are you doing here in the corner?" asked a teasing female voice with a heavy French accent.

Kendra had not identified the stranger as a woman until she spoke. A good answer refused to enter her mind—she felt much too self-conscious. "Just waiting for the meeting."

"But the small talk is part of the meeting!" the woman enthused. "Where have you been lately?"

A direct question. Should she lie? She settled on vagueness. "Here and there."

"I recently returned from the Dominican Republic," the

woman said. "Absolutely perfect weather. I was tracking an alleged member of the Society, a man who was asking questions about acquiring a dullion." Kendra had seen a dullion before, made of straw, when she was fleeing her home earlier in the summer. Vanessa had explained that they were like golems, although not quite as powerful. "Rumor has it there is a warlock on the island who can create them. Can you imagine the implications if that art has survived? I have been unable to confirm the tale, so who knows. I don't recognize you, and you sound young, are you new?"

The woman spoke so frankly that Kendra felt considerable pressure to open up. Besides, it would be almost impossible for Kendra to disguise her youth. "I'm fairly young, yes."

"I started young myself, you know—"

"There you are," Warren interrupted. Beside him stood a tall figure in a silver mask with gold trim.

"If you will excuse us," the Lieutenant apologized to the Frenchwoman. "This young lady has an appointment with the Captain."

"I was about to guess she was a novice," the woman gushed. "So nice to meet you, hopefully we can work together sometime."

"Nice to meet you," Kendra replied as Warren took her elbow and guided her away.

The three of them exited the room and strode down the grandiose hallway to a smaller corridor. Some distance down the corridor, they stopped at a mahogany door. "Your presence is irregular," the Lieutenant informed Warren.

"Inducting a minor is irregular as well," Warren said. "I promised her grandfather she wouldn't leave my sight."

"You know me, Warren," the Lieutenant said. "Where would the child be safer than here?"

"Again, the operative word is *child*," Warren insisted.

The Lieutenant gave a curt nod and opened the door. The three of them entered. Three people were already in the room. One stood over by a wide fireplace, wearing a silver robe and a golden mask. The other two people wore silver masks and robes like Kendra's.

"Warren?" asked the figure in the gold mask in a feminine Southern accent. "What are you doing here?"

"Captain, this candidate is a minor," Warren said. "I have been mandated by her guardian not to let her out of my sight. It is the condition of her attendance."

"Understandable," the figure in the golden mask said. "Very well, I suppose we are ready to begin."

Kendra leaned over to Warren. "How did she know who you—"

"You're curious how I knew it was Warren entering with you?" the Captain asked. She tapped her mask. "This golden mask sees through all the silver ones. I have to know all the Knights under my command. I hand select them, and I keep watch. In case any of you are wondering, no, this is not my real voice, it's another special feature of my mask. Lieutenant, shall we proceed?"

The Lieutenant removed his mask. He had bushy red hair and freckles on his broad brow. He looked oddly familiar, but Kendra could not place him. "You three novices are receiving knighthood today. Today's recruits have been assigned to the East, and so I am your Lieutenant, Dougan Fisk. You will know my face, and I yours. Please remove your masks."

Kendra looked to Warren. He nodded, taking off his own mask. Kendra pulled hers off as well.

One of the other people wearing a silver mask was shorter than Kendra. Without her mask, Kendra saw that she was quite elderly, probably older than Grandma, with a narrow, wrinkled face and steel gray hair pulled into a bun. The other person in the room was a boy a few inches taller than Kendra. He was slim, and could not be past his teenage years, nice-looking, with tan, flawless skin, thin lips, and dark eyes. He looked at Kendra and for a moment appeared absolutely awestruck, staring at her with such naked admiration that she wanted to hide behind her mask before she blushed. After the initial stunned reaction, he managed to regulate his expression. He raised his eyebrows slightly, the corners of his mouth twitching toward an uncertain smile.

"The Captain almost always keeps the mask on," Dougan explained. "Our brotherhood exists mainly to combat a secretive and subtle organization, the Society of the Evening Star, and so secrecy is required on our part as well. We use checks and balances to monitor one another. The Captain knows all of the Knights. The four Lieutenants each know the Knights assigned to them, along with the identity of the Captain. Each Knight knows the Lieutenant he or she reports to, as you now know me. And each of the Knights knows some other Knights, as you are now meeting one another. Be most careful about revealing your membership in this brotherhood to others, even after they have reason to guess it."

"Wh-wh-wh-why are we East?" the teenage boy asked, tripping painfully over the first consonant.

"No good reason, just a tool of delegation," the Captain said. "Despite being called the Knights of the Dawn, this is not a military body. Titles like 'Captain' and 'Lieutenant' are strictly for organizational purposes. We compartmentalize information for the security of all. Your participation in this group is strictly voluntary. You can quit the brotherhood at any time. We do demand secrecy, however. If we did not trust that you could handle that requirement, you would not be here."

"As part of agreeing to be a Knight, you'll occasionally receive assignments specific to your area of expertise," Dougan said. "Generally, until you resign, by accepting membership in the brotherhood, you are committing to come when called and to serve where needed. All costs incurred will be reimbursed. In addition, you will receive a stipend to more than cover lost wages. If you betray secrets or perform in a manner that causes us unusual concern for the safety of the Knights, we reserve the right to expel you from the brotherhood."

"We are friends to all magical creatures and to the refuges where they dwell," the Captain said. "We are foes to all who seek to harm and exploit them. Have you any questions?"

"D-d-don't you find it peculiar that we can't know who our leader is?" the teenage boy asked.

"Not ideal," the Captain admitted. "But, regrettably, necessary."

"The word that comes to mind is *cowardly*," the teenager said.

Kendra felt her pulse quicken. She would never have expected such boldness from a teenager with a stuttering problem. It made her feel simultaneously excited and uncomfortable. The Captain was about the right height to be the Sphinx. How would he react?

"I've been called worse," the Captain said, remaining friendly. "You are not the first Knight to suggest dispensing with the masks. But given a recent breech in security that I am not at liberty to discuss, compartmentalizing our information has become more crucial than ever."

"I get not sharing everything with everybody," the teenager said. "I j-j-j, j-j-j, I only wish I knew who was giving me assignments."

"I suspect, were our positions reversed, I would feel as you do, Gavin," the Captain said. "Have you paused to consider that perhaps behind this mask is a person known to the Society? Perhaps I wear this mask not for my benefit, but to protect the other Knights, to prevent the Society from using me to get to them?"

Gavin stared at his feet. "M-makes sense."

"Chin up, I called for questions. Are there any other concerns?"

"I beg your pardon," said the older lady, "but aren't these two a little young for this kind of service?"

The Captain picked up a poker and jabbed a log in the fire, sending up a flurry of sparks. "Given these dangerous times, we've tightened our entry requirements more than ever. On top of a spotless background, and overwhelming evidence of reliable character, prospective Knights must also have unique strategic value. Kendra and Gavin both possess unusual talents that qualify them to lend highly specialized assistance. Not unlike your usefulness, Estelle, as a gifted archivist and researcher."

"Don't omit my world-renowned expertise with a broadsword," the elderly woman bragged. She winked at Kendra and Gavin. "That was a joke."

"Anything else?" the Captain asked, facing each of them in turn. None of them volunteered any further questions or comments. "Then I will formally induct you and leave you to mingle. Keep in mind, now as always, you are welcome to decline the invitation to join our community. If you wish to proceed, raise your right hand." The Captain raised his.

Kendra, Gavin, and Estelle lifted their hands.

"Repeat after me. I pledge to keep the secrets of the Knights of the Dawn, and to aid my fellow Knights in their worthy goals."

They repeated the words, and then lowered their hands. "Congratulations," the Captain said. "Your knighthood is official. Glad to have you on our side. Take a few minutes to get acquainted before we begin the gathering." The Captain crossed to the door and exited the room.

"Not so bad, was it?" Warren said over Kendra's shoulder, patting her on the back. "I'm Warren Burgess, by the way," he said to the other new Knights.

"Estelle Smith," the elderly woman said.

"Gavin Rose," the teenager said.

"Kendra Sorenson," Kendra said.

"Warren and I go way back," Dougan said.

"Since before you were a Lieutenant." Warren lowered his voice slightly. "Since we last spoke, you've seen the Captain without his mask. Just between the five of us, who is he?"

"You sure it's a he?" Dougan asked.

"Ninety percent. Manly build, manly walk."

"You've been out of touch for a while," Dougan said. "I thought you'd abandoned the cause."

"I'm still around," Warren said, not elaborating that he had spent the previous few years as a catatonic albino. "Kendra, you've met Dougan's brother."

"His brother?" Kendra asked. Then she realized why Dougan looked familiar. "Oh, Maddox! That's right, his last name was Fisk."

Dougan nodded. "He's not officially a Knight, hears his own drum beating too loudly for that, though he's helped us out on occasion."

"But here we are, monopolizing the conversation!" Warren apologized. "Gavin Rose, you say? Any relation to Chuck Rose?"

"M-m-my father."

"No joke? I never knew Chuck had a kid. He's one of our best guys. Why isn't he here with you?"

"He died seven months ago," Gavin said. "Christmas day, in the Himalayas. One of the Seven Sanctuaries."

Warren's smile vanished. "I'm sorry to hear that. I've been out of the loop."

"P-p-p-people wonder why I want to follow in his footsteps," Gavin said, looking at the floor. "I never knew Mom. I have no siblings. Dad kept me a secret from all of you because he didn't want me to get involved, at least not until I was eighteen. But he shared what he did with me, taught me a lot. I have some natural aptitude for it."

"There's an understatement," Dougan chuckled. "Chuck's best friend, Arlin Santos, brought Gavin to our attention. You remember Arlin, don't you, Warren? He's here tonight. We had been hearing rumors for years that Chuck was secretly raising a child. Little did we know how much he took after his old man, and then some. We actually have assignments for Gavin and Kendra immediately following the gathering."

"An assignment she can do here?" Warren asked.

Dougan shook his head. "Going someplace. Tomorrow morning."

Warren scowled. "Not without me, and not unless I sign off. Dougan, she's fourteen."

"I'll fill you in," Dougan promised. "It's important. We'll keep her safe."

There was a knock at the door.

"Masks," Dougan said, covering his face. "Enter," he called, once the others had done likewise.

A figure in a silver mask peered in. "Time for the gathering," a nasally male voice announced.

"Thank you," Dougan nodded at the speaker. "Off we go, then."

CHAPTER FIVE

First Assignment

Dougan and Warren led the way down the lavish main hall. As Kendra passed a suit of armor, she glimpsed her warped reflection in the breastplate, an anonymous silver mask under a hood. Gavin fell into step beside her.

"Nice how we got to know each other so well," he said bitterly.

"They didn't leave us much time," Kendra agreed.

"I don't always stutter, you know. It gets worse when I'm uncomfortable. I hate it. Once I get going, I focus on my words too much, and the problem snowballs."

"It isn't a big deal."

They advanced down the hall in silence. Eyes aimed downward, Gavin rubbed the sleeve of his robe between his fingers. The quietness became awkward.

"Kind of a cool castle," Kendra said.

"Not bad," he replied. "It's funny, I thought for sure I'd be the youngest Knight, and then pretty much the first person I meet has me beat by two years. Maybe it will turn out that the Captain is really just a freakishly tall third-grader."

Kendra smiled. "I turn fifteen in October."

"Eighteen months younger, then. You must have quite a talent."

"I guess somebody thinks so."

"Don't feel any pressure to talk about it. I can't really share mine either." They were almost to the end of the hall. Gavin rubbed the side of his mask. "These masks are the worst. Instant claustrophobia. I'm still not sold on the idea. It seems to me like masks would make it easier for traitors to hide. But I guess these guys have been at it longer than I have. The system must have some benefits. You know what the assembly is about?"

"No. You?"

"A little. D-d-d-dougan mentioned they're concerned about the Society and tightening security."

At the end of the hall they passed through a grand doorway into an airy ballroom. Strands of tiny white lights illuminated the room, the glossy wood floor gently reflecting the mellow luminance. Twenty round tables stood around the ballroom, positioned to make every seat as close as possible to a lectern on a stage. Each table had six chairs, and most were occupied by Knights. Kendra estimated there were now at least a hundred present.

Only the tables farthest from the stage had vacant

chairs. Warren and Dougan claimed the last two seats at a table toward the middle of the room. Kendra, Gavin, and Estelle crossed to the rear table farthest from the entrance, filling in the remaining three seats. Kendra had scarcely scooted her chair forward when the Knights arose together. The Captain, spotlighted, strode to the lectern, golden mask flashing. The Knights burst into applause.

The Captain motioned for the Knights to be seated. The clapping subsided and the Knights sank back into their chairs.

"Thank you all for assembling on such short notice," the Captain said into a microphone, his voice now a dignified male with a clipped English accent. "We try to keep united gatherings to a minimum, but I felt recent circumstances warranted a special convocation. Not all eligible Knights were able to attend. Seven were unreachable, two were hospitalized, and twelve were engaged in activities that I granted priority over today's gathering."

"You know I do not relish wasting words. Over the past five years, the Society has become more active than during any other period in history. If preserves keep falling at the present rate, none will be functional within two decades. Furthermore, we know that our brotherhood has been infiltrated by members of the Society. I am not referring to leaked information—I am referring to full-fledged members of the Society wearing masks and robes among us."

This last remark caused a stir as Knights throughout the room murmured to each other. Kendra heard more than one exclamation of outrage.

The Captain raised his hands. "The confirmed traitor has been apprehended, and the worst damage she intended to do was curtailed. Some of you may have noticed old friends who are not present tonight. Some of those may be among the twenty-one Knights unable to attend for legitimate reasons. Others may be among the seventeen Knights I have discharged over the past two months."

This announcement initiated another round of hushed comments. The Captain waited for the whispered remarks to end.

"I am not saying all seventeen of these Knights are traitors, but they are Knights with suspicious ties, who have spent too much time fraternizing with questionable individuals. They are Knights who have been unnecessarily free with covert information. Let their fate serve as a warning to us all. We will not tolerate the sharing of secrets, and we will not endure even the appearance of disloyalty. The stakes are too high, the danger too real. Allow me to read the names of the discharged Knights, in case they try to solicit further information from any of us." He went on to list seventeen names. None were familiar to Kendra.

"If any of you know concrete reasons why I should reconsider the ruling against a certain individual, please feel at liberty to consult with me after this meeting. I take no joy in disenfranchising allies. All of these Knights could have been useful to us in the coming days, weeks, months, and years. My intent is not to deplete our ranks. But I would rather be weakened than crippled. I ask each of you to set a new standard in loyalty, in discretion, and in vigilance. Do not share secrets, even with other Knights, unless the information is desperately relevant to the recipient. Please report any suspicious activities, along with any new intelligence you encounter. Despite our most diligent efforts, traitors could remain among us."

He paused, letting his words sink in. The room was silent.

"I also gathered you here tonight to petition you for information. Each of you is familiar with the preserves hidden across the globe. Beyond these, there are certain refuges not commonly known, even among the Knights of the Dawn. Not even I know all of them. Some of you know about some of these places. To my unspeakable alarm, even our most hidden sanctuaries are now coming under attack. In fact, they are rapidly becoming the focus of Society activity. I ask those of you who can identify the locations of any of these special refuges, or even rumors as to where they may be, to report such information to your Lieutenant or directly to me. Even if you feel sure we are already aware of all you know, I encourage you to come forward. I would rather hear redundant reports than risk missing anything. Since the Society is successfully finding these most confidential refuges, it is time for the Knights to take a more active role in protecting them."

Another round of discussion began. One of the masked figures at Kendra's table muttered, "I knew this was coming."

Kendra did not like it. If the Sphinx was the Captain, as well as a traitor, this would all be working to his advantage. He would be able to pass along everything the Knights of the Dawn knew to the Society of the Evening Star. All she could do was hope she was wrong.

"Allow me to conclude my remarks dwelling on the positive. All signs indicate that we are entering the darkest chapter of our long history. But we are rising to the occasion. Amid our increasing trials, we continue to score key victories, and we remain a step ahead of our adversaries. We must not relax our efforts. Only with relentless diligence and daily acts of heroism will we overcome our opponents. They are determined, they are patient, they are smart. But I know each of you, and I know we are up to the challenge. The coming season may be our darkest, but I am convinced it will also be our greatest. Preparations are in motion to weather the coming storm. Many of you will receive new assignments tonight. Much has been asked of you. Much is being asked of you. Much will be asked of you. I salute your past, present, and future valor. Thank you."

As the Captain strode away from the lectern, Kendra rose to join the standing ovation. She clapped with her hands but not her heart. Were they really a step ahead of the Society of the Evening Star? Or had she just heard the leader of the Society preaching in disguise?

Gavin leaned toward her. "Pretty good speech. Nice and short."

She nodded.

The applause died and the Knights began strolling away from the tables. Gavin and Estelle wandered off, and Kendra found herself surrounded by masked strangers. She moved toward a nearby curtained wall and found glass doors that opened to the outside. Kendra tried the handle, found it unlocked, and slipped out into the night.

Overhead, beyond a mesh roof, stars brightened a moonless sky, countless pinpricks of light. Kendra found herself in a small, screened room with a screen door on the far side. Passing through the door, Kendra entered an enormous screened cage. Lush foliage, including numerous trees and ferns, thrived all around. A man-made stream wound among the vegetation, bridged by meandering paths. A rich perfume of blossoms saturated the air.

Throughout the caged wilderness, glowing softly among the branches and fronds, glided an exotic variety of fairies. Several congregated above a place where the stream pooled, gazing down at their luminous reflections. Most of the fairies had extravagant wings and unusual coloring. Long, gauzy tails shimmered in the darkness. A fuzzy gray fairy with mothlike wings and tufts of pink fur perched on a nearby branch. A white, sparkling fairy drifted into a bulbous blossom, turning the flower into a delicate lantern.

A pair of fairies sped over to Kendra and floated in front of her. One was large and feathery, with elaborate plumage fanning out around her head. The other had very dark skin and fanciful butterfly wings with tiger stripes. At first Kendra thought they were paying her unusual attention, before she recognized that they were enjoying their reflections in her mask.

Kendra remembered that Mr. and Mrs. Fairbanks were fairy collectors. Of course, the fairies could not be kept indoors—if a captured fairy remained inside overnight, she changed into an imp. Apparently the vast cage did not qualify as indoors.

"The curve of the mask makes your head look fat," the feathery fairy giggled to the other.

"From my perspective, your rump looks rather blimpish," the striped fairy snickered.

"Now, girls," Kendra said, "be kind."

The fairies appeared dumbstruck. "Did you hear that?" the feathery fairy said. "She spoke in perfect Silvian!"

Kendra had spoken English, but something about her being fairykind caused many magical creatures to hear her words in their native tongues. She had conversed that way with fairies, imps, goblins, naiads, and brownies.

"Take off your mask," the striped fairy ordered.

"I'm not supposed to," Kendra said.

"Nonsense," the feathery fairy insisted, "show us your face."

"No humans are around," the striped fairy added.

Kendra raised her mask, giving them a peek before covering her features again.

"You're *her*," the feathery fairy gasped.

"It's true, then," the striped fairy squealed. "The Queen has selected a human handmaiden."

"What do you mean?" Kendra wondered.

"Don't play coy," the feathery fairy chided.

"I'm not," Kendra said. "Nobody ever said anything about being a handmaiden."

"Take off your mask again," the striped fairy said.

Kendra lifted the mask. The striped fairy extended a hand. "May I?" she asked.

Kendra nodded.

The fairy laid a tiny palm against her cheek. Gradually, the fairy grew brighter, until she was beaming orange stripes onto the surrounding foliage. Kendra squinted her eyes against the fiery brilliance.

The striped fairy removed her hand and drifted away, the intensity of her radiance fading only slightly. Other fairies flocked to them, hovering curiously.

"You're dazzling," Kendra said, holding up a hand to shield her eyes.

"Me?" the striped fairy laughed. "None of the others are looking at me. I'm barely the moon reflecting the light of the sun."

"I'm not glowing," Kendra said, noticing that the twenty fairies surrounding them were indeed all staring at her.

"Not on the same spectrum as I am," the striped fairy said. "But you shine much, much brighter. If you were radiating on my spectrum, we would all be blinded."

"Are you all right, Yolie?" the feathery fairy asked.

"I may have overdone it, Larina," the striped fairy answered. "Care to share the spark?"

The feathery fairy streaked over to the striped fairy. Yolie kissed the feathery fairy on the forehead. Larina flared brighter as the striped fairy dimmed. When they parted, their luminance was about equal.

Larina examined the intensified vibrance of her

multihued feathers. A bright aura shone around her like a rainbow. "Magnificent!" she cried.

"This is more manageable," Yolie said, still gleaming.

"Is she truly a mortal handmaiden?" asked the sparkling white fairy who had illuminated the blossom.

"Can there be any doubt?" Larina exclaimed.

"You got brighter because you touched me?" Kendra asked.

"You are a reservoir of magical energy like I have never encountered," Yolie said. "Surely you can feel it?"

"I can't," Kendra said. Yet she knew she had magical energy inside of her. How else could she recharge depleted magical relics? Kendra glanced over her shoulder at the screen door behind her and the curtained glass doors of the ballroom. What if somebody came out while her mask was off and she was speaking to fairies? Kendra replaced her mask. "Please don't tell any of the other people about me. I have to keep my identity a secret."

"We won't tell," Larina pledged.

"We had better diffuse our energy," Yolie suggested. "We're too bright. The difference is too plain."

"In the plants?" Larina proposed.

Yolie tittered. "The garden would flourish too quickly. The surplus energy would be unmistakable. We should spread it among ourselves, then share just a little with the plants."

The surrounding fairies cheered, then closed in on the two brightest. Kisses were exchanged until all the fairies shone only mildly brighter than they had originally.

"Have you any words for us?" Larina asked.

"Thank you for keeping my secret," Kendra said.

"You could make it an order in the name of the Queen," Yolie prompted.

"An order?"

"Sure, if you want the secret kept."

Several of the other fairies glared at Yolie. A few quivered with rage.

"Okay," Kendra said uncertainly. "I order you in the name of the Queen to keep my identity a secret."

"Is there anything else we can do for you?" Larina asked. "Life here is so frightfully tedious."

"I can always use information," Kendra said. "What do you know about the Captain of the Knights of the Dawn?"

"Knights of the Dawn?" Larina asked. "Who pays them any mind?"

"I'm a Knight," Kendra said.

"Forgive us," Yolie said. "We consider most mortal affairs somewhat . . . trivial."

"I promise the question is not trivial," Kendra said.

"We haven't paid enough attention to the Knights to know what you're asking," Larina apologized. "All we know about the Knights is that Wesley Fairbanks would trade all his wealth to be one."

"Are Mr. and Mrs. Fairbanks good people?" Kendra asked.

"As far as we can tell," Yolie said. "They treat us kindly and give us every possible consideration. Some of us have even condescended to speak with Marion in English on occasion."

"Do they know any secrets?" Kendra asked.

The fairies all looked at one another, as if hoping one of them might be aware of something. "I'm afraid not," Yolie finally said. "The couple knows little about our kind. We are simply wondrous novelties to them. Maybe we can put the word out to seek the identity of the Captain of the Knights of the Dawn."

"I'd appreciate it," Kendra said. "You don't happen to know anything about secret fairy preserves, do you?"

Kendra heard a door open behind her. Jumping and turning, she saw a figure in a cloak and a silver mask hurry to the screen door. Behind her mask, she licked her lips. Who could it be?

"Kendra?" asked Warren. "They want to issue your assignment."

"Okay," she said, whirling to face the fairies. "Secret preserves?"

"Sorry," Larina said. "We don't really know about secret preserves. Most of us are from the wild."

"Thanks for being so helpful," Kendra said.

"Our pleasure," Yolie chirped. "Come visit again."

Warren held the screen open and Kendra exited. "Be glad you weren't spotted surrounded by chatty fairies," he said.

"It just sort of happened," Kendra apologized.

"Tanu and I saw you go out. We got into a conversation

blocking the door. I kept an eye on you through the curtains. Learn anything?"

"Not much. Except that these fairies apparently didn't get the memo to give me the cold shoulder." Part of her wanted to say more, but only Grandpa, Grandma, Seth, and the Sphinx knew that Kendra was fairykind. Disclosing what the fairies had said about her being the Queen's handmaiden might give too much away. Most of her friends at Fablehaven thought that her abilities were a consequence of being fairystruck, which was somewhat less unheard of than her actual condition.

Nobody had become fairykind in more than a thousand years, so nobody could fill Kendra in on all the specifics. Although she knew it meant that the fairies had shared their magic with her in a way that caused it to dwell inside of her as it did in them, she had never heard herself referred to as the Queen's handmaiden, and was unsure what the expression meant. She knew being fairykind enabled her to see in the dark, understand languages related to Silvian, resist certain forms of mind control, recharge magical objects, and apparently transfer some of her energy to fairies. The Sphinx had implied that she probably had other abilities waiting to be discovered. Because her abilities could make her a target of people wishing to exploit her talents, Grandpa insisted on keeping her fairykind status a secret even from trusted friends.

Warren opened the door into the ballroom, where a tall, broad figure awaited. "Is everything all right?" Tanu asked.

Warren nodded. He led Kendra across the crowded room and back into the grand hallway.

"Who's meeting with us?" Kendra asked.

"Your Lieutenant," Warren said. "The quick appointment must mean the mission is important. All of the Knights are eager to speak with the Captain and their Lieutenants."

"What do you make of everything the Captain shared in his speech?" Kendra asked.

"We'll discuss that when we have more privacy."

They returned to the same room where they had met the Captain earlier. A person in a gold-trimmed mask stood by the fireplace. Once Warren and Kendra closed the door, Dougan removed his mask, prompting Kendra and Warren to do the same.

"How did you like your first meeting as a Knight?" Dougan asked Kendra.

"It made me nervous," she admitted.

"Good, that was part of the aim," he said. "We need to keep on our toes now more than ever. Are you ready for your assignment?"

"Sure," Kendra said.

Dougan gestured toward a sofa. Warren and Kendra sat down together. Dougan remained standing, hands clasped behind his back. "Warren, have you ever heard of Lost Mesa?"

Warren's eyebrows knitted together. "Can't say I have."

"Clearly you know about some of the secret preserves,

like Fablehaven," he said. "Lost Mesa is another of the secret preserves."

"The refuge in Arizona," Warren deduced. "I know of it, though I hadn't heard the name. I've never been there."

"Lost Mesa is on Navajo land. What do you know about the objects hidden on the secret preserves?"

"There are five secret preserves, each with a hidden artifact," Kendra said. "Together, the artifacts can open Zzyzx, the main demon prison."

"The Captain told me you would know," Dougan said. "Protecting these artifacts from exploitation is the top priority of the Knights of the Dawn. We have strong reason to suspect that the Society has learned the location of Lost Mesa. We sent in a small team to recover the artifact there, in order to transfer it to a safer repository. The team has encountered some trouble, so I am personally going there to complete the operation. I need Kendra to come with me, so that she can recharge the artifact before we extract it. We understand she has that ability."

Warren held up his hand. "A few questions. First off, what sort of trouble did the current team encounter?"

"They found the caverns where the artifact lies hidden," Dougan said. "The traps guarding the prize proved too much for the three of them. One of the team members perished, and a second was badly injured."

"Sounds like an ideal situation for involving a fourteen-year-old girl," Warren said. "Why exactly do you need to charge the artifact?"

"The Captain thinks that if the artifact is operational, we can use its power to better conceal it."

"Does he know which artifact it is?"

"He or she does not," Dougan answered.

"Won't activating the artifacts make them that much more dangerous if they fall into the wrong hands?"

Dougan folded his arms. "Do you really think the Society won't find a way to charge them if they ever lay hands on them? If anything, charging the artifacts now will make Kendra safer. The Society won't be after her to jump-start their prison keys."

Warren got up from his seat and wiped his hands down his face. "Dougan, level with me, is the Captain the Sphinx?" He stared at the Lieutenant intently.

"That's one of many popular theories," Dougan smiled. "No theory I've heard has it right."

"That is exactly what I would say if I were trying to conceal the truth, especially if one of the theories were accurate."

"It's also what you'd say if the theories were all false," Dougan said. "Warren, I have to warn you, this line of questioning is unacceptable."

Warren shook his head. "I can't elaborate why, but the question is important. I don't care who the Captain is, as long as he isn't the Sphinx. Just swear that to me."

"I'm not swearing one way or the other. Don't push me, Warren. I'll already have to converse with the Captain about your sudden interest in his or her identity. Don't make it worse. I took an oath. For all of our sakes, I can't expose anything about the leader of the Knights."

"Then Kendra isn't going to Lost Mesa," Warren said. "If necessary, she'll resign her knighthood." Warren turned to face her. "Would you mind having the shortest career in the history of the Knights of the Dawn?"

"I'll do whatever you think is best," Kendra said.

"I don't appreciate being strong-armed," Dougan growled.

"I don't like being kept in the dark," Warren countered. "Dougan, you know me. I don't ask for intelligence just to satisfy my curiosity. I've got a reason."

Dougan rubbed his forehead. "Look, will the two of you swear to keep the following information private? Not a word to anyone!"

"I promise," Warren said.

Kendra nodded.

"The Captain is not the Sphinx," Dougan said. "We like that rumor, because it distracts people from the truth, so don't spoil it. Now you tell me, what would it matter if the Captain were the Sphinx?"

"What do you know about the events at Fablehaven earlier this summer?" Warren asked.

"Were there events out of the ordinary?" Dougan asked.

"Then I can't tell you," Warren said. "None of this is a huge deal, just me being overly cautious. Which I tend to be when the fate of the world is on the line. If the Captain sees fit to fill you in on what happened, maybe we can talk more."

"I hear you. I told you what you wanted. Are you ready to step aside and allow Kendra to come to Lost Mesa with me?"

"Who else is going?"

"Just me, Kendra, and Gavin."

"The new kid?"

"Gavin was recruited because we need his help negotiating the caverns," Dougan explained. "Will you step aside?"

"No. But if you promise to keep Kendra far from the caverns, and if you let me join you, and if she agrees, I'll think about it. I may even come in handy. I'm not too shabby at bypassing traps myself."

"I'll have to check with the Captain," Dougan said.

"Understandable," Warren allowed. "I'll need to speak with Kendra privately to gauge her willingness."

"Very well," Dougan said, replacing his mask and striding to the door. "Sit tight. I'll be back soon." He exited.

Warren crouched next to Kendra. "What do you think?" he whispered.

"Could the room be bugged?"

"Doubtful. But not impossible."

"I don't know," Kendra said. "I keep worrying that Vanessa may have us jumping at shadows. If the Sphinx were a friend, and if you came along, I would totally go, no hesitation."

"Here's my take," Warren whispered. "If the Sphinx is a friend, sure, I'll be glad to help, but if he's an enemy, it will be even more important for me to get onto that preserve. I find the fact that they are after another artifact incredibly suspicious, especially since they seem intent on charging it. I'm still not convinced that the Captain is not the Sphinx. Dougan is a good guy, but he would lie to protect a secret of such magnitude. Even if the Captain isn't the Sphinx, he could just as easily be a puppet. At the very least, the Sphinx frequently trades secrets with the Knights."

"The Sphinx might be on our side," Kendra reminded him.

"He might," Warren said. "But if he were on our side, I don't picture the Sphinx wanting anyone, himself included, to know the location of so many artifacts. On top of Vanessa's accusations, the idea of seeking multiple artifacts in such a short period of time smells fishy. After all, they were hidden separately for a reason." He leaned closer, his lips almost touching her ear, and spoke in the quietest whisper Kendra could imagine. "I need to get onto the preserve, not to help them recover the artifact, but to recover it myself. It will surely mark the end of my association with the Knights of the Dawn, but no one person should know the location of so many artifacts, especially when there is an implication that he may be our enemy."

"So we should go," Kendra concluded.

"This makes things very complicated for you," Warren continued in his faint whisper. "It would be risky to simply go to Lost Mesa and help them extract the artifact, let alone to try to steal it from them! You can play innocent. I won't involve you directly. I'll make it look like I was using this role as your protector for my own ends. There's a chance Dougan may try to hold you responsible. I can't guarantee your safety, but we'll make sure Tanu, Coulter, and Stan all know where you are, so they can ensure that you end up back home."

Kendra closed her eyes and pressed a hand to her forehead. The thought of trying to pull this off made her stomach twist. But if the Society ended up opening Zzyzx, it would mean the end of the world as she knew it. Preventing that was worth taking a gut-wrenching risk, right?

"Okay," Kendra said. "If you can come, let's do it."

"I hate to put you in this position," Warren whispered. "Stan would wring my neck. But even though I hate the risk, and even though we might be wrong, I think we have to try."

Kendra nodded.

They sat in silence, listening to the logs snap and pop in the fireplace. Although the wait stretched much longer than Kendra had anticipated, she experienced no boredom. Her mind continued reexamining the situation, trying to foresee how everything would play out. It was impossible to predict, but she found herself holding firm to the resolution that she and Warren had to go to Lost Mesa and see what they could learn. And perhaps what they could steal.

Nearly an hour later, Dougan returned, removing his mask as he came through the door. "Sorry about the wait," he said. "The Captain is swamped right now. The Captain mentioned that there were circumstances I could not know involving trouble at Fablehaven that would have justifiably made you extra cautious. Warren, if Kendra is willing to embark for Lost Mesa in the morning, you will be welcome to join her."

Warren and Dougan looked to Kendra. "Fine with me," she said, feeling a little sorry for Tanu and Coulter. No matter how this was explained to Grandpa and Grandma, they were going to be furious!

CHAPTER SIX

Plague

S eth threw the baseball as high and hard as he could, deliberately making it a tough catch for Mendigo. The primitive wooden puppet sprang into action the instant the ball took flight, dashing across the lawn. The human-sized limberjack wore a baseball glove on one hand and a cap on his head. The golden hooks that served as joints jingled as he dove over a hedge, stretching out to trap the ball in his mitt.

The nimble puppet landed in a somersault, then whipped the ball back at Seth as soon as he rolled to his feet. The ball hissed through the air, streaking straight instead of arcing high, and slapped into Seth's glove, sting-ing his hand. "Don't chuck it so hard," Seth instructed. "My hands have nerves!"

The limberjack stood in a crouch, ready to make the next impossible grab. After playing catch with Mendigo in the yard and having a few rounds of batting practice, Seth was convinced Mendigo could land a multimillion-dollar contract in the major leagues. Mendigo never dropped the ball and never threw wild. When pitching to Seth, the puppet would put the ball wherever Seth asked, at whatever speed he wanted. Batting, Mendigo could smack line drives in any direction he was told, or he could just as easily smash home runs with his quick, fluid swing. Of course, eligibility might be an issue. Seth wasn't sure about Major League Baseball's policy regarding giant magical puppets.

"Showboat," Seth called, throwing the baseball high. Mendigo was already running before the ball left Seth's hand. As the puppet closed in on the baseball, he shifted the glove from his hand to his foot and performed a smooth cartwheel, catching the ball with his gloved foot while upside down. The limberjack tossed the ball back to Seth, still with some zip, but not as hard as his previous throw.

Seth winged the ball sidearm in a new direction. Playing with Mendigo was a fun distraction, even though he knew the puppet was really his baby-sitter. Things had been tense since Coulter and Tanu had returned with news that Warren and Kendra had embarked on a mission for the Knights of the Dawn. Even without knowing all of the details, Seth felt sick with envy.

Grandpa and Grandma had taken the news hard, becoming even more protective of Seth than usual. Technically, his three-day period prohibiting even chaperoned excursions was over, but they had forbidden him from accompanying Coulter and Tanu on their assignment this afternoon.

Grandpa had been monitoring the nipsies while the others were gone, and had found that the warlike nipsies were relentless in their thirst to conquer the others. Nothing he tried could dissuade them. In the end he decided that the only way to save the untainted nipsies was to relocate them. Coulter and Tanu were currently searching for a new habitat for the good nipsies. A routine assignment, but Grandpa had suspended Seth from the woods until they figured out the story behind the new subspecies of dark creatures.

Mendigo returned the ball to Seth, who threw it to the right, lower than his previous toss. Mendigo started after it and then halted, letting the ball drop to the grass and roll into a flower bed. Seth put his hands on his hips. Unlike Hugo, Mendigo had no will—he only followed orders. And the current order was to play catch.

Continuing to ignore the ball, Mendigo rushed toward Seth at full speed. The action was baffling. Once, Mendigo had served Muriel the witch, but some fairies had helped Kendra break that connection earlier in the summer. Mendigo only took orders from the staff of Fablehaven now. He had proven so useful that Grandpa had arranged for Mendigo to be allowed past the barriers protecting the yard and house.

So why was Mendigo charging him? "Mendigo, stop!" Seth cried, but the puppet paid him no heed. Grandpa had issued Mendigo a standing order not to allow Seth out of the yard. Was the limberjack confused? Seth was nowhere near the edge of the lawn.

When Mendigo reached Seth, he dipped a shoulder, wrapped both arms around his legs, hoisted him into the air, and sprinted for the house. Slung over the wooden shoulder, Seth looked up and saw a group of dark fairies streaking toward them. They were unlike any fairies Seth had ever seen. Their wings did not glisten in the sunlight. Their raiment did not sparkle. In spite of the clear sky and the hot sun, each of the dozen fairies was shrouded in shadow. Faintly, a thin, dark contrail followed each one. Instead of light, these fairies radiated darkness.

The fairies gained swiftly, but the house was not far away. Mendigo swerved to avoid inky streaks of shadow hurled from the fairies. Wherever the black energy struck, vegetation instantly withered. Grass turned white and sere, blossoms wilted and faded, leaves crumpled and dried. A dark streak zapped Mendigo on the back, and a black circle appeared on the brown wood.

Bypassing the stairs, Mendigo clambered over the railing of the deck and clattered to the back door. The puppet dropped Seth, who thrust the door open and ordered the limberjack inside. Yanking the door shut, Seth hollered for Grandpa.

Seth now understood Mendigo's behavior. The puppet had one permanent command above all others—to protect the people of Fablehaven. The limberjack had sensed the fairies coming, and had known they meant trouble. Seth had a queasy feeling that if not for Mendigo, he might be a brown, shriveled corpse out on the lawn, the human version of a spoiled banana.

"What is it, Seth?" Grandpa asked, emerging from the study.

"I was just attacked in the yard by evil fairies," Seth gasped.

Grandpa glowered at him. "Have you been trapping fairies again?"

"No, I promise, I didn't do anything to provoke them," Seth insisted. "These fairies are different. They're wild and dark. Look out the window."

Seth and his Grandpa went to a window. The dismal flock of fairies were working their magic on a row of rosebushes, turning green leaves brown and vivid petals black. "I've never seen such a thing," Grandpa breathed, reaching for the door.

"Don't!" Seth warned. "They'll come after you."

"I have to see," Grandpa said, pushing the door open.

At once the fairies darted toward the deck, firing shadowy streaks. Grandpa promptly retreated indoors. The fairies hovered just beyond the deck. Several were laughing. A couple made faces. They desiccated a few potted plants on the deck before flitting away.

"I've never heard of anything like these creatures," Grandpa said. "How did they get in the yard?"

"They flew in as if they belonged," Seth replied, "just like any fairy would."

"Fairies are creatures of light." Grandpa spoke weakly, uncertainly, as if hesitant to believe what was happening.

"Some of the nipsies turned dark," Seth reminded him.

Frowning, Grandpa rubbed his chin. "These fairies aren't in a fallen state. When a fairy falls she becomes an imp, and would be banned from the yard. These fairies are in a darkened state—an undefined alteration that leaves them with full access to the gardens. I've never heard of anything like it. Perhaps I ought to place a temporary ban on all fairies, until we get this sorted out. I'm not sure I can exclude only the dark ones."

"Is Grandma still shopping?" Seth asked.

"Yes," Grandpa said. "She won't be back for at least an hour. Dale is down at the stable. Tanu and Coulter are still out scouting for a place to relocate the good nipsies."

"What should we do?" Seth inquired.

"I'll telephone Ruth," Grandpa said. "Warn her to be careful when entering the yard. I'll send Mendigo to fetch Dale."

"Can we get in touch with Tanu and Coulter?" Seth asked.

"No, but they have Hugo with them," Grandpa said. "We'll have to trust that they can take care of themselves." He turned to address the big puppet. "Mendigo, at full speed, go retrieve Dale from the stables, keeping him safe from harm. Steer clear of any dark creatures like those fairies."

Grandpa opened the door, and Mendigo raced out onto the deck, vaulted the railing, and sped across the lawn. "What should I do?" Seth asked.

"Keep watch from the windows," Grandpa said. "Don't go outside. Let me know if you see anything unusual. After I call your grandmother, I'm going to make a more concerted effort to get the Sphinx on the line."

Grandpa hurried away, and Seth went from room to room, checking through all of the windows, trying to spot the dark fairies. After three laps, he gave up. Apparently they had flown away.

To test his assumption he opened the door and ventured out onto the deck. Hadn't Grandpa done the same thing a moment ago, but with the fairies in sight? Seth was ready to retreat, but no gloomy fairies attacked. Had Grandpa already banished them from the yard? Seth sat down in a chair, gazing out at the garden.

He realized this was the first time he had been outside unsupervised since getting busted for visiting the nipsies. He felt an instant itch to bolt into the woods. Where would he go? Maybe to the tennis court to check in on how Doren and Newel were doing. Or to the pond to chuck rocks at the naiads.

No. After the scare with the fairies, he had to grant reluctantly that Grandpa was probably right about this being a foolish time to roam the woods. Besides, if he got caught, he would probably lose Grandpa's trust forever and end up grounded for all eternity.

He noticed a few normal fairies fluttering around the yard. They approached the dead roses and began healing them with glittering flashes. Wilted petals blushed. Curled leaves unfurled. Brittle limbs became supple and green.

The fairies were evidently not banned yet—the others must have voluntarily deserted the yard. Seth watched the fairies continue restoring the damaged vegetation. He did not try to move in for a closer look. Even the pretty fairies had no fondness for him. They were still resentful that he had accidentally turned one of them into an imp the previous summer. They had punished him, the fairy had been restored, and he had apologized a lot, but the fairies still mostly spurned him.

As his excitement over the dark fairies wore off in their absence, Seth ached with boredom. If Grandpa would trust him with keys to the dungeon, he could probably find a way to pass the time down there. He wished Mendigo would return. He wished he could switch places with Kendra, off on an adventure so secretive nobody had trusted him with the details. He even almost wished he was shopping with Grandma!

What could he do? There were toys in the attic bedroom, lots of them, but he had played with them so much over the summer that they failed to entice him anymore. Maybe he could rip up some of his clothes and leave them for the brownies to mend. It was always interesting to see the improvements they made.

Seth stood up, ready to go inside, when a vaporous personage emerged from the woods. The misty, translucent figure glided toward the deck. Seth realized to his horror that the ghostly apparition looked like Tanu, except wispy and insubstantial.

Had Tanu been killed? Was this his spirit come to haunt them? Seth watched as the gaseous form drew nearer. Its face looked grave.

"Are you a ghost?" Seth called.

The vaporous Tanu shook his head, and motioned as if drinking something from a bottle.

"A potion?" Seth asked. "That's right, you have a potion that turns you into gas, like the one Kendra said Warren used when you were battling the giant panther!"

Tanu nodded, drifting nearer. A light breeze arose, forcing him off course and temporarily dissipating his misty body. When the breeze died, Tanu re-formed and continued until he reached the deck. Unable to resist, Seth passed a hand through the insubstantial Samoan. The gas felt more like powder than mist. None of it stuck to his hand.

Tanu gestured for Seth to open the back door. Seth complied and followed Tanu into the house. "Grandpa, Tanu came back! He's made of gas!"

Indoors, Tanu held together better, which made him look more solid. Seth swatted a hand through Tanu's stomach, making the vapor shift and swirl.

"What is it, Tanu?" Grandpa asked, hustling into the room, cell phone in hand. "Was there trouble?"

The Samoan nodded.

"Where's Coulter? Is he all right?"

Tanu shook his head.

"Dead?" Grandpa asked.

Tanu shook his head slightly and shrugged.

"Does he need our help?"

Tanu tilted a hand from side to side.

"He doesn't need our help immediately."

Tanu nodded.

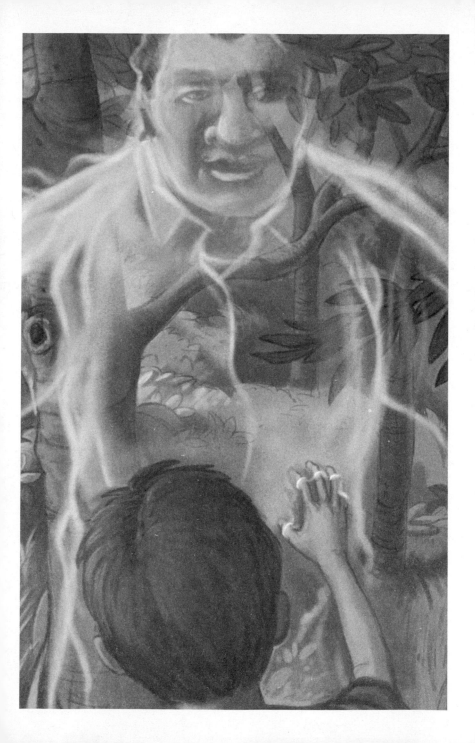

"Are we in immediate danger?"

Tanu shook his head.

"How long before you're back to normal?"

Tanu scrunched his brow, then held up one hand, the fingers spread wide.

"Five minutes?" Grandpa verified.

Tanu nodded.

The back door opened, and Dale entered with Mendigo. "What's going on?" Dale asked, taking in Tanu's altered state. "Mendigo showed up at the stables and abducted me."

"We have a problem," Grandpa said. "Dark fairies attacked Seth in the yard."

Eyes wide, Tanu gestured vigorously.

"Dark fairies attacked you too?" Seth asked.

Tanu stabbed a finger at Seth, nodding emphatically.

"Have you noticed anything unusual with any of the creatures today?" Grandpa asked Dale.

"Nothing like dark fairies," he replied.

"I called Ruth. She'll be careful coming into the house. I still can't reach the Sphinx."

"When will he solidify?" Dale asked, his eyes flicking over to Tanu.

"In a few minutes," Grandpa said.

"Mind if I grab some water?" Dale asked.

"Might do us all some good," Grandpa said.

They went to the kitchen, where Dale poured each of them a tall glass of cool water from the fridge. While Seth sipped at his drink, Tanu coalesced into his old self. A brief fizzing sound accompanied the rapid transformation.

"Sorry about that," Tanu said. "I'm not sure I would have escaped without the aid of a potion."

"What happened?" Grandpa asked calmly.

Tanu took a sip of water. "As planned, we were scouting for a new home for the gentle nipsies. We were investigating that crescent-shaped meadow near where the Forgotten Chapel used to stand. You know the one?"

"Sure," Dale said.

Grandpa nodded.

"I would, if I was ever allowed to explore," Seth grumbled.

"We came across a swarm of squabbling fairies, weaving around like dogfighters, some light, some dark. From what we saw, when the dark ones got their mouths on the light ones, the light fairies were extinguished—they became dark. But the light fairies didn't appear to be converting any dark ones."

"How many fairies?" Grandpa asked.

"Must have been nearly thirty," Tanu answered. "The brawl looked about even at first, but before long, the dark outnumbered the light three to one. Coulter and I decided we ought to break it up before all the fairies were changed. He has that crystal that makes people dizzy, and thought he might be able to disrupt the battle enough to give the light fairies a chance to escape.

"The instant we stepped into the clearing, the dark fairies left off tangling with the light ones and swarmed us. There was almost no time to think. Coulter urged me to go gaseous. Hugo put himself between us and the onslaught, and they hit him hard with murky magic that withered the grass on his body and left him spotted with black marks. Holding his crystal high, Coulter ordered Hugo to retreat to the barn, which was the right call. There was little Hugo could do against so many tiny enemies. The golem obeyed, and the fairies swooped at Coulter. The crystal disrupted their flight. Most crashed to the ground. A few managed to land on Coulter. They started biting him, and then he vanished."

"Did he put on his invisibility glove?" Seth asked hopefully.

"No glove," Tanu said. "He just disappeared. I drank the potion as the fairies came at me, and dissolved into a gaseous state just in time. They were mad, darting through me, shooting bursts of blackness at me, but when they saw that it was in vain, they flew away."

"They couldn't have killed Coulter," Dale said. "Dark or not, the treaty would still bind them. You were on neutral ground. They couldn't kill Coulter unless he had killed somebody at Fablehaven."

"For that very reason, I don't think he's dead," Tanu said. "But they placed some sort of curse on him that either made him invisible or teleported him away. I stayed and scoured the area, but found no evidence that he was invisible. No depressions in the grass where he might have been lying or standing. I would have heard him if he made a sound, but I detected nothing. That's all I know. I came straight here."

"You're sure Coulter didn't change into a darkened state himself?" Grandpa asked. "He simply vanished?"

"That's what I saw," Tanu said. "Maybe he turned into grass, or into a mosquito, or into oxygen. Maybe he shrank. I suppose there's a chance that somehow the rules don't apply to these dark creatures, and Coulter no longer exists in any form."

Grandpa sighed, bowing his head. When he raised it, he looked wretched. "I worry that I'm unfit to continue as caretaker. Have I grown too old? Have I lost my touch? Perhaps I should resign and ask the Conservators' Alliance to appoint a new overseer in my stead. It seems we've had one catastrophe after another lately, with the people I love most paying the price for my incompetence."

"This isn't your fault," Tanu said, resting a hand on his shoulder. "I know you and Coulter are old friends."

"I'm not asking for sympathy," Grandpa said. "I'm simply trying to be objective. I've been captured twice in the past year. The preserve was taken to the brink of collapse each time. I may have become more of a hindrance than a help to Fablehaven and those who live here."

"A fellow can't always avoid tough circumstances," Dale said. "But you can weather the trouble and come out on top. You've done it before, and I expect you'll do it again."

Grandpa shook his head. "I haven't solved anything lately. If not for my grandchildren risking their lives, along with help from the rest of you and a healthy dose of good fortune, Fablehaven would be in ruins."

Seth had never seen Grandpa Sorenson look so defeated. How could he revive him? He spoke up quickly.

"The first time, I caused all the trouble. The second time, Vanessa betrayed us. You never did anything wrong."

"And this time?" Grandpa asked, his voice calm and sad. "Not only did I inadvertently let your sister end up on a dangerous mission thousands of miles away, I also sent my oldest friend to his grave. How did I miss the warning signs?"

"The only thing that could make you unfit to lead would be belief in such nonsense," Tanu said gently. "Nobody could have seen this coming. You think Coulter or I would have approached the fairies so haphazardly had we sensed the danger? These are turbulent times. Fablehaven has been under deliberate assault from formidable foes. You've come through it so far, and so have we. I've traveled far and wide, and I can't think of anybody I would rather have watching over this preserve than you, Stan."

"I'll second that," Dale said. "Don't forget who'd most likely end up assigning the new caretaker if you resigned without appointing a successor."

"The Sphinx?" guessed Seth.

"His is the most trusted voice among the conservators," Grandpa admitted.

"Coulter is probably alive somewhere," Tanu said. "Pull yourself together, Stan. We need a plan."

"Thanks, Tanu, Dale, Seth." Grandpa pursed his lips, his eyes hardening. "We need information. The Sphinx is proving to be unreachable. Given the extremity of our circumstances, I think it's time to investigate what else Vanessa knows."

※ ※ ※

Slaggo and Voorsh led a skinny, birdlike humanoid down the dank dungeon corridor. The manacled prisoner had a head like a seagull and was covered with gray, molting feathers. Slaggo held a torch, and Grandpa walked alongside, shining a flashlight on the threesome. When the flashlight beam strayed too high, reflecting off the birdman's beady black eyes, he threw his head back and let out a fierce squawk. Voorsh yanked on a chain fastened to an iron collar, making the grungy birdman stumble sideways. Grandpa switched off the flashlight.

"Ready?" Grandpa asked, eyeing Tanu, Dale, and Grandma. Tanu held handcuffs, Dale clutched a truncheon, and Grandma gripped a crossbow. They each gave a single nod.

Grandpa opened the front of the Quiet Box, revealing an empty space where a person could stand. The goblin wardens guided the birdman into the compartment. Grandpa closed the door and the box rotated halfway around, exposing an identical door on the opposite side. Grandpa opened the door and revealed Vanessa standing inside, wearing one of Grandma's old housecoats, a faint smile on her lips, the torchlight accenting her elegant features. Her skin had less color than the last time Seth had seen her, but her dark eyes smoldered. He had to admit she remained strikingly beautiful.

"How long has it been?" she asked, stepping out of the box and extending her hands so Tanu could cuff them.

"Six weeks," Grandpa said, as Tanu secured the handcuffs.

"Where are my animals?"

"We released some," Grandpa said. "Others we gave away to those capable of caring for them."

Vanessa nodded as if satisfied. Her faint smile stretched into a smirk. "Let me guess. Kendra is no longer here, and some disaster is transpiring at Fablehaven."

Grandpa and Grandma exchanged a wary glance. "How did you know?" Grandma asked.

Vanessa stretched her cuffed hands high above her head and arched her back. She closed her eyes. "Certain precautions the Sphinx takes are predictable once you understand how he operates. It's the same way I anticipated that he was going to backstab me and lock me away in that miserable box."

"How did you predict this?" Grandpa asked.

Keeping her legs straight, Vanessa bent forward and touched the ground between her feet. "You released me from the box, and you all look serious, so obviously there has been trouble. Consider the circumstances. The Sphinx cannot afford to let his identity as the leader of the Society of the Evening Star be discovered. Even without the note I left, there were enough clues to what he was doing that you might have eventually become suspicious. He successfully acquired the artifact and freed the previous occupant of the Quiet Box. He had no more use for this preserve. Therefore, his next move would probably be to set some plan in motion to destroy Fablehaven and all of you with it—except

Kendra, who he suspects may still be useful. I'm sure he created an excuse to get her away from here just in time. You're all in tremendous danger. You see, when the Sphinx commits a crime, he disposes of all the evidence. Then, to be safe, he burns down the neighborhood." Vanessa swung her handcuffed arms from side to side, twisting at her waist. "I can't tell you how nice it feels to stretch."

"Can you guess how he is trying to destroy Fablehaven?" Grandpa asked.

Vanessa arched an eyebrow. "Some of the Sphinx's strategies are predictable. His methods are not. But whatever he has set in motion will probably be impossible to stop. Fablehaven is doomed. I expect I would be safer if you just put me back in the Quiet Box."

"Don't worry, Vanessa," Grandma said. "We will."

"I take it you don't fully comprehend the current threat?" Vanessa asked Grandpa.

"It is like nothing we've ever seen."

"Tell me about it; maybe I can help. I've been working for the Society for some time now." Vanessa started jogging in place, lifting her knees high.

"Creatures at Fablehaven are turning dark," Grandpa said. "The change has been most evident in the nipsies and fairies so far—creatures of light who are transforming in appearance and attitude into creatures of darkness. I'm not talking about fairies falling and becoming imps. We've seen fairies draped in shadow using their magic to wither and ruin rather than to nourish and beautify."

"And the condition is spreading?" Vanessa asked, legs pumping rapidly.

"Like a magical plague," Grandpa said. "Making matters worse, the dark fairies can cross all the same boundaries as the light fairies, including into the yard."

An expression of admiration appeared on her face. "Leave it to the Sphinx to invent new ways to eradicate preserves. I've never heard of an epidemic like you're describing. Let me guess. Even doubting the Sphinx, you've turned to him for help, but heard nothing."

Grandpa nodded.

"He is not replying because he expects you will soon be dead. You have two options. Abandon the preserve. Or try to figure out how to stop this plague the Sphinx has created, fail, and then abandon the preserve. My guess is you'll go with the second choice."

"Abandoning Fablehaven is not an option," Grandpa said. "Not until we do all we can to save it. Certainly not until we learn the secret behind this plague so we can prevent it from recurring elsewhere."

Vanessa stopped high-stepping, panting lightly. "Whether or not you can salvage Fablehaven, trying to discover the nature of the plague makes sense. Any leads?"

"Not yet," Grandpa said. "Only today did we realize how virulently the condition is spreading."

"I could help if you let me," Vanessa offered. "Magical creatures are my specialty."

"Along with controlling victims in their sleep," Grandma reminded everyone.

"You could post a guard," Vanessa suggested.

"We promised ourselves before we opened the box that you would be going back inside," Grandpa said.

"Very well, when all else fails and you change your minds, you'll know where to find me," she said. "The Quiet Box isn't as bad as I expected, really. After standing there waiting in the darkness for a while, you slip into a trance. Not full sleep, but you shut down, lose all sense of time. I was never hungry or thirsty—although I could use a drink now."

"Can you offer us sure evidence that the Sphinx is a traitor?" Grandma asked.

"Proof will be hard to come by. I know the names of other traitors. I was not the only one to infiltrate the Knights of the Dawn. And I know one secret that would absolutely blow your minds. But of course I'll divulge further information along those lines only in exchange for my freedom. Where is Kendra, by the way?" She asked the question with pretended innocence.

"Helping with a covert mission," Grandpa said.

Vanessa laughed. "Is he extracting another artifact so soon?"

"I said nothing about—"

Vanessa laughed louder, cutting him off. "Right," she chuckled. "Kendra's not in Arizona or Australia. Still, hard to believe, after all this time, the Sphinx has stopped pacing himself and is sprinting for the finish line. Any clue who went with her?"

"We've told her enough," Grandma said.

"Fine," Vanessa said. "Good luck with the Sphinx. Good luck with the plague. And good luck with seeing Kendra again." She stepped backwards into the Quiet Box, regarding them smugly.

"And good luck with getting out of there," Grandma said. Vanessa's eyes widened as Grandma slammed the door. Grandma turned to the others. "I'll not have her trying to use our fears to hold us hostage."

"We may eventually need her help," Grandpa said.

The Quiet Box turned, and Grandma opened the door. Slaggo and Voorsh took custody of the birdlike man. "I'm willing to work twice as hard in hopes of avoiding that eventuality."

"We lack communication with Warren, so Vanessa's knowledge of possible traitors won't help Kendra in the near future," Grandpa said. "Vanessa can offer no proof that the Sphinx is the leader of the Society. And it sounds like she'd be guessing as much as we are as to how to combat this plague. I suppose we can refrain from further questions for now."

"What now?" Seth asked.

"We need to determine how this plague started," Grandpa said, "in order to find a way to stop it."

CHAPTER SEVEN

Lost Mesa

The empty dirt road extended into the distance ahead of Kendra until it faded in a blur of shimmering heat. Her view of the desert landscape wobbled as the pickup jounced over the washboard surface of the desolate lane. It was rough country—uneven plains interrupted by rocky gorges and sheer plateaus. Lukewarm air gushed from the dashboard vents, refusing to actually get cool.

They had not stayed on roads the entire time. Part of the ride had taken them over miles of trackless terrain, emphasizing the isolation of their hidden destination. Driving directions from an Internet search were not going to lead a traveler anywhere near Lost Mesa.

The driver was a quiet Navajo man with leathery skin, probably in his fifties. He wore a spotless white cowboy hat and a bolo tie. Kendra had tried to engage him in conversation—he answered all direct questions, but never elaborated or made inquiries of his own. His name was Neil. He had been married once for less than a year. He had no kids. He had worked at Lost Mesa since his teenage years. He agreed that the day was hot.

Warren, Dougan, and Gavin all reclined in the bed of the pickup with the luggage, wearing hats that shielded their faces from the sun. All Kendra had to do was remember how hot and dusty they were to silence any possible complaints about the truck's feeble air conditioner.

"Almost there," Neil said, the first unsolicited words he had uttered since "I'll take your suitcase" back at the small airport in Flagstaff.

Kendra leaned forward, scanning up ahead for a landmark besides sun-baked dirt and turquoise sagebrush. The only feature out of the ordinary was a low barbed-wire fence coming into view, with a battered wooden gate that spanned the road. The three-wire fence stretched out of sight in either direction. A faded No Trespassing sign hung on the gate, red background with white letters.

"I don't see much besides a fence," Kendra said.

Neil glanced at her, eyes so squinted they looked closed. "You see the fence?"

"Sure. Barbed wire. Does it keep anybody out?"

"I've been driving this road thirty years," he said. "I still can't see the fence till after I pass it. Powerful distracter spell. I have to focus on the road. It's tough every time, fighting the urge to turn around, even though I know exactly where I'm going."

"Oh," Kendra said. Her goal had not been to advertise that distracter spells had no effect on her, but she could think of no false explanation to explain how she had seen the fence so easily. There it was, three parallel strands of barbed wire affixed to slim, rusted posts.

When the truck reached the gate, Neil slowed to a stop, climbed down, opened the gate, climbed back up, and drove through. The instant the car passed the fence line, a massive plateau sprang into view up ahead, so dominating the landscape that Kendra could not fathom how she had failed to notice it up until now. The looming mesa was not only enormous, it was striking, with bands of white, yellow, orange, and red coloring its steep sides.

"Welcome to Lost Mesa," Neil said, stopping the truck again.

"I've got it!" Warren called as Neil opened the door to climb down again. Warren ran over and shut the gate. Neil closed his door as Warren leapt back into the truck.

Kendra began to notice that the imposing plateau was not the only variation in the landscape on this side of the fence. Tall saguaro cacti were suddenly plentiful, rounded green arms pointing skyward. Joshua trees mingled with the saguaros, contorted limbs twisting into unlikely shapes.

"There weren't cactuses like this a minute ago," Kendra said.

Neil shook his head. "Not like these. We have a diverse forest here."

The truck sped up. The road was now paved. The asphalt looked dark enough to have been recently laid. "Is that *the* lost mesa?" Kendra asked, looking up at the plateau.

"The table that went missing when the preserve was founded. Here we call it Painted Mesa. Almost nobody knows, but part of the reason the Navajo people ended up with the largest reservation in the country was to conceal this hallowed place."

"Do Navajos run it?" Kendra asked.

"Not solely. We Diné are new here compared to the Pueblo people."

"Has the preserve been here long?" Kendra asked. She finally had Neil on a roll!

"This is the oldest preserve on the continent, founded centuries before European colonization, first managed by the ancient race outsiders call Anasazi. Persian magi actually established the preserve. They wanted it to stay a secret. Back then, this land was unknown across the Atlantic. We're still doing a good job at remaining off the map."

"Painted Mesa can't be seen from outside of the fence?" Kendra asked.

"Not even by satellites," Neil said proudly. "This preserve is the opposite of a mirage. You don't see us, but we're really here."

Kendra glimpsed fairies flitting among the cacti. A few were bright, with butterfly or dragonfly wings, but most were colored in more earthy shades. Many had scales or spines or protective carapaces. Their wings reminded Kendra of locusts and beetles. One furry brown fairy flapped leathery bat wings.

As the truck rounded a corner, new species of cacti came into view. Some had leaves like swords; others had long, spindly arms; still others had reddish needles. Sitting up next to a clump of spherical cacti, nose twitching as it tested the air, a large rabbit with a short pair of forked antlers caught Kendra's eye.

"That rabbit has horns!" Kendra exclaimed.

"Jackalope," Neil said. "They bring good luck." He glanced at Kendra without moving his head. "You had milk this morning?"

"Warren has some buttery stuff that works like the milk," Kendra said evasively. Warren did have a substance like that, derived from the milk of a giant walrus on a preserve in Greenland. He had even eaten some today, so his eyes would be open to the magical creatures of Lost Mesa. Kendra neglected to mention that Warren had not shared any with her because she no longer required milk to observe magical beings.

The truck topped a rise, and the main buildings of Lost Mesa came into view. Kendra first noticed the huge pueblo complex, which looked like two dozen boxy adobe homes artfully stacked together. The windows were dark, with no glass. Wooden beams jutted from the reddish-brown walls. Beside the pueblo stood a white hacienda with a red-tiled roof. The horseshoe-shaped hacienda looked considerably more modern than the pueblo complex. A tall water tower overshadowed the hacienda, built on long stilts.

Across a vacant area from the houses stood two other structures. One was a vast wooden building with a curved aluminum roof. Even though she saw no runway, Kendra wondered if it might be an airplane hangar. The other was a low, domed structure that sheltered a wide area. The gigantic black head of a cow even bigger than Viola protruded through a large opening just above ground level. The cow was munching hay from a vast trough. Seeing that enormous head at ground level revealed to Kendra that the domed roof must cover a tremendous pit where the colossal cow lived.

The truck snaked along the curvy road, pulling to a stop on a tiled area outside the hacienda. Before Neil had cut the engine, the main door opened, and a short Native American woman emerged. Her silver hair was pulled up in a round bun, and she wore a colorful shawl across her shoulders. Although her copper skin was seamed, her eyes were lively, and she walked with vigor.

Several other people followed the woman out the door. A potbellied man with narrow shoulders, long limbs, and a heavy gray mustache walked alongside a tall, slender Native American woman with a broad jaw and high cheekbones. Behind them came a freckly woman with short brown hair pushing a pudgy, round-faced Mexican man in a wheelchair.

Kendra dropped down from the truck, while Warren, Dougan, and Gavin hopped out of the bed. "Welcome to Lost Mesa," said the older woman with the bun. "I am Rosa, the caretaker here. We're glad to have you with us."

They exchanged introductions. The tall younger woman was Rosa's daughter, Mara. She said nothing. The gangly man with the mustache was named Hal. Tammy was the woman pushing the wheelchair, and she seemed to know Dougan. The guy in the wheelchair was named Javier. One of his legs was missing. The other was in a splint.

It was decided that Warren and Dougan would go talk to Rosa, Tammy, and Javier inside the hacienda. Neil and Mara helped Warren and Dougan tote their bags into the house, leaving Kendra and Gavin alone with Hal, who had been appointed to show them around the preserve.

"Don't that beat all," Hal said once the others were out of sight. "The sky starts falling around here, and they send us a couple of teenagers. No disrespect intended. First thing an able mind learns at Lost Mesa is that looks can deceive."

"Wh-wh-who died?" Gavin asked.

Hal raised his eyebrows. "If they didn't tell you, I'm not sure it's my place."

"Javier was injured at the same time?" Gavin wondered.

"So I'm told," Hal said, hooking his thumbs into the belt loops of his jeans. The movement made Kendra notice his heavy silver belt buckle with a majestic elk engraved on the front.

"Hot today," Kendra said.

"If you say so," Hal allowed. "Monsoon season is under way. We saw rain two nights this week. Things have cooled off a few degrees since July."

"Wh-what are you going to show us?" Gavin asked.

"Whatever you like," Hal said, flashing a smile that showed a gold tooth. "You two are getting the V.I.P.

treatment, in part because you could end up with the R.I.P. treatment. Heaven forbid."

"D-d-do you know why we're here?" Gavin asked.

"None of my affair. Some foolishness up on Painted Mesa, I expect. Something risky, judging from Javier. I'm not one to pry."

"Tammy was working with Javier and whoever died?" Kendra asked.

"That she was," Hal affirmed. "Things went awry, so they called in the cavalry. You kids been to a preserve like this before?"

Gavin nodded.

"Yeah," Kendra said.

"Then I reckon you can guess what the cow is for." He jerked his head toward the domed structure. "We call her Mazy. She's been skittish lately, so don't slide up too close, especially when she's eating. A few folks live in the pueblo over yonder, but you'll have rooms in the house, for which you'll be grateful, once you feel the draft from the swamp coolers."

"What about the building that looks like a hangar?" Kendra asked.

"That's the museum," Hal said. "One of a kind, for all I know. We'll save it for the finale." He picked up a covered white plastic bucket with a metal handle and slung it into the bed of the truck Neil had driven. Pulling a set of keys from his pocket, Hal opened the passenger door. "Let's take a ride. We can all squeeze up front."

Kendra climbed up and scooted into the middle. Hal

sauntered around to the driver's side, using the steering wheel to pull himself up. "Nice and cozy," Hal said, turning the key in the ignition. He glanced over at Kendra and Gavin. "Don't tell me you two are sweethearts."

They both hastily shook their heads.

"Now, don't go protesting too much," he laughed, backing up the truck before starting down a dirt road. "Aside from the buildings and Painted Mesa, I know this place looks like a whole lot of nothing. But you'd be surprised at the hidden springs and ravines and sandstone mazes. Not to mention that most of the activity around here takes place beneath the surface."

"Caves?" Gavin asked.

"Caverns that would put Carlsbad to shame," Hal exclaimed. "Some individual chambers could house an entire football stadium with room to spare. I'm talking about no fewer than seven elaborate cave systems that go on for hundreds of miles all told. I expect one day we'll find how they all interconnect. If this place were open to the public, it'd be the caving capital of the world. 'Course, as you might expect, you never know what a spelunker might run across in the tunnels below Lost Mesa. Better to stay on the surface, enjoy the gorgeous gorges and the beautiful buttes."

"What kind of creatures are in the caves?" Kendra asked.

"I make a point of not knowing. One of these days I'll kick the bucket, sure enough, but curiosity will not be my downfall. That said, you don't have to go looking to know those caverns teem with every manner of haunt and bugaboo that have plagued the human race since time began. Here we go. Take a gander up ahead."

They came around the side of a bluff, bringing into view an old Spanish mission with a single belfry. The brown walls of the building rose and fell in gentle curves. The truck drove around to the back, where they found a cemetery enclosed by a low wall.

Hal brought the truck to a stop. "This and the pueblo are the oldest structures on the property," he said. "One of the most memorable features is the boneyard. It not only houses the biggest zombie collection in the world, it's one of the oldest to boot!" He opened his door and got out.

Kendra turned to gauge Gavin's reaction, but he was already climbing down as well. She heard the tinkling of many bells coming from the graveyard. "Zombies?" Kendra asked incredulously, sliding out of the truck, soles slapping the dirt. "As in dead people?"

"Not people," Hal clarified. "Not like you and me." He retrieved the plastic bucket from the back of the truck. "They don't have any more brains than a leech. And they aren't any more human either."

"Is this safe?" Kendra asked.

Hal led the way to a short iron gate in the cemetery wall. "Zombies have only one drive. Hunger. Satisfy that drive, and they aren't too harmful. We've got as good a system here as I've ever heard of."

Kendra followed Hal and Gavin through the gate and into the graveyard. None of the headstones were ostentatious. They were small and old, white as bone, worn so smooth that only a few occasional letters or numbers were faintly visible. Planted beside each grave was a bell on a small pole with a cord attached. Each cord disappeared underground. Of the nearly two hundred bells in the grave-yard, at least thirty were ringing.

"Took some doing," Hal said, "but they got these zombies pretty well trained. It was done before my time. When the zombies get hungry, they ring their bells. If they ring long enough, we bring them some mash." He held up the bucket. "Long as we satisfy their hunger, they stay put."

Hal walked over to the nearest clanging bell. He crouched, lifted up a clear tube that ran into the ground, and unstopped it. Then he took a funnel from his back pocket. "Mind holding this?" he asked Gavin.

Gavin held the funnel in the tube while Hal took the lid off the bucket and began pouring goopy red fluid. Kendra looked away as the chunky liquid sluiced through the tube. Hal quit pouring, stopped up the tube, and moved to the next active bell. Kendra noticed that the first bell was no longer ringing.

"What if you quit feeding them?" Gavin asked, inserting the funnel into the next tube.

"I expect you can guess," Hal said, pouring the gruesome sludge. "The hunger would build until they clawed their way to the surface to find food on their own."

"Why not get them nice and full, then dig them up and burn them?" Kendra asked.

"That wouldn't be very charitable," Hal scolded, pro-ceeding to a new grave. "Maybe you don't understand.

Unlike some of the undead, zombies have no human spark. Ending the suffering of a human trapped in a state like this, I could view that as mercy. But a zombie has no humanity. A zombie is something else. An endangered species, truth be known. Not pretty or cuddly, not very bright, not very quick. Tenacious predators, deadly under certain circumstances, but not overly adept at defending themselves. We found a way to keep zombies satisfied without letting them harm anyone, a way to preserve the species, so we do it, unsavory or not. We're not much different from a wildlife conservationist trying to protect ugly bats or spiders or mosquitoes from extinction. These refuges exist to protect all magical creatures, the fair ones and the foul ones alike."

"Makes sense, I guess," Kendra said. "Mind if I go wait in the truck?"

"Suit yourself," Hal said, tossing her the keys. They glanced off her fingers and fell to the dry ground beside one of the tubes. After a brief hesitation, Kendra snatched them and trotted out of the graveyard.

As she walked to the car, she fleetingly wished she could trade places with her brother. Feeding bloody meals to subterranean zombies would probably be a favorite pastime in Seth's version of paradise. And she would be more than happy to hang out with her grandparents, read old journals, and sleep in a familiar bed.

Inside the truck, Kendra blasted the air conditioner, aiming the tepid currents from all the vents directly at herself. It was only a slight improvement over trying to cool down using a hair dryer. She pictured herself running from a hoard of ravenous zombies on a hot day, eventually collapsing from heatstroke and getting devoured. Then she imagined Hal giving a rousing eulogy at her funeral, explaining how Kendra's death was a beautiful sacrifice allowing the noble zombies to live on, delighting future generations by mindlessly trying to eat them. With her luck, it could totally happen.

Hal and Gavin finally returned from the cemetery. Hal tossed the bucket into the back and climbed into the driver's seat. "Almost used up all my mash," Hal said. "Good thing I normally bring more than I need. Twenty bells is what I consider a busy day. Thirty-two is close to the record."

"Wh-wh-wh-wh-where to now?" Gavin asked. Kendra noticed one of his hands clenching into a fist as he stuttered.

"We'll hit a few sights, then wind up back at the museum." Hal drove them to an old mill with a covered well out front. Then he showed them the irrigated fields where a group of men and women toiled to raise corn and other crops. He pointed out a bowl-shaped cavity in the ground where a meteor had supposedly landed, and drove them around a tremendous Joshua tree with hundreds of limbs. At last, they came back into sight of the hacienda and the pueblo complex. Hal pulled the truck to a stop in front of the museum.

Kendra and Gavin followed Hal to a small door beside a pair of larger doors on rollers. Hal unlocked the door and they entered. The hangar contained a single cavernous room. Daylight flooded in through high windows.

Hal reached over and flipped on the lights, banishing the remaining shadows.

"Welcome to the Museum of Unnatural History," Hal said. "The world's largest collection of freestanding magical creature skeletons and other related paraphernalia."

Directly in front of Kendra loomed a humanlike skeleton more than twice the height of a man. The skull tapered to a blunt point and had three eye sockets arranged like the points of a triangle. A bronze plaque labeled the creature a Mesopotamian Triclops.

Beyond the nearest skeleton were many others: the bones of a horse supporting the bones of a human upper body instead of an equine head and neck; the skeleton of an ogre positioned as if combating nine dwarfish skeletons; a cow skull the size of a motor home; a mobile suspending delicate fairy skeletons; and a titanic humanoid skeleton with curved fangs and disproportionately thick bones that extended over half the distance to the high ceiling.

Kendra also beheld other exotic displays. A huge, scaly skin hung on hooks, limp and dry, apparently shed by a creature with four arms and a serpentine body. A vibrant collection of eggshells, large and small, was arranged inside a glass case. Strange weapons and armor lined an entire wall. Enormous golden antlers branched outward above a doorway.

Despite the numerous eye-catching exhibits in the room, Gavin immediately stalked toward what was undoubtedly the main attraction. Kendra and Hal jogged after him, catching up as he stopped in the center of the room with his hands on his hips.

Protected by a circular railing, taking up one quarter of the total floor space, was the skeleton of an immense dragon. Kendra gazed at the long, slender bones of the wings, the razor claws on the four feet, the vertebrae of the winding tail and elegant neck, and the vicious teeth on the massive horned skull. The milky bones were semitransparent, as if made of clouded glass or quartz, giving the tremendous skeleton an ethereal appearance.

"Who would dare put actual dragon bones on display?" Gavin seethed through clenched teeth.

"Actual bones is right," Hal said. "Unlike some of the exhibits, which are re-creations and whatnot, this is entirely the original skeleton of a single dragon. Good luck finding another like it."

"Who did this?" Gavin reiterated, eyes blazing.

Hal finally seemed to notice he was upset. "There's a plaque right in front of you."

Gavin stormed forward to read the bronze plaque attached to the railing.

WORLD'S ONLY COMPLETE SKELETON
OF AN ADULT MALE DRAGON
BELIEVED BY SOME TO BE
RANTICUS THE INVINCIBLE
DONATED BY PATTON BURGESS
1901

Gavin gripped the railing, tendons standing out on the backs of his hands. He took a shuddering breath and then whirled, body tensed, eyeing Hal like he was ready to throw a punch. "Have none of you ever heard that the remains of a dragon are sacred?"

Hal returned his gaze, unperturbed. "You have some special connection with dragons, Gavin?"

Gavin lowered his eyes, his body going slack. After a moment, he spoke, his voice calmer. "My-my dad worked with dragons."

"No fooling," Hal said with admiration. "Not many men have the constitution for that kind of work. Mind if ask your dad's name?"

"Charlie Rose." He did not lift his eyes.

"Your dad is Chuck Rose?" Hal gasped. "He's the closest thing we've had to a dragon tamer since Patton himself! I never knew Chuck had a kid! 'Course, he always was a mite secretive. How's your old man?"

"Dead."

Hal's face fell. "Oh. Hadn't caught wind of that. I'm sorry to hear it, I truly am. No wonder the sight of a dragon skeleton would put you ill at ease."

"Dad fought hard to protect dragons," Gavin said, finally lifting his gaze. "Their welfare was his top priority. He taught me a lot about them. I don't know much about Patton Burgess."

"Patton ain't exactly news no more. Passed on more than sixty years ago. Makes sense that your father wouldn't have brought him up too much. Those who love dragons would avoid the subject. Rumor has it—never confirmed, mind you—that Patton was the last living person to slay a full-grown dragon."

Kendra tried to keep her expression steady. If she revealed how she knew about Patton Burgess, it would tie her to Fablehaven. Better to avoid the appearance of knowing anything about the topic.

"Slayed a full-grown dragon?" Gavin asked with a smile, clearly not believing a word. "Did he claim to have killed this dragon?"

"Way my granddad tells it, and my granddad met him, Patton never claimed to have killed a dragon. Fact is, he claimed the opposite. In this case, Patton said he found old Ranticus by following shady merchants who were pillaging his organs and selling them off piece by piece."

"Ranticus was numbered among the twenty lost dragons," Gavin said. "One of the minority who never sought refuge in a sanctuary."

"We don't mean any harm keeping him on display," Hal said. "It's out of respect more than anything. Preserving what we can. Ain't like we charge admission."

Gavin nodded. "B-b-because of my dad, dragons mean more to me than any other creature. I'm sorry if my reaction was out of line."

"No harm done. Sorry I didn't know your pedigree—I would have handled that differently."

"Like not brought me in here?" Gavin asked.

"You're onto me," Hal admitted.

"The bones are beautiful," Kendra said, turning her attention back to the fantastical skeleton.

"Lighter and stronger than anything I can think of," Hal said.

Gavin turned to face the exhibit as well. "Only other dragons can properly dispose of them. Time and the elements are no match."

They regarded the dragon remains in silence for several minutes. Kendra felt as though she could stare at the skeleton for the rest of the day. It was as if dragons were magical right down to their bones.

Hal rubbed his round belly. "Anybody else itching for some grub?"

"I could eat," Gavin said.

"How do you eat with that mustache?" Kendra asked as they started toward the exit.

Hal stroked the whiskers lovingly. "I call it my flavor saver."

"Sorry I asked," Kendra said, scrunching her face.

They passed out of the warehouse in silence. Hal ignored the truck and ambled toward the hacienda. "I can honestly say that I'm glad to have met you two," Hal said as they approached the front door. "One of you may be a little squeamish about zombies, and the other a mite sympathetic to dragons, but we've all got our oddities. Come to mention it, I'm doubly glad you're here, since Rosa never lays quite as full a table as when we have company."

"You like Rosa?" Gavin asked.

"Like her fine," Hal said. "What with her being my

spouse and all I oughtn't complain. Lost Mesa is different from some preserves in that it has always been managed by a female caretaker. Comes from Pueblo culture, where the women inherit the property. I expect Mara will take over the position before long. She's a tough one—loyal as they come, but none too friendly."

Hal opened the door and led them down a hall to an airy dining room. The hacienda was less hot and more humid than outside. Kendra noticed a large evaporative cooler humming in a window. Warren and Dougan already sat at the table with Rosa and Mara.

"We wondered when you'd show up," Rosa said. "Where'd you take them, Colorado?"

"Here and there," Hal said unflappably. "Fed the zombies and such." He stole a blue corn chip from a basket on the table, jerking his hand away before Rosa could swat it with a ladle.

"That must have been appetizing," Warren said, shooting Kendra a glance.

"W-w-we're ready for food," Gavin said.

"We're ready to feed you," Rosa said with a smile. "Enchilada soup, tamales, and corn casserole."

Tammy wheeled Javier into the room, and they started passing the food around. Kendra tried to put zombies out of her mind when Rosa ladled the reddish soup into her bowl. The food looked and tasted different from other Mexican fare Kendra had eaten. Even though she found it a little too spicy, she enjoyed it.

The conversation during dinner was all small talk,

with Hal saying the most, and Mara saying nothing. After the meal, Warren and Dougan excused themselves, taking Kendra and Gavin with them. Warren led Kendra into a bedroom with a view of the courtyard and closed the door.

"Dougan is filling in Gavin," Warren said. "This will be your room. We should be out of here in no time. We're going after the artifact tomorrow. They agreed to let me tag along. All you'll have to do is sit tight."

"What happened last time?" Kendra asked.

Warren moved closer and spoke lower. "It was Javier, Tammy, and a guy named Zack. The entrance to the vault is up on top of Painted Mesa, and I guess getting there is a pain. Neil knew a way, so he guided them up, but waited outside the entrance. Rosa had entrusted them with the key to the vault, so they got inside without much trouble and made it past a couple of traps. Then they ran into a dragon."

"A live one?" Kendra said.

"Zack, the leader, was dead before they knew what was happening. Javier lost a leg and injured the other one. He wasn't bitten—he got swiped by the tail. He and Tammy were lucky to escape with their lives. They couldn't relate much about what the dragon looked like, but they both act certain about what attacked them."

"Gavin's dad worked with dragons," Kendra said.

"Which is why they brought him along. Apparently Gavin is a natural dragon tamer. You need to keep that quiet for his sake. It's the main reason his father kept him a secret. It could make him as big a target as you."

"What's a dragon tamer?"

Warren sat down on the bed. "To understand that, first you have to understand dragons, arguably the most powerful race of magical creatures. They live for thousands of years, they can grow to the size of apartment buildings, they have frighteningly keen intellects, and they have deep magic woven into every fiber of their bodies. Just about any mortals who try to converse with dragons find themselves instantly transfixed and rendered utterly powerless. A dragon tamer can avoid this effect and actually hold a conversation."

"And then they can control the dragon?" Kendra asked.

Warren chuckled. "Nobody controls a dragon. But dragons are so accustomed to overpowering all other beings simply with their gaze that they find a human who they cannot break most intriguing. It's a dangerous game, but sometimes dragons will grant favors to such individuals, including allowing them to live."

"So Gavin will try to talk his way past the dragon?" Kendra asked.

"That's the idea. I just found out about the dragon, but they informed him earlier. I guess he's game to try. And I'm fool enough to tag along."

"What if talking fails? Could you guys kill it?"

"Are you serious? With what? Their scales are like stone, their bones like adamant. They each have a unique arsenal of powers at their disposal, not to mention teeth, tail, and claws. And keep in mind, all but a select few people become petrified in their presence. Dragons are the supreme predator."

"Hal acted like Patton Burgess might have killed a dragon," Kendra said.

"How'd you end up talking about slaying dragons?"

"They have a dragon skeleton in their museum. Donated by Patton."

"Patton always denied the rumors that he ever killed a dragon. I see no reason to doubt him. In olden times, great wizards learned how to use magic to destroy dragons, which was how they persuaded them to take refuge in the Seven Sanctuaries. But a wizard who could slay a dragon has not walked the earth for hundreds of years. The only people I've heard of killing dragons in our times are poachers abusing hatchlings. Poachers of that sort are rare, courtesy of their short life spans."

"What are the Seven Sanctuaries?" Kendra asked.

"Higher preserves than the kind you have seen," Warren said. "Some magical creatures are too powerful to endure human supervision. These are sent to the Seven Sanctuaries. Almost nobody knows their locations, myself included. But we're straying from the topic."

"You're going to try to steal an artifact from a dragon," Kendra said.

"Close. I'm going to sneak past a dragon in order to help Dougan obtain an artifact in order to steal it from Dougan in order to hide it in a better spot."

"You think Gavin can really talk his way past a dragon?" Kendra asked.

"If he's everything Dougan claims, maybe. His father was the most renowned dragon expert in the world. Even among caretakers and Knights of the Dawn, dragons remain the stuff of legend. I've never seen a live one. Almost none of us have. But Chuck Rose lived among them for months at a time, studying their habits. He even photographed one."

"How'd he die?"

Warren sighed. "A dragon ate him."

CHAPTER EIGHT

Shadowman

S eth squeezed toothpaste onto his brush and started scrubbing his teeth. He hardly saw his reflection in the bathroom mirror. Things at Fablehaven were getting so intense he had almost stopped envying Kendra for being away. Almost. He still sometimes pictured her and Warren rappelling into an Egyptian tomb, mowing down mummies and cobras with machine guns. An adventure that awesome would outshine a mysterious plague making the fairies lose their light.

After spitting into the sink and splashing water on his face, Seth headed out of the bathroom and up the attic stairs. He had just participated in a long conversation with Grandpa, Grandma, Tanu, and Dale, and he was trying to sort through all the new information so he could figure out a way to save everybody. If only he could prove that his defeating the revenant hadn't been a fluke, the next time a secret mission became necessary, maybe they would bring him along.

At the top of the stairs he paused, leaning against the side of the doorway. The fading light of dusk glowed purple through the window of the attic playroom. Grandpa and the others had been trying to list all the possible sources of the plague. According to them, there were four major demons at Fablehaven: Bahumat, who was trapped in a secure prison under a hill; Olloch the Glutton, who was frozen in the woods until some idiot fed him; Graulas, a very old demon who was basically hibernating; and a demon nobody had ever seen named Kurisock, who lived in a tar pit.

Against his will, Seth glanced at the journals piled beside Kendra's bed. She had known about the tar pit already because of reading. Could those pages contain info Grandpa and the others might have overlooked? Probably not. And if so, they were welcome to do the reading themselves.

The adults had expressed the opinion that, of the four demons, Bahumat and Olloch were currently the most dangerous, because they had never agreed to the Fablehaven treaty. Normally, all of the magical creatures admitted to Fablehaven had to pledge to abide by the treaty, which established boundaries for where they could roam and limits to how much they could harm other creatures. There were borders that Graulas and Kurisock had sworn not to cross, rules they had made binding vows not to break. Only people foolish enough to enter their domains were at serious risk from those two. But Bahumat had been at Fablehaven since before the treaty was established, and Olloch had come to Fablehaven as a guest, which imposed certain automatic restraints but left room for him to cause trouble if he gained enough power. At least that was how Seth understood it.

The important part was that the plague probably wasn't caused by any of the four demons, at least not acting directly. None of them had sufficient access. There were some candidates in the dungeon, but Dale had checked, and they were all still safely imprisoned. There was a hag in the swamp who had helped train Muriel, but Grandma had maintained that starting the plague was far beyond her abilities, and the others agreed. There was a poisonous bog full of evil creatures, but their boundaries were clearly defined. Same with the inhabitants of a tunnel not far from where Nero lived. Grandpa had named many other dark creatures on the preserve, but none that were strong enough in dark magic to have possibly initiated the plague.

In the end, with no viable suspects, Seth had asked what creature haunted the old Fablehaven mansion. Before responding, the adults wanted to know how he knew a creature dwelled there. He had never brought up how he had visited the manor after escaping from Olloch, worried that everyone would be angry at him for choosing to go inside. He explained how he had been lost, and how he had hoped that from the roof he could get some perspective regarding his location. Then he told how a mysterious whirlwind arose, chasing him from the house, leaving him shaken and terrified.

Grandpa explained that they weren't sure what dwelled in the mansion. Apparently the manor had been overthrown on Midsummer Eve more than a hundred years ago. The acting caretaker at the time, Marshal Burgess, lost his life, and caretakers had been warned ever after to avoid the old manor.

"Whatever found a new home in the mansion," Grandpa had concluded, "was something from this preserve. Even if it escaped from the poisoned bog, it should not have the power to create a plague like we're witnessing. An advantage to the treaty is that we know what creatures are here. We have them catalogued."

"How could any creature have remained in the mansion after Midsummer Eve?" Tanu had inquired. "The culprit should have been forced to return to its proper dwelling once the night ended."

"Theoretically any of them could remain if they managed to change the register, which appears to be what happened," Grandpa had explained. "The register is used to alter certain boundaries and grant access. Patton Burgess managed to tear the treaty from the register and escape with those essential pages. Otherwise the preserve might have fallen. The treaty now resides in the current register. But the damage done to the old manor was irreparable."

So the whirlwind wasn't the answer. The demons weren't the answer. None of the creatures at Fablehaven were apparently the answer. And yet the plague was happening. They had eventually decided to sleep on it, leaving the problem unresolved. The only decisive action taken all day was when Grandpa used the register to prohibit all fairies from entering the yard.

Seth wandered to the window to gaze out at the purple evening, and jumped back when he saw a black figure silhouetted against the glowing sky. Seth jostled against the nearby telescope, embracing the expensive piece of equipment before it could topple. Then Seth turned back to the window, half expecting the figure to be gone.

The figure remained, crouching, not a silhouette—a human-shaped, three-dimensional shadow. The shadowman waved at Seth. Hesitant, Seth waved back.

The shadowman shook his fists as if excited, then motioned for Seth to open the window. Seth shook his head. The shadowman pointed at himself, then pointed into the room, then once again pantomimed opening the window.

Seth had gotten into major trouble the previous summer for letting a creature into the house by opening that same attic window. The creature had been disguised as a baby, but turned out to be a goblin, and once inside, the treacherous intruder had let other monstrosities in. Before the night was over, Grandpa had been kidnapped, and Dale had been temporarily turned to lead. Seth had learned his lesson. This year, he had stayed in bed on Midsummer Eve. Peeking out the window had hardly been a temptation.

Of course, Midsummer Eve was different from most days, being a night when the boundaries of Fablehaven were dissolved and all sorts of nightmarish monsters could come into the yard. But today was ordinary. On a regular evening, dangerous creatures should not have access to the yard in order to crouch outside Seth's window. Did that mean the shadowman was a friendly creature?

Then again, nice creatures had become menacing lately. Maybe this shadowman had once been able to enter the yard, and now that he was evil, he was using that status to trick Seth! Or maybe this was whoever had started the plague! The thought made Seth shiver. It had a ring of truth to it—the inky black figure looked like a likely candidate for starting a plague that replaced light with darkness.

Seth tugged the curtains shut and backed away from the window. What should he do? He had to tell somebody!

Seth clomped down the attic steps and raced to his grandparents' room. The door was shut, so he banged on it. "Come in," Grandpa invited.

Seth opened the door. Neither Grandpa or Grandma had changed into their nightclothes yet. "There's something outside my window," Seth whispered hastily.

"What do you mean?" Grandpa asked.

"A shadowman. A living shadow in the shape of a man. He wanted me to let him in. What creatures can enter the yard besides fairies?"

"Hugo and Mendigo," Grandma said. "And of course the brownies live under the yard and have access to the house. Anything else, Stan?"

"Everything else is by invitation only," Grandpa said. "I've let satyrs into the yard on occasion."

"What if this shadow guy started the plague?" Seth

speculated. "A creature we didn't know was on the preserve, some shadowy enemy who can come into the yard but not the house."

Grandpa scowled thoughtfully. "The yard has failsafes to prevent most creatures, even surprise guests, from entering. Whatever the nature of this shadowman, not all of the rules seem to apply."

"At least it couldn't enter the house," Grandma said.

Grandpa started toward the door. "We had better fetch Tanu and Dale."

Seth followed Grandma and Grandpa as they collected Tanu and Dale and explained the situation. They mounted the steps to the attic in a line, Grandpa in front, Seth at the rear. Moving the telescope out of the way, they gathered around the curtained window, Grandma with her crossbow, Tanu holding a potion ready.

Grandpa pulled aside the curtains to reveal an empty stretch of roof barely visible in the dying twilight. Seth pushed his way forward to the glass, peering in all directions. The shadowman was gone.

"He was here," Seth promised.

"I believe you," Grandpa said.

"He really was," Seth maintained.

They waited, watching as Grandpa shone a flashlight through the slightly warped panes. They located no sign of an intruder. Grandpa clicked off the flashlight.

"Keep the window closed tonight," Tanu admonished. "If he returns, come for me. If not, I'll search the roof in the morning."

Tanu, Dale, and Grandpa left the room. Grandma waited at the top of the stairs. "You'll be all right?"

"I'm not scared," Seth said. "I just hoped I'd found something useful."

"You probably have. Keep that window shut."

"I will."

"Good night, dear. You did the right thing to come and tell us."

"'Night."

Grandma left.

Seth changed into his pajamas and flopped onto his bed. He began to suspect that the shadowman had returned, perching outside the window. The fiend had probably not wanted the others to see him. But now if Seth peeked, he would be there, silently asking to enter.

Unable to banish the suspicion, Seth went to the window and threw aside the curtain. The shadowman had not returned.

⚶ ⚶ ⚶

The next morning, Tanu crept around on the roof outside the window but found no trace of a visitor. Seth was unsurprised. Since when did shadows leave footprints?

At breakfast, Grandpa tried to inform Seth he would be restricted to the house all day. After Seth's persistent complaining, Grandpa agreed to let him play with Mendigo in the yard if somebody supervised them from the deck.

Grandpa, Grandma, Tanu, and Dale spent the day poring over journals and other books from their extensive library, trying to find any hint of something like the plague afflicting the creatures of Fablehaven. They took turns reading on the deck. Mendigo had orders to bring Seth inside at the first appearance of anything suspicious.

The day passed uneventfully. Seth played football and baseball with Mendigo, and went swimming in the afternoon. At lunch and dinner, Seth listened as the adults discussed how frustrated they were about the lack of any information that explained what was transpiring at Fablehaven. Grandpa had still been unable to get a call through to the Sphinx.

After dinner, Seth begged his way outside for a few minutes. Hugo was there, having recently finished some chores in the barn, and Seth wanted to see what happened if Mendigo pitched to the golem.

The baseball bat looked tiny clutched in Hugo's massive hand. Seth told Hugo to hit the ball as hard as he could, then instructed Mendigo to throw a fastball right down the middle. Seth moved out of the way, worried about getting brained by a foul ball. He didn't think they would need a catcher.

Mendigo hurled a blazing pitch, and Hugo, swinging one-handed, whaled the ball into the sky. Seth tried to follow the baseball as it shrank into the distance, but failed. He knew the ball had still been rising when it cleared the trees on the far side of the yard, so it had to have landed a good ways into the woods.

Seth turned to Tanu, who was sitting on the deck,

enjoying the sunset as he sipped herbal tea. "Can I send Mendigo to fetch it?"

"Go ahead," Tanu said, "if you think the ball is worth fetching."

"It might just be a pile of mush," Seth laughed.

"That was quite a blast."

Seth told Mendigo to quickly retrieve the ball, but the puppet did not respond. When Tanu repeated the command, the limberjack dashed across the yard and into the woods.

That was when Seth saw the shadowman coming into the yard not far from where Mendigo had entered the trees. The phantom moved toward Seth with swift, deliberate strides. Seth retreated toward the deck. "There he is," Seth told Tanu, pointing. "The shadowman."

The Samoan stared in the direction Seth was indicating, looking perplexed. "In the trees?"

"No, right there, in the yard, coming through that flower bed!"

Tanu stared for a moment longer. "I don't see anything."

"He's on the lawn now, getting close to us, walking fast."

"I still don't see it," Tanu said, giving Seth a worried glance.

"You think I'm crazy?" Seth asked.

"I think we better get inside," Tanu said, backing toward the door. "Just because I can't see him doesn't mean you don't. Where is he now?"

"Almost to the deck."

Tanu motioned for Seth to follow and went in the back

door. Seth entered after Tanu and they shut the door. "We have a situation," Tanu called.

The others hurried into the room.

"What now?" Grandpa asked.

"Seth sees the shadowman in the yard," Tanu said. "I don't."

"He's on the deck," Seth said, looking out a window by the door.

"Where?" Grandpa asked.

"Right there, by the rocker."

"Anybody else see it?" Grandma asked.

"Not me," Dale said.

"He's motioning for us to come outside," Seth said.

Placing her hands on her hips, Grandma regarded Seth suspiciously. "You're not leading us on, are you? This would be a terrible joke, Seth. The situation at Fablehaven is much too—"

"I'm not making this up! I would never lie about something so important. I can't imagine why you guys can't see him!"

"Describe him," Grandpa said.

"Like I said last night, it looks like the shadow of a man, but three-dimensional," Seth said. "There isn't much else to describe. He's holding up his left hand, pointing at it with the other hand. Oh my gosh!"

"What?" Grandma prodded.

"He's missing his pinky and part of his ring finger."

"Coulter," Grandpa said. "Or some form of him."

"Or something that wants us to believe it's some form of him," Grandma added.

Grandpa strode to the door. "Warn us if he moves toward me," Grandpa told Seth, cracking the door open. Leaning forward, Grandpa spoke through the opening. "If you're a friend, stay where you are."

"He's not moving," Seth said.

"Are you Coulter Dixon?" Grandpa asked.

"He nodded," Seth said.

"What do you want?"

"He's motioning for us to come with him."

"Can you speak?"

"He shook his head. He's pointing at me, and motioning for me to come."

"Seth's not going with you," Grandpa said.

"He's pointing at himself and then into the house. He wants to come inside."

"We can't invite you in. You could be our friend, with your mind intact, simply in an altered state, or—"

"He's giving a thumbs-up and nodding," Seth interrupted.

"Or you could be a twisted version of Coulter, with all his knowledge, but sinister intentions." Grandpa closed the door and turned to the others. "We can't risk letting him inside, or being led into a trap."

"He's making a pleading gesture," Seth reported.

Grandpa closed his eyes, steadying himself, then opened the door again. "Help me understand what is happening. You are free to roam the preserve?"

"Thumbs-up," Seth said.

"Even places where we normally would be unable to go?"

"Two thumbs up," Seth said. "That one must be important."

"And you have found something we need to see."

"He's shaking his hand like so-so."

"You can lead us to vital information."

"Two thumbs up."

"And it is urgent? The situation is dire?"

"Thumbs-up."

"What if only I come?" Grandpa offered.

"Thumbs-down."

"Seth has to come?"

"Thumbs-up."

"Could Tanu and I come with Seth?"

"He's shrugging," Seth said.

"You don't know? Can you find out?"

"Thumbs-up."

"Go find out if we can come. I can't send Seth with you alone, I hope you understand. And none of us can accompany you until we can confirm you are not an evil version of yourself seeking to betray us. Give us some time to deliberate. Can you come back in the morning?"

"He's shaking his head," Seth relayed. "He's pantomiming a ball. Now he's shielding his eyes. I think he means he can't go out in the sunlight. Yep, he heard me, he's giving a thumbs-up."

"Tomorrow evening, then," Grandpa said.

"Thumbs-up."

"Try to think of a way to prove we can trust you."

"He's tapping a finger to the side of his head, like he'll think about it. Now he's walking away."

Grandpa closed the door. "I can't foresee a way to prove he's the same Coulter we love and trust. He could have all of Coulter's knowledge yet still be a threat."

"Why can't he come into the house on his own?" Dale asked.

"I think he could if we left the door open," Tanu said. "He's insubstantial right now. Not immaterial enough to pass through a door, but he can't open one on his own."

"How do we confirm he's on our side?" Seth asked.

"Your grandfather may be right," Grandma said. "I'm not sure there's a way."

"The situation is dire enough that if he would let me go with him, I would simply take the risk," Grandpa said. "But I'll not let Seth do it."

"I'll take the risk," Seth said. "I'm not afraid."

"Why is he insisting Seth comes?" Dale asked.

"Only Seth can see him," Tanu said.

"Of course," Grandpa said. "No wonder he was adamant that we couldn't come without Seth. I was too busy trying to find a deeper purpose in it."

"Still," Grandma said, "he was hesitant to allow others to join Seth. Why could it be that only Seth can see him?"

Nobody ventured a guess.

"You're sure you aren't making fools of us?" Grandma asked Seth again, studying him shrewdly.

"I promise," Seth said.

"This isn't a trick to get out of the house and into the woods?" Grandma pressed.

"Trust me, if all I wanted was to get into the woods, I'd already be there. I swear I would never make up a story like this. And I have no idea why only I can see him."

"I believe you, Seth," Grandpa said. "But I don't like any of this. I wonder if our shadowy Coulter could reveal himself to more of us if he wanted? Could he be choosing to let only Seth see him? We need to do all we can to make sense of this. Unanswerable questions are piling up. I propose we speak with Vanessa again. If she can be of any service, now is the time to call upon her. Perhaps in her work for our enemies she has witnessed something like this shadowman phenomenon."

"She's not a cure-all," Grandma said. "Odds are all she'll be able to do is imitate the same guesses we're making."

"Our guesses aren't adding up to much," Grandpa said. "Time could be running out. We should at least check."

"I'll go in the box, if it will speed things up," Dale volunteered. "Long as you let me out."

"She'll be going back inside," Grandma promised.

Grandma got her crossbow and Grandpa grabbed a flashlight. Tanu went to retrieve his handcuffs but returned empty-handed. "Anybody seen my handcuffs? All I can find are the keys."

"Did you ever take them off of her?" Grandma asked. Something about the way she asked the question hinted that she already knew the answer.

They descended the steps to the basement. When they

reached the Quiet Box, Dale opened the door and stepped inside. Grandma closed the door, the Quiet Box rotated, and when she opened it, Vanessa stood there with her wrists cuffed together.

"Thanks for leaving me shackled," she said, stepping out of the box. "As if I didn't already feel like part of a cheap magic act. What's the latest?"

"Coulter is in some sort of darkened, shadowy state," Grandpa said. "He can't speak. He seems to want to share information with us, but we don't know if we can trust him."

"Neither do I," Vanessa said. "Have you any guesses how the plague originated?"

"Do you?" Grandma responded, her tone accusatory.

"I've had some time to mull it over. What have you come up with?"

"Honestly, we can't fathom how it could have originated here," Grandpa said. "Bahumat is imprisoned, Olloch is frozen, the other major demons are bound by the treaty. We can't think of any being at Fablehaven with the ability to initiate something like this."

As he spoke, a smile appeared on Vanessa's lips, gradually widening. "And the obvious conclusion hasn't occurred to any of you?"

"That it came from outside of Fablehaven?" Grandma guessed.

"Not necessarily," Vanessa said. "I have a different possibility in mind. But I don't want to go back into the box."

"There is no way for you to undo the connection you forged when you bit us?" Grandpa asked.

"I could lie and say there was," Vanessa said. "You know the link is permanent. I would be happy to take an oath never to use those connections again."

"We know what your word is worth," Grandpa said.

"Considering that the Sphinx is now more my enemy than yours, you can rely on me much more than you know. I'm enough of an opportunist to recognize when the time has come to trade sides."

"And to recognize when you can commit a large enough betrayal for the Sphinx to welcome you back," Grandma said. "Or perhaps the Sphinx really is on our side, and whoever employs you would be glad for your return as soon as you manage to slip away."

"Makes it complicated," Vanessa admitted.

"Vanessa," Grandpa said, "if you don't help us rescue Fablehaven, you might be stuck in that box for the rest of eternity."

"No prison lasts forever," Vanessa said. "Besides, as blind as you seem, sooner or later you'll arrive at the same conclusion I did."

"Let's make it sooner," Grandpa said, raising his voice for the first time. "I'm on the verge of deciding the Quiet Box is too good for you. I could arrange a stay in the Hall of Dread. Your ability to haunt our sleep wouldn't remain a concern for long."

Vanessa paled.

Seth did not know too much about the Hall of Dread. He knew it was on the other side of the dungeon behind a bloodred door, and that the prisoners there required no food. Apparently Vanessa knew more details than he did.

"I'll tell you," Vanessa relented. "Granted, I'd rather go to the Hall of Dread than give away the key knowledge that might buy my freedom. But this is not that information. Nor does it get you much closer to comprehending how the plague began, although it sheds some light on whom to blame. Are you sure the Sphinx took the previous occupant of the Quiet Box off the preserve with him?"

"We watched them drive away . . ." Grandma's voice trailed off.

"Did you observe them from all angles the entire time?" Vanessa pursued. "Is it possible the Sphinx might have released the prisoner before passing through the gate?"

Grandma and Grandpa looked at each other. Then Grandpa looked at Vanessa. "We watched them depart, but not closely enough to guarantee you're wrong. Your theory is plausible."

"Given the circumstances," Vanessa said, "I'd say probable. There is no other explanation."

The thought of that secret prisoner bundled in burlap roaming the preserve turning nipsies and fairies dark made Seth shudder. He had to admit, it was the most likely propo-sition they had considered.

"What do you know about the prisoner?" Grandma asked Vanessa.

"No more than you," Vanessa said. "I have no clue who the prisoner was, or how he or she or it started the plague, but the process of elimination sure makes the prisoner look like the culprit. And it definitely doesn't reflect well on the Sphinx."

"You're right, we should have seen this possibility," Grandpa said. "I wonder if, deep down, I still haven't come to terms with the reality that the Sphinx might be our greatest enemy."

"This is still all conjecture," Grandma reminded them, although without much conviction.

"Have you any other information that might help us?" Grandpa inquired.

"Not with solving the mystery of this plague," Vanessa said. "I would need time to study it firsthand. If you let me help, I'm sure I could be of service."

"We're shorthanded enough without having to stand guard over you," Grandpa replied.

"Fine," Vanessa said. "Could you take the shackles with you this time?"

Tanu unlocked and removed the handcuffs. Vanessa stepped back into the box. She winked at Seth. He stuck out his tongue. Grandma closed the door, the box rotated, and Dale emerged.

"I was starting to worry this was all an elaborate setup to get rid of me," Dale said, shaking his arms as if clearing off invisible cobwebs.

"Did it feel like a long time?" Seth asked.

"Long enough," Dale answered. "You lose your senses in there. Can't hear a thing, can't see a thing, can't smell a thing. You start losing all sensation. You feel like a disembodied mind. It's almost relaxing, but not in a good way.

You start losing your grip of who you are. I can't figure how Vanessa manages to string words into sentences after spending weeks in that emptiness."

"I'm not sure anything could put her at a loss for words," Grandma said. "She's as slippery as they come. Whatever we do, we must place no trust in her."

"No trust," Grandpa said. "But she may be of further use for information. She acts like she still has a card to play, and she's no fool, so she probably does. How can we discover the identity of the hooded prisoner?"

"Could Nero have seen something in his stone?" Grandma asked.

"Possibly," Grandpa said. "If not, there's a chance he still could."

"I'll go ask him," Seth offered. His previous visit with the cliff troll had been exciting. The greedy troll had wanted to acquire him as a servant in exchange for using a seeing stone to locate Grandpa.

"You'll do nothing of the kind," Grandma said. "A massage enticed him into helping us once. The same offer might tempt him again."

"Knowing Nero, having sampled your skills once, he'll want you to sign on as his permanent masseuse before he'll assist us," Grandpa said. "Last time, he had never had a massage. The novelty of it was the key. You proved that curiosity will motivate him more than riches."

"A special potion, perhaps?" Tanu suggested.

"Something modern?" Seth tried. "Like a cell phone or a camera?"

Grandpa put his hands together against his lips as if praying. "It's hard to say what might do the trick, but something along those lines is worth a try. With creatures transformed by the plague lurking about, simply getting to Nero might be the hardest part."

"What if Nero has been affected by the plague?" Dale wondered.

"If it turns light creatures dark, it might turn dark creatures darker," Tanu speculated.

"Maybe we'd have better luck following Coulter," Seth reminded them.

"We won't be able to answer those questions until we make a choice and take a risk," Grandpa said. "Let's sleep on it and decide tomorrow."

CHAPTER NINE

Pathways

Asqueal escaped Kendra when she awoke in the night, the roar of the thunderclap fading. She felt flustered and disoriented. The noise had jolted her out of sleep as abruptly as a punch in the face. Although this was her second night at Lost Mesa, the dark room initially appeared unfamiliar—it took a moment to make sense of the rustic furniture fashioned from knotty wooden posts.

Had the house been struck by lightning? Even though she had been asleep, Kendra felt certain she had never heard thunder that loud. It had been like dynamite exploding inside her pillow. She sat up and swung her legs over the edge of the bed. A brilliant strobe flickered, bright enough to throw shadows, accompanied almost instantaneously by another deafening detonation of thunder.

Covering her ears, Kendra walked to the window, staring out into the dim courtyard. With clouds blotting out all starlight and no lights on in the hacienda, the courtyard should have looked totally black.

She could make out cactus shapes in the dimness. The courtyard had a fountain in the center, tiled paths, gravel paths, and a variety of desert flora. She expected to see one of the taller cacti in flames from a lightning strike, but that did not appear to be the case. No rain was falling. The courtyard was still. Kendra felt tense, awaiting the next flash of light and crash of sound.

Instead of more lightning and thunder, rain began to fall. For a few seconds it pattered lightly; then it really began to pour. Kendra opened her window, enjoying the aroma the rain released from the desert soil. A fairy with wings like a june bug alighted on the windowsill. Glowing a soft green, she had an exquisite face and was pudgier than any fairy Kendra had seen.

"Got caught in the rain?" Kendra asked.

"I don't mind the water," the fairy chirped. "Freshens things up. This little cloudburst will pass in a few minutes."

"Did you see the lightning?" Kendra asked.

"Hard to miss. You shine almost as brightly."

"I've been told that before. Do you want to come into my room?"

The fairy giggled. "The windowsill is as close as I can come. You're up late."

"The thunder woke me. Do fairies often stay up all night?"

"Not all of us. Not me, usually. But I hate to miss a rain-storm. We get so few. I adore the monsoons."

The rain was already falling more gently. Kendra stretched out a hand to feel the fat drops on her palm. Lightning flared up in the clouds, farther away than before, muted by the intervening mist. Thunder followed a couple of heartbeats afterward.

Kendra wondered what Warren was doing at the moment. He had departed for the vault with Dougan, Gavin, Tammy, and Neil about an hour before sunset. He might have returned already, for all she knew. Or he could be in the belly of a dragon.

"My friends might be out in this weather," Kendra said.

The fairy tittered. "The ones trying to climb the mesa?"

"You saw them?"

"Yes."

"I'm worried about them."

The fairy sniggered again.

"It isn't funny. They're on a dangerous mission."

"It *is* funny. I don't think they went anywhere. They couldn't find a way up."

"They didn't climb the mesa?" Kendra asked.

"Getting up there can be problematic."

"But Neil knows a way."

"*Knew* a way, from the look of things. The rain is relenting."

The fairy was right. It was barely sprinkling now. The earthy, humid air smelled wonderful. "What do you know about Painted Mesa?" Kendra asked.

"We don't go up there. Near the mesa, sure, the whole formation has a lovely aura. But there is old magic woven into that place. Your friends are lucky they couldn't climb it. Good night."

The fairy leapt from the windowsill and buzzed off into the night, veering up over the roof and out of sight. After the company, Kendra felt lonely. Lightning pulsed somewhere above her. Thunder growled a few seconds later.

Kendra closed the window and slid back into bed. Part of her wanted to check if Warren was safe in his room, but she felt uncomfortable intruding if he was asleep. She was sure to hear in the morning about what had happened.

⚹ ⚹ ⚹

Kendra had never tried huevos rancheros, but found she liked them a lot. The thought of mixing eggs with fresh guacamole had never occurred to her, and she had been missing out. Warren, Dougan, and Gavin sat eating with her while Rosa puttered in the kitchen.

"So you couldn't find a way up," Kendra said, cutting into her food with the side of her fork. She had found them eating after she awoke and showered. None of them had mentioned the mission yet.

"What tipped you off?" Warren asked.

"No bite marks," Kendra said.

"Very funny," Dougan said, checking over his shoulder as if worried somebody might be eavesdropping.

"Seriously," Warren said.

Kendra realized she shouldn't be telling Dougan and

Gavin that she could talk to fairies. "One look at your faces told the whole story. You were acting too normal."

"Neil said the mesa can be fickle," Warren explained. "There are many ways up, but none are constant. They open only to certain people at certain times."

"Rent a helicopter," Kendra said, taking another bite.

"Neil says the mesa would never allow it," Dougan said.

"I believe him," Gavin said. "Y-y-y-you can feel the magic of the place; it makes you drowsy. You should have seen Tammy's face when the path wasn't there. She said it was unmistakable last time."

"Neil didn't like it either," Warren said. "I guess his way up has been pretty reliable."

"Ascending the mesa has always been a challenge," Rosa said, wiping her hands on a dishtowel as she approached the table. "I warned you it might not be easy. Especially after the others went and disturbed things."

Kendra thought of the revenant guarding the entrance to the vault at Fablehaven. Here, was the mesa itself the guard?

"The way to the top may be closed for some time," Neil said, coming into the room, holding his white cowboy hat in one hand. He was wearing jeans and hiking boots. "There have been periods lasting fifty years or more when no pathway was available."

"We can't wait," Dougan said. "We need to get up there."

"Forcing the mesa is impossible," Neil said. "Don't lose hope yet. I want to take Kendra and scout around the base."

"Kendra?" Warren asked.

"She saw the fence around Lost Mesa before we entered the preserve," Neil said. "If the Twilight Way is closed, eyes like hers might help spot one of the other paths."

Kendra noticed Gavin and Dougan regarding her with interest. "I'd be happy to look, if you think it might help," she said.

"I'll come with you," Warren said.

Neil nodded. "Mara will join us as well. When will you be ready to leave?"

"Give us twenty minutes," Warren said, glancing at Kendra to make sure that was acceptable.

"Sounds good," she said.

Warren hurried through the rest of his food, and Kendra did likewise. When they were done, she followed him to her room. He closed the door.

"How did you really hear we couldn't find a pathway up Painted Mesa?" Warren asked.

"A fairy told me last night," Kendra said.

"I'm sure the others didn't believe your comment was based solely on intuition, but I doubt they'll openly pry. Remember to be careful about hinting at your powers. Dougan knows you can recharge magical items. That's it. The others don't even know that much."

"Sorry," Kendra said. "I'll be careful."

"We have to be cautious. I think we can trust Dougan and Gavin, but I don't want to take anything for granted. I'm positive the Society has people in place to make sure the artifact ends up in their hands. Remember, at Fablehaven,

the original plan was for Vanessa and Errol to steal the artifact themselves. The traitor here might be somebody who
has lived on the preserve a while. Or it could be Tammy or
Javier."

"Hopefully it was Zack," Kendra said.

Warren grinned. "Wouldn't that be nice? I've done
some digging. Tammy is along because she has a talent for
finding and disabling traps. Javier is a seasoned ingredient
collector, used to work for a couple of the top dealers. He
has a lot of experience getting out of dodgy situations. Their
reputations are solid, but so was Vanessa's."

"Are you worried about Neil or Mara?" Kendra asked.

"If the Sphinx is a suspect, anyone is a suspect," he said.
"Trust no one. Try to stay inside the hacienda unless I'm
with you."

"Think I'll be able to find a trail?" Kendra asked.

Warren shrugged. "You can see through distracter spells.
You've got a better shot of finding a secret path than I have."

"We should probably get going."

Neil and Mara were outside in a dirty Jeep with the
engine running. Warren and Kendra climbed in back.
They did not keep to roads for long. Out the front window,
Painted Mesa loomed ever larger. During one stretch, Neil
forced the Jeep up such a steep grade that Kendra worried it
would rear up and tip over backwards. The bumpy, jarring
drive ended in a flat area strewn with jagged boulders.

A few hundred yards of rugged terrain separated them
from where a sheer stone face of the mesa rose into the sky.
"It's so high," Kendra said, using her hand as a visor as she

stared up at the colorful plateau. There was hardly a cloud in the bright blue sky.

Neil came up beside her. "You'll be looking for handholds, a rope, a cave, a stairway, a path—anything that might grant access. To most eyes, most of the time, there appears to be no possible route to the top, even for an experienced climber. The pathways become available only at certain moments. For example, until lately, the Twilight Way appeared at sunset. We'll circle the mesa multiple times."

"Do you know of other paths besides the Twilight Way?" Warren asked.

"We know of others, but not where to look," Neil said. "The only other reliable route is the Festival Road. It opens on festival nights. The next opportunity would be the autumnal equinox."

"Scaling the mesa on a festival night would be madness," Mara said, her voice a resonant alto. "Suicide."

"Sounds like my kind of party," Warren joked. Mara did not acknowledge that he had spoken.

"What if you get up there and can't find a way down?" Kendra asked.

"There are normally many ways down," Neil said. "The mesa is happy to see visitors leave. I've never had trouble, nor have I heard stories of others facing difficulties descending."

"Those people might not be around to tell the stories," Warren pointed out.

Neil shrugged.

"Could the Twilight Way open up again?" Kendra asked.

Neil tossed up his hands. "Hard to say. My guess would be not for many seasons. But we'll check this evening— maybe your sharp eyes will catch sight of something I missed."

Kendra noticed beige rabbit feet dangling from Neil's pierced earlobes. "Are those lucky?" Kendra asked, indicating the earrings.

"Jackalope," Neil said. "If we're going to find a pathway, we'll need all the luck we can get."

She refrained from telling Neil the obvious—that the feet had clearly not been very lucky for the jackalope.

They hiked around the mesa. Little was said. Neil mostly studied the sheer rock faces from several paces away. Mara got up close, caressing the stone, sometimes leaning her cheek against the unyielding surface. Kendra scrutinized the mesa as best she could, from near and far, but noticed no evidence of a path.

The sun beat down relentlessly. Neil loaned Kendra a wide-brimmed hat and some sunscreen. When they finally circled back to the Jeep, Neil retrieved a plastic cooler. They ate sandwiches and trail mix in the shade.

During the afternoon, a warm breeze began to blow. Kendra saw the most interesting things when she faced away from the mesa and glimpsed an occasional fairy or jackalope in the distance. She wondered if the jackalopes resented Neil for his earrings. No creatures, insects included, ventured right up to the mesa. The atmosphere was heavy. Gavin had been right, there was something in the air that lulled you, made you drowsy.

They completed another meticulous lap around the mesa before hunkering down in the shade and eating the dried fruit and jerky Neil had brought for dinner. He told them a final loop around the mesa would put them in about the right spot to look for the Twilight Way when the sun went down.

As they hiked, leaden thunderheads began to blow in from the south. When they paused for a water break, Mara surveyed the oncoming clouds. "Going to be a real storm tonight," she predicted.

By the time the sun neared the horizon, the wind was whistling through the rocks, a constant, eerie moan that rose to shrill hoots and shrieks during gusts. Ominous clouds obscured much of the sky, shot through with magnificent colors where the sun was sinking.

"It should be here," Neil said, staring up at a blank cliff. "A winding trail."

Mara leaned against the base of the precipice, eyes closed, palms pressed against the stone. Kendra stared hard, trying to will her eyes to see through whatever spells might be concealing the path. Neil paced around the area, clearly frustrated. Warren stood with his arms folded, nothing moving but his eyes. Behind them, the sun finally disappeared below the horizon.

A particularly strong gust blew Kendra's hat off and made her stagger. The wind cried out in disharmonious howls.

"We should get back to the Jeep," Neil said, eyes sweeping the mesa one last time.

"The Twilight Way is closed," Mara declared solemnly.

As they hiked back to where they had parked the Jeep, rain began to patter on the rocks around them, leaving dime-sized splotches on the stone. Within minutes, the rocks had darkened with wetness, becoming slick and treacherous in places.

Coming into sight of the Jeep, they scrambled over and around jumbled piles of damp stone. The rain fell hard now. Although her clothes were soaked, the warm air kept Kendra from shivering. She glanced back over her shoulder and saw a waterfall streaming down the side of the mesa. The sight made her pause. The water was not falling straight; it was coming at an angle, leaping and rolling, the lively rapids of a steep stream. Not a natural stream—the water was tumbling down a steep stairway, carved into the face of the mesa.

"Stop," Kendra called, pointing. "Look at that waterfall!"

The other three turned and stared at the mesa. "Waterfall?" Warren asked.

"Not a true waterfall," Kendra amended. "Water racing down a stairway."

"You see stairs?" Neil asked.

Kendra pointed from the base of the mesa to the top. "Looks like they run all the way up. They're so obvious now, I can't believe they were hidden before! You'll want to wait until they dry off. It would be a tough climb with all that water."

"The Flooded Stairs," Mara said with wonder in her voice.

"I still don't see anything," Warren said.

"Neither do we," Neil replied. "Take us to the foot of the stairs."

The others followed Kendra as she led them back to the base of the mesa. Reaching the stairs did not take long. Just beyond the end of the stairs, the water slurped into a dark fissure in the ground. Kendra edged up to the crevice and peered down. There was no end in sight. She could hear water churning in the distant depths.

"I'm surprised we didn't fall in the hole when we were circling the mesa earlier," Kendra said, turning to the others.

"I don't see a hole," Warren said.

"Can you lead me onto the stairs?" Neil asked.

Taking his hand, Kendra led him around the opening in the ground and along a rocky shelf until they stood together at the bottom step. Cold water gushed around their shins. "Do you see it now?" Kendra asked.

"Lead me up a few steps," Neil said.

Treading carefully, for though the water was not deep, it was coming fast, Kendra placed her foot onto the first slick stone step. With Neil in tow, she climbed four stairs before she slipped, plunging a hand and both knees into the frigid stream before Neil hoisted her up.

"Enough," Neil said.

They carefully returned to the shelf, then walked around the crevice to rejoin Warren and Mara. "I didn't see the stairway until you started climbing," Warren said. "And then it only seemed to go about five steps beyond the point you reached. I had to focus hard to keep my eyes on you."

"I saw fifteen steps ahead of me before the stairs ceased," Neil said.

"It keeps going and going," Kendra verified, "turning here and there, reaching landings or ledges in some places. The stairs lead all the way to the top. Will the storm be over by morning?"

"When the rain ends, the stairs will be gone," Mara said. "That is why, even with your gifted sight, you did not perceive the stairs or the fissure earlier. None have found the Flooded Stairs in centuries. Many assumed the pathway existed only in lore."

"You have to climb the stairs in the rain?" Kendra asked. "That is going to be tough!"

"This could be our only opportunity," Neil said to Warren.

Warren nodded. "We should get the others."

"We'll need Kendra to guide us," Neil said. "I felt the strength of the spell. It took all I had to follow her lead. Without her, we have no chance."

Warren frowned, water trickling down his face from his damp hair. "We'll have to find another way."

Neil shook his head. "This was a long shot, a miracle. Don't count on finding another way, not for years. Maybe we should leave whatever is up there alone. It is well guarded."

"I'll lead you up, if you need me," Kendra said. "I'll need somebody near me who can keep the water from sweeping me away."

"No, Kendra," Warren said. "There is no imminent danger compelling us. You don't need to do this."

"If we don't recover what we came for, someone else might," Kendra said. "I don't have to go into the vault. Just up the mesa."

"She could wait outside with me," Neil offered.

"There can be strange activity on the mesa during a storm," Mara warned. The wind wailed, underscoring her words.

"We'll take refuge in the old weather room," Neil said. "I passed the time quietly there on the last trip."

Kendra looked at Warren. He did not look fully unwilling. She suspected he wanted her to do it, but not because he pushed her. "This is important," Kendra insisted. "Why am I here if not to help where I can? Let's do it."

Warren turned to Neil. "You met no trouble on top of the mesa last time?"

"No real danger," Neil said. "That may have partially been luck. The mesa is certainly not always safe."

"Do you think you can protect Kendra?"

"I expect so."

"Will this rain last a while?" Warren asked Mara.

"Off and on, for a few hours at least."

They started back toward the Jeep. "We could round up the others and be ready to return within half an hour," Warren said. "Do you have climbing equipment? Ropes? Harnesses? Carabiners?"

"For six of us?" Neil asked. "Maybe. I'll gather all we have."

They fell silent. That was it. The decision had been made. They were going to give it a try.

As Kendra followed the others, picking her way over and around wet rocks, she tried not to picture herself frozen with fear high on a watery stairway, a magnificent desert vista overwhelming her with paralyzing vertigo. In spite of Warren's faith in her, she wished she could retract her offer.

CHAPTER TEN

Shadow Wounds

Seated on a chair on the deck, Seth examined the checkerboard in disbelief. Tanu had just jumped two of his checkers, and now outnumbered Seth seven pieces to three. But that was not the cause of his amazement. Seth reexamined his potential move, put his hand on one of his two kings, and jumped six of Tanu's pieces, zigzagging around the board.

He looked up at Tanu. The Samoan stared back with wide eyes. "You asked for it," Seth laughed, removing all but one of Tanu's red checkers. Tanu had already beaten him twice in a row, and things had been looking grim until the coolest move he had ever found opened up. "I used to think triple jumps were the ultimate."

"I've never seen so many jumps in one move," Tanu said, a smile creeping onto his face.

"Wait a minute," Seth said. "You set me up! You did that on purpose!"

"What?" Tanu asked with too much innocence.

"You wanted to see if you could create the biggest jump in the history of checkers. You must have been maneuvering the whole time to set that up!"

"You're the one who found the move," Tanu reminded him.

"I know pity when I see it. I'd much rather strike out than have somebody pitch to me underhand. Is this your way of getting back at me for always going first?"

Tanu grabbed a handful of popcorn from a wooden bowl. "When you're black you say 'coal before fire.' When you're red you say 'fire before smoke.' How can I keep up with that?"

"Well, even if you staged it, jumping six guys felt pretty good."

Tanu's smile revealed part of a kernel caught between his teeth. "The longest possible jump would be nine, but I'm not sure I could make that happen during an actual game. Five was my previous best."

"Hello!" came a voice from the edge of the yard, made smaller by the distance. "Stan? Seth? Are you there? Hello?"

Seth and Tanu both looked toward the woods. Doren the satyr stood beyond the perimeter of the lawn, waving both arms.

"Hi, Doren," Seth called.

"What do you think he wants?" Tanu asked.

"We better go check," Seth said.

"Hurry!" Doren urged. "Emergency!"

"Come, Mendigo," Tanu said. The overgrown puppet followed as Seth and Tanu vaulted the deck railing and ran across the yard to the satyr. Doren's face was red, and his eyes were puffy. Seth had never beheld the jovial satyr in such a state.

"What is it?" Seth asked.

"Newel," the satyr said. "He was napping. Those foul little nipsies had their revenge on him, accosted him in his sleep."

"How is he?" Tanu asked.

Doren grabbed fistfuls of his hair and shook his head. "Not good. He's changing, I think, like the nipsies changed. You've got to help him! Is Stan around?"

Seth shook his head. Grandpa had gone with Grandma, Dale, and Hugo to negotiate with Nero, hoping the cliff troll could provide some information by using his seeing stone.

"Stan is away for the afternoon," Tanu said. "Describe what is happening to Newel."

"He woke up screaming with evil nipsies on him like fleas. I helped him brush them off, but not before they inflicted lots of tiny wounds on his neck, arms, and chest. Once we drove them out, careful not to kill them, we thought all was well. His injuries were plentiful but miniscule. We even had a laugh about it, and started laying plans for a counterattack. We figured we could pack their grandest palaces with dung."

"Then Newel took a turn for the worse," Tanu prompted.

"Not long afterward, he started sweating and acting delirious. Felt like you could fry an egg on his forehead. He lay down, and soon he started moaning. When I left him, he seemed tormented by dark dreams. His chest and arms were looking hairier."

"We might be able to learn something by observing him," Tanu said. "How far away is he?"

"We have a shelter over by the tennis courts," Doren said. "He wasn't too far gone when I left him. Maybe we can reverse it. Potions are your specialty, right?"

"I'm not sure what we're up against, but I'll try," Tanu said. "Seth, go back to the house and wait for—"

"No way," Seth said. "He's my friend, it isn't far, I've been good lately, I'm coming."

Tanu tapped a thick finger against his chin. "You've been more patient than usual these past few days, and it might be unwise to leave you alone. Your grandparents might have my head, but if you promise to let Mendigo return you to the house without complaint on my order, you can join us."

"Deal!" Seth exclaimed.

"Lead the way," Tanu told Doren.

The satyr took off at a brisk pace. They raced along a path that Seth knew, having visited the tennis court many times over the summer. Newel and Doren had built the grass court, and Warren had provided top-notch equipment. Both of the satyrs were quite adept at the sport.

Before long Seth had a stitch in his side. For such a big man, Tanu could cover ground quickly. The run did not seem to tire him.

"Newel is in the shed?" Seth panted as the tennis court drew near.

"Not the equipment shed," Doren replied, not at all winded by the running. "We keep shelters all over the preserve. Never know where you might decide you want to rest your head. It isn't far from the court."

"Mendigo, carry Seth," Tanu ordered.

The wooden puppet scooped Seth into his arms. Seth felt mildly offended—Tanu hadn't even bothered to ask his permission! The court was not much farther. Even though being carried was a relief, and it allowed Tanu and Doren to pick up their pace a little, Seth wished he had been the one to suggest it. He disliked feeling underestimated.

They left the path, tromped through some undergrowth, and emerged on the immaculate lawn of the freshly chalked tennis court. Without pause, Doren dashed across the court and plunged into the trees beyond. Branches whipped past Seth as Mendigo raced along behind the others, dodging around trees and bushes.

Finally a tidy wooden shack came into view. The walls looked weathered and splintery, but there were no gaps or cracks, and the solid door fit snugly. There was a single window beside the door with four panes and green curtains behind it. A stovepipe protruded through the roof. When they reached the tiny clearing where the shack stood, Mendigo dumped Seth on his feet.

"Keep your distance, Seth," Tanu warned, approaching the shack with Doren. The satyr opened the door and entered. Tanu waited on the threshold. Seth heard a vicious snarl, and Doren came flying out the door backwards. Tanu caught him, stumbling away from the doorway as he absorbed the airborne satyr's momentum.

A shaggy creature emerged from the shack. It was Newel, and yet it was not Newel. Taller and bulkier, he still walked upright like a man, but dark brown fur covered him from horns to hooves. The horns were longer and blacker, corkscrewing up to sharp points. His face was almost unrecognizable, the nose and mouth having fused into a snout, quivering lips peeled back to reveal sharp teeth like a wolf's. Most disturbing were his eyes: yellow and bestial, with horizontally slit pupils.

Growling savagely, Newel pounced from the doorway, hurling Tanu aside and tackling Doren. Newel and Doren rolled across the ground. Doren gripped Newel by the neck, muscles straining to keep those snapping teeth away.

"Mendigo, immobilize Newel," Tanu called.

The limberjack raced toward the struggling satyrs. Just before Mendigo reached them, Newel wrenched free from Doren, caught one of the puppet's extended arms, and flung him through the air into the shack. Then Newel charged Seth.

Seth realized he had no way to fend off the vicious satyr. Running would buy him only a few seconds, and would take him farther from the help of the others. Instead, he

crouched, and when Newel had almost reached him, he dove forward at his legs.

The tactic surprised the raging satyr, who tripped over Seth and did a somersault before regaining his feet. The side of Seth's head throbbed where a hoof had clubbed him. He looked up at Newel in time to see Tanu slam into him from the side, smashing the satyr to the ground like a linebacker with permission to kill.

Newel recovered swiftly, rolling away from Tanu and rising to a crouch. Newel leapt at Tanu, who sidestepped the lunge and wrapped the crazed satyr in a full nelson, arms twined under Newel's armpits and locked behind his neck. Newel struggled and squirmed, but Tanu bore down on him ruthlessly, using brute strength to maintain the hold. Mendigo and Doren rushed toward the combat.

After a loud cry between a roar and a bleat, Newel craned his head and sank his teeth into Tanu's thick forearm. Jaws clamped shut, Newel twisted and ducked, heaving Tanu over the top of himself, breaking the hold and sending the Samoan sprawling.

Doren charged his mutated friend, but Newel backhanded him with a crack like a gunshot, and Doren flopped to the ground. Then Newel danced away from Mendigo. Twice Newel grabbed for the giant puppet, but Mendigo dodged him. Dropping to all fours, Mendigo skittered back and forth in a spidery crawl before moving in and entangling Newel's legs. Stomping and kicking, the enraged satyr broke free, leaving Mendigo with a splintered arm.

"Go!" Doren shouted, rising, his cheek already swelling. "We can't win this. It's too late. I'll hold him off!"

Tanu tossed a small, unstopped bottle to Seth. Liquid sloshed from its mouth as he caught it. "Drink," Tanu said.

Seth upended the bottle and guzzled the fluid. It fizzed and bubbled as it went down with a sour, fruity taste. Newel rushed at Doren, who turned, planted his hands on the ground, and bucked his friend in the chest with both hooves. The blow sent Newel soaring.

"Run, Doren," Tanu urged. "Don't let him bite you. Mendigo, help me back to the yard as fast as you can."

The limberjack dashed to Tanu, who climbed on piggyback. Mendigo did not look sturdy enough to carry such a large man, but he took off at a fast pace.

Seth felt tingly all over, almost as if the carbonation of the potion was now gurgling through his veins. Snorting and rising, Newel directed his attention toward Seth, pouncing with teeth bared and arms outstretched. Seth tried to run but, although his legs moved, his feet could get no traction.

Newel passed right through him, and bubbling tingles erupted through Seth's body. As the effervescent sensation subsided, Seth noticed that his body was pulling back together. He was in a gaseous state!

"Newel!" Doren said sharply, backing away from his deranged friend. "Why are you doing this? Come to your senses!"

Newel sneered. "You'll thank me later."

"Leave me be," Doren said gently. "We're best friends."

"Won't take long," Newel growled in his guttural voice.

Seth tried to say, "Come and get me, you goat-faced psycho," but, though his mouth could make the right shapes, no sound came out.

Roaring, Newel rushed at Doren, who turned and ran in the opposite direction from where Tanu was heading. Apparently Newel was more interested in chasing his friend than pursuing the Samoan, because he did not even glance at Tanu and Mendigo. Doren crashed away through the undergrowth with Newel in close pursuit. Seth noticed for the first time that a slender cord of shadow was connected to Newel. The curling black line wound out of sight into the trees.

Seth was left alone in the small clearing, hovering a few inches above the ground, wispy particles of himself steaming from his body without ever truly dissipating. He tried again to move, swinging his arms and legs. Although he did not generate any more traction than he had previously, Seth began to glide forward. He soon found that it was not moving his arms or legs that mattered. All it took was the intent to move in a certain direction, and he gradually began to drift that way.

Arms hanging at his side, legs dangling motionless, Seth slowly glided after Tanu, hoping to reach the house before solidifying in case Newel decided to return. In his gaseous state, Seth could have abandoned paths and traveled in a straight line through the woods, but the paths were fairly direct, and he didn't particularly enjoy the sensation of dissolving around branches and other obstructions.

With his top speed barely matching the pace of a

leisurely stroll, he remained anxious throughout the tedious journey. He worried about how Tanu was doing, and whether Doren had outrun Newel, and what to do if Newel reappeared. But Newel did not return, and Seth remained gaseous until he drifted across the yard and up onto the deck.

Tanu opened the door and admitted Seth to the house. Mendigo waited nearby, a deep split in one wooden forearm. Tanu looked worried. "Did Doren make it away?" he asked.

Unable to speak, Seth shrugged and crossed his fingers.

"I hope so too. I think my wound is going to be a problem. Look."

Tanu held up his beefy arm. There was no blood, but much of the forearm looked like shadow instead of flesh. "Oh, no!" Seth mouthed.

"It's turning invisible," Tanu said. "Like what happened to Coulter, only slower. The invisible portion has been spreading. I have no idea how to slow it."

Seth shook his head.

"Don't worry. I didn't expect you to have the answer."

Seth shook his head more vigorously, making the particles of his face disperse with fizzy tingles. He drifted over to a shelf and pointed at a black binder, then pointed at Tanu's arm.

"You want me to take notes about my arm? I'll let you inform the others. You'll solidify soon."

Seth looked around the room. He glided over to a window, where the light of the sun was making a flowerpot cast a shadow. He pointed at the shadow, then indicated Tanu's arm.

"Shadowy?" Tanu asked. Understanding suddenly registered in his expression. "My arm looks shadowy to you, not invisible. Like how you see Coulter as a shadowman."

Seth gave Tanu a thumbs-up.

"I'd better go outside, in case I turn evil like Newel."

Tanu walked out to the deck. Seth floated along behind him. They stood together, silently staring into the yard. A frothy sensation surged through Seth, tickly tingles everywhere, as if he were a bottle of soda that somebody had shaken until it was wildly foaming over. After a fizzy hiss, the tingling stopped, and he found himself standing on the deck, his body solid once more.

"That was pretty cool," Seth said.

"Unique sensation, isn't it?" Tanu said. "I have only one gaseous potion left. Come with me, I want to try something."

"I'm sorry about your arm," Seth said.

"Wasn't your fault. I'm glad you avoided getting nipped." They descended the stairs from the deck, passing from underneath the overhang into direct sunlight. Wincing and clutching his shadowy forearm, Tanu fled into the shade. "I was afraid of that," he growled through clenched teeth.

"Did it hurt?" Seth asked.

"Coulter said he couldn't visit us until sundown. I think I just confirmed why. When the sunlight hit my arm, the invisible part burned with unbearable cold. I can hardly imagine how that would feel spread over my whole body.

Maybe I should wrap my arm and go find a shady spot far from the house."

"I don't think you'll turn evil," Seth said.

"You have a reason?"

"Newel didn't behave like himself," Seth said. "He was out of control. But Coulter acted calm. He seemed normal, except for being a shadow."

"Coulter may just be more devious than Newel," Tanu said. "He might have pounced on us if we'd given him the chance." Tanu held up his arm. The area from his wrist to his elbow was lost in shadow. "It's spreading faster." Sweat beaded on his forehead. He sat down heavily on the deck stairs.

Across the lawn, Seth saw Grandpa Sorenson emerge from the woods. Behind him came Dale, and then Hugo giving Grandma a ride on his shoulder. "Grandpa!" Seth called. "Tanu got hurt!"

Grandpa turned and said something inaudible to Hugo. The golem picked him up, steadied Grandma, and loped across the lawn. Dale ran along behind. Hugo set Seth's grandparents down beside the deck. Tanu raised his injured arm.

"What happened?" Grandpa asked.

Tanu recounted the incident with Newel, telling how the satyr had changed, how he had attacked them, how they had gotten away, and how the injury looked shadowy to Seth. Grandma knelt by Tanu, inspecting his arm.

"A single bite did this?" she asked.

"It was a big bite," Seth said.

"Small injuries from nipsies were enough to transform Newel," Tanu said.

"How are you feeling?" Grandma asked.

"Feverish." The shadow had cloaked all of his hand except the fingertips and was also spreading up his arm. "I don't think I have much time. I'll give Coulter your best."

"We'll do all we can to restore you," Grandpa promised. "Try to resist any evil inclinations."

"I'll give you two thumbs up if you can trust me," Tanu said. "I'll try with everything I have not to deceive you with that gesture. Can you think of a better way to prove I'm still on your side?"

"I can't think of much else you could do," Grandpa said.

"He'll have to stay out of the sun," Seth said. "It's painfully cold to him."

"The sun didn't appear to affect Newel?" Grandma asked.

"No," Seth said.

"Nor did it slow the fairies who came after Seth," Grandpa said. "Tanu, stay on the deck until sundown. Confer with Coulter when he arrives."

"Later, if I can hang on to my wits, I'll explore the preserve, see what I can find," Tanu mumbled, his mouth twisted into a grimace. "Did you learn anything from Nero?"

"We found him injured on the floor of the ravine, pinned beneath a heavy log," Grandpa said. "Apparently he had been set upon by dark dwarfs. They stole his seeing stone and much of his treasure. He couldn't tell us how the plague originated. The injuries he had sustained did not appear to be transforming him in any way. Hugo moved the log and Nero was able to scramble back up to his lair."

Tanu began breathing heavily, eyes squeezed shut, sweat trickling down his face. His entire arm was lost in shadow. "Sorry to hear . . . it was a bust," he wheezed. "Better . . . get inside . . . just in case."

Grandpa placed a reassuring hand on Tanu's healthy shoulder. "We'll get you back. Good luck." He stood up. "Hugo, I want you in the barn standing guard over Viola. Be ready to come if we call."

The golem strode away toward the barn. Dale patted Tanu's good shoulder. Grandpa led the others into the house, leaving Tanu groaning on the deck steps.

"Can't we do anything for him?" Seth asked, peeking out the window.

"Not to prevent what is happening," Grandma said. "But we won't rest until we get Tanu and Coulter back."

Dale busied himself examining Mendigo's fractured arm.

"Did you see any darkened creatures on your way to Nero?" Seth asked.

"Not one," Grandpa said. "We kept to paths and moved quickly. I didn't realize how fortunate we were until now. If we determine that we can trust Tanu and Coulter, we may attempt a final excursion in the morning before sunrise. If not, it may be time to consider abandoning Fablehaven until we can return armed with a plan."

"Don't ignore help from Tanu and Coulter just because you need me there in order to see them," Seth pleaded.

"Like it or not, I must take that into consideration," Grandpa said. "I'll not place you in jeopardy."

"If I'm the only one who can see them, maybe it means there is something only I can do to help them," Seth reasoned. "There may be more important reasons for having me come than simply as a means to follow them. It may be our only hope for success."

"I won't rule it out," Grandpa said.

"Stan!" Grandma said reproachfully.

Grandpa turned to face her, and her expression softened.

"Did you wink at her?" Seth asked. "Are you just trying to shut me up?"

Grandpa regarded Seth with an amused expression. "You get more perceptive every day."

CHAPTER ELEVEN

The Old Pueblo

Gavin joined Kendra in the entry hall toting a wooden spear with a head crafted from black stone. Despite the primitive design, the weapon looked sleek and dangerous, the head affixed securely, the tip and edges sharp. Still, Kendra wondered why he preferred the spear to a more modern weapon.

Kendra wore sturdy boots and a hooded poncho over her fresh, dry clothes. "Expect we'll see any mammoths?" she asked.

Gavin grinned, hefting the spear. "You weren't with us yesterday, so you didn't hear all the details. Technically, the mesa isn't part of the preserve. It's older. Untamable. The t-t-treaty that founded this preserve won't protect us while we're up there. Rosa said that only weapons fashioned by the people who used to live on Painted Mesa are of any use against the creatures we'll encounter. This spear is more than a thousand years old. They use special treatments to keep it like new."

"Did the others have to use weapons last time?" Kendra asked.

"Supposedly not," Gavin said. "They took them, but made it to the vault with no problem. The trouble came when they reached the dragon. But I worry that things may have changed since last time. The path they used has vanished. Plus, there was a disturbing weight to the air when we tried to climb the mesa yesterday. Honestly, I think you should back out of this, Kendra."

Kendra felt like she was back at Fablehaven earlier in the summer, when Coulter refused to include her on certain excursions with Seth simply because she was a girl. Her hesitations about scaling the mesa suddenly fled. "How do you expect to find the stairs without me?"

"I don't mind you guiding us to the bottom of the stairs," Gavin said. "But if we can't climb them without you, maybe we don't have any business being up there."

Kendra took a slow breath. "Even though I'm the only one who can find the way up, you somehow think you belong on the mesa more than I do?"

"I don't mean it as an insult," he said, holding up his free hand. "I just suspect you haven't had much combat training." He twirled the spear casually, making it swish through the air.

"That would look really nifty in a parade," Kendra said

flatly. "You're sweet to worry." With no particular training, hadn't she led fairies in an assault that captured a powerful demon? Hadn't she helped Warren retrieve the artifact from the vault at Fablehaven? What had Gavin done?

Gavin fixed her with an intense stare and spoke with conviction. "You think I'm a dumb teenage boy spouting off about girls having no business on an adventure. Not so. I'm worried about whether *I'll* survive. I would hate to see you get hurt. Kendra, I insist you tell Warren you would rather stay behind."

Kendra could not resist laughing. The surprise on his face, the way he went from so intense to so unsure, only added fuel to the fire. It took a moment to regain the power of speech. Gavin looked so crushed that she wanted to reassure him. "Okay, I was being sarcastic before, but you really are sweet. I appreciate the sentiment. I'm scared too—part of me would love to follow your advice. But I won't be going into the vault, just camping on the mesa with Neil. I wouldn't do this just for kicks. I think it's worth the risk."

Tammy entered the hall wearing a lightweight hooded jacket and carrying a tomahawk. She had tightened the hood so that only her eyes, nose, and mouth were visible. "I can't believe we're hiking up a waterfall," she said. "The trail was tiring enough."

"You didn't see anything on top of the mesa last time?" Kendra asked.

"We saw something," Tammy corrected her. "Something big. It had at least ten legs and it rippled when it moved. But it never came too close. The mesa shouldn't be a problem. I'm worried about negotiating some of those traps again, though."

Warren, Neil, Dougan, Hal, and Rosa came down the hall to the door. Dougan held a bulky stone axe. Warren carried a spear.

Hal sauntered over to Kendra, thumbs hooked in the belt loops of his jeans. "You're really going to lead these nutcases up the mesa?" he asked.

She nodded.

"Reckon I could lend you this." He held out a stone knife in a buckskin sheath.

"I'd rather she went weaponless, like Neil," Warren said.

Hal scratched his mustache. "Neil does have a talent for staying alive. Live by the sword, die by the sword, is that it? Might not be a bad idea." He tucked the knife away.

"We only have climbing gear for five," Warren announced. "I'll ascend at the rear without a harness, just keeping hold of the rope."

"You have the key?" Rosa asked.

Dougan patted his backpack. "Wouldn't be much use to reach the top without it."

"We should get under way," Neil recommended.

Outside, rain continued to drizzle. Neil drove the Jeep with Kendra, Warren, and Tammy. Dougan followed in the truck with Gavin as copilot. Windshield wipers swaying hypnotically, the Jeep sloshed through puddles and occasionally fishtailed in the mud. At one point, Neil gunned the engine and they roared through a stream, water spraying up from both sides of the Jeep like wings. They approached the mesa from a less direct route than before, winding more, and not climbing as steeply. The drive took almost twice as long.

At length they stopped in the same flat, boulder-strewn area where they had parked earlier. Neil cut the engine and killed the headlights. Everyone exited the vehicles and shouldered their gear. Warren, Dougan, and Gavin turned on large waterproof flashlights.

"You see the stairs?" Dougan asked Kendra, squinting into the rainy darkness.

"Barely," Kendra said. She actually discerned the Flooded Stairs more clearly than she admitted, but wanted to avoid making it obvious that she could see in the dark.

They picked their way forward over wet rocks, looping around several depressions where water had pooled. Part of Kendra wondered why they bothered avoiding the water, considering the climb they were about to undertake. The hood of her poncho magnified the patter of the rainfall.

As they neared the fissure at the foot of the stairs, Kendra found herself beside Neil. "What happens if the rain stops while we're on the stairway?" she asked.

"Truthfully, I have no idea. I would like to think the stairs will persist while we remain on them. We should probably hurry just in case."

Warren helped Kendra into a harness, tightened some straps, and wound a rope through some metal clasps. Once they were all linked together, Kendra led the others along the narrow shelf between the cliff and the fissure.

"Don't focus on the stairs," Neil instructed the others.

"Put your attention on following the person in front of you. It may take some effort."

Kendra stepped into the rushing water at the base of the stairs and started climbing. The boots gave her better footing than the tennis shoes she had worn earlier. As the steps became steeper, it became impossible to ascend without using her hands. Her sleeves and pant legs became soaked. The rushing water made each step forward feel unstable.

After at least a hundred stairs, they reached the first landing. Kendra turned and looked down, shocked by how much steeper the ascent looked from this perspective than it had felt as she climbed. If she fell, she would undoubtedly tumble all the way down the crude stone stairway, and her corpse would be washed away into the fissure. She backed away from the edge, fearful of hurtling down the most painful waterslide of her life.

Kendra turned. Ahead, the water fell straight for about a hundred feet before noisily splashing on the landing. The stairs became as steep as a ladder, rising to the side of the cascade.

Kendra guided the others forward and started mounting the steepest steps yet, trying to ignore the sound and spray of the waterfall beside her. No stair was wide enough to place her entire sole on it, and the steps were often separated by more than two feet. She moved cautiously upward, always keeping her hands on a higher step as she climbed, the aroma of wet stone filling her nostrils. She concentrated on nothing but the next step, ignoring the void behind her, ignoring the thought of slipping and peeling everyone off the stairs with her. The wind picked up, blowing her hood back and making her long hair flutter like a banner. Her arms trembled with fear and exertion.

Why had she volunteered for this? She should have listened to Gavin. He had tried to give her an out, but pride had prevented her from considering it.

She reached for the next step, got the best hold she could, lifted her right foot, and then her left foot. She pretended that she was only a few feet off the ground as she repeated the tiring process.

At last Kendra reached the top of the waterfall and another broad ledge. Neil boosted himself up behind her. Looking up, there remained a long distance to climb. She denied the impulse to look back or down.

"You're doing well," Neil encouraged. "Do you need a break?"

Kendra nodded. She had been so full of adrenaline while climbing beside the waterfall that she had not noticed how fatigued her limbs felt. Kendra pulled her hood up and waited a few minutes on the ledge before proceeding onward.

The stairway now rose back and forth in many short flights. Sometimes the flowing water followed the path of the stairs; sometimes it spilled over and took a shortcut. They scaled flight after flight to landing after landing. Kendra's legs ached, and she started running out of breath, requiring more frequent pauses the longer she climbed.

The wind began to blow harder, lashing at her poncho, hurling the rain against her, making even the most stable flights of stairs feel treacherous. It was hard to tell if the storm itself was worsening, or if the wind was just more violent at the higher elevation.

After inching along a narrow ledge, Kendra found herself at the base of the last flight of steps, the wind whipping her hair sideways. The final flight was almost as steep as the stairs beside the waterfall, except this time they would have to climb up directly through the cascade.

"These are the last stairs!" Kendra shouted to Neil over the tempest. "They're steep, and the water is falling fast. Should we wait and see if the storm dies down?"

"The mesa is trying to drive us back," Neil replied. "Lead on!"

Kendra sloshed forward and started up, climbing with hands and feet. Water sucked at her legs and sprayed off her arms into her face. Whether she was moving or at rest, it felt like the rushing stream was on the verge of tearing away her hold on the slick stairs. Each step was a risk, taking her higher, increasing the distance that she would fall. The others followed in her wake.

One foot slipped as she trusted her weight to it, and her knee smacked down painfully against a step, water gushing around her thigh. Neil placed a steadying hand against the small of her back and helped her rise. Higher and higher she climbed, until the top was ten steps away, then five, then her head saw above the edge of the mesa, and she mounted the final few stairs. Kendra walked away from the stairway and the stream to solid rock strewn with puddles.

The others finished the climb and gathered around her,

the wind buffeting them even more violently now that they huddled atop the mesa. Lightning blazed across the sky, the first Kendra had noticed since setting out. For a moment, the entire expanse of the mesa flashed into view. In the distance, toward the center, Kendra saw ancient ruins, layer upon layer of crumbling walls and stairs that must once have formed a more impressive pueblo complex than the structure neighboring the hacienda. Briefly her eye was drawn to the movement of many dancers prancing wildly in the rain on the near side of the ruins. Before she could consider the scene, the lighting flash ended. The distance and the darkness and the rain combined to obscure the revelers even from Kendra's keen eyes. Thunder rumbled, muffled by the wind.

"Kachinas!" Neil cried.

The middle-aged Navajo rapidly loosed Kendra from the climbing gear, not bothering to remove her harness. Lightning flared again, revealing that the figures were no longer engaged in their frenzied dance. The revelers were charging toward them.

"What does this mean?" Warren shouted.

"These are kachinas or other kindred beings," Neil yelled. "Ancient spirits of the wilderness. We've interrupted a ceremony welcoming the rain. We must get to the cover of the ruins. Keep your weapons handy."

Tammy was having trouble loosening the rope tied to her, so she hacked it away with her tomahawk.

"How do we get there?" Warren asked.

"Not through them," Neil said, starting to run in a

crouch along the perimeter of the mesa. "We'll try to loop around."

Kendra followed, not liking the fact that the lip of the precipice was no more than ten yards away. Flashlight beams swayed and bobbed in the rain, making strips of shining drops visible along with oval patches of ground. Kendra chose not to turn her flashlight on; she found the light distracting. She could see at least fifty feet in all directions.

"We've got company!" Dougan called, his voice almost lost in the gale. Kendra looked over her shoulder. The beam of his flashlight was trained on a lean, shaggy figure with the head of a coyote. The humanoid creature clutched a staff topped with rattles and wore an elaborate beaded necklace. He threw back his head and howled, a high, warbling cry that pierced the tempestuous night.

Neil skidded to a halt. Ahead of him, blocking their progress, his flashlight lit up an eight-foot-tall, bare-chested oaf wearing a huge painted mask. Or was that his actual face? He brandished a long, lopsided club.

Swiveling, Neil charged toward the interior of the plateau. Suddenly, bizarre figures were everywhere. A tall, feathery being with the head of a hawk seized Tammy by one arm, dragged her several paces, twirled as if hurling a discus, and flung her off the edge of the mesa. Kendra watched in horror as Tammy spun through the air, arms flailing as if she were trying to swim, and disappeared from view. The creature had hurled her so far, and most of the mesa was so steep, that Kendra imagined the stricken woman might freefall the entire way to the bottom.

Kendra dodged away from a leering, humpbacked man carrying a long flute, and found herself in the grasp of a sleek, furry creature with the body of a human female and the head of a bobcat. Crying out, Kendra struggled, but the bobcat woman had a crushing grip on her upper arm and hauled her toward the rim of the mesa. The heels of her boots slid over the slick, rocky ground. She could smell the creature's wet fur. What would it feel like, plunging toward the ground through the stormy night alongside the raindrops?

Then Gavin appeared out of the darkness, swinging his spear. The bobcat woman yowled and recoiled, dropping Kendra, clawed hands raised protectively, a diagonal wound gaping across her feline face. Gavin stabbed and whirled and slashed, driving the fierce creature back, deftly avoiding counterattacks, slicing and piercing her as she slowly retreated, fangs bared.

From her hands and knees, Kendra saw Dougan wielding his axe to drive back the coyote man. There was Warren, using his spear to keep a gigantic bronze scorpion at bay. And here came Neil, rushing toward her. Glancing over her shoulder, Kendra saw that she was only a few feet from the brink of the lofty precipice. She scrambled away from the edge.

The feathery, hawkish man had joined the bobcat woman in attacking Gavin. Gavin used the butt of his spear to thump the bobcat woman while jabbing with the other end to wound the screeching, feathered attacker.

Neil reached Kendra and hauled her to her feet. "Climb on my back and hold on," he ordered breathlessly.

Kendra was unsure how Neil would outrun their many enemies with her riding piggyback, but clambered onto him without argument. As soon as her legs wrapped around his waist, he began to change. He fell forward as if he meant to crawl, but did not drop as near to the ground as Kendra expected. His neck thickened and elongated, his ears slid higher on his head, and his torso swelled. In an instant, Kendra found herself astride a cantering chestnut stallion.

With no saddle or bridle, there was not much to cling to, and Kendra found herself bouncing further out of position with each stride the horse took. The giant man with a face like a mask obstructed their escape, heavy club poised to strike. The stallion slowed and reared, thrashing the large man with flailing front hooves. The massive figure toppled, but Kendra failed to maintain her grip and fell to the ground also, landing in a muddy puddle.

The stallion curveted around the area, bucking and plunging, trampling the fallen enemy and scattering others. Kendra looked around, and saw Gavin do a handspring to retrieve Tammy's fallen tomahawk. Twirling his spear adroitly, he now held off four opponents. A pair of motionless bodies lay crumpled near him.

His gaze met hers, and after a final wide sweep of his spear, he sprinted toward her. The creatures gave chase. Kendra rose to her feet. As Gavin neared her, he hauled back one arm and flung the tomahawk in her direction. The weapon missed her by inches, the black stone bit embedding in the shoulder of a broad, lumpy man with a towering fore-head and a deformed face. Kendra had not sensed him coming up behind her. The disfigured man fell with a throaty bellow, and then Gavin had her hand, and they were racing together through the rain.

Kendra heard hooves pounding off to one side. Handing Kendra the spear, Gavin seized her waist and heaved her up onto the chestnut stallion with astonishing strength. An instant later he had vaulted up behind her. He reclaimed the spear, using his free hand to steady her. "Go, Neil!" he cried.

Neil increased his speed to a furious gallop, tearing across the blustery mesa at a speed Kendra would not have thought possible. Blinded by the heavy rain, she was grateful to have Gavin stabilizing her. He appeared to have no trouble remaining astride the charging stallion, clutching the spear in his free hand as if he were jousting.

Blinking rapidly to try to peer ahead through the downpour, Kendra recognized the ruins coming into view. The horse leapt over a low fence, sending tingles through Kendra's stomach, and then they were swerving around rubble and broken walls. With a clatter of hooves on stone, the horse came to a stop outside the empty doorway of the most intact building among the ruins.

The horse melted away beneath Kendra and Gavin, leaving them standing beside Neil in the rain. His former clothes were gone. All he wore now were animal pelts. "Stay in here until I return," he ordered, jerking a thumb at the yawning doorway. He rubbed his side as if in pain.

"Are you all right?" Gavin asked.

"Holding my other form is hard," Neil said, nudging Kendra toward the building.

Lightning dazzled across the sky, throwing strange highlights and shadows across the ruins. Explosive thunder followed immediately, and Neil was a horse again, galloping off into the storm.

Gavin took Kendra's hand, and she led him into the shelter of the building. Part of the roof had collapsed, but the walls were whole, keeping the wind out except when it gusted through the doorway. "I lost my flashlight," Gavin told her.

Kendra had hers dangling from her climbing harness. It was not as big as some of the others, but when she switched it on, the beam was bright. The water pouring through the open portion of the roof was running across the mud-streaked floor and trickling down through an open hatch into an underground chamber.

"Look at you," he admired, "holding on to your gear even when savage rain dancers are trying to toss you off of cliffs."

"It was fastened to my harness," she said. "Thanks for saving me. You were great back there."

"It's wh-wh-wh, wh-wh-wh. It's wh-why they brought me along. Everybody has their thing. This is where I shine, whacking monsters with primitive spears."

Kendra felt embarrassed. Her behavior when they were attacked had made it apparent that she had no idea how to handle herself in a fight. She braced herself, realizing she had better 'fess up before he could point out her deficiencies.

"You were right, Gavin, I shouldn't have come. I don't know what I expected. You had to watch out for me instead of helping the others."

"Wh-what do you mean? Because of you, I had an excuse to ride out of danger on Neil. You did much better than I expected."

Kendra tried to smile. He was kind not to rub it in, but she knew she had been a liability. "I can't believe Tammy is gone," she said.

"I hope you don't blame yourself for that," he said. "It happened too quickly for anyone to have saved her. We didn't really know what they had in mind until the hawk guy sent her soaring." He shook his head. "They definitely wanted us off of their mesa. We crashed the wrong party."

To make the loss less painful, Kendra found herself hoping that Tammy had been secretly working for the Society of the Evening Star. They waited without speaking, listening to the wind outside keening stridently among the ruins. The storm raged more forcefully than ever, as if exerting a final effort to sweep them off the plateau.

Somebody strode through the doorway. Kendra swung the flashlight over, expecting Neil. Instead the coyote man stood on the threshold, an angry gash visible beneath the wet, matted fur of his chest. She gasped and nearly dropped the flashlight. The intruder shook his staff. Even with the wind howling, Kendra could hear the rattles. The coyote spoke in a human voice, chanting in a strange, warbling language.

"C-c-catch any of that?" Gavin asked softly.

"Nope."

The coyote man sidled into the room, snarling. Gavin stepped in front of Kendra, and then advanced with his spear. As the coyote and Gavin drew close to each other, Kendra wanted to look away. Instead, squeezing the flashlight like a lifeline, she shifted the beam so it shone right in the coyote man's eyes. He wove his head to avoid the glare, but she kept the beam on him, and Gavin poked at him with the spear.

Slowly Gavin prodded the intruder back. With a sudden grab, the coyote man seized the spear just below the head and yanked Gavin toward him. Instead of resisting, Gavin sprang forward and nimbly kicked the coyote man right where his chest was injured. Staggering back and whining in pain, the coyote man relinquished the spear and dropped his staff. Gavin charged, the stone spearhead biting into his enemy until the coyote man fled the room nursing new wounds.

Panting, Gavin backed away from the doorway. "If he returns, I'm going to make you a souvenir—coyote-on-a-stick."

"He already left behind a souvenir," Kendra said.

"Does that mean you're claiming it?" Gavin asked, stooping to pick up the staff with the rattles attached. He shook it gently. "It's certainly magical." He tossed it to Kendra.

"Will he hunt me down to retrieve it?" Kendra asked apprehensively.

"If he ever tracks you down, give it back. I wouldn't

worry. Since the preserve surrounds this mesa, I imagine the coyote guy is stuck here."

"What if he comes to retrieve it tonight?"

Gavin smirked. "Coyote-on-a-stick, remember?"

Kendra shook the stick hard, listening to the crackle of the rattles. Outside, the wind rose, lightning flashed, and thunder erupted, drowning out the rattling. She kept shaking it briskly, trying to hear the rattles over the wailing gusts outside. The wind shrieked even louder. Hail began drumming against the roof and pelting through the broken portion. Ice pellets skittered across the floor.

"I'd be careful how you shake that," Gavin said.

She stopped, holding the rattle still. Within a few seconds, the hail stopped, and the wind wasn't gusting as hard. "This is controlling the storm?" Kendra exclaimed.

"Influencing it, at least," Gavin said.

Kendra studied the staff with amazement. She held it out to Gavin. "You earned it, you should keep it."

"N-n-nope," Gavin said. "It's your souvenir."

Kendra held the staff carefully, keeping it still. Over the next minute the storm went into a lull. The wind no longer blew as hard. The rain diminished to a sprinkle.

"Do you think the others are okay?" Kendra wondered.

"I hope so. Dougan has the key. If they don't show, we may have to fight our way back to the stairs." Leaning on the spear, Gavin glanced over at Kendra. "The way things played out, I know it seems like I made a good call about the danger, but this is much worse than I'd guessed, or I would have been more forceful with everyone about you not coming. Are you hanging in there?"

"I'm okay," she lied.

"That was smart, shining the light in the coyote's eyes. Thanks."

The wind and rain picked up again, but still didn't lash the mesa as furiously as earlier. Sheet lightning started flickering regularly, accompanied by growls of thunder. On the fifth flash, three men staggered through the doorway. Warren, Dougan, and Neil crossed the room to Kendra and Gavin. Dougan no longer had his axe. Warren held the top half of his broken spear. Neil limped between them, supported by the other men.

"Ugly business out there," Dougan said. "Have you had any visitors?"

"C-c-coyote man dropped by," Gavin said.

"He came inside the room?" Neil asked, his face haggard.

Gavin nodded. "I had to repel him with the spear."

"Then Kendra and I won't be safe here after all," Neil said. "In times past, the creatures who haunt the mesa would not have dared set foot here in the weather room. Then again, I know little about the rite we interrupted. We must have rendered all protections ineffectual."

"He definitely came inside," Kendra said. "He left this behind." She held up the staff. Neil frowned at it.

"It's her souvenir," Gavin insisted.

"We need to get inside the vault," Neil said. "Anywhere will be safer than this mesa tonight." Dougan and Warren helped him toward the hatch in the floor.

"Sorry I wasn't much of a bodyguard," Warren apologized to Kendra. "They struck so suddenly, and I saw Gavin taking much better care of you than I could have. Gavin, I've never met a man who could top your dad in a brawl, but you would have given him a run for his money."

"Only thanks to all he taught me," Gavin said with a proud grin.

Below them gaped the hatch. A long, upright log with pegs in it functioned as a ladder. Shining flashlights into the void, they saw the floor about twelve feet below. Gavin descended the ladder first, holding Kendra's flashlight. Then came Dougan, then Kendra, then Neil lowering himself with his arms and one leg. After Neil reached the ground, Warren did not follow, and they heard the sounds of a scuffle. Spear in hand, Gavin raced up the ladder with incredible speed.

After a few tense moments, Warren and Gavin descended the ladder.

"What happened?" Kendra exclaimed. "Are you two all right?"

"No coyote-on-a-stick," Gavin said regretfully. "He didn't show up."

"But others did," Warren said. "The hawkman and a freakish oaf. I'm with Neil. We can't leave anyone above ground. There are too many enemies abroad."

"Will a dragon be any safer?" Kendra questioned.

Warren shrugged. "Neither option is inviting, but at least the vaults are designed to be potentially survivable."

Kendra hoped Warren was right. She could not help

remembering that only one and a half of the three people who had entered this vault last time had emerged.

Dougan removed the key from his bag. It was a thick silver disk the size of a dinner plate. The underground room had a spacious circular depression in the center. Water flowed into the depression but, instead of pooling there, continued to drain deeper. With Warren helping Neil, they all stepped down into the circular recess.

"This room was a kiva," Neil explained. "A site for sacred ceremonies."

Dougan pressed a small protuberance on the disk, and several oddly shaped metal teeth clicked out of the sides like blades from a pocket knife. When he released the button, the jagged teeth retracted. Kneeling in the center of the circular depression, he set the disk into a round indentation where it fit snugly. Then he pressed the center of the disk and twisted it.

With a jolting clack and a subterranean rumbling, the floor of the circular depression began to rotate. Dougan had taken his hand off of the key, but still the floor turned, and as it turned, it sank, as if they stood on the head of a gigantic screw. Ever rotating, they gradually descended into a vast chamber, where the irregular walls had the appearance of a natural cavern. Looking up, Kendra watched the round hole in the ceiling grow distant. The sounds of the storm faded. Announced by a final echoing thud, the turning floor came to a halt.

CHAPTER TWELVE

Obstacles

Dougan squatted beside Neil. "How's your leg?"

Brow crinkled, Neil probed his knee. "I think I tore a tendon. I won't be walking normally anytime soon."

"Who injured you?" Kendra asked.

"I did," Neil said ruefully. "This was an old man's injury, earned by running too far too fast over ground that was too firm."

"Call it a hero's injury," Warren said. "You should have seen him bowl over some of the creatures who had me pinned."

"You can use my spear as a crutch," Gavin offered.

"We all stand a better chance of surviving if the spear stays in your hands," Neil said.

Gavin handed Neil the spear. "When trouble arrives, pass it back to me."

"If it would be better for the mission, I could stay behind with Neil," Kendra offered.

Warren shook his head. "If we could have left you safe up top, fine. In here, our best hope for survival is to stick together."

"Tammy mentioned a hulking beast covered by so many knives that they looked like feathers," Dougan said. He shone his flashlight around the vast chamber, showing the mouths of three different caves. "The beast should be down that passageway, the widest one. She said it prowled along behind to prey on stragglers."

"Speaking of Tammy," Kendra said, "can we do this without her? Wasn't her job to get us past the traps?"

Dougan stood and stretched. "Losing her was a tragedy, and a serious blow to the mission, but she shared enough information that we won't be wandering blind, at least not until after the dragon." He swiveled his flashlight to illuminate the narrowest exit from the chamber. "For example, that tunnel gets gradually steeper until it falls away to unfathomable depths. We want the medium-sized cave."

"W-w-w-we should get moving," Gavin suggested.

Warren stepped off the circular platform that had lowered them into the room, tapping with the broken end of his spear to test the ground. The others followed. Dougan tried to assist Neil, but the Navajo man quietly refused any aid, preferring to limp forward leaning heavily on the spear. Though Neil uttered no complaint, the set of his jaw and the tightness around his eyes made the pain he was suffering evident.

Warren held a flashlight, as did Dougan. Gavin, bringing up the rear, retained Kendra's light. Gavin shone his light on a glistening stone formation against one wall shaped like a melting pipe organ. The mouth of the medium-sized passage was guarded by tall stalagmites, tapered stone projections the color of caramel reaching for the stalactites above.

After weaving through the stalagmites, they descended into the steep, winding passageway. Tiny, soda-straw stalactites hung in fragile clusters. The contorted walls were a burnt yellow. Some portions of the descent were so steep that Neil sat down and scooted forward. Kendra crouched, grabbing knobs of stone with her free hand, clutching the staff with the rattles in the other, trying to keep it quiet.

From up ahead, Kendra heard the sound of water flowing. The steady rushing grew louder until they found their way blocked by a chasm with a swift, deep stream at the bottom. The only way to get across was by hopping along the tops of a staggered collection of rough stone columns, none of them quite the same height.

Warren shone his flashlight on the three broadest, most inviting columns. "Tammy warned that these three are traps, rigged to collapse if you step on them. As you can see, there are enough other columns to take alternate routes around the three biggest."

Warren uncoiled a length of rope, handed one end to Dougan, and set off across the columns, bounding from one to the next without any significant pauses or missteps.

Despite his confidence, Kendra felt tense inside until he stood safely on the far side of the chasm.

"Fasten the rope to Kendra's harness," Warren called.

Dougan knelt and secured the rope to her metal buckles and carabiners. "You saw how he did it?"

Kendra nodded.

"Don't think about the drop," Gavin suggested, returning her flashlight. "I'll hold your rain stick." She handed him the coyote man's staff.

Kendra moved to the edge of the chasm. The flat top of the first column was a short step away. She tried to imagine she was stepping onto a rock in a shallow stream, and strode forward. The next column was more rounded, and she would have to jump in order to reach it, but there was easily room for both feet on it. If it weren't for the gloomy void beneath, the leap would not have been intimidating, but she could not make herself move.

"Place a hand on the rope," Warren called to her. "Remember, if you fall, I'm here to pull you up."

Kendra compressed her lips. If she fell, she would swing to the far side of the chasm and smash into the wall, probably striking columns along the way. But holding the rope did provide an illusion of security. Admonishing herself to think like Seth, which to her meant not to think at all, she leaped to the next column, wobbled, and righted herself.

Jump after jump, step after step, she made her way around two of the three biggest columns. Near the far side of the chasm, to get around the final inviting, traitorous column, she would have to use columns so small that each would support only one foot at a time.

"Do these all in a row, Kendra," Warren advised. "Five quick steps, just one brief game of hopscotch. You're almost to me. If you fall, no big deal."

Kendra planned her steps. Warren was right, if she fell now, the swing to the far wall of the chasm was no longer as threatening. Mustering her courage one last time, she leaped, leaped, leaped, leaped, leaped, and stumbled off-balance into Warren's outstretched arms.

Dougan, Neil, and Gavin cheered from the far side of the chasm. Warren untied Kendra, fastened the climbing rope to his large flashlight, and flung it across the gulf to Dougan, who caught it.

"Neil doesn't want to try crossing the columns on one foot," Dougan called. "He thinks a deliberate swing across the chasm is best, which means I had better cross next to help you anchor him."

"All right," Warren replied.

"I think I can carry him," Gavin interjected. Nobody responded. "It wouldn't be too different from one of the training exercises my dad used to make me do. I'm stronger than I look."

"Either way, I had better come across to help belay you," Dougan said, tying the rope to himself.

"How did Javier get back across with his injured legs?" Kendra wondered.

"Tammy carried him," Warren said. "Javier had a potion that reduced his weight."

"For that matter, how did they get out at all?" Kendra continued. "I thought these vaults were designed to keep people from going back unless they claimed the treasure."

Warren nodded, watching Dougan as he started across. "That was my understanding as well. Tammy and Javier felt like the dragon meant certain death, so they risked back-tracking, and the gamble paid off."

Although his movements were not graceful, Dougan traversed the chasm without mishap. Warren threw the flashlight with the rope attached to Gavin, who caught it with one hand and began affixing the rope to Neil.

"Are you sure Neil won't be too heavy?" Dougan shouted.

Gavin stooped and hoisted Neil over one shoulder. Without responding, he stepped onto the first column, and then hopped to the second. Besides Neil on his shoulder, Gavin held the staff, which rattled every time he jumped. Kendra felt her insides clench with each small leap, and then lurch violently when he swayed awkwardly while perched on a small, rounded knob. Gavin hesitated where Kendra had last paused, studying the five consecutive jumps that would complete the crossing. Shifting Neil slightly, Gavin sprang from column to column, tumbling to his knees when he reached the far ledge.

"Well done!" Dougan enthused, slapping Gavin on the back. "I may never again underestimate the strength of youth."

"It w-w-w-was harder than I expected," Gavin panted. "At least we made it."

Warren helped Neil off Gavin's shoulder. He coiled up the rope, then led the way deeper into the cave, which continued to descend, although not as steeply as previously. Gavin used his flashlight beam to point out sparkling patches of calcite on the moist cave walls. He also spotlighted colorful ripples that looked like bacon. Kendra could practically taste stone with each breath she drew. The air was uncomfortably cool. She wished her clothes would dry.

The passage grew narrower until they all had to turn sideways to proceed. Then suddenly it widened into a spacious cavern. Warren halted and motioned for the others to do likewise.

"Chokepods?" Dougan asked.

"You won't believe how many," Warren said. "Come forward slowly. Don't fully emerge from the cover of the passageway."

The others crept forward until they all had a view of the congested cavern. Thousands of bulbs floated in the air. Mottled with shades of cinnamon, brown, and black, they were mostly spherical, though the tops looked a bit pinched. Their texture was fibrous, like cornhusks. The smallest were the size of softballs, the largest more like beach balls. All remained in constant motion, drifting lazily until they floated close together, in which case they gently repelled one another.

"What are they?" Kendra asked.

"If you touch them, they burst, releasing a highly toxic gas," Dougan explained. "The gas can get into your system through respiration or even just contact with your skin.

You'll die almost instantly, and the toxin will gradually liquefy you. Eventually your remains will vaporize into fumes that can be absorbed by other chokepods."

"If one of us touches even a small chokepod, everyone in the cavern will perish, and it will be unsafe to enter for hours," Warren said.

Kendra tried to imagine weaving across the room. The chokepods floated from a foot or two above the floor to up near the ceiling, never quite brushing up against the walls. There was space between them, but not much, and the constant drifting meant that gaps big enough to accommodate a person were constantly opening and closing.

"Where are we trying to go?" Kendra asked.

"There are several false passageways around the perimeter of the room," Dougan said. "But the true way forward is through a hole in the center."

Kendra saw a raised area in the center of the cavern. Surrounded by rocks, the hole was not visible. It was a good hiding place for the passage, especially since the chokepods were most densely gathered in the middle of the room.

"Tammy explained that the key is to stay low," Warren related. "The chokepods never strike the ground, nor the ceiling, nor the walls, nor the stalagmites, nor the stalactites, nor each other. She said the chokepods rarely dip low enough to touch a person lying flat on the floor of the cavern. So we'll squirm forward, staying near stalagmites wherever possible."

"Can you manage this, Neil?" Dougan asked.

Neil nodded stoically.

"I'll try first," Warren said. "You all back away into the corridor. I'll cry out a warning if I brush up against a choke-pod and pollute the cavern. If I do, fall back to the chasm and wait. Otherwise, I'll call out once I'm safely in the hole."

The others retreated deeper into the narrow passage-way, fending off the darkness with two flashlights. "You'll go next, Kendra," Dougan informed her.

"Shouldn't Gavin go next?" Kendra suggested. "If all else fails, he and Warren could go on ahead and retrieve the artifact. Then you, Dougan, so you can help them, then me and Neil."

"Makes sense," Neil agreed.

"Except I'm the biggest, and therefore most likely to touch a chokepod even lying prone," Dougan said. "Gavin next, then Kendra, then me, then Neil."

They waited in silence. From behind, Kendra heard a distant roar, faint as the last rebound of an echo. "Did you hear that?" Kendra whispered to Gavin.

"Yeah," he whispered back, squeezing her hand con-solingly.

Even in a dark cave surrounded by the likelihood of death, Kendra could not help wondering if maybe there were romantic overtones to the gesture. She left her hand in his, enjoying the contact, thinking of the contrast between his stuttering speech and the confidence with which he had protected her on the mesa.

"I'm clear," Warren finally hollered.

"Guess I'm up," Gavin said. "I'll take the staff, Kendra. And the spear, Neil—it might trip you up in there. S-see you guys on the other side." Handing Kendra her flashlight, he raised his voice. "Warren, can you light the way for me?"

"Sure," Warren replied.

He slipped out of sight down the passageway. It seemed much less time had elapsed than Warren had taken before Gavin called out, "Kendra's turn!"

Mouth dry, palms wet, Kendra crept forward. Where the passageway ended, she stared into the cavern, watching chokepods dreamily rise and fall and drift laterally in every possible combination. She could see Warren's head in the center of the room. He held a flashlight.

"Kendra," Warren said, "I'll be your spotter. Just squirm on your belly and follow the beam of my flashlight. Let me tell you how to move. I have the advantage of being able to see your whole body all at once, along with all of the choke-pods near you. It worked well with Gavin."

"But if I pop a pod, you'll die with me."

"If you burst a chokepod, and the gas doesn't get me, your grandfather will. Come on."

Kendra prostrated herself and wormed forward. The floor of the cavern was neither smooth nor particularly jag-ged. She slithered along slowly, using her knees and elbows and wiggling her waist, grateful to have Warren's flashlight beam to follow. She kept her eyes down, hardly aware of the bulbs bobbing above her like grotesque balloons.

She was more than halfway to the center of the cavern when she heard a sharp intake of breath from Warren. "Lie flat, Kendra, flat as you can!" She laid her cheek against the stone, exhaling the air from her lungs, willing herself to sink into the rock. "On my command, roll onto your back to your left. Think about which way left is for you; don't roll right. Ready, almost, almost, now!"

Kendra rolled to her left onto her back, keeping her body as close to the ground as possible. Although she wanted to close her eyes, she could not help looking. Chokepods crowded all around her. She watched a huge pod dip low beside her, inches from the cavern floor, precisely where she had been, before bobbing up just high enough to clear her waist.

"Keep still," Warren ordered, voice taut.

Although the huge chokepod did not touch any of the others, its passage stirred the surrounding pods in new directions. A pair of chokepods the size of basketballs nearly collided directly above Kendra's nose, so close to her face that she expected both of them to brush against her skin and rupture. Instead, they drifted apart, missing her by a fraction of an inch.

Trembling, Kendra slowly inhaled, watching the cluster of chokepods above her leisurely disperse. A tear leaked from the corner of one eye.

"Well done, Kendra," Warren said, sounding relieved. "Roll to your left again and keep following the beam of my flashlight."

"Now?" Kendra asked.

"Sure."

She rolled over and inched forward, trying to calm her breathing.

"Scramble forward quickly," Warren instructed. "You've reached a clear area."

Her elbows ached as she propelled herself rapidly across the cavern floor. The flashlight beam guided her right, then left.

"Slow down," Warren said. "Wait, stop, back up a little."

Kendra glanced up and saw a chokepod the size of a volleyball falling toward her head at a diagonal. It was definitely on a collision course!

"Don't roll!" Warren warned. "They're on both sides! Blow at it!"

Puckering her lips, Kendra emptied her lungs at the oncoming chokepod. The stream of her breath sent the dappled bulb veering off course.

"Lie flat!" Warren commanded.

This time she did close her eyes, waiting in the darkness for a chokepod to kiss her skin and burst.

"Okay," Warren said. "Almost there, Kendra. Squirm forward."

She opened her eyes and followed the beam to the rocky barrier at the edge of the hole. Warren was so close! He had her wait, and then scuttle over the rocks when the air was momentarily clear. Then he was helping her take hold of iron rungs bolted into the stone wall of the hole. Surprised to be alive, quivering in shock, she descended the rungs to where Gavin stood waiting.

"Sounded like you had some close calls," Gavin said.

"I hated it," Kendra admitted. "I thought I was a goner. I had to blow one away."

"I b-b-blew three," Gavin said. "I got cocky and tried to hurry. Almost cost me. Maybe you should sit down."

Kendra plopped down with her back to the wall and drew her knees up to her chest. She still could not believe she had survived. A couple of times the chokepods had come unbearably close. She bowed her head, striving to steady herself. The adventure was not over yet.

Before she knew it, Dougan had descended the rungs and stood beside Gavin. "Could have gone my whole life without that experience." He sounded shaken. "I've been in some tight spots, but death has never felt so near."

Kendra felt relieved that she was not the only person who had found the experience of scooting across the cavern floor traumatizing.

"Isn't the dragon our next major problem?" Gavin asked.

"According to Tammy," Dougan affirmed. "She's been right this far."

That was when they heard an explosion, followed by Neil's strangled voice crying, "Run!"

An instant later, Warren slapped to the ground at the base of the ladder. "Go, go, go," he urged, yanking Kendra to her feet. They charged recklessly down the uneven passageway, rounding several corners before they slowed.

"Are you all right?" Dougan asked Warren, placing an arm around his shoulders.

"I think so," Warren said. "I saw it coming, too many chokepods converging on Neil. I warned him, then started down just in case, leaving the flashlight propped up on the rocks by the top of the hole. When I heard the chokepod burst, I dropped, and somehow landed without spraining an ankle. I think we're clear." Turning, he punched the wall of the cave hard enough to make his knuckles bleed.

"Y-y-y-y-you did well," Gavin told Warren. "If not for you, I wouldn't have made it through the cavern."

"Me neither," Kendra said.

"We owe you," Dougan agreed.

Warren nodded, shrugging gently away from Dougan. "I owed Neil. He saved my skin. Dangerous place. Bad luck. We should keep moving."

The others followed Warren as the cave began sloping up for the first time. Kendra tried not to think of Neil lying inert in the cavernous room full of bizarre, floating bulbs. She understood what Warren meant about owing him. If not for Neil, she would be dead as well. And now Neil had lost his life.

Gavin shouldered past Kendra and Dougan, grabbing Warren. "Wait," he said in an urgent whisper.

"What is it?" Warren asked.

"I smell dragon," Gavin responded. "Time for me to earn my keep. If I can secure us safe passage, I'll whistle. When you enter the room, don't look at the dragon, especially not into her eyes."

"*Her* eyes?" Dougan asked.

"Smells female," Gavin said. "No matter what happens, don't even consider attacking her. If things go wrong, run."

Warren moved aside. Gavin walked past him and around a corner. Warren, Dougan, and Kendra waited silently. They did not wait long.

An earsplitting screech rent the air, prompting all three of them to clamp their hands over their ears. A succession of roars and shrieks followed, seemingly too powerful to proceed from any animal. The only creature Kendra had ever heard make sounds at that volume was Bahumat, which was not a cheery thought.

The deafening bellows persisted, making the stone vibrate underfoot. To Kendra, the tumult sounded like a hundred dragons rather than one. Finally the clamor subsided, the silence now seeming much quieter than it had before. They uncovered their ears. A moment later, they heard a high, shrill whistle.

"That's the signal," Dougan said. "Me first. Warren, hang back with Kendra."

Dougan took the lead, while Warren and Kendra trailed at a distance. Soon they saw light up ahead. Dougan switched off his flashlight. They reached the opening of a chamber so vast that Kendra had trouble envisioning how it could fit inside the mesa. The tremendous room reminded her of when Hal had described caverns large enough to contain an entire football stadium. She had assumed he was exaggerating. Apparently not.

The colossal chamber was lit by glowing white stones set in the walls, making Kendra recall the stones inside the inverted tower. The high roof was so far away, Kendra doubted whether even Hugo could throw a rock high enough to reach it. She and Warren watched Dougan, who proceeded farther into the room, surveyed the scene, then waved them forward.

The room was wider and longer than it was tall. Some stalagmites rose over forty feet into the air. Although she knew she was not supposed to look, Kendra could not help shifting her gaze to Gavin, who stood fifty yards away, his back to her, arms and feet spread wide, facing a dragon perched above him on an oblong boulder. They appeared to be locked in an intense staring contest, both holding perfectly still.

The dragon gleamed like a new penny, overlapping copper scales encasing her in metallic armor. A tall fin ran from the top of her fierce head to the base of her neck. Not including the whiplike tail and the long, arched neck, the body of the dragon was the size of an elephant. A pair of shiny wings were folded at her sides.

The eyes of the dragon shifted to Kendra. They were bright, like molten gold. The dragon's mouth cracked open in a fang-filled imitation of a smile. "You dare to meet my gaze, little one?" the dragon asked, her silky words ringing like struck metal.

Kendra did not know what to do. She felt foolish for disobeying her instructions. She had been concerned about Gavin, and then the dragon had looked so fascinating. The heat of the stare made her feel cold. Her limbs went numb. What was it Warren had said about dragon tamers? Most people froze when dragons spoke to them. Dragon tamers spoke back.

"You are very beautiful," Kendra said in the loudest voice she could manage. "My eyes could not resist!"

"This one is almost eloquent," the dragon mused, keeping her eyes locked on Kendra. "Come closer, my pet."

"Kendra, look away!" Gavin demanded. "Chalize, do not forget our arrangement."

Kendra tried to turn her head, but the muscles in her neck would not respond. She tried to close her eyes, but her eyelids refused to operate. Although she felt immobilized by fear, her mind remained clear.

"Your companions were not to gaze upon me," Chalize sang, bright eyes still skewering Kendra. The dragon moved for the first time, crouching lower, as if coiling to spring.

"Do not forget yourself, worm!" Gavin yelled.

The dragon looked back at him, eyes narrowed. "Worm, is it?"

Kendra dropped her gaze to the floor. Warren appeared at one elbow, Dougan at the other, hurrying her along. She shuffled forward, listening to the conversation without raising her eyes.

"She spoke to you politely, Chalize," Gavin said. "Your kind are not meant to devour such without cause."

"She broke your promise and laid eyes on me. What further cause should I require?" The words were as harsh as swords clashing.

Gavin began speaking an unintelligible language, as distinct from a human tongue as the squeals of dolphins or the moans of whales. The dragon replied in similar fashion. The volume of the conversation was louder than when they had used English.

Kendra felt an impulse to look back. Was the dragon

still influencing her, or was she simply insane? Resisting the urge, she kept her eyes averted from Gavin and Chalize.

Presently Kendra, Warren, and Dougan reached the base of a long, wide stairway. As they climbed, the argument ended. Kendra could imagine Gavin staring down the dragon again. How had he gotten away with insulting her? How was he able to converse in her own language, a language that evidently not even the fairies knew, since Kendra had not understood any part of the exchange? There was certainly more to Gavin than met the eye.

Legs burning, they arrived at the top of the stairwell and beheld a deeply recessed alcove with an iron door. Advancing to the door, they found it locked, with no key in sight. They waited, none of them daring to look back.

Finally they heard rapid footfalls on the stairs. Gavin approached from behind, plunged a golden key into the lock, and opened the door. "Hurry," he said.

They rushed through the door into a corridor walled with stone blocks. Gavin paused to close the door behind them and then hurried to catch up. The floor was tiled. Glowing stones shone from sockets in the walls.

"You spoke like a dragon," Dougan said in wonder.

"Starting to see why Dad kept me a secret?" Gavin asked.

Dougan remained amazed. "I understood you were a dragon tamer, a natural, but this . . ."

"If you care for me at all, please never share what you heard."

"I'm sorry I looked at the dragon," Kendra said.

"D-d-d-don't mention it," Gavin said. "How did you manage to reply?"

"I don't know," Kendra said. "My body couldn't move, but my mind stayed clear. I remembered that dragon tamers spoke to dragons, so after I got caught in her stare, I gave it a try. Every other part of me was frozen, but my mouth still worked."

"Usually the mind is paralyzed along with the body," Gavin said. "You have serious potential as a dragon tamer."

"How were you able to look in her eyes?" Warren asked. "I've always understood that dragon tamers avoid eye contact."

"Y-you were peeking as well?" Gavin accused.

"Just enough to see you."

"I challenged Chalize to try to break my will without touching me," Gavin said. "Our arrangement was that if she failed, she would let us pass in and out freely."

"What made you think you could succeed!" Dougan exclaimed.

"I've always been immune to the charms of dragons," Gavin said. "Through some inborn quirk, their stares do not mesmerize me. She could have decapitated me with a flick of her tail, but she is young and has lived in solitude, so she relished the challenge. Surely, to her, it seemed a contest she could not possibly lose."

"From what I half-glimpsed, she did look rather small," Warren said.

"V-v-v-v-very mysterious," Gavin said. "Chalize is a youngling, with most of her growth ahead of her. She can't be much more than a hundred years old. Yet this vault has been here at least ten times that long. The cavern where she dwells was raked with claw marks and gouges from a much larger, older dragon."

"I noticed," Warren said. "So where was the parent?"

"I inquired how she came here," Gavin said. "She refused to respond. Something about the whole situation seems shady. At least she surrendered her key as promised."

"Her youth explains why she attacked the others so quickly," Dougan said.

"Right," Gavin agreed. "Normally dragons prefer to toy with their food. The young ones are more impulsive."

"Are all dragons as metallic as she is?" Kendra asked. "She almost looked like a robot."

"Each dragon is unique," Gavin said. "I have seen others with metal scales, but Chalize was the most metallic I've seen. Her entire body is sheathed in a copper alloy. You can even hear it in her voice."

Dougan laid an arm across Gavin's shoulders. "I suppose it goes without saying, but well done back there. You're a marvel."

"Th-th-thanks," Gavin said, lowering his eyes shyly.

As they proceeded down the corridor, Warren led the way, probing the ground with his broken spear. He warned them not to touch the walls, and to keep an eye out for trip-wires. Now that they had passed beyond the limits of where Tammy had scouted, any danger was possible.

The hall ended at a bronze door. Behind it they found a spiral staircase leading downward. Testing every step before trusting their weight to it, they wound ever deeper into the earth. After hundreds of uninterrupted steps, the stairs ended at another bronze door.

"This could be the abode of the guardian," Warren whispered. "Kendra, hang back."

Warren led the way through the unlocked door, followed by Dougan and Gavin. Kendra peered in after them. The lofty room made Kendra think of the inside of a cathedral without pews or windows. Statues stood in elevated niches; small rooms housing various ornaments branched out from the main chamber; fading murals decorated the walls and ceiling; and a tremendous, ornate altar dominated the far end of the room.

Warren, Dougan, and Gavin crossed the room cautiously, all facing in different directions, as Kendra watched from the door. They reached the altar and looked around, gradually relaxing. They started searching all of the side rooms, handling various treasures, but found no guardian to oppose them.

Weary of waiting, and doubting the presence of danger, Kendra entered the room. Warren was giving the altar a closer examination, hesitantly touching jewels. "Nothing?" Kendra asked.

Warren looked up. "Possibly we have not yet awakened or activated the guardian. But if you ask me, I think somebody made off with the artifact a long time ago. I see nothing suspicious. This room should have held our most fearsome challenge, unless the guardian has already fallen."

"It might explain why Tammy and Javier were able

to exit the caves without finding the artifact," Kendra observed.

"Right, and why a new dragon was placed here a century ago," Warren agreed.

Kendra came around to the far side of the altar and froze, reading what had been inscribed there in silver letters. "Did you read this?" Kendra asked softly.

"It isn't a language I'm familiar with," Warren said.

"Must be a fairy language," Kendra whispered. "It looks like English to me."

"What does it say?"

Peering around to make sure Dougan and Gavin were out of earshot, she quietly read the words aloud:

Courtesy of the world's greatest adventurer,
this artifact has a new home at Fablehaven.

CHAPTER THIRTEEN

Secret Admirer

S eth lay under the covers in his bed, fully dressed except for his shoes, fingers laced behind his head, staring up at the slanted ceiling of the dark attic room. He was contemplating the difference between courage and stupidity, a distinction Grandpa Sorenson had repeatedly tried to emphasize. He considered himself armed with useful definitions. Stupidity was when you took risks for no good reason. Courage was when you took a calculated risk in order to accomplish something important.

Had he been stupid in the past? Sure! Peeking out of the window on Midsummer Eve when he had been warned not to look had been stupid. The only benefit had been to satisfy his curiosity, and he had nearly gotten his family killed. This summer he had taken some risks for flimsy reasons as well. Of course, when the risk seemed small, sometimes he didn't mind acting a little stupid.

But he had also acted courageously. He had overdosed on courage potion to confront the revenant in hopes of saving his family. That risk had paid off.

Was sneaking out of the house to follow the shadowy manifestations of Coulter and Tanu into the woods going to be dangerous? Absolutely. The question was whether the risk was justified.

Earlier that afternoon, Tanu had completed his transformation into a shadowman just outside the window. He had waited in the shade on the deck until sundown, when he had ventured off into the woods. A few hours later, with evening deepening, the silent shadows of Tanu and Coulter had returned. Visible only to Seth, they had stood halfway across the yard from the house, allowing Grandpa to address them from the deck. Tanu had indicated that all was well with two thumbs up, and they had gestured for Seth to follow them, inviting Grandpa to come along as well. Through pantomime, Coulter had expressed that he would scout ahead as they traveled in order to prevent encounters with dangerous creatures.

But Grandpa had declined the invitation. He had stated that if Tanu and Coulter could devise a way for him to follow them without Seth, he would consent to accompany them. As he told them this, Seth stood behind him making subtle gestures, stealthily pointing at Grandpa and shaking his head, then pointing at himself, then pointing at them, then winking. None but Seth could see Tanu salute that he had received the message.

The house had been still for some time. If he was going to follow through on the message he had mimed to Tanu and Coulter, the moment had arrived. But he hesitated. Was he actually going to disregard a direct order from Grandpa and entrust his life to the shadowy versions of Tanu and Coulter? If Tanu and Coulter had his best interests in mind, would they be willing to let him sneak away with them against Grandpa's wishes? Hopefully they were certain he would be safe and confident that Grandpa would thank them all later.

What were the possibilities? They might lead him into a trap. He might die or be transformed into a shadow himself. Then again, he might solve the mystery of the plague, restore Tanu and Coulter, and save Fablehaven.

Seth scooted out from under his covers, pulled on his shoes, and started tying the laces. The bottom line was that Grandpa would have been willing to risk his life on the gamble that the shadows of Tanu and Coulter meant to offer meaningful assistance. He would have followed them if he could have done so alone. He simply was not willing to risk Seth's life. To Seth, this proved that the risk was worth taking. If Grandpa loved him too much to let him take a worthwhile risk, then he would bypass Grandpa.

Shoes secure, Seth slid his emergency kit out from under the bed. Then he tiptoed down the attic stairs, flinching at every creak. At the bottom of the steps the house remained dark and quiet. Seth hurried along the hall and down the stairs to the entry hall. He stole into Grandpa's study, tugged a chain to turn on a desk lamp, and rummaged through Tanu's bag of potions. After examining several bottles, Seth found the one he wanted, grabbed it, and closed the bag.

He switched off the light and crept to the back door. Unlocking it, he slipped outside, where moonlight bathed the yard in silver highlights. "Tanu?" Seth hissed in a forced whisper. "Coulter?"

A pair of humanoid shadows emerged from behind a hedge, one taller and bulkier than the other. Seth climbed over the deck railing and dropped to the lawn. Immediately, two additional figures streaked toward him, one much bigger than Tanu, the other a little taller than Coulter.

Seth uncapped the potion he had swiped and guzzled the contents. By the time Mendigo and Hugo reached him, an effervescent tingling raced through his limbs, and he hovered in the air, a vaporous rendition of himself. Mendigo and Hugo tried in vain to lay hands on him.

Of course Grandpa hadn't trusted him. Of course Mendigo and Hugo had been stationed with orders to prevent him from leaving the yard. Was it Seth's fault that Grandpa had neglected to hide Tanu's potions?

Coulter and Tanu motioned for Seth to follow. Willing himself forward, Seth drifted behind them as quickly as he could. Mendigo stayed with him, ceaselessly trying to seize him, causing bubbly tingles wherever his wooden hands grabbed. His progress was frustratingly slow. Hugo went to the house and started thumping on the wall. Seth tried to ignore the lights turning on inside.

He was most of the way to the woods when Dale called

out after him. "Seth, you mind your grandfather and come back right away." Refusing to even look back, Seth shook his head.

When Seth reached the edge of the woods, Grandpa spoke from the deck. "Wait, Seth, come back! Tanu! Coulter! Hold on, listen, if you're going to do this, at least let me join you." The shadowy figures stopped. Shaking his head emphatically, Seth crossed and uncrossed his arms. This was a trick. As soon as he became solid, Grandpa would drag him home. He waved a hand, goading them to continue.

"Seth," Grandpa demanded, "don't wave them onward. Tanu, Coulter, if you really are in possession of yourselves, wait for me."

The shadowy figures shrugged at Seth and stood their ground. He waved more frantically for them to proceed. Did they know his grandfather at all?

"Mendigo," Grandpa called. "Stand down. You will accompany Seth and me. Hugo, fetch the cart. I take it the cart would be the quickest means to reach our destination?"

Tanu nodded. Seth turned and nodded at Grandpa.

"We'll have to wait for you to solidify," Grandpa said. "Let me grab a flashlight and put on more appropriate clothing."

He went back inside. Seth waved for Tanu and Coulter to lead on, but they shook their heads.

"I saw that," Dale called from the deck. "Don't keep egging them on. Your Grandpa is as good as his word. He means to come with you, and if you ask me, you'll fare better with him than without him."

Seth relaxed, hovering in the darkness near the shadows of his friends. If Grandpa was tricking him, he supposed he could always devise a fresh strategy for running away.

Grandpa returned dressed for travel. He instructed Dale to wait with Grandma, and to flee Fablehaven if they failed to return or returned as shadows. Seth glided over to where Hugo stood ready to pull the wooden cart like a giant rickshaw. Tanu and Coulter climbed up into the wagon, as did Grandpa and Mendigo. Seth floated alongside, waiting to transform.

At last the tedious wait ended in a fizzy rush, and Seth boosted himself up into the cart with the others. The shadowmen sat up front. Grandpa and Seth hunkered down in the rear.

"I do this against my better judgment," Grandpa said.

"We need to take the risk," Seth maintained in his best grown-up voice. "I'm not going to abandon Tanu and Coulter when I might be able to help them."

"Let's go, Hugo," Grandpa commanded.

The cart lurched forward and Hugo bounded down the path, setting a brisk pace. The warm night air washed over Seth as the cart advanced through the darkness. When the trail forked, Tanu indicated which direction to take, Seth relayed the gesture, and Grandpa issued a directive to Hugo.

With Hugo lolloping tirelessly in front of the cart, they traveled down the road toward where the Forgotten Chapel once stood, then took several other paths, until they ended up on a rugged, overgrown track that Seth had never traveled. The cart bounced and jolted over the uneven lane, until Tanu and Coulter waved them to a halt.

Grandpa switched on his flashlight, revealing a gradual, grassy slope that led to a steep hill with a cave in the side. "Tell me they aren't pointing at the cave," Grandpa said.

"Yes," Seth replied. "They already jumped down from the cart."

"We may as well turn around right now," Grandpa said. "That is the lair of Graulas, one of the major demons of Fablehaven. To enter his lair would place us in his power. It would be suicide."

Coulter gestured at the cave, then tapped a shadowy finger against his temple.

"Graulas knows something important," Seth relayed.

Tanu and Coulter both nodded and motioned for them to follow.

Grandpa leaned close to Seth, speaking for his ears only. "Graulas is arguably the most powerful demon at Fablehaven, although he has hibernated in recent years. He would be the last being to share information with us willingly."

Tanu pointed at the cave, gave a thumbs-up, opened and closed his free hand like a mouth talking, and pointed to Seth.

"Graulas wants to speak with me?" Seth asked. "Grandpa, they're both giving me a thumbs-up. This is where they meant to take me. You wait here, and I'll go see."

Grandpa gripped Seth's arm. "I came along to see what

they had in mind. If the venture held promise, I would continue. But this is folly. Mendigo and Hugo won't be able to set foot on his territory. The treaty will offer us no protection. We're turning back."

"Okay," Seth said, slouching against the back of the cart.

Grandpa relaxed his hold on Seth's arm. "Tanu, Coulter, this is too much to ask. We are going to return."

Tearing free from Grandpa's grasp with a sudden lunge, Seth sprang off the cart and started running up the slope toward the mouth of the cave. If Mendigo and Hugo couldn't follow, then Grandpa couldn't stop him.

"Mendigo, bring Seth back here!" Grandpa barked.

The wooden puppet vaulted from the cart, rapidly gained on Seth, then came to an abrupt standstill about fifteen paces from the road. Seth continued up the slope, but the puppet could proceed no farther.

Grandpa stood up, fists on his hips. "Seth Andrew Sorenson, you return to this cart this instant!"

Seth glanced back but did not slow. The shadowy Coulter and Tanu jogged along at either side of him. The mouth of the cave drew near.

"Seth, wait," Grandpa shouted anxiously from down the slope. "I'm coming with you." Seth did not like the resigned tone in his voice.

Seth paused, watching Grandpa trudge through the tall grass, flashlight in hand. "You can come, but don't get close enough to touch me."

Grandpa glared, the muscles in his jaw tightening. "The

only thing more alarming than what is in that cave will be your punishment if we somehow survive."

"If we survive, I'll have made a good choice." Seth waited until Grandpa was about ten paces away, then started toward the cave again.

"You realize we are going to our deaths?" Grandpa said grimly.

"Who better to tell us about an evil plague than a demon?" Seth countered.

A tall wooden post stood outside the cave. Rusted iron shackles dangled from the top. Evidently victims had once been chained there. The thought made Seth shiver. The shadows of Tanu and Coulter did not proceed beyond the post. Seth waved for them to follow. They shook their heads and motioned him forward.

The mouth of the cave was large enough to accommodate a school bus. As Seth tromped inside, he realized that worrying about Grandpa stopping him from saving Fablehaven had partly distracted him from properly thinking through whether he should be stopping himself. He hoped that Tanu and Coulter were not enslaved to the will of this demon.

The smooth dirt walls and floor gave Seth the impression that the cave had not formed naturally—it was an excavation. As he continued forward, the cave curved twice and then widened into a single, stuffy room with a domed ceiling through which protruded a few twisted roots.

Rotten, broken furniture mingled with disorderly piles of pale bones. A huge, sagging table bore numerous moldy books and the waxy puddles of melted candles. Ruptured barrels were heaped haphazardly against one wall, leaking rancid contents. Amid a jumble of crushed crates, Seth noticed the glint of jewels.

Against the far, curving wall of the room, cobwebs veiled a huge, hunched shape. The lumpy figure sat on the floor, back to the dirt wall, slumped to one side. Seth glanced over his shoulder at Grandpa. He stood motionless except for the quivering hand clutching the flashlight.

"Shine the light on the thing in the corner," Seth said. The beam was currently aimed at the cluttered table.

Grandpa offered no response. He did not move.

And then a voice spoke, deeper than any voice Seth had ever imagined, slow and labored, as if on the brink of death. "You . . . do . . . not . . . fear . . . me?"

Seth squinted at the web-shrouded shape in the corner. "Of course I do," he said, stepping closer. "But my friends said you wanted to speak with me."

The figure stirred, making the cobwebs ripple and dust plume into the air. "You . . . do not . . . feel . . . fear . . . as you did . . . in . . . the grove?" The speaker sounded sad and tired.

"With the revenant? How do you know about that? I don't feel fear like I did there. The fear there was uncontrollable."

The figure shifted again. One of the largest sheets of cobweb tore, billowing lazily. The rumbling voice gained a little strength. "Your grandsire . . . is in the grip of such fear now. Take . . . his light . . . and come closer."

Seth walked over to Grandpa, who had yet to move. Seth poked him gently in the ribs, but got only a slight twitch as a reaction. Why was Grandpa so incapacitated? Was Graulas directing magic specifically at him? A devious part of Seth's mind wished that Grandpa would remain like this, so he wouldn't get in trouble if they made it out alive. Seth yanked the flashlight from his grasp.

"Will Grandpa be all right?" Seth asked.

"He will."

"You're Graulas?"

"I am. Come closer."

Picking his way through the decaying debris, Seth drew nearer to the demon. With one thick, gnarled hand, the demon was peeling away cobwebs. Dust fumed up from his clothes. Gagging, Seth covered his nose and mouth against the putrid stench. Although the demon was sitting on the floor and hunched to one side, Seth came no higher than his bloated shoulder.

Seth took an involuntary step back when the flashlight illuminated the demon's face. His skin was like the head of a turkey, red and folded and droopy, as if horribly infected. He was bald, and he had no visible ears. A pair of curled ram horns projected from the sides of his broad skull, and a milky film clouded his cold, black eyes.

"Would you believe . . . I was once . . . one of the six . . . most feared . . . and respected . . . demons . . . in the world?" he asked, his breathing labored. His entire body rocked with the effort of each wheezing inhalation.

"Sure," Seth said.

The demon shook his saggy head, folds of red flesh swaying. "Do not patronize me."

"I'm not. I believe you."

Graulas coughed. Webs flapped and dust swirled. "Nothing . . . has caught my interest . . . in hundreds of years," he growled wearily. He closed his eyes. His breathing slowed, and his voice became steadier. "I came to this pitiful zoo to die, Seth, but dying comes slowly for my kind, so very slowly. Hunger cannot conquer me. Disease is no match. I slumber, but I do not rest."

"Why did you come here to die?" Seth asked.

"To embrace my fate. I have known true greatness, Seth. To fall from greatness, from the dizziest heights to the deepest depths, knowing one might have prevented it, certain one will never reclaim what one has lost, cripples the will. Life holds no more meaning than one chooses to impose, and I quit pretending long ago."

"I'm sorry," Seth said. "You have a big spider on your arm."

"No matter," the demon wheezed. "I did not summon you here to pity my condition. As dormant as I have become, I cannot submerge all of my gifts. Without conscious effort, without tools or spells, this preserve is open to my scrutiny, all save a few select locations. I dread the futile monotony of all that is out there and endeavor to ignore it, to turn inward, and even so I cannot help perceiving much that transpires. Nothing has intrigued me . . . until you." Graulas opened his filmy eyes.

"Me?"

"Your courage in the grove surprised me. Surprise is a reaction I had all but forgotten. I have seen enough that I always know what to expect. I assess the odds of various outcomes, and my predictions are never thwarted. Before you were finished confronting the revenant, the potion failed. I saw the artificial bravado leave you. Your demise was certain. Yet, despite my certainty, you removed the nail. Had you been full-grown, a seasoned hero of legendary renown, well-trained, armed with charms and talismans, I would have been deeply impressed. But for a mere boy to perform such a feat? I was truly surprised."

Seth was unsure what to say. He watched the demon and waited.

Graulas leaned forward. "You wonder why I brought you here."

"To find out what I taste like?"

The demon regarded him morosely. "I brought you here to thank you for my first surprise in centuries."

"You're welcome."

The demon shook his head slightly. Or had only his eyes moved? "I intend to thank you by bestowing what you currently need. Knowledge. It will probably not save you, but who can say? Perhaps you will amaze me again. Based on your performance in the grove, it might be poor judgment to consider you incapable of anything. Sit down."

Seth squatted on a corroded, overturned bookcase.

"The revenant was nothing without the nail," Graulas rasped. "A feeble being fortified by a talisman of tremendous dark power. Your friends should have striven more earnestly to recover it."

"Tanu searched for it for hours," Seth said. "He finally decided it must have been destroyed when I pulled it out."

"A talisman of such potency is not easily unmade. By the time your friend started looking, he was too late."

"What happened to it?"

"First consider what happened to you. Why do you suppose that only you can discern the shades of your friends?"

"Did the nail do that to me?"

Graulas leaned back and closed his eyes, a pained expression flashing across his revolting features, as if he was coping with a sudden surge of agony. After a moment, he spoke, dark eyes still squeezed shut. "The talisman left its mark on you. Be glad you did not touch the nail with your flesh, or it would have taken possession of you. You have been enabled to see certain dark properties that are invisible to most eyes. And you have acquired an immunity to magical fear."

"Really?"

"My presence inspires a paralyzing horror in humans, similar to the aura that surrounded the revenant. Exuding terror is part of my nature. Look to your grandsire if you harbor any doubt."

Seth stood up, shaking his arms and flexing his fingers. "I really don't feel scared. I mean, I'm worried that you might be tricking me, and that you might kill me and Grandpa, but I don't feel petrified like with the revenant."

"This sight you have been endowed with might help you

locate the source of the magic transforming the creatures of Fablehaven," Graulas said. "Your darkened friends remain reliable. For such fragile creatures, humans sometimes have surprising strengths. One is self-possession. The same magic that has altered the creatures of Fablehaven has failed to overthrow the minds of Coulter and Tanugatoa."

"Good to know," Seth said.

Graulas paused, eyes still shut, his breathing loud. "Would you care for my insights on how the current trouble at Fablehaven originated?"

"Did it have something to do with the prisoner the Sphinx released?"

Graulas opened his eyes. "Very good. Do you happen to know the identity of the captive?"

"So the Sphinx really is a traitor?" Seth exclaimed. "No, none of us know who the prisoner was. Do you?"

Graulas licked his lips, his tongue a bruised color and marked by sores. "His presence was unmistakable, although most would not have been able to sense his true identity. He was Navarog, the demon prince, lord of the dragons."

"The prisoner was a dragon?"

"The foremost of all dark dragons."

"He looked human-sized."

"He was in disguise, naturally. Many dragons can assume a human form when it suits them. Navarog did not revert to his true shape while on this property. His business at Fablehaven was of a stealthier nature."

Seth sat back down on the corroded bookcase. "You say 'was.' Did he leave?"

"He left Fablehaven on the same day the Sphinx set him free," Graulas said. "He was never formally admitted to the preserve, and so the walls could not hold him. But he did not depart until after performing some mischief. First he went to the grove and retrieved the nail. The dark talisman had already burrowed deep into the ground, which is why Tanugatoa missed it, but it surfaced when summoned. Then Navarog took the nail to Kurisock."

"The other demon?"

"There are a few places my senses cannot penetrate at Fablehaven. One is the house and yard where you live with your grandparents. Another is the mansion that was once the residence of the caretaker. And a third is the tiny domain ruled by Kurisock. I cannot say precisely what Navarog did with the nail, but he had it when he entered Kurisock's domain, and when he left, the talisman was no longer in his possession. After delivering the nail, Navarog fled the preserve."

"Where'd he go from here?" Seth asked.

"Ever since I tied myself to this preserve, my sight does not carry beyond the boundaries," Graulas explained. "I have no guess where a dragon as mighty as Navarog might have gone."

"So to save Fablehaven, I have to stop Kurisock," Seth said.

"It would be intriguing to watch how you fared against him," Graulas mused with a glint in his eye. Something about the stare convinced Seth that the demon was somehow toying with him. "Do not ask me why Navarog went to Kurisock.

If Kurisock has accomplished great deeds, I have not heard of them. He has wrought devastation on occasion, but lacks the faculties of a master strategist. There was a time when Navarog would have brought the talisman straight to me."

"Do you just want to use me to trip up a rival?"

"Rival?" Graulus rumbled, almost chuckling. "I long ago ceased measuring myself against others."

"How do I stop Kurisock?"

"Kurisock is more shadow than substance. To interact with the material world, he binds himself to a host. In return for a borrowed physical form, he imbues the host with power. Depending on whom Kurisock symbiotically unites with, the results can be impressive."

"Then he's not working alone."

"In my long years, I have never seen darkness transform beings as infectiously as is happening on this preserve. I do not know how it is being accomplished. By binding oath, Kurisock cannot go beyond the limits of his domain here at Fablehaven. He must have partnered with a powerful entity, and the nail must be amplifying his abilities."

"Would the nail do different things for Kurisock than it did for the revenant?"

"Undoubtedly," Graulas agreed. "The nail is a reservoir of dark power. Without it the revenant would not have been very intimidating. With it he was among the most dangerous and powerful creatures at Fablehaven. Kurisock was formidable without the nail. With the talisman, his abilities may have become sufficiently augmented to explain this virulent darkness."

"You're a demon, right?" Seth said dubiously. "No offense, but shouldn't you be happy about this plague?"

Graulas coughed, moribund body heaving. "The pendulum swings back and forth between light and darkness. I lost interest long ago. What rekindled my interest was you, Seth. I am curious to see how you fare against this threat."

"I'll do my best. What else can you tell me?"

"You must figure out the rest with the help of your friends," Graulas said. "You do not have much time. The infectious darkness is spreading inexorably. There are only two safe refuges on the preserve, and even they cannot hold out indefinitely. I cannot see the shrine of the Fairy Queen. It repels darkness. Many of the creatures of light have sought sanctuary around her pond. And the centaurs, among others, have withdrawn to protected ground in a far corner of the preserve, within a ring of stones that will not admit darkness. Those will be the last places to fall."

"And the house," Seth added.

"If you say so," Graulas said. "Now I must rest. Take your grandfather and go. This is another triumph you can add to your list: Few mortals have entered my presence and lived to tell the tale."

"One more thing," Seth asked. "How did Coulter and Tanu know I could trust you?"

"Coulter was exploring, searching for the cause of the plague. He came to me. In his current state, though I can see and hear him clearly, I cannot harm him. I told him that I had information to share with you, and convinced him that I was a sincere admirer. Later I persuaded Tanugatoa as well.

Fortunately for you, I was telling the truth. Go and rescue this wretched, ridiculous zoo, if you dare."

Graulas closed his eyes. His mushy, crinkled face drooped, and then slumped forward, as if he had lapsed into unconsciousness.

Letting the flashlight dangle from a cord around his wrist, Seth returned to Grandpa and grabbed him under his arms. The contact seemed to stir Grandpa out of his trance, and Seth helped him walk out of the cave. Coulter and Tanu were waiting outside. Once they were back in the moonlight, Grandpa flinched wildly, flailing his arms, and Seth released him.

"We're outside!" Grandpa gasped.

"Graulas let us go," Seth said. "Did you catch any of what he told us?"

"Bits and pieces," Grandpa said, brow knitted. "It was hard to focus. How did you withstand the fear? The cold?"

"Actually, it was kind of stuffy in there," Seth said. "I guess I'm immune to magical fear. Something to do with surviving the revenant. We need to have a long talk."

Grandpa bent over and brushed off his pants. "You realize we can't trust what Graulas told you."

"I know. But we need to consider it. I'm pretty sure he told me the truth. If he meant us harm, all he needed to do was sit back and watch us fail. At least this gives us some leads to pursue."

Grandpa nodded, walking toward Hugo and the cart. "First things first. Let's hurry home."

CHAPTER FOURTEEN

Homecoming

The rising sun bathed the top of Painted Mesa in golden light, the pueblo ruins casting long shadows beyond the brink of the nearest precipice. A scrawny lizard skittered along the top of a crumbling wall, its progress interrupted by unpredictable pauses. The thirsty ground and arid air had already sapped away the rainfall. A warm breeze and a few fluffy clouds suggested that the storm might have been nothing more than a dream.

Kendra, Dougan, Gavin, and Warren tramped across reddish stone away from the ruins. When they reached the edge of the mesa, Kendra peered down at a bird of prey wheeling in a wide circle, brown wings tilting in the breeze. The air was shockingly clear. The desert panorama—expanses of dirt and stone gouged by gorges and overseen by craggy buttes—looked so crisp that Kendra felt as though she had put on a pair of much-needed prescription glasses.

Getting out of the cave had proven nearly as arduous as getting in. After extensive searching and experimentation, they had concluded that the artifact was not hidden or disguised—it really was gone. Warren had cautioned Kendra not to share her translation of the inscription on the altar with Dougan or Gavin. In the end, they each claimed several treasures from the chamber and departed.

Upon returning to Chalize's lair, Kendra had managed to keep her eyes off the metallic dragon, and Gavin had presented the coppery beast with a selection of the loveliest treasures they had pilfered. Later, Warren successfully tested the air in the cavern with the chokepods. Crossing the cavern was dodgy, but they all made it. Kendra had avoided looking at Neil, who Warren had reported was already mostly liquefied.

At the chasm, Kendra had fallen, but the swing to the wall had not been far, and Warren had pulled her up. The others traversed the gap without incident. When they reached the platform where they had started, Dougan inserted the key, and they spiraled up into the kiva.

Uncertain what enemies they might find waiting, venturing out onto the mesa was tense. But, with Gavin leading the way, they were relieved to find no trace of the creatures who had attacked them the night before.

Now, traipsing along the rim of the mesa, Kendra clung to the rain staff stolen from the coyote man. Jewels rattled in her pockets. Gavin had retained a heavy golden crown set with sapphires, which he now wore on his head. Dougan bore a chalice wrought of crystal and platinum. Warren wore several new rings and clung to a sheathed sword with a pearly hilt.

About halfway around the perimeter of the mesa, they found a pathway that descended the plateau in a steep series of switchbacks. They encountered no trouble on the way down. As the day grew hotter and the balmy breeze faltered, the mesa remained tranquil.

Once they reached the base of the mesa, Kendra was unsurprised when they looked back to see that the zigzagging path they had descended was gone. They hiked around the mesa toward the vehicles, until Gavin spotted Tammy's corpse lying between a pair of tall, bullet-shaped boulders. While Dougan and Gavin moved in for a closer inspection, Warren escorted Kendra along a route that kept the body out of view.

The Jeep and the truck were parked not too far beyond where Gavin had found Tammy. Warren and Kendra waited by the vehicles until Dougan and Gavin showed up carrying a bundled load between them. Warren jogged over to help. Together they carefully placed Tammy's remains in the bed of the truck.

"We don't have keys to the Jeep," Dougan said. "Those were lost with Neil."

"I'll ride in back," Gavin offered.

"Before we return to the hacienda, I have a proposal," Dougan said. "In case we still have a traitor in our midst, someone who works at the preserve, for example, I say we pretend the mission was a success." Dougan held up the platinum and crystal chalice. "I recommend we secure this item in our strongbox as if it were the artifact, on the chance that the decoy helps flush out an enemy." He wrapped it tightly in his poncho.

"Great idea," Warren approved.

"Plus, it can't hurt to send the message that the artifact was recovered," Kendra said. "The misinformation might prevent the Society from hunting for it elsewhere."

"If they weren't the ones who already snatched it," Gavin murmured.

"A possible scenario," Dougan acknowledged. "But until we learn more about the missing artifact, our best hope to mislead the Society is to claim victory."

Kendra sat between Dougan and Warren on the ride back to the hacienda. She felt a little guilty about not telling Dougan and Gavin that the artifact was probably not in the hands of the Society of the Evening Star, that it had been relocated to Fablehaven. They had paid a high price to reach the final chamber of the vault, and Kendra loathed leaving them with the feeling that the mission had been a total failure. But if the Sphinx was a traitor, she and Warren could not risk allowing vital information to reach him through Dougan and Gavin.

Kendra tried not to think about Tammy lying in the bed of the truck. She felt bad for Gavin riding back there with the corpse. She refused to think of Neil, brave and quiet, whose reward for a heroic rescue was to be slowly devoured by strange cave balloons.

Kendra had spoken little all morning, and did not deviate from her pattern during the drive. She felt stretched. Her eyes itched. Danger had kept her on edge all night. Now that the peril had passed, her fatigue became harder to ignore.

Rosa, Hal, and Mara came out of the hacienda as the truck pulled to a stop. Hal sauntered forward, glancing in the bed of the truck as the others got out.

"Tammy?" Hal asked, his attention on the bundled corpse.

Dougan nodded.

"No Jeep," Hal remarked. "I take it Neil ran into trouble."

"Chokepods," Dougan reported.

Hal nodded, averting his eyes. Biting her knuckles, Rosa choked back sobs. She leaned against Mara, who kept a stoic expression, her dark eyes hard. Witnessing their grief made Kendra teary.

"He went inside the vault," Hal said, a statement with an implied question.

"We ran into serious trouble on the mesa," Warren explained. "Neil was a real hero. None of us would have made it to the cave without him. Weathering the night outside the vault would have meant certain doom, so he and Kendra entered with us."

"I reckon you saw he was a skinwalker," Hal said.

"He became a chestnut stallion and ferried us to safety," Gavin said.

"Did you find what you were after?" Hal asked.

Dougan hefted the chalice, which was still wrapped in his poncho. "We'll leave you in peace as soon as we can schedule a flight."

"We'll radio Stu," Hal offered. "He can hop on the Internet and book your flights. You must have endured quite a night." He laid a hand on the side of the truck. "Go on inside; I'll take care of the young lady."

Kendra followed Warren into the hacienda, avoiding eye contact with Rosa and Mara. What must they think of them? Strangers who came to their preserve, dragged one of their friends onto a dangerous mesa to recover some artifact, and returned bearing news of his death, without so much as a body to bury.

"You okay?" Warren asked.

Kendra could not imagine that he actually wanted the truth. She nodded instead.

"You did great," Warren said. "That was a nightmare. Get some rest, all right? Let me know if you need anything."

"Thanks," Kendra said, entering her room and closing the door. After pulling off her boots and socks, she dove onto her bed, buried her face in the pillow, and cried. Her tears and muffled sobs helped purge the fear and sorrow of the previous night. Soon exhaustion overcame her, and Kendra sank into a dreamless sleep.

※ ※ ※

Rosy light glowed through her window when Kendra awoke. She wiped crust from her eyelids and smacked her lips. Her mouth tasted dry and stale. Sitting up, she felt woozy and had a slight headache. Irregular sleep patterns had never agreed with her.

Someone had left a glass of water on her nightstand. Kendra sipped from the glass, grateful to wash away the unpleasant taste in her mouth. She padded across the floor, went out into the hall, and walked to the kitchen. Mara looked up. She had been wiping the table.

"You must be hungry," Mara said in her husky voice.

"Sort of," Kendra replied. "I'm so sorry about Neil."

"He knew the risks," she said evenly. "Would you prefer something light? Soup and toast?"

"Don't fuss over me. I'll grab a bite later. Have you seen Warren?"

"He's in the courtyard."

Kendra hurried down a corridor, the tiles cool against her bare feet, and stepped out into the courtyard. Although the sun was setting, the pebbles of the gravel pathway remained warm, crunching underfoot and prickling her soles. Several fairies buzzed in the air. Warren stood on a tiled path beside a flowering cactus, hands clasped behind his back. He turned and smiled at Kendra. "You woke up."

"I'll probably be awake all night."

"Maybe not. I bet you're more fatigued than you realize. We have a flight booked tomorrow at eleven in the morning."

"Great."

He walked toward her. "I've been thinking. Without divulging all we know, I want to warn Dougan about the Sphinx, just tell him enough to get him paying attention."

"Okay."

"We don't want to notify the Sphinx that we're onto him, but I think we can also err by keeping our suspicions too private. I was waiting for you. I want you there to corroborate the story. Don't tell him more than I do. Does that sound foolish?"

Kendra thought about it for a moment. "Telling anyone is a risk, but I think we need somebody like Dougan keeping an eye on him."

"I agree. As a Lieutenant of the Knights of the Dawn, Dougan is very well connected, and I can think of no other high-ranking Knight who strikes me as more trustworthy." He led her back inside the house. They walked to a closed door and knocked.

"Come in," Dougan invited.

They entered a tidy bedroom not unlike Kendra's. Dougan sat at a desk writing in a notebook.

"We need to talk," Warren said.

"Sure." Dougan gestured at his bed. He was sitting on the only chair. Kendra and Warren sat down on the mattress.

"These are uncertain times," Warren began. "I need to run something by you. Kendra is here to verify my words. You recall when I grilled you about the identity of the Captain."

"Right," Dougan said, his tone hinting not to ask again.

"We ended up discussing the Sphinx. Whatever his relation to the Knights of the Dawn, at the very least, he has long been one of our more trusted collaborators. As a

Lieutenant, you're close to the Captain, so there is something I want you to know. You're aware that Fablehaven is
one of the five secret preserves."

"Yes."

"Are you aware that the Sphinx removed the artifact
hidden at Fablehaven earlier this summer?"

Dougan stared at him silently, lips slightly puckered. He
shook his head almost imperceptibly.

"Then I doubt you heard he also took with him a prisoner who had been confined in the most secure cell on the
property? A detainee who had been there ever since the
preserve was founded? An anonymous captive with an infa-
mous reputation."

Dougan cleared his throat. "I was unaware."

"There were some shifty circumstances surrounding the
whole event," Warren said. "Nothing to prove the Sphinx
is a traitor. But given the high stakes, together with the
nature of our current mission, I want to be sure the Sphinx
is not the only person aware that the Fablehaven artifact
was removed, if you take my meaning."

Dougan nodded. "You saw the artifact?" he asked
Kendra.

"I saw it in use," she said. "I recharged it myself. The
Sphinx came to Fablehaven and took it personally."

"If what you told us before was true, and the Sphinx
is not leading the Knights, you'll want to make sure the
Captain knows about this," Warren said. "If you misled us,
and the Sphinx is the Captain, make sure at least one of the

other Lieutenants knows the details we're sharing. No one person should have control over multiple artifacts."

"I understand the implications," Dougan said, voice steady.

"Implications are all we have," Warren said. "This is merely precautionary. We have no desire to wrongly accuse an innocent ally. Still, in case the Sphinx really is working for the other side, please don't let our concerns get back to him. If he is a traitor, he has covered the secret well, and will stop at nothing to keep it from leaking."

"One way to protect yourselves against him would be to accuse him openly," Dougan said.

"Which we hesitate to do . . ." Warren began.

"Because if he is on our side, we desperately need him," Dougan finished. "Spreading false accusations about his dis-loyalty would provoke widespread distrust and dissension."

"And if as our true ally he is successfully concealing the artifacts, hopefully taking measures so no one person knows where multiple items are housed, we don't want to frus-trate his efforts. Dougan, we hope our suspicion is wrong. But I can't ignore the smallest chance we may be right. The results would be devastating."

"Catastrophic," Dougan agreed. "Now I understand why you were asking about the Captain. I'll keep a lid on this, and I'll keep an eye open."

"That's all we ask," Warren said. "I felt we could rely on you. Sorry to trouble you with this."

"Don't apologize," Dougan said. "This is how the Knights police themselves. Nobody is above suspicion.

Sharing your concerns with me was the correct choice. Anything else?" He studied both Warren and Kendra.

"Not that I can think of," Kendra said.

"For the record," Warren mentioned, "we know four of the five hidden preserves. This one, Fablehaven, Brazil, and Australia. We can't come up with the fifth."

"Honestly, neither can we," Dougan said soberly. "Which is why we're aggressively soliciting knowledge about the hidden preserves. For so long our policy was to leave those mysteries alone. Although the secret preserves were seldom discussed openly, most of us assumed that if we pooled our knowledge, all five would be known to the Knights collectively. Word is that you have been conducting some private research on the matter."

Standing up, Warren chuckled softly. "Apparently not as private as I supposed. The four preserves I named are all I've come up with, and I knew about them before I really started digging."

"I'll delve into this matter of the Sphinx, and I'll alert you of any significant findings. Let me know if you uncover any new information."

"Count on it," Warren said, leading Kendra out of the room.

✳ ✳ ✳

Kendra awoke the following morning just after dawn. Beside her on the bed lay a Louis L'Amour hardcover borrowed from a bookshelf in the living room. She had ended up needing the companionship of the novel much less than she had expected. Before midnight, when she was only a third of the way through the western, her eyes had grown weary and she had rested her head on her pillow. That was the last thing she remembered.

Kendra placed the novel on her nightstand and switched off her reading light. She felt too perfectly rested to attempt any further sleep, so she put on her clothes. Would the others be up yet?

The hallway outside her room was quiet. She walked to the kitchen and found nobody. She had never been the first to awaken at the hacienda, and could not imagine that everyone had slept past dawn.

She opened the front door and found Gavin walking across the driveway. "Good morning," Kendra called.

"If you say so," he replied.

"What happened?"

"Javier is gone, along with the strongbox."

"What?"

"Check out the Jeep."

Kendra looked beyond Gavin at the Jeep parked in the driveway. Hal and Mara had used spare keys to retrieve the vehicle the previous evening. All four tires were flat. "He slashed the tires?"

"And they couldn't find the pickup," Gavin said. "They're all out searching for clues on motorcycles and horseback."

"So Javier was a spy?"

"L-1-1-looks that way. At least the artifact he took was a decoy. Still, Dougan acted really worried. Even though

Javier had a questionable past back when he was selling his services to the highest bidder, he had proven himself extremely reliable in recent years. Dougan said if Javier was secretly working for the Society, anyone could be."

"What now?" Kendra wondered.

"We'll still leave as planned. I was coming to grab some breakfast."

"Why didn't anyone wake me up?" Kendra asked.

"Nobody specifically woke me up either," Gavin said. "They wanted to let us rest after yesterday. The revving motorcycles got me out of bed. M-m-my window looks out the front. Hungry?"

He walked into the hacienda and strode to the kitchen, taking milk from the fridge and cereal from the pantry. "I'll have a bowl," Kendra said. "Want some orange juice? Toast?"

"Please."

While Kendra poured the juice and put bread into the toaster, Gavin set the table, placing the milk between the bowls of cereal and locating boysenberry preserves. Kendra buttered the toast and set it on the table, splashed milk onto her cereal, and started eating.

They were rinsing their bowls in the sink when Dougan entered the hacienda with swift strides. Warren followed at his heels.

"Any luck?" Gavin asked.

"We found the truck abandoned near the entrance to the preserve," Dougan reported bitterly. "He mutilated the tires. He must have had an accomplice waiting on the far side of the fence."

"Will we still make it to the airport?" Kendra asked.

"Hal has spare tires." Dougan poured himself a glass of water. "We should still get away on schedule." He took a long drink. "After all that's happened, it almost seems appropriate that we should end our stay here on another sour note. I won't be surprised if the Knights of the Dawn are never permitted on the premises again."

"We seem to be the opposite of jackalope feet," Warren agreed. "On the bright side, at least we're not about to confess to our evil employer that we ruined our legs and blew our cover in order to steal a phony artifact. I think old Javier might end up having the worst day of all of us." He clapped his hands together and rubbed them. "Time for some culinary therapy. What's for breakfast?"

* * *

On the floor beside his bed, Seth hunched over a musty journal, scanning page after page for words like *Graulas* and *Kurisock*. He glanced at the clock. Almost midnight. Kendra could show up at any minute. He did not want her to discover that he had started reading Patton's journals. She would never let him live that down.

His eyes found the word *Kurisock*, and he slowed down to study the passage:

Today I revisited the territory allotted to Kurisock. I still suspect that the demon played a central role in the tragedy that destroyed my uncle, the details of which I do not intend to relate in a volume as unguarded as this journal. In truth, if my grief over the calamity does not diminish, I may never impart the particulars.

Let it suffice to convey that I traversed the frontier into Kurisock's realm and spied on his smoldering pit, a malodorous venture that yielded no revelations. I dare not venture deeper into his territory, lest stripped of all protection I render myself defenseless and trade my life for naught. I reluctantly concede that investigating Kurisock in this manner is a fruitless enterprise, and intend at last to acquiesce to the advice that I refrain from further encroachments into his domain.

I hesitate to abandon my aunt to her fate, but the woman I knew no longer exists. I fear that her horrific condition may be irreversible.

Seth had found references to Kurisock and his tar pit before, although no passage revealed nearly as much about the nature of the demon as Graulas had shared. Seth had also encountered multiple mentions of a tragedy involving Patton's uncle. But this was the first entry where Patton had let slip that Kurisock might have been involved in his uncle's downfall. And until now, Seth had never read anything about a strange condition afflicting Patton's aunt.

Footsteps thumped up the attic stairs. Seth started, fumbling with the journal before sliding it under his bed. He tried to assume a casual pose as the door opened and Dale poked his head in. "They're back."

Seth got to his feet, grateful that the person on the stairs had been Dale and not Kendra. His sister had an uncanny ability to guess when he had been up to something, and he did not want her to know that he had broken down and turned into a bookworm while she was off having adventures.

Seth followed Dale down to the main level, reaching the entry hall just as Grandma came through the front door with her arm around Kendra. Warren and Grandpa entered carrying luggage and closed the door.

Seth crossed to Kendra and reluctantly accepted her hug. Stepping back, he scowled at his sister. "If you guys fought another three-headed flying panther, you're going to have to buy me antidepressants."

"Nope," Kendra said. "Just a dragon."

"A dragon!" Seth gasped enviously. "I missed out on a dragon fight?"

"Not a fight," Warren clarified. "We had to sneak past it."

"Where'd you guys go that you had to sneak past dragons?" Seth moaned, afraid of the answer, but unable to resist asking.

"Another secret preserve," Kendra said vaguely, glancing at Grandma.

"You can tell him," Grandma said. "We're all going to have to share information tonight. Much has happened here, and I'm sure you have stories to tell. We need to piece it all together in order to move forward."

"We were at a preserve called Lost Mesa in Arizona," Kendra said. "We went after another artifact. I got to help feed zombies."

Seth paled. "You fed zombies," he whispered in awe. He

hit the side of his leg with his fist. "Why do you torture me like this! You probably didn't even like it!"

"I didn't," Kendra admitted.

Seth covered his eyes with his hands. "It's like the awesomest stuff happens to you just because you're too girly to enjoy it!"

"You did converse with an ancient and powerful demon," Grandpa reminded him.

"I know, which was so cool, but she won't even care," Seth complained. "She'll just be glad it wasn't her. The only thing that would make her jealous would be if I led a parade riding a unicorn while ballerinas sang love songs."

"Don't try to pin your secret dreams on me," Kendra said with a smirk.

Seth felt his cheeks grow a little warm. "Don't try to pretend you'd rather see a dragon than a unicorn."

"Maybe you're right," she admitted. "Especially if the unicorn wouldn't try to hypnotize and eat me. But the dragon was pretty amazing. She shone all coppery."

"She?" Seth said. "It was a girl dragon? Well, that makes me feel a little better."

"I know the hour is late," Grandpa interrupted, "but I don't feel we can wait until tomorrow to exchange information and begin devising a plan. Shall we adjourn to the living room?"

Leaving the luggage in the hall, Grandpa, Grandma, Kendra, Seth, Warren, and Dale found seats in the living room. To the astonishment of everyone except Kendra, Warren shared the information that the artifact at Lost Mesa had been taken to Fablehaven by Patton Burgess, along with the details about Javier stealing the decoy artifact. Grandpa related to Warren and Kendra how Coulter and Tanu had become shadows along with all the specifics of what Seth had learned from Graulas.

"I can't believe that old demon let the two of you go," Warren said. "You really think you can trust him?"

"I'm sure we can't trust him," Grandpa said. "But after some thought and research, I now believe he may have been telling the truth—perhaps out of boredom, or as part of a convoluted Society scheme, or even to exact some kind of personal revenge against a rival."

"Maybe he really was impressed by my heroics," Seth added, mildly offended.

"I suspect he was, or he would not have taken notice of you in the first place. Yet I'm skeptical that admiration alone prompted him to volunteer such crucial information."

"I'm skeptical whether he was telling the truth at all," Grandma said. "Graulas is a conniver. We have no way to corroborate any of the assertions he presented about Kurisock."

"At the same time, nothing we have found disproves anything he told Seth," Grandpa rebutted. "A demon like Graulas does not invite humans into his lair and allow them to leave alive. He has been inactive for centuries, and hibernating for decades. Something must have genuinely sparked his interest and roused him from his stupor."

"The plague itself may have penetrated his hibernation," Grandma said. "His sole motive may be to participate in the

destruction of this preserve. Have we read the same journals? Graulas has never hidden his disdain for Fablehaven.
He views this preserve as his disgraceful tomb."

"I can't make complete sense of his actions either,
but there are many plausible aspects of his explanation,"
Grandpa maintained. "It harmonizes with what Vanessa
told us about the Sphinx. It agrees with the fact that we
never found the corrupt nail Seth extracted from the revenant. It names a viable source of the plague. This afternoon,
Hugo and I investigated the pond where Lena now dwells,
and the magic guarding that sanctuary is indeed holding off
the darkness. As Graulas claimed, many of the remaining
creatures of light have gathered there."

"You don't think desperation might be tainting your
opinion?" Grandma asked.

"Of course it is! In order to grasp at straws, we need
straws! This is our first reasonable lead since Vanessa suggested that the prisoner of the Quiet Box might be involved.
It gives us a place to focus, and it has a ring of credibility to
it."

"You spoke with Vanessa?" Kendra asked.

"Twice," Seth said smugly, enjoying Kendra's glare.

"What did she say?" Kendra inquired.

Grandma explained how Vanessa had implicated the
prisoner as a probable source of the plague, offered her assistance in finding a cure, and hinted that she knew of other
spies among the Knights of the Dawn.

"I thought she might have useful information," Kendra
said.

"What's the next step to follow up on Kurisock?" Warren asked.

"That is the question," Grandpa said. "If the demon can bind himself to other creatures, in effect producing a new being, we suddenly have to reconsider every entity on the preserve as a possible source of the plague. Who can say what relationship might have spawned this evil?"

Seth had something to contribute, but wanted to phrase it carefully. "When I was playing up in the attic earlier, I knocked over a journal, and it fell open to a page about Kurisock." Everyone was watching him. He swallowed and continued. "Patton thought that Kurisock was involved in destroying his uncle."

"One of Patton's great secrets," Grandma murmured. "He never fully explained how his uncle met his demise, but it was evidently connected with the fall of the old mansion, and the reason none are to trespass there. Could Kurisock have somehow reached beyond the boundaries of his realm?"

Grandpa shook his head. "He could not have personally left his domain. Like Graulas, he is bound to the parcel of land he governs, even on festival days. But he certainly could have orchestrated the mayhem from afar."

"My question is whether we abandon Fablehaven for the present," Grandma said. "This plague has enveloped so much in such a short time."

"I was ready to leave if we found no new leads," Grandpa said. "But two new reasons to stay have arisen. We have a possible source of the plague to investigate, and we have reason to suspect a second artifact may be hidden on the property."

Grandma sighed. "There is nothing in the journals or histories—"

Grandpa held up a finger. "Patton would never have passed on such sensitive information, at least not openly."

"But he passed it on at the scene of the crime?" Grandma asked dubiously.

"In a runic language that neither Warren, Dougan, nor Gavin even recognized," Grandpa reminded her. "Some obscure fairy tongue that only Kendra could decipher. Ruth, if an artifact might be here, I must remain until we either recover it or disprove its presence."

"Should we at least send the kids away?" Grandma asked.

"There remains great danger for the children beyond the walls of Fablehaven," Grandpa said. "We may reach a point when they must flee the preserve, when all of you must, but for now, as long as the kids stay in the house, I think they're safer here."

"Except for me," Seth corrected. "I can't stay indoors. Graulas said I need to figure out how to stop Kurisock."

Grandpa reddened. "Which is precisely why you shouldn't be involved. Graulas was likely luring you into peril. If the nail opened your eyes to certain dark elements, who knows how else it might be able to influence you. More than any of us, you must not take any chances."

Warren chuckled. "Then we better lock him in the Quiet Box."

Seth grinned.

"So help me, Seth, for your own good, if you don't behave with maturity through this crisis, I'll take Warren up on that," Grandma vowed.

"What about our parents?" Kendra asked. "Have you heard more from them?"

"I told them we would send you home on Thursday," Grandpa said.

"Thursday!" Kendra exclaimed.

"Today is Friday," Seth said. "We're going home in less than a week?"

"Today is early Saturday morning, technically," Dale pointed out. "Midnight has passed us by."

"It was the only way to stall them," Grandpa said. "Your school starts the week after next. We'll figure out something between now and then."

Seth tapped his temple thoughtfully. "If it means getting out of school, maybe we should lock Mom and Dad in the dungeon."

"We'll do what we must," Grandpa sighed, not seeming to take the comment quite as jokingly as Seth had intended.

CHAPTER FIFTEEN

Brownie Sunday

K endra sat before a plate of hot apple pancakes dusted
with powdered sugar, already satisfied after her third
swallow. Smiling at Grandma, she cut away another bite
with the side of her fork and swirled it in syrup. Grandma
beamed at her. Saturday morning pancakes were a Sorenson
tradition, and apple pancakes were Kendra's favorite.

Kendra's meager appetite had nothing to do with the
food. She was still trying to shake off the dream from the
previous night.

Kendra had been back at the carnival, the same one
from the limo dream, the same one where she had wandered lost as a child, except this time she was riding the
Ferris wheel, rising high until the festive lights twinkled far
below and the calliope music became faint, then plunging

back into the smells and sights and sounds of the lively fairground. She was alone on her bench, but other friends and family were also riding the attraction. In alternating positions above and below her sat her parents, Seth, Grandpa, Grandma, Lena, Coulter, Tanu, Vanessa, Warren, Dale, Neil, Tammy, Javier, Mara, Hal, and Rosa.

As the ride went on, the speed of the Ferris wheel increased alarmingly, until Kendra was rocking precariously with wind washing over her as she repeatedly fell forward, fell backward, rose backward, and rose forward, the machine's gears squealing, riders screaming. The enormous wheel had shuddered and tilted, no longer rotating vertically. With the sound of shattering wood and groaning metal, individual seats began breaking free and plummeting to the fairground below.

Kendra had not been able to make out which of her friends and family were falling. She tried to force herself to wake up, but it was hard to cling to the slippery notion that the frightening scene was imaginary. As she ascended toward the apex of her rotation, the wheel canted even more, threatening to collapse completely at any moment. She noticed Seth beneath her, clinging to a pole, legs swinging.

And then the wheel tipped over sideways, and she fell away from her seat, tumbling through the darkness with her loved ones, the colorful carnival lights growing brighter as she neared the ground. She had awakened an instant before impact.

Kendra didn't need a professional analysis to arrive at an interpretation. The tragic escapade on Painted Mesa had left her traumatized, and then to come home and learn how the plague had spread, infecting not just the creatures of Fablehaven but Coulter and Tanu as well, she felt like danger was encroaching from all sides. Bad people were after her. Too many people who were supposed to be good couldn't be trusted. It wasn't safe to go home to her parents. It wasn't safe to hide at Fablehaven. She and everyone she loved was in peril.

"Don't eat more than you want," Grandma said. Kendra realized she had been toying with her pancakes, procrastinating the next bite.

"I'm kind of tense," Kendra confessed, eating another forkful, hoping her face looked pleasant as she chewed.

"I'll have hers," Seth offered, having almost finished his stack.

"When your growth spurt ends, you're going to get fat as a blimp," Kendra predicted.

"When my growth spurt ends, I won't eat as much," he said, wolfing down the last of his pancakes. "Besides, I'm not watching my figure for Gavin."

"It isn't like that," Kendra protested, trying not to blush.

"He battled his way past the cheetah lady and tamed the dragon to save you," Seth accused. "Plus he's sixteen, so he has his driver's license."

"I'm never telling you anything ever again."

"You won't have to—you'll have Gavin."

"Don't pester your sister," Grandma chided. "She's had a hard week."

"I bet I could tame dragons," Seth said. "Have I mentioned that I'm immune to fear?"

"About a hundred times," Kendra muttered, sliding her plate over to him. "You know, I was wondering, Seth, it seems like a big coincidence that one of those journals fell open to a page about Kurisock. In fact, I'm having a hard time picturing a game that makes books fall open in the first place. How does that happen? If I didn't know how useless reading was, I might suspect you were studying those journals on purpose."

Seth kept his eyes on his plate, wordlessly shoveling food into his mouth.

"You don't need to act shy about your new love of reading," Kendra continued. "You know what? I could help you get a library card, then you can add some variety to all those boring old—"

"It was an emergency!" Seth blurted. "Read my lips—*emergency reading*—not some demented idea of fun. If I were starving, I would eat asparagus. If somebody held a gun to my head, I would watch a soap opera. And to save Fablehaven, I would read a book, okay, are you happy?"

"You had best be careful, Seth," Grandma said. "The love of reading can be very contagious."

"I just lost my appetite," he declared, rising from the table and storming out of the room.

Kendra shared a laugh with Grandma.

Grandpa came into the kitchen, glancing over his shoulder in the direction Seth had departed. "What's eating him?"

"Kendra accused him of voluntarily reading," Grandma said gravely.

Grandpa raised his eyebrows. "Should I telephone the authorities?"

Grandma shook her head. "I'll not have my grandson subjected to the humiliation of his reading habit becoming public. We have to cope with this disgrace discreetly."

"I have an idea, Grandpa," Kendra announced.

"Board up the windows so the paparazzi won't catch him in the act?" Grandpa guessed.

Kendra snickered. "No, a real idea, about Fablehaven."

Grandpa motioned for her to proceed.

"We should talk to Lena. If what happened to Patton's uncle is a secret, and Kurisock was involved, maybe Lena could fill in some details. We need to find out all we can about the demon."

Grandpa wore a knowing smile. "I agree so much that I've already planned to stop by the pond for that very reason. Not to mention that I'd love to learn whether she has heard of the artifact Patton supposedly brought here."

"I speak their language," Kendra said. "I could talk to her directly."

"I wish I could accept your help," Grandpa said. "You're bright and capable. I expect you would be an asset in reaching Lena. But this plague is too dangerous—we could both be transformed into shadows en route. The provision under which I am allowing you and your brother to remain at Fablehaven is that you not venture outdoors until we better understand what is happening out there. You two have already jeopardized your safety too much."

"You're the boss," Kendra said. "I just thought I might have better luck getting Lena to talk. We need information."

"True," Grandpa said. "But I must decline the offer. I will not allow you to become a shadow. Do I see extra pancakes?"

"You already had plenty," Grandma said.

"More than three hours ago," Grandpa replied, sitting down in the seat Seth had vacated. "Even after a late night, we old-timers rise with the sun." He winked at Kendra.

Warren came into the room carrying a coiled rope. "More pancakes?"

"Just working on some leftovers," Grandpa said.

"Are you heading to the pond with Grandpa?" Kendra asked.

"At first," Warren replied. "Then Hugo and I are going on a reconnaissance mission. I'll get as close to Kurisock as I can."

"Don't get so close that you return as a shadow," Kendra admonished.

"I'll do my best to remain intact," he said. "If I do become a shadow, don't worry, I won't be resentful that my final wish for a few more apple pancakes went unfulfilled."

"All right," Grandpa said. "Grab a plate. I'll share."

❉ ❉ ❉

That night Kendra reclined in bed scanning a journal, stealing glances at Seth, who was leafing through pages of his own at a brisk pace, pausing occasionally to study a passage. She tried to focus on her reading, but the sight of him hunched forward intently kept drawing her gaze.

"I can see you watching me," he said without looking up. "I should start charging admission."

"Find anything interesting?"

"Nothing useful."

"Me neither," Kendra said. "Nothing new."

"I'm surprised you ever find anything, you go through the book so slowly."

"I'm surprised you don't miss everything, flipping through pages so fast."

"Who knows how much time we have?" Seth said, closing the journal and rubbing his eyes. "Nobody found anything today."

"I told Grandpa he should let me talk to Lena," Kendra said. "She wouldn't even make an appearance for him."

"We could sneak down to the pond tonight," Seth offered.

"Are you insane?"

"I'm kidding. Mostly. Besides, Hugo and Mendigo would never let us out of the yard. I was relieved to hear Grandpa saw Doren at the pond. I was sure Newel would have caught him."

Kendra closed her book. "Grandpa got good info from some of the satyrs and dryads."

"Just confirming what we already know," Seth argued. "News flash—the plague is everywhere."

"Warren made it back safe from Kurisock's domain."

"With no new info except that a fog giant is standing guard. He didn't even reach the tar pit."

Kendra reached for the bedside lamp. "Should I turn off the light?"

"Might as well. I think my eyes will melt if I try to read any more."

She clicked off the light. "I don't get why you were so upset about being caught reading."

"It was just embarrassing. What if people found out?"

"They'd just think you were normal and smart. Most people worth knowing enjoy reading. Everyone in our family does it. Grandma taught college."

"Yeah, well, I was making fun of you before, so now I look like a hypocrite."

Kendra smiled. "No, you look like you finally wised up." He gave no reply. Kendra stared at the ceiling, assuming the conversation had ended.

"What if we can't fix this problem?" Seth asked as she was starting to fade off to sleep. "I know we've survived some scary situations in the past, but this plague feels different. Nobody has ever seen anything like it. We don't really know what it is, let alone how to repair the damage. And it spreads so fast, turning friends into enemies. You should have seen Newel."

"I'm worried too," Kendra said. "All I know for sure is that Coulter was right—even when you try your best to prepare, these preserves can be deadly."

"I'm sorry some of the people at Lost Mesa didn't make it," Seth said softly. "I'm glad I wasn't there for that."

"Me too," Kendra said quietly.

"Good night."

"'Night."

✣ ✣ ✣

"Kendra, Seth, wake up, don't be afraid." The voice boomed through the dark room, as if emanating from the walls.

Kendra sat up bleary-eyed but alert. Seth was already propped up on one arm, blinking in the darkness.

"Kendra, Seth, this is your grandfather," the voice said. It did sound like Grandpa, only magnified. "I'm speaking from the secret attic, where Dale, Warren, your grandmother, and I have taken refuge. The brownies have become infected, and have turned against us. Do not open your door until we come for you in the morning. Without adults in your room, you will be totally safe from harm. We expect to pass the night without incident here as well."

Seth stared at Kendra, not quite into her eyes. She realized that he could not see her as distinctly as she could see him.

Grandpa repeated the message, using the same words, presumably in case they had not been awake the first time. Then he reiterated the message a third time, adding more at the end. "The brownies are only permitted in the house from sunset to sunrise, so we'll evacuate in the morning. We're sorry we didn't see this coming. The brownies are an insular community, virtually never in contact with other creatures at Fablehaven. Their habitations beneath the yard enjoy many of the same protections as this house. Even so, we should have known the plague would find a way. Sorry to disturb you. Try to get some sleep."

"Yeah, right," Seth said, switching on the bedside lamp.

"Just what we needed," Kendra sighed. "Evil brownies."

"I wonder what they look like."

"Don't even consider peeking!"

"I know, of course not." Seth got out of bed and jogged to the window.

"What are you doing?"

"Checking something." He pulled the curtains aside. "Tanu is out here. His shadow."

"Don't you dare open the window!" Kendra commanded, rising from her bed to join her brother.

"He's motioning for us to stay put," Seth reported.

Looking over Seth's shoulder, Kendra saw nothing on the roof. Then a fairy glided into view, glowing a deep violet shade as if illuminated by a black light.

"He's pointing at the fairies and signing to keep the window closed," Seth said. "See, there are more fairies just beyond the roof. They're tough to make out, they're so dark." He gave Tanu a thumbs-up and closed the curtain. "No evil fairies have shown themselves for a while. I bet this was a trap. The brownies were supposed to flush us out so the fairies could transform us."

"I thought Grandpa banned fairies from the yard," Kendra said, returning to her bed.

Seth started pacing. "It must not have worked for some

reason. I never knew Grandpa could make announcements to the whole house."

"They have all sorts of cool stuff in the secret attic."

"Too bad they don't have a door to our side."

"It doesn't matter. They'll come get us in the morning. We should try to sleep. Tomorrow will probably be hectic."

Seth put his ear against the door. "I can't hear anything."

"There are probably ten of them patiently waiting on the far side, ready to pounce."

"Brownies are shrimps. All I'd need are some heavy boots, a pair of shin guards, and a weed whacker."

The image made Kendra giggle. "You said the nipsies are much smaller than brownies, but that didn't stop them from contaminating Newel."

"I guess," Seth said. He opened a wardrobe and pulled out some clothes.

"What are you doing?" Kendra asked.

"I want to get dressed in case we have to make a hasty getaway. Don't watch."

When Seth was done, he returned to his bed. Kendra gathered her clothes, turned off the lamp, warned Seth not to peek, and changed. She climbed into bed with her shoes on.

"How am I supposed to sleep?" Seth asked after a couple of minutes.

"Pretend nothing is happening. They're so quiet, it could just be a regular night."

"I'll try."

"Good night, Seth."

"Don't let the brownies bite."

※ ※ ※

Seth slept lightly the rest of the night, often waking with a jolt, body rigid, feeling flustered and disoriented. A few times he clicked on the lamp to make sure there were no savage brownies scampering around on the floor. He even leaned down to peer under the bed, just in case.

Finally he awoke to find pink light bleeding through the curtains. He got out of bed without disturbing Kendra, crossed to the window, and waited for the increased light of the sun clearing the horizon. He noticed no fairies while he waited.

A few minutes after direct sunlight brightened the morning, Seth heard the attic stairs creaking. He shook Kendra awake, then went to the door. "Who's there?"

"Glad you're awake," Warren called. "Don't open the door."

"Why not?"

"It's been booby-trapped. Actually, on second thought, if you want, you can pull the door open swiftly, just stay behind it and off to the side. Make sure Kendra is positioned out of the way as well."

"Okay." Kendra got out of bed and stood beside the door. Seth gripped the knob, turned it slowly, then yanked the door open, staying behind it as he lunged to the side. Three arrows whistled into the room and thudded high against the far wall.

"Nicely done," Warren approved. "Take a look at the stairway."

Seth peeked through the doorway. Numerous wires crisscrossed the stairs, high and low, horizontal and diagonal. Many of the wires ran through pulleys or hooks that had been affixed to the walls. Several crossbows had been rigged in high corners of the stairwell, most pointing at the attic door, others defending it. Down in the hall, a shotgun propped on a cleverly designed rack was aimed up the stairs. Warren crouched against the wall a third of the way up the steps, having already threaded past several tripwires.

"Where did all the weapons come from?" Kendra asked from behind Seth.

"The brownies raided an arsenal in the dungeon," Warren said. "Many additional weapons were custom-made. This stairway is only the beginning. The whole house has been booby-trapped. I've never seen anything like it."

"How do we get down the stairs?" Kendra asked.

Warren shook his head slightly. "I was planning to disable the traps, but the cords are complicated. Some are rigged to trigger multiple traps at once; some are decoys. I'm having a hard time making sure which wire does what. When you pulled the door open, one of the arrows grazed my ear. I didn't see it coming."

"Maybe we could go out on the roof and get down that way," Seth suggested.

"At least a dozen dark fairies are waiting in ambush. Going outside is not an option right now."

"Didn't Grandpa ban fairies from the yard?" Kendra asked.

Warren nodded. "Before he banned them, dark fairies

must have hidden near the house. The register won't expel creatures who have already accessed the yard. It will only prevent new ones from entering."

"Tricky," Seth said.

"Last night was well planned," Warren said. "This plague is not spreading randomly. Somebody directed a deliberate, coordinated assault. Worst of all, before your grandparents awoke, the brownies got hold of the register."

"Oh, no!" Kendra groaned. "If the brownies altered the register, that might also explain the dark fairies."

"Good point." Warren backed down a step and stretched. "Anything may be able to access the house soon. We have to clear out of here."

"Is Hugo all right?" Seth asked.

"The golem has been spending the nights in a safe room inside the barn. Your Grandpa is doing everything he can to prevent Hugo from becoming infected. Hugo will come when we call. He should be fine in the barn until we do."

"So now we have to limbo down the stairs with our lives at stake," Kendra said.

"Why don't I just shove the rocking horse down the stairway," Seth suggested. "We could all just stand back and let most of the traps go off."

Warren stared at him for a moment. "That actually might work just fine. Give me a minute to backtrack. Duck away from the door in case I accidentally set off a trap or two."

Seth went to the unicorn rocking horse and dragged it over near the doorway. He thought the curved runners under the horse would help it sled down the stairs quite well. In fact, under other circumstances, he might have tried riding the rocking horse down the stairs for fun. Why did fabulous ideas tend to occur to him at the wrong time?

"I'm ready," Warren called. "Stay well away from the doorway. I expect it will be bombarded by a volley of quarrels, darts, and arrows."

Seth positioned the rocking horse at the top at the stairs and lay down behind it. "I'll shove it with my feet, then roll out of the way."

Kendra stood off to the side of the door. "I'll slam the door as soon as it's through, then dive clear."

Seth placed the soles of his shoes on the unicorn's rump. "One . . . two . . . three!" He gave the rocking horse a push and rolled sideways. Kendra heaved the door closed and lunged away.

A gunshot rang out, blasting a hole in the door. A crossbow quarrel zinged through the hole and stuck quivering into the opposite wall. Seth heard the rocking horse clattering down the staircase, the twang of bowstrings, and the overlapping beat of several other projectiles thudding against the door.

"That was awesome," Seth told Kendra.

"You're psychotic," Kendra replied.

"Well done!" Warren called from below. "The horse tipped and missed a few of the higher cords, but the way is now fairly clear."

Looking down the stairs, Seth saw several feathered shafts embedded in the floor around where Warren now

stood. The rocking horse lay on its side leaning against the bottom step, bristling with arrows and missing its horn. "Wasn't that awesome?" Seth asked.

Warren cocked his head, his expression mildly embarrassed. "I'm sorry, Kendra—it was pretty cool."

"All boys belong in insane asylums," Kendra said.

"Watch your step on the way down," Warren instructed. "At least two of the crossbows are still armed. And see the ax tied to that rope? It will come free and swing toward you if you touch that steep cord on the left."

Seth started down the stairs, ducking wires as he went, trying to avoid even the slack cords the rocking horse had already tripped. Kendra waited until he was standing beside Warren, and then carefully descended the staircase.

The hall at the bottom of the stairs contained a new web of wires. Although there were some crossbows, most of the traps involved curiously designed catapults meant to hurl knives and hatchets.

Seth noticed a tiny piece of brown wood hanging on the wall from a golden hook. "Is that part of Mendigo?"

Warren nodded. "I've seen a few pieces of him around. He's been staying the night inside the house. The brownies dismantled him."

Seth reached for the piece of the puppet. Warren put an arm on his elbow to stop him. "Wait. All the pieces of Mendigo are rigged to traps."

Grandma and Grandpa Sorenson appeared farther down the hall. "Thank goodness you're all right," Grandma said, placing a hand over her bosom. "Don't come this way. Our room is a nest of nasty traps. Besides, we all need to end up downstairs eventually."

"You should have seen the attic stairway," Warren said. "It was crammed with more deathtraps than any other part of the house so far. Seth pushed the rocking horse down the stairs to deliberately set off the majority."

"We heard the clamor and were concerned," Grandpa said. "How do we proceed, Warren?"

"It will be hard to spring all the traps on purpose," Warren said. "Many are protected by countertraps. Our best bet is to make our way downstairs one at a time, individually navigating the obstacles. I'll help coach each of you through."

"Me first," Grandpa said.

"Where's Dale?" Kendra asked.

"He was with me," Warren replied. "While I helped you escape the attic, he continued along the hall, heading for the garage. He wants to make sure the vehicles are in order."

"Everyone else out of the hall," Grandpa said.

Grandma stepped out of sight. Seth and Kendra sat at the foot of the attic stairs.

"Be watchful, Stan," Warren said. "Some of the trip-wires are more apparent than others. Most are fairly visible, but a few are fashioned out of fishing line or thread. Like the one right in front of you, at the height of your knees."

"I see it," Grandpa said.

"If you accidentally brush a wire, fall flat. Most of the traps appear to be designed to strike an upright target."

Warren proceeded to guide Stan down the hall. Seth

and Kendra listened to Warren's instructions as Grandpa descended the stairs to the entry hall. Grandpa made an increasing number of snappy comments as impatience eroded his composure.

Finally Grandpa reached the living room and Warren began directing Grandma. While Grandma was on the stairs, there was a tremendous crash in the entry hall. Warren called out that nobody had been injured. Soon he came and got Kendra, and Seth found himself waiting alone on the bottom step.

At last Warren returned for him. Seth did not find dodging over and under the cords in the hall very difficult, although a few were difficult to see. Upon reaching the top of the stairs to the entry hall, Seth chuckled. A grandfather clock, an armoire, a display case, a suit of armor, and a heavy rocking chair covered with spikes were all suspended from the roof of the entry hall. A china cabinet had apparently also been suspended there, but had fallen, accounting for the crash he had heard.

Seth picked his way carefully down the stairs, heeding Warren's counsel on which wire to go over, which to go under, and how to position his body. The wires were more prevalent on the stairs than they had been in the hall, and a few times Seth felt like a contortionist. He was impressed that Grandma and Grandpa had been able to manage the descent.

When he reached the living room, Seth was relieved to find there were fewer traps on the ground floor than had crowded the upstairs hall and stairways. Any pieces of furniture unaffiliated with traps had been reworked into tortured, unusable shapes. "Some of those wires were too close together," Seth commented, wiping perspiration from his forehead.

"I thought you were immune to fear," Kendra teased.

"Magical fear," Seth clarified. "I still have regular emotions. I'm no more eager than the next guy to get squished by a grandfather clock."

Simultaneously ducking a thick cord and stepping over a threadlike wire, Dale entered the living room. "The vehicles have been sabotaged," he said. "The engine parts are all over the garage, connected to traps."

"What about the phone?" Grandpa asked.

"The lines are down," Dale reported.

"Don't you have your cell?" Kendra asked.

"The brownies stole it off of my dresser," Grandpa said. "Your grandmother and I are lucky we didn't get contaminated. There were several brownies in the room when we awoke. If Warren and Dale hadn't barged in and raised the alarm, I'm sure the little monsters would have transformed us into shadows in our sleep."

"Your grandpa was impressive," Warren said. "He used the bedspread to hold them at bay while we retreated into the attic through the door in his bathroom closet."

Grandpa waved a dismissive hand. "What of the front gate, Dale?"

"I went as far down the driveway as I dared, holding the fairies off with flash powder, like you told me. The gate is shut and barred, with loads of creatures guarding it."

Grandpa scowled, pounding a fist into his palm. "I can't believe I lost the register. They've used it to lock us in."

"And they could let anybody they want into Fablehaven now," Kendra said.

"If they so choose," Grandpa said. "I expect Vanessa had it right. The Society is finished with Fablehaven. They have no idea that a second artifact may be hidden here. Nobody will be coming in. The Sphinx simply wants this preserve to self-destruct."

"What do we do?" Seth asked.

"We retreat to the nearest bastion of relative safety," Grandpa said. "Hopefully at the pond we can formulate a plan."

"We should have gotten you kids out of here when we had the chance," Grandma lamented.

"We wouldn't leave you even if we could," Seth assured her. "We'll figure out a way to stop this plague."

Grandpa frowned pensively. "Can we get to the tents?"

"I think so," Dale said. "They're in the garage."

"What else should we bring?" Grandpa asked.

"I have extra flash powder from the attic and my cross-bow," Grandma said.

"Tanu's potions are all over his room, attached to traps," Warren said. "I'll try to retrieve some."

"While you're up there, see if you can grab a picture of Patton," Kendra said. "We need bait for Lena."

"Good idea," Grandpa said.

"What about Mendigo?" Seth asked, nodding toward the corner of the room where the limberjack's torso dangled from the ceiling, connected by a network of wires to two crossbows and two small catapults.

"Too many pieces to that puzzle," Grandma said. "We'll put him back together if we ever get out of this."

"You and the kids stay put," Grandpa told Grandma. "I'm going to get some provisions from the pantry. Ruth, give Seth some walrus butter."

Seth slapped his forehead. "No wonder I didn't see any dark fairies in the yard out the window this morning. How come I saw them last night, after sleeping for a while?"

"It can be hard to predict at what hour of the night the milk will stop working," Grandma said. "The only sure way to keep it functioning is to stay awake. We keep a stash of walrus butter in the attic, so we already had our dose for the day."

Seth dipped a finger in the butter she offered and tasted it. "I prefer the milk."

Warren patted Seth on the arm. "When opening the fridge might mean an arrow in your throat, stick with the butter."

"Let's split up and gather what we need," Grandpa said. "This house is no longer a reliable shelter. I don't want to remain here a minute longer than necessary."

Seth squatted on the floor beside Kendra while Warren, Dale, and Grandpa departed. Grandma leaned against the wall. Bristling with spikes and blades and barbs, none of the furniture was fit to hold them.

CHAPTER SIXTEEN

Refuge

Hugo tromped swiftly across the backyard, hauling the empty cart through hedges and over flower beds, finally backing it up against the deck. Warren opened the back door and leapt from the deck into the cart, scanning the air for fairies, his fists full of flash powder. After a moment he motioned for the others to follow.

Grandpa, Grandma, Kendra, Seth, and Dale piled into the cart, each lugging a tent or some sleeping bags. "Hugo, race to the pond as quickly as you're able," Grandpa directed.

The cart lurched forward, bucking and swaying as Hugo pounded across the yard at a furious pace. Kendra lost her footing, dropping to her knees. She dug a handful of flash powder out of the bag Grandma had entrusted to her. The others got powder ready as well, except Dale, who held a net in one hand, a compound bow in the other, and had a quiver of arrows slung over one shoulder.

They rumbled across the yard without seeing any fairies, then Hugo charged down a dirt road. Kendra knew that the entrance to the pond was not very far. She was beginning to hope they might reach their destination without encountering any resistance when a group of dark fairies swarmed into view up ahead.

"Right in front of us," Grandpa said.

"I see them," Dale said.

"Wait until they get close," Warren warned. "At this speed the powder won't hang in the air to protect us. We need direct hits."

The fairies fanned out and swooped at the cart from all directions. Standing at the front of the cart, Grandpa hurled his powder forward, spreading it wide. Some of the incoming fairies veered away as light flashed and sparks sizzled. Kendra flung her handful of glittery silver dust. Electricity crackled, zapping fairies from the air as they came into contact with the volatile substance.

Hugo raced onward, swerving periodically to help avoid the darting fairies. Dark fairies squealed as more handfuls of powder were thrown. The fairies fired shadowy streaks at the cart. Blinding flashes flared whenever the dark energy struck the powder.

The tall hedge enclosing the pond came into view. A footpath diverged from the road and led through a gap in the hedge. Three dark satyrs guarded the entrance to the pond, their heads as goatlike as their legs.

Dale swung his net to bat away fairies. A tight formation of shadowy fairies whizzed toward them from the side, but Grandma fried them with powder.

"Hugo, ram through the satyrs!" Grandpa shouted.

Hugo lowered his head and dashed for the entrance. Two of the satyrs grabbed the third and launched him acrobatically into the air, then sprang out of the path of the oncoming golem. The airborne satyr soared over Hugo, furry arms outstretched, teeth bared. Warren yanked Grandpa out of the way just in time. The goatman landed nimbly in the bed of the cart an instant before Dale hit him with a flying tackle that sent both of them tumbling over the side.

Without an order, Hugo leaped away from the front of the cart, giving the wagon a final push to ensure it would coast through the gap in the hedge. The golem loped toward Dale, who was still rolling on the ground with the goatman. About half the arrows had spilled from the quiver on Dale's back. The two other dark satyrs rushed at Hugo from either side. Without breaking stride, the golem made a motion like an umpire calling a runner safe, simultaneously backhanding both assailants and sending them cartwheeling through the weeds.

Dale managed to roll free from the goatman and was scrambling to his feet when Hugo seized the dark satyr by one arm, hoisted him high, and punted the snarling fiend halfway to the main road. Cradling Dale, Hugo ran past the hedge and into the meadow surrounding the pond.

Kendra cheered along with the others as the cart coasted to a stop. Dozens of dark fairies flew to different points along the hedge, hovering above it, but none crossed over. The tainted satyrs rose and stood at the gap in the hedge snarling in frustrated fury. Hugo gently set Dale on his feet. Dale looked shaken, his clothes torn and smudged with dirt, one elbow scraped and bleeding.

"Nice work, big brother," Warren said, vaulting down from the cart. He started examining Dale. "The brute didn't bite you, did he?"

Dale shook his head. Warren embraced him.

Grandpa climbed down from the cart and began inspecting Hugo, studying the splotches where the fairies had discolored him with their dark energy.

"Way to go, Hugo!" Seth cheered.

"Quick thinking, Hugo," Grandpa approved.

The golem gave a gaping, craggy smile.

"Will he be all right?" Seth asked.

"Much of the dirt and stone composing Hugo is temporary," Grandpa said. "He sheds and gains soil all the time. As you've seen, he can even gradually regrow a limb. The plague would have to work in deep to affect him."

As Grandpa spoke, Hugo brushed away the discolored soil, leaving his body unmarked.

From her elevated position in the cart, Kendra surveyed the scene. The pond looked the same as she remembered, enclosed by a whitewashed wooden boardwalk connecting twelve elaborate gazebos. The interiors of the hedges were meticulously trimmed, and the lawn of the meadow appeared freshly clipped.

But the familiarity ended there. The parklike clearing around the pond had never been nearly so crowded. Fairies fluttered everywhere, hundreds of them, in all shades and varieties. Exotic birds perched in the trees above the pond, including a few golden owls with human faces. Satyrs romped on the boardwalk and in the gazebos, hooves clacking against wooden planks as they chased merry maidens who looked no older than high school seniors. Off to one side of the pond was a tidy encampment of short, stocky men and women in homespun clothing. On the other side several tall, graceful women stood conversing, dressed in flowing robes that reminded Kendra of foliage. In a far corner of the field, right up against the hedge, Kendra observed a pair of centaurs staring back at her.

"Seth, Stan, Kendra!" yelled a jovial voice. "Glad you dropped in!"

Kendra turned and saw Doren gamboling toward the cart, followed by an unfamiliar satyr whose wooly white legs had brown spots.

"Doren!" Seth cried, leaping from the cart. "I'm so glad you outran Newel!"

"I led him on an epic chase," Doren bragged, beaming. "Sharp turns saved me. He got bigger, but wasn't quite as fleet. Tenacious, though. If I hadn't thought to come here, he would have snared me in the end."

Kendra climbed down from the cart.

The satyr with the white legs elbowed Doren.

"This is Verl," Doren said.

Verl took Kendra's hand and kissed the back of it. "Enchanted," he simpered in a smarmy voice, wearing a ridiculous half-grin. He had stubby horns and a childish face.

Doren punched Verl on the shoulder. "She's off limits, you blockhead! Caretaker's granddaughter."

"I could be your caretaker," Verl persisted, limply retaining her hand.

"Why don't you take a swim, Verl," Doren said, ushering him away several steps before returning. Kendra ignored Verl when he turned and winked at her, fluttering his fingers. "Don't mind Verl," Doren told her. "He's a little intoxicated by all these nymphs trapped in the same space as him. They normally won't come within shouting distance. The guy makes a career out of striking out."

"I can't believe how many creatures are here," Seth said.

Kendra followed his gaze to where a group of shaggy, tawny, monkeylike creatures were leaping acrobatically along the top of a gazebo. Each seemed to have a few extra arms or legs.

"Not many safe places left," Doren said. "Even some of the nipsies found shelter here—the only ones who didn't go dark, not quite half a kingdom. They're erecting a village underneath one of the gazebos. They work fast."

"Who are those tall women over there?" Kendra asked.

"Those stately ladies are the dryads. Wood nymphs. More approachable than the water nymphs, but not nearly as lively as the hamadryads, who love to flirt."

"What are hamadryads?" Seth asked.

"Dryads are beings of the forest as a whole. Hamadryads are linked to individual trees. The hamadryads are the more spirited girls you see socializing with the satyrs among the pavilions."

"Can you introduce me to a centaur?" Seth asked.

"You'd have better luck introducing yourself," Doren replied sourly. "Centaurs are very self-important. They've adopted the notion that satyrs are frivolous. Apparently having a bit of fun on occasion renders us unfit for fellowship. But be my guest, go say hello, maybe you can join them in standing around glaring at everyone."

"Are those little people dwarfs?" Kendra asked.

"They're none too happy about being driven above ground. But any port in a storm. All sorts have sought shelter here. We even had a few brownies turn up, which can't bode well for you."

"We lost control of the house," Seth said. "Evil brownies snagged the register."

Doren shook his head sadly. "Some situations have a nasty way of going from bad to worse."

"Doren," Grandpa said, approaching from one side, "how are you holding up? I really am very sorry about Newel."

Grief flickered across Doren's features. "I'm getting by. He was a straw-brained, long-winded, skirt-chasing rascal, but he was my best pal. Sorry about your big islander friend."

"We need to get these tents set up," Grandpa announced. "Would you care to lend us a hand?"

Doren suddenly appeared uncomfortable. "Right, about

that, I'd love to, but the thing is, it turns out I promised a few of the dwarfs I'd swing by to see how they're settling in." He started backing away. "You all mean much more to me than they do, but I can't let our special bond interfere with an ironclad commitment, especially when the little fellows are out of their element."

"Understandable," Grandpa said.

"We'll catch up more later, after you get the—um—after you get more settled." He turned and trotted away.

Grandpa brushed his hands together as if wiping off dust. "The most surefire way to part company with a satyr is to mention work."

"Why'd you scare him off?" Seth asked.

"Because satyrs can chatter for hours, and I need Kendra to join me on the pier."

"Now?" Kendra asked.

"There's no reason to delay."

"Let me guess," Seth said. "I'm not invited."

"Too many spectators may impede contact," Grandpa said. "You're welcome to assist Warren and Dale with the tents. Kendra, let's not forget that photograph of Patton."

* * *

Seth walked with Kendra and Grandpa toward the cart before veering away, hustling to join a line of dwarfs trooping by. None stood much taller than his waist. "How are you men doing?" he asked.

When they looked up, he saw that despite their sparse

whiskers, they were all women. One of them spat at his feet. He hopped away from the loogie.

"Sorry, I'm nearsighted," Seth said.

The dwarfs continued on their way, paying him no further heed. Seth jogged toward the pond. Who wanted to set up tents when all these amazing creatures were corralled for his enjoyment? Besides, it would give Warren and Dale an occasion for brotherly bonding.

Seth was impressed by the quantity of satyrs. He had vaguely assumed Newel and Doren might be the only ones. But he counted at least fifty trouncing about, some older than others, some shirtless, others wearing vests, their fur ranging from black to brown to red to gold to gray to white.

The satyrs possessed boundless energy. They chased hamadryads, danced in clusters, wrestled, and played spontaneous acrobatic games. Although their boisterous antics were inviting, Seth's association with Newel and Doren had stripped away some of the satyrs' mystique. He was more curious to interact with the creatures he had never seen.

He sidled up to the gathering of dryads. There were about twenty of the slender ladies, not one of them shorter than six feet. Several had the bronze skin of Native Americans. Some were pale, others ruddy. They all had leaves and twigs twined in their long tresses.

"You've got the right idea, brother," said a voice in his ear. Startled, Seth turned and found Verl beside him, gawking at the dryads. "The hamas are girls—these are women."

"I'm not after a girlfriend," Seth assured him.

Verl smiled wolfishly and winked. "Right, none of us

are, we're well-traveled gentlemen, above all that. Look, if you need backup, just give me the signal." He nudged Seth toward the regal women. "Save the redhead for me."

The two redheads Seth could see were at least a head taller than Verl. Having the love-starved satyr at his side made him suddenly self-conscious. The women were not only lovely—they were intimidating in their numbers and their uncommon height. He backed away sheepishly.

"No, Seth, no!" Verl panicked, falling back with him. "Don't waffle now. You were there! The black one on the left was giving you the eye. Do you need an icebreaker?"

"You got me flustered," Seth muttered, continuing his retreat. "I just wanted to meet a dryad."

Verl shook his head knowingly and clapped him on the back. "Don't we all?"

Seth shrugged away from him. "I need some alone time."

Verl lifted his hands. "The man needs some space. I can relate. Want me to run interference for you, keep away the hangers-on?"

Seth stared at the satyr, uncertain what he meant. "I guess."

"Consider it done," Verl said. "Tell me, how did you meet Newel and Doren?"

"I was accidentally stealing stew from an ogress. Why?"

"Why, he asks. Are you pulling my leg? Newel and Doren are only the coolest satyrs in all of Fablehaven! Those guys can land babes with a wink at fifty yards!"

Seth was beginning to grasp that Verl was the satyr equivalent of a nerd. If he wanted to get away, it would require some finesse. "Hey, Verl, I just caught the redhead staring at you."

Verl blanched. "No."

Seth tried to keep his face composed. "Absolutely. Now she's whispering to her friend. Her eyes are still on you."

Verl smoothed a hand over his hair. "What's she doing now?"

"I almost don't know how to describe it. She's smoldering at you, Verl. You should go talk to her."

"Me?" he squeaked. "No, no, not yet, I better let this simmer for a while."

"Verl, this is your moment. The timing will never be better."

"I hear you, Seth, but honestly, I don't feel right about horning in on your territory. I'm no claim jumper." He raised a fist. "Good hunting."

Seth watched Verl scamper hastily away, then set his eyes on the centaurs. They had not moved since Seth had spotted them. Both were men from the waist up, astonishingly broad and muscular, with brooding expressions. One had the body of a silver horse; the other was chocolate brown.

After the dryads, the surly centaurs suddenly seemed much less intimidating.

Seth started toward them. They watched him approach, so he kept his eyes lowered most of the way. There was no denying it—these were the most impressive creatures within view.

As he drew near, Seth looked up. They glowered down at him. Seth folded his arms and glanced over his shoulder, trying to act jaded and casual. "These idiotic satyrs are driving me nuts."

The centaurs regarded him without comment.

"I mean, a guy can hardly find any peace to process all the recent trouble around here. And to dissect the important issues. You know?"

"Are you making sport of us, young human?" asked the silver centaur in a melodious baritone.

Seth decided to break character. "I just wanted to meet you two."

"We don't commonly socialize," said the silver centaur.

"We're all stuck here," Seth replied. "Might as well get acquainted."

The centaurs considered him grimly. "Our names are difficult to pronounce in your language," said the brown centaur, his voice deeper and gruffer than the other's. "Mine translates as Broadhoof."

"Call me Cloudwing," the other said.

"I'm Seth. My grandfather is the caretaker."

"He needs more practice taking care of things," Broadhoof scoffed.

"He's saved Fablehaven before," Seth countered. "Give him time."

"No mortal is fit for such a task," Cloudwing asserted.

Seth batted at a fly. "I hope you're wrong. I haven't noticed many centaurs around here."

Cloudwing stretched his arms, triceps bulging. "Most of our kind assembled at a different refuge."

"The ring of stones?" Seth asked.

"You know of Grunhold?" Broadhoof sounded surprised.

"Not the name. I just heard there was another place at Fablehaven that repelled dark creatures."

"We belong there, with our kind," Broadhoof said.

"Why not make a run for it?" Seth asked.

Cloudwing stamped a hoof. "Grunhold is far from here. Considering how the darkness has spread, it would be irresponsible to attempt the journey."

"Have any of your kind been contaminated?" Seth asked.

Broadhoof scowled. "Some. Two who were scouting with us were changed and chased us here."

"Not that any portion of Fablehaven will serve as a refuge much longer," Cloudwing said. "I question whether any magic can indefinitely withstand such pervasive darkness."

"We have introduced ourselves," Broadhoof declared. "If you will excuse us, young human, we prefer conversing in our own tongue."

"Okay, good to meet you," Seth said with a small wave.

The centaurs gave no response, nor did they proceed to speak with each other. Seth walked away, disappointed not to hear what their language sounded like, certain their stern eyes were boring into his back. Doren was right. Centaurs were jerks.

※ ※ ※

Kendra gazed down at the framed sepia photograph. Even with old-fashioned hair and a heavy mustache, Patton had been a strikingly handsome man. He was not smiling, but something in his expression screamed playful cockiness. Of course, her perception might be tainted by her having read so many entries in his journals.

Grandpa walked beside her onto the little pier that projected from the base of one of the gazebos. On one side of the pier floated the boathouse Patton had constructed. The pond was basically smooth. She saw no sign of the naiads. Her gaze wandered to the island at the center of the pond, where the tiny shrine to the Fairy Queen lay hidden among the shrubs.

"I think I'll also ask Lena if we can get the bowl back," Kendra said.

"The bowl from the shrine?" Grandpa asked.

"I was talking to a fairy earlier this summer, Shiara, who told me the naiads claimed the bowl as a trophy."

Grandpa frowned. "They guard the shrine. I assumed that trusting the bowl to their care would be the best way to ensure it was returned, since treading on the island is forbidden."

"Shiara said I wouldn't have been punished for personally returning it. Her words felt true. I was thinking, if I could get the bowl—"

"—maybe you could use it as an excuse to safely gain access to the island and approach the Fairy Queen about the plague. The odds for success aren't terrific, but we can at least inquire about the bowl."

"Right," Kendra said. She strode down the pier, glancing back when Grandpa did not accompany her.

"I'll hang back and let you call to Lena," Grandpa said. "I had no luck last time."

Kendra walked to the end of the quay, stopping a few feet from the edge. She knew not to get near enough to the water for the naiads to grab hold of her. "Lena, it's Kendra! We need to talk."

"Look who blew in with the homeless land-plodders," said a snide female voice from below the water.

"I thought that puppet would have strangled her by now," responded a second speaker.

Kendra scowled. Upon one of her previous visits to the pond, the naiads had released Mendigo. Still under orders from Muriel the witch, the limberjack had snatched Kendra and taken her to the hill where the Forgotten Chapel once stood.

"You might as well summon Lena," Kendra stated. "I brought her a present she'll want to see."

"You may as well hobble away on your clumsy stilts," admonished a third voice. "Lena wants nothing to do with ground-stalkers."

Kendra raised her voice even more. "Lena, I brought a picture of your favorite land-plodder. A photograph of Patton."

"Go dig a hole and lie in it," hissed the first voice with a hint of desperation. "Even a dull-witted air-gulper should recognize when her company is undesired."

"Grow old and die," spat another naiad.

"Kendra, wait!" called a familiar voice, dreamy and musical. Lena drifted into view, her upturned face just below the surface of the water. She looked even younger than the last time Kendra had seen her. Not a trace of gray remained in her black hair.

"Lena," Kendra said, "we need your help."

Lena regarded Kendra with her dark, almond-shaped eyes. "You mentioned a photograph."

"Patton looks very handsome in it."

"What would Lena care about some dry old picture?" squealed a voice. Other naiads tittered.

"What do you need?" Lena inquired sedately.

"I have good reason to believe Patton brought a second artifact to Fablehaven. I'm talking about the serious artifacts, the ones the Society wants. Do you know anything about it?"

Lena stared at Kendra. "I remember. Patton made me pledge not to share the secret unless it was absolutely necessary. That man was so funny about his mysteries. As if any of it really mattered."

"Lena, we absolutely need to locate the artifact. Fablehaven is on the brink of collapse."

"Again? Do you hope to trade the photograph for information about the artifact? Kendra, the water would ruin it."

"Not the photo itself," Kendra said. "Just a peek. How long has it been since you've seen his face?"

For an instant, Lena looked wounded, but her serenity returned almost immediately. "Don't you see that finding the artifact is irrelevant? Everything up there ends. Everything is fleeting, illusory, temporary. All you can show me is a flat image of my beloved, a lifeless memory. The real man is gone. As you will be also."

"If it truly doesn't matter, Lena," Grandpa said from farther back on the pier, "why not tell us? The information means nothing to you, but here, now, for the short time we live and breathe, it matters to us."

"The old one is yapping now," complained an unseen naiad.

"Don't answer him, Lena," encouraged a second voice. "Wait him out. He'll be dead before you know it."

Several voices giggled.

"Have you forgotten our friendship, Lena?" Grandpa asked.

"Please tell us," Kendra said. "For Patton." She held up the picture.

Lena's eyes widened. Her face broke the surface of the water and she mouthed Patton's name.

"Don't make us drag you under," warned a voice.

"Touch me and so help me I'll abandon you," Lena murmured, entranced by the image Kendra held.

Lena's gaze shifted to Kendra. "All right, Kendra. Perhaps this is what he would have wanted. He hid the artifact in the old manor."

"Where in the manor?"

"It will be hard to find. Go to the northernmost room on the third floor. The safe with the artifact inside appears every Monday at noon for one minute."

"Does the safe have a key?"

"A combination: right twice to 33, left once to 22, then right to 31."

Kendra glanced back at Grandpa. He was jotting down the numbers. "Got that?" she asked.

"33–22–31," he said, giving Lena a funny look.

His former housekeeper averted her eyes shyly.

"I have another question," Kendra asked. "What did Kurisock do to Patton's uncle?"

"I don't know," Lena said. "Patton never shared that story. It plainly pained him, so I never pressed. He meant to tell me, I think, in his later years. He repeatedly told me I would hear the tale one day."

"So you know nothing about Kurisock?" Kendra asked.

"Only that he is a demon on this preserve. And he may have been somehow affiliated with the apparition who usurped the manor."

"What apparition?" Kendra asked.

"It happened before my fall to mortality. Like I said, I never learned the details. The apparition who destroyed Marshal no doubt still resides in the manor. Patton hid the artifact there because it would be well guarded."

"Marshal was Patton's uncle?"

"Marshal Burgess."

"One last thing. There is a silver bowl. The Fairy Queen gave it to me."

Lena nodded. "Forget the bowl. You cast it into the pond, and we have claimed it."

"I need it back," Kendra said. There was a chorus of hearty laughter from the other naiads. "It's the key for me to safely approach the Fairy Queen again. She may be our only hope of overcoming the plague."

"Come over to the edge and I'll hand it to you," taunted an unseen naiad. Several other voices tittered.

"The bowl is their most treasured keepsake," Lena said. "They, we, will never relinquish it. I had best go. My sisters become skittish when I spend too much time near the surface."

Kendra felt tears well in her eyes. "Are you happy, Lena?"

"Happy enough. My sisters have striven to rehabilitate me. The glimpse of Patton was thoughtful, although it made old wounds ache. For the kindness of the gesture, I told you what you wanted. Enjoy what time you have."

Lena sank into the pond. Kendra stared after her, but the pond was deep, and Lena was soon out of sight.

Grandpa approached behind Kendra, placing his hands on her shoulders. "Well done, Kendra. Very well done."

"The withered one grabbed the obnoxious one," observed a voice.

"Push her in!" cried another.

"Let's get away from here," Kendra said.

CHAPTER SEVENTEEN

Preparations

The largest of the three tents Dale had brought from the house was the biggest privately owned tent Seth had ever seen. The square monstrosity had broad purple and yellow stripes and a steep, curving roof that sloped up to a high central pole with a banner at the pinnacle. The flap over the wide entrance was propped on rods to form a sizable awning. The smaller tents were also fairly roomy, but their dimensions and coloring were less eccentric.

Seth sat in the entrance of the tent where he, Warren, and Dale would be staying. Grandma and Grandpa were sharing the big one. And Kendra got her own, which Seth did not like, but sadly he could think of no reasonable arguments why the arrangements should be otherwise. He had resolved that if the weather stayed pleasant, he would go sleep in one of the gazebos.

A barefooted dryad approached Grandpa's tent. Her long, auburn hair hung past her waist, and her robes evoked memories of bright autumn leaves. She crouched to duck through the entrance. How tall did that make her? Seven feet? More?

Seth had seen several interesting characters come and go from Grandpa's tent over the past hour. But when he had sought admittance, Grandma had shooed him away, promising that he would soon be part of the conversation.

A red fairy with wings like flower petals shot through the air. Seth could not tell whether she had emerged from Grandpa's tent or had come whizzing over the top from behind. She hovered for a moment not far from Seth before streaking out of view.

Absently uprooting handfuls of grass, Seth resolved not to be excluded any longer. Clearly Grandpa and Grandma preferred to gather news and opinions in a way that would allow them to regulate the information, sharing only those facts and ideas deemed suitable for his frail brain. But hearing the unedited details from the actual creatures was half the fun, and whether his grandparents believed it or not, Seth knew he was mature enough to handle anything they could hear. Besides, was it his fault that the walls of a tent were so thin?

He rose and strolled to the back of the yellow and purple tent, sitting in the shade on the lawn with his back to the fabric wall. Straining to listen, he tried to look idle and bored. He heard only the clamor of the satyrs playing on the boardwalk.

"You won't hear anything," Warren said, coming around the side of the tent.

Seth hopped guiltily to his feet. "I just wanted to relax in the shade."

"The tent is magically soundproof—a fact you might have known if you'd helped us set it up."

"I'm sorry, I was—"

Warren held up a hand. "If our roles were reversed, I would have been anxious to meet all the creatures here too. Don't worry, I would have come and nabbed you had we really needed your help. Have you enjoyed yourself?"

"The centaurs weren't very nice," Seth said.

"It looked like they spoke to you. That alone is a feat."

"What's with them?"

"In a word, arrogance. They see themselves as the apex of all creation. All else lies beneath their notice."

"Kind of like fairies," Seth said.

"Yes and no. Fairies are vain, and find most of our affairs boring, but whatever they pretend, they care what we think of them. Centaurs neither seek nor appreciate our admiration—if anything, they take it for granted. Unlike fairies, centaurs sincerely perceive all other creatures as inherently lower than themselves."

"They sound like my math teacher," Seth said.

Warren grinned.

Seth noticed some dark fairies floating just beyond the

nearest portion of the hedge wall. "This plague got to the centaurs just like it affected everyone else."

"Had it not, I doubt they would display any interest," Warren said. "In fairness, they have some excuse for their haughtiness. Centaurs tend to be brilliant thinkers, gifted artisans, and formidable warriors. Pride itself is their greatest flaw."

"Seth!" Grandma called from the other side of the tent. "Dale! Warren! Kendra! Come counsel with us."

"There you go," Warren said, sounding relieved himself. "The wait is over."

Part of Seth wondered if Warren had wandered to the back of the tent in order to quietly verify whether it was actually as soundproof as purported. They walked around to the front of the tent, passing the towering dryad with the autumnal robes and an aged satyr with a white goatee and deep laugh lines. Kendra unzipped her tent and came outside. Dale jogged toward them from the direction of the dwarf encampment. Grandma and Grandpa waited at the entrance of the tent and welcomed them inside. Both Stan and Ruth looked tired and careworn.

The tent was so large that Seth half expected to find it furnished, but there were only a pair of rolled sleeping bags in the corner and some gear. They all sat on the floor, which was quite comfortable, thanks to the springy turf underneath. The sunlight filtering through the yellow and purple fabric gave the room an odd cast.

"I have a question," Kendra said. "If the evil brownies

stole the register, can't they just change the rules and let dark creatures come in here?"

"Most of the boundaries and borders of Fablehaven are fixed by the treaty that established the preserve and are therefore unchangeable while the treaty stands," Grandma explained. "The register simply allowed us to regulate access to the preserve as a whole and to dictate which creatures could cross the barriers guarding our home. The magical barriers protecting this area are different from most of the boundaries at Fablehaven. Most boundaries are established to limit access by particular types of creature—there are certain sectors where fairies are allowed, and satyrs, and fog giants, and so forth. Some creatures are granted more area to roam than others, based on how potentially harmful they are to others. Since most of the boundaries are divided according to species, when the light creatures started turning dark, they retained access to the same areas."

"But the border around the pond and this field functions according to affiliation with light or darkness," Grandpa said. "Once a creature starts drawing more upon darkness than light, that creature can no longer enter here."

"How long will this place hold off the darkness?" Seth asked.

"We wish we knew," Grandma said. "Perhaps for a good while. Perhaps for another hour. We can be certain only that our backs are to the wall. We're almost out of options. If we fail to take effective action, the preserve will soon fall."

"I conferred with my most trustworthy contacts from among the creatures gathered here," Grandpa said, his demeanor becoming more official, "in an effort to gauge the level of support we could expect from the various races. I traded words with at least one delegate from most of them, excluding the brownies and the centaurs. As a whole, the creatures here feel sufficiently cornered and intimidated by this plague that I believe we can count on considerable assistance as needed."

"But we did not want any of them here while we discuss strategy," Grandma said. "We withheld certain key information. If they should become contaminated, most, if not all, would utterly betray us."

"Why do the creatures all change so completely?" Kendra asked. "Seth said that Coulter and Tanu kept helping us after they transformed."

"You ask a difficult question," Grandpa said. "The short answer is that as nonmagical, mortal beings, humans are affected differently by the plague. The rest requires speculation. For the most part, unapologetically, magical creatures are what they are. They tend to be less self-aware than humans, relying more on instinct. We humans are conflicted beings. Our beliefs don't always harmonize with our instincts, and our behavior doesn't always reflect our beliefs. We constantly struggle with right and wrong. We wage war between the person we are and the person we hope to become. We have a lot of practice wrestling with ourselves. As a result, compared to magical creatures, we humans are much more able to suppress our natural inclinations in order to deliberately choose our identities."

"I don't get it," Seth said.

"Each human being has significant potential for light *and* darkness," Grandpa continued. "Over a lifetime, we get a lot of practice leaning toward one or the other. Having made different choices, a renowned hero could have been a wretched villain. My guess is that when Coulter and Tanu were transformed, their minds resisted the darkness in a way most magical creatures can't imagine."

"I still don't see how somebody nice like Newel could instantly become so evil," Seth said.

Grandpa held up a finger. "I don't view most magical creatures as good or evil. What they are largely governs how they act. In order to be good, you must recognize the difference between right and wrong and strive to choose the right. To be truly evil you must do the contrary. Being good or evil is a choice.

"Instead, the creatures of Fablehaven are light or dark. Some are inherently builders, some are nurturers, some are playful. Some are inherently destroyers, some are deceivers, some crave power. Some love light, some love darkness. But change their nature, and without much resistance, their identities follow. Like a fairy becoming an imp, or an imp regaining her fairyhood." Grandpa looked at Grandma. "Am I waxing too philosophical?"

"A little," she said.

"Questions that start with 'why' are the toughest to answer," Dale said. "You end up guessing more than knowing."

"I think I get what you mean," Kendra said. "A demon like Bahumat automatically hates and destroys because he sees no other option. He isn't questioning his actions or resisting a conscience. Someone like Muriel, who deliberately chose to serve darkness, is more evil."

"So Newel acted differently because he isn't Newel anymore," Seth concluded. "The plague totally overwhelmed him. He's something else."

"That's the basic idea," Grandpa said.

Warren sighed. "If a starving bear ate my family, even though he may have had no wicked intentions, even though he was just being a bear, his nature has made him a menace, and I'm going to shoot him." He sounded exasperated by the conversation.

"The bear would have to be stopped," Grandma agreed. "Stan is just making the distinction that you wouldn't blame the bear the same way you would blame a responsible person."

"I get the distinction," Warren said. "I have a different opinion about magical creatures. I can think of many creatures who have chosen to carry out good or evil actions, regardless of their nature. I hold dark creatures more accountable for what they are and what they do than Stan does."

"As is your right," Grandpa said. "The issue is largely academic, although some who share your view would use it as an excuse to eradicate all dark creatures, a notion I find detestable. I'll agree that creatures of light can be deadly—consider the naiads, who drown the innocent for sport. The Fairy Queen herself strikes down those who tread near her shrine uninvited. And creatures of darkness can be helpful—

look at Graulas, supplying key information, or the goblins who reliably patrol our dungeon."

"This fascinating debate aside," Grandma said testily, "the matter at hand is to halt the plague at any cost. We're on the brink of destruction."

Everyone nodded.

Straightening his shirt, looking somewhat chagrined, Grandpa shifted gears. "Lena didn't know much more about Kurisock, except to confirm that he was involved with the fiend who now controls the old manor. But she was able to tell us much about the second artifact." He related the details about the location of the safe, the time it would appear, and the combination.

"Any guess which artifact it is?" Warren asked.

"She didn't say," Kendra answered.

"The artifact could wield power over space or time," Grandma said. "It could enhance vision. Or it could bestow immortality. Those are supposedly the powers of the four that remain unclaimed."

"Do you think the artifact might help us reverse the plague?" Seth asked.

"We can hope," Grandpa said. "For now, recovering it is the most pressing task. On top of claiming the artifact, risking an excursion to the manor would also serve as useful reconnaissance. Anything we can discover about Kurisock and those associated with him could help us unravel the mystery of the plague."

Dale cleared his throat. "Not to gainsay you, Stan, but

considering what we know about the old manor, the odds may not be good that any of us will return."

"We know that a dreaded presence haunts the property there," Grandpa admitted. "But those rumors were started by Patton, who had good reason to scare people away."

"Because he hid the artifact there," Kendra said.

"Furthermore," Grandpa continued, "we know of somebody who unwittingly entered the manor and survived to tell the tale."

All eyes turned to Seth. "I guess I did. I hadn't drunk milk yet that day. I had just escaped from Olloch, so I couldn't see what anything actually was. In fact, maybe that's the only reason I got out of there at all."

"I've wondered the same thing," Grandma said.

"Roaming the preserve without consuming milk has advantages and drawbacks," Grandpa said. "There is evidence that if you are unable to perceive magical creatures, they must exert greater effort in order to perceive you. In addition, many of the dark creatures feed on fear. If you fail to recognize them for what they are, the fear is diminished, and their motivation to inflict harm is reduced."

"But just because you can't see magical creatures doesn't mean they aren't there," Dale interjected. "Wandering the preserve without milk is a fine way to stroll blissfully into a death trap."

"Which is the downside," Grandpa affirmed.

Grandma leaned forward eagerly. "But if we know where we're going, and have an idea what awaits us, and we stick to the path on the way there and back, not drinking the milk may give us the advantage we need to sneak past the apparition and reach the safe. Seth, how long were you in the manor before the whirlwind pursued you?"

"Several minutes," Seth said. "Enough time to climb to the top floor, step out onto the roof, get my bearings, come back into the room, and start down the hall."

"Forgoing the milk sounds like our best option," Warren said. "You say the safe will appear tomorrow?"

"At noon," Grandpa said. "And then not for another week. We can't afford to wait."

"What about daylight saving time?" Grandma asked. "This time of year, we recognize noon standard time as one o'clock."

"With an apparition guarding the safe, timing will be essential," Grandpa said. "When did daylight saving time go into effect?"

"Around World War I," Grandma said. "Probably after the safe was created."

"Let's go by standard time, then, and hope the safe isn't as smart as my cell phone, automatically updating itself," Grandpa said. "We want to reach that room at one o'clock tomorrow afternoon."

"Dale and I can tackle this," Warren offered.

"I should come," Seth said. "If I'm there, Coulter and Tanu can scout for us."

"They can't be out under the sun," Grandpa reminded him. "And we have to do this around midday. In fact, in the interest of caution, since they can't help, don't mention any of this to them."

"Maybe tomorrow will be cloudy," Seth tried. "Besides, I'm the only one who has been inside the manor before. I know where Lena was talking about. And what if the apparition uses magical fear? I may be the only one of us not paralyzed!"

"We'll consider your courageous offer," Grandpa said.

"I don't see how we'll succeed without incurring some losses," Grandma said, her brow scrunched. "Too much is riding on this for us to fail. We need multiple people going after the safe from multiple directions. Some of us will fall, but others are bound to get through."

"I agree," Grandpa said. "Dale, Warren, Ruth, and I should combine in a united offensive."

"And me," Seth insisted.

"I could come too," Kendra offered.

"Your eyes can't be closed to magical creatures," Grandpa reminded Kendra. "Your ability to see and be seen might inadvertently give us away."

"It might be handy to have somebody along who can tell what is actually happening," Kendra maintained.

"We'll bring walrus butter," Warren said. "We'll unveil our eyes if the need arises."

"So the five of us," Seth said as if the matter were decided. "Plus Hugo."

"Hugo, yes," Grandpa said. "Five, I'm not so sure."

"I'll even hang back if you want," Seth proposed. "I'll only go inside if it makes sense. Otherwise I'll retreat. Think about it. If this fails, we're all doomed anyhow. I might as well be there to help it succeed."

"He makes a good case," Warren conceded. "And we'll be glad to have him if fear overcomes us. We know such fear exists."

"All right," Grandpa said. "You can join us, Seth. But not Kendra. Nothing personal, dear. Your ability to see really could spoil our one possible advantage."

"Do we want help from any of the other creatures?" Seth asked.

"I doubt they could enter the manor," Grandma said.

"But they could create a diversion," Warren suggested. "Draw attention elsewhere. Many dark creatures await us beyond the hedge."

"Good thinking," Grandpa said, becoming animated. "We could send out several parties in different directions. Fairies and satyrs and dryads."

"Ideally centaurs," Grandma added.

"Good luck," Dale harrumphed.

"Seth spoke with them earlier today," Warren said. "Perhaps if we tickled their pride."

"Maybe coming from the children, if they sounded sufficiently desperate," Grandpa mused. "Regardless, I'll speak with representatives from the other creatures here. We'll drum up enough help to cause a commotion tomorrow. Remember, no walrus butter in the morning. Tomorrow the pond should appear encompassed by butterflies, goats, groundhogs, and deer."

"What about the golden owls?" Kendra asked. "The ones with faces?"

"The astrids?" Grandma said. "Little is known about them. They rarely acknowledge other creatures."

"I'll prepare the cart," Dale said. "If we're all blind and covered, Hugo might be able to smuggle us to the manor unnoticed."

"Won't they go after Hugo?" Seth asked.

"A golem is not an easy target," Grandma said. "Many potential enemies may not care to bother him if he appears to be alone."

Grandpa clapped his hands together and rubbed them briskly. "Time is short. Let's start making the arrangements."

※ ※ ※

The sun was setting as Kendra and Seth trudged across an empty expanse of lawn toward the centaurs. The golden glow highlighted the bloated muscles of their chests, shoulders, and arms as the pair stood gazing stoically toward the pond.

"I don't think you should come," Kendra hissed. "You have too much of a temper. We need to sincerely beg."

"How dumb do you think I am?" Seth replied. "Anyone can beg!"

Kendra gave him a dubious glance. "Can you humbly plead for a favor from a jerk who rubs your nose in it?"

He hesitated. "Of course."

"You better not blow this," Kendra warned, lowering her voice to a whisper. "Remember, by groveling, we're manipulating them. Pride is their weakness, and we're exploiting that in order to get what we need. They may gloat, but if they do what we ask, we're the ones in charge."

"And if they turn us down flat?" Seth asked.

"We'll have tried," Kendra said simply. "And we'll leave it at that. We can't afford extra problems, not with so much riding on tomorrow. Can you behave?"

"I will," he said, sounding more certain than he had earlier.

"Follow my lead," Kendra said.

"Let me introduce you first."

As they approached, the centaurs did not watch them. When Kendra and Seth finally stood directly before them, the centaurs kept their solemn eyes steadily fixed upon some inscrutable subject of interest elsewhere.

"Broadhoof, Cloudwing, this is my sister, Kendra," Seth said. "She wanted to meet you."

Cloudwing glanced down at them. Broadhoof did not.

"We come to you on an urgent errand," Kendra said.

Cloudwing regarded her momentarily. The silver fur on his quarters twitched. "We already declined the invitation to counsel with your grandsire."

"This isn't a repeated invitation," Kendra said. "We've devised a plan to recover an item that may help reverse the plague. Many of the other creatures here have offered their help, but without you, we're leaderless."

Now both of the centaurs regarded her.

Kendra continued. "We need to divert the attention of the darkened creatures watching this area so my grandpa and a few others can slip away to pursue the item. None of the other creatures have the speed or ability to lead the charge through the main gap in the hedge."

"Only tainted centaurs could truly challenge us," Cloudwing considered, eyes on Broadhoof.

"We could outdistance the satiric sentries at will," Broadhoof said.

"How do we know this scheme warrants our leadership?" Cloudwing asked.

Kendra faltered, glancing at Seth.

"My grandpa is willing to risk his life, and the lives of his family, to carry out the plan," Seth said. "We can't guarantee it will work, but at least it gives us all a chance."

"Without your help, we'll never know," Kendra exaggerated. "Please."

"We need you," Seth said. "If the plan works, you'll have rescued Fablehaven from my grandfather's incompetent management." He glanced at Kendra for approval.

The centaurs leaned together, conferring inaudibly.

"Your lack of leadership is indeed a problem," Broadhoof pronounced. "But Cloudwing and I do not perceive it as our problem. We must decline."

"What?" Seth cried. "Are you serious? Then I'm glad half the preserve is here to watch who stood idly by when Fablehaven was endangered."

Kendra glared at her brother.

"We care little for the fate of satyrs and humans, and less for their reactions to our indifference," Cloudwing stated.

"Thanks anyhow," Kendra said, grabbing Seth's arm to pull him away. He shook free of her.

"Fine," Seth spat. "But I'll be going out there tomorrow. Good luck ignoring the fact that you don't even have the courage of a human boy."

The centaurs stiffened.

"Am I deceived, or did the whelp label us cowards?" Cloudwing asked in a dangerous tone. "Our verdict not to lead your diversion had nothing to do with fearfulness. We recognized the activity as futile."

Broadhoof fixed Seth with a fierce stare. "Surely the human youth misspoke."

Seth folded his arms and stared back silently.

"If he means to stand by his insult," Broadhoof said forebodingly, "I will demand immediate satisfaction. No one, great or small, tramples my honor."

"You mean a duel?" Seth asked incredulously. "You're going to prove your courage by beating up a kid?"

"He raises a valid concern," Cloudwing said, laying a hand on Broadhoof's shoulder. "Consorting with hogs will only leave us soiled."

"The two of you are dead to us," Broadhoof declared. "Depart."

Kendra tried to drag Seth away, but he was too strong.

"All muscle and no backbone," Seth snarled. "Let's go find some satyrs to lead us. Or maybe a dwarf. Leave the frightened ponies to pretend they have honor."

Kendra wanted to strangle her brother.

"We overlooked your insult out of pity," Broadhoof fumed. "Yet you persist?"

"I thought I was dead," Seth said. "Keep it straight, you nag."

Broadhoof balled his fists, huge muscles bunching in his forearms. Veins stood out in his beefy neck. "Very well. Tomorrow at sunrise, you and I will resolve the issue of my honor."

"No we won't," Seth said. "I don't fight with mules. The fleas are my biggest concern. That, and the actual problems that need solving. You're welcome to murder me in my tent."

"Broadhoof is within his rights to challenge you to a duel after a deliberate insult," Cloudwing asserted. "I stand as a witness of the exchange." He extended a hand, indicating the surrounding area. "Furthermore, this place is a refuge for creatures of light. As a human, you are a trespasser here. Like the naiads in the pond, Broadhoof could slay you at will with utter impunity."

Kendra felt her stomach drop. Seth looked shaken.

"Which would prove nothing about your honor," Seth said, his voice almost steady. "If you care about honor, lead the diversion tomorrow."

The centaurs put their heads together and spoke quietly. After a moment they parted.

"Seth Sorenson," Broadhoof intoned weightily. "Never in my long years have I been so openly affronted. Your words are unforgivable. And yet I am not ignorant to the reality that they were spoken in a misguided ploy to gain my assistance, in counterpoint to the awkward flattery you attempted at first. For the insolence of denying my challenge, I should strike you down where you stand. But in acknowledgment of the desperate valor behind your words, I will stay my hand for the moment, and forget this conversation ever occurred if you drop to your knees, beg my forgiveness, claim insanity, and declare yourself a craven coward."

Seth hesitated. Kendra elbowed him. He shook his head. "No. I won't do that. If I did, I really would be a coward. All I take back is saying my grandfather mismanaged the preserve. You're right that we were pretending to flatter you."

With a ring of metal, Broadhoof unsheathed an enormous sword. Kendra had not previously noticed the scabbard hanging at his side. The centaur held the blade aloft.

"This brings me no pleasure," Broadhoof growled broodingly.

"I have a better idea," Seth said. "If you lead the diversion tomorrow, and I come back alive, I'll duel with you. Then you can satisfy your honor the right way."

Kendra thought the centaur appeared relieved. He spoke briefly with Cloudwing.

"Very well," Broadhoof said. "You have accomplished your aim, though not without a price. Tomorrow we will spearhead your diversion. The day afterward, at dawn, we settle the matter of your impudence."

Kendra seized Seth's hand. This time he allowed her to conduct him away. She waited to speak until they were far from the centaurs. "What's the matter with you?" It required all of her control to resist screaming the words.

"I got them to help us," Seth said.

"You knew they were arrogant, you knew they might not

help, but you insisted on insulting them! Not only is getting yourself killed a bad idea, it hurts our chances of saving Fablehaven!"

"But I'm not dead," he said, patting his torso as if shocked to find himself intact.

"You should be. And you probably will be."

"Not for two days."

"Don't speak so soon. We haven't told Grandma and Grandpa what happened yet."

"Don't tell them," Seth pleaded, suddenly desperate. "Things are bad enough. I'll do whatever you want, just don't tell."

Kendra threw up her hands. "*Now* you beg."

"If you tell, they won't let me go to the manor, but they'll need me. Also, they'll worry needlessly. They'll lose focus and make mistakes. Listen. You can tell them eventually. You can make me look as stupid as you want. Just wait until after we raid the manor."

The reasoning behind his plea made some sense. "All right," Kendra consented. "I'll wait until tomorrow afternoon."

His grin tempted her to change her mind.

CHAPTER EIGHTEEN

The Old Manor

Alone, Kendra leaned against the smooth gazebo railing watching dozens of creatures take up positions around the field. Dryads and hamadryads clustered around indentations where the hedge was penetrable. Doren led a band of satyrs to the main gap by the path. Groups of fairies patrolled the air in glittering formations. Broadhoof and Cloudwing took up positions in the center of the field near Hugo and the cart.

Not all of the creatures were participating. The majority of the fairies flitted about the trellises of the boardwalk, playing among the blossoms. The dwarfs had unanimously taken refuge in their tents, having complained to Grandpa that running was not their strong suit. The more animal-like creatures had gone into hiding. Many satyrs and nymphs observed the proceedings from other gazebos.

Even in the shade, the midday heat was uncomfortable. Kendra limply fanned herself with one hand. She could not see Seth, Grandma, Warren, or Dale. They had collapsed a tent, and lay hidden beneath it in the bed of the cart. Grandpa stood in the front of the cart, supervising the final preparations, hands on his hips.

Kendra had kept her word and refrained from telling anyone about Seth's agreement with Broadhoof. Grandma and Grandpa had been overjoyed to hear that the centaurs would assist with the diversion. Kendra had done her best to appear equally pleased.

Grandpa raised a handkerchief in the air, waved it briefly, and then let it fall. As the silky square fluttered to the ground, Cloudwing reared, equine muscles churning beneath his silver fur. He clutched a huge bow in one hand, and across his broad back hung a quiver of arrows the size of javelins. Broadhoof unsheathed his tremendous sword with a flourish, the burnished blade catching the sunlight.

Together the centaurs raced across the grass toward the gap in the hedge, blurred hooves flinging up tufts of turf, galloping with such fluid speed that Kendra found herself breathless. Shoulder to shoulder they charged through the gap, stampeding over the dark satyrs who sought to impede their passage.

With a victorious shout, twenty satyrs detached themselves from the hedge at either side of the gap and followed the centaurs through, spreading out in all directions. A few hamadryads ran with them. While the satyrs were quick and nimble, the nymphs put them to shame, seeming more to fly than to run, effortlessly outdistancing any pursuers.

Kendra smiled to herself. No smitten satyr would ever chase down a hamadryad who did not wish to be caught!

Around the field, dryads and satyrs snuck through hidden openings in the hedge, often on hands and knees. Fairies flew over the hedge wall, angling skyward as their shadowy sisters gave chase. The satyrs watching from the boardwalk whistled, stamped, and shouted huzzahs. Many naiads surfaced, heads dripping, eyes wide as they observed the tumult.

Amid the commotion, Hugo charged forward, towing the cart. Grandpa had hidden himself under the tent with the others. Kendra held her breath as the hulking golem stormed through the gap in the hedge unmolested and the cart rumbled out of sight.

After the cart passed through the main gap, a few tall dryads followed, splitting off in different directions, their flowing robes and long hair trailing behind. Satyrs and hamadryads began returning under the hedge and through the gap. Some laughed; others appeared flustered.

Kendra glanced back at the naiads, their weedy hair glossed with slime, their wet faces surprisingly fragile and young for beings whose favorite pastime was drowning humans. Kendra locked eyes with one of them and waved. In response, they all hastily plunged under the water.

Over the next several minutes, more fairies, satyrs, and dryads returned. As they reentered the field, they were welcomed by embraces from friends. Most then turned to anxiously await the arrival of other loved ones.

More minutes passed, and arrivals grew sparse. Running hard, flanks lathered, the centaurs galloped though the gap, forcing a cluster of dark fairies to abandon their pursuit. Only two arrows remained in Cloudwing's quiver.

Less than a minute later, dodging and fighting several dark satyrs, Doren reappeared in the gap, leading a desperate knot of satyrs. Shoving opponents aside, a half dozen satyrs stumbled through the gap into the arms of friends.

Kendra saw a familiar figure standing at the threshold of the field. Verl, snowy fur matted with dirt, chest and shoulders marred by bites and scratches, strained to take a step forward. He had won through to the field, but his eyes widened with panic as an unseen barrier prevented his entry. Kendra saw his childish face begin to contort into a more goatlike countenance, watched his white fur begin to darken. Bleating black satyrs hauled him down from behind, piling on him. Moments later, when Verl arose, he had the head of a goat and fur as black as sable.

The satyrs and hamadryads withdrew from the gap. Kendra descended the gazebo steps and ran to Doren.

"Did they get away all right?" the satyr panted.

"Yes," Kendra said. "How awful about Verl."

"Nasty business," Doren agreed. "At least most of us made it back. The worst trouble came after a flock of dark fairies cornered one of the most powerful dryads. They changed her swiftly, and she went on to nab a bunch of us. I see the centaurs made it back." He nodded toward where

Broadhoof and Cloudwing stood ringed by animated satyrs, grimly enduring the adulation.

"They were fast," Kendra said.

Doren nodded as he tried to wipe mud from his collarbone. "They can run. And they can fight. Cloudwing pinned a pair of dark satyrs to a tree with a single arrow. Broadhoof hurled the dark dryad into a ditch. Toward the end, a dark centaur showed up and forced them to retreat."

Broadhoof and Cloudwing trotted away from their admirers. Kendra gazed despairingly at the heavily muscled topography of Broadhoof's back. If Seth survived the escapade at the manor, the brawny centaur would be waiting. Kendra wondered whether her brother might be better off as a shadow.

※ ※ ※

Beneath the tent with four other bodies, Seth breathed hot, stale air. He closed his eyes and tried to focus on something other than his discomfort, imagining how refreshing it would feel to poke his head out and feel the wind rushing by as Hugo loped down the road. The day was hot and muggy, but nothing compared to the stifling atmosphere under the tent.

The morning had felt surreal for Seth, watching goats and deer roaming about the field, and groundhogs congregating in their camp by the pond. Grandpa had spent a good deal of time going over plans with a pair of horses and issuing commands to a strangely mobile pile of rocks.

Kendra had pointed out which goat was Doren, and had

served as translator when they wished each other good luck. All Seth heard was baaing and bleating.

The entire scene around the pond looked so ridiculous that Seth had briefly wondered whether the milk simply made everyone crazy. But when the rock pile lifted him off his feet and gently set him in the cart, it was plain there was more much going on than his eyes could distinguish.

The cart jounced sharply, and Seth rapped his head against the side. Cradling his cranium, he wormed toward the center of the crowded cart, then rested his head on his folded arms, trying to relax as he inhaled the warm, stifling air.

For the first leg of the cart ride, he had been anxious, aware that dark creatures could fall upon them at any moment. But as the journey progressed, interference seemed less likely. The plan was apparently working. All they had to do was reach the manor without suffocating.

The uncomfortable tedium of the ride became Seth's chief concern. Lying virtually motionless, his body slick with sweat, he pictured his face over the vent of an air conditioner, the coolness washing over him. He imagined himself gulping down a tall glass of ice water, the glass so cold it hurt his hands, the water so frigid it made his teeth tingle.

He was stretched out beside Warren, and wanted to make conversation, or at least exchange a few whispered complaints, but he had been strictly admonished not to utter a word. He resolutely followed orders, holding still and keeping silent, even choking back coughs when the urge arose. Meanwhile, the cart rolled endlessly forward.

Seth slipped a hand into his pocket, fingering the dollop of walrus butter wrapped in plastic film. They each had a little, in case the time arrived when seeing magical creatures became preferable to deliberate blindness. He wished he could eat it simply for a sensation to divert his mind from his unfortunate surroundings. Why hadn't he brought candy? Or water? He lamented to think of his precious emergency kit sitting under his bed. How had he forgotten to bring it when he had gone down the trapped staircase? He had jelly beans in there!

The ride became more jarring, as if Hugo were dragging the cart over a giant washboard. Seth clenched his jaw to prevent his teeth from clacking. The stuttering vibrations made it difficult to think.

At last the cart came to an abrupt stop. Seth heard rustling as Grandpa peeked out.

"We're at the edge of the yard," Grandpa announced quietly. "As I feared, Hugo can go no farther. Out we go; I see no present threat."

Seth gratefully crawled out from under the tent, feeling validated that the others were at least as red-faced and drenched in sweat as he was. His clothes felt clingy and sticky, and although the air was not as fresh as he had hoped, it was still much preferable to the stuffiness in the cart.

Behind the cart stretched a weathered flagstone road, flanked by the remnants of old cabins and shacks. Many of the flagstones were out of place, and tall weeds throve in the gaps. The uneven stone road explained the washboard feeling at the end of the ride. Seth had walked that road before—he should have guessed!

Ahead of them, the road doubled back on itself to form a looping driveway that granted access to an impressive manor. Compared to the timeworn road and the decrepit shelters bordering it, the manor was in excellent repair. The building rose three stories, with four stately pillars out front. Climbing plants had invaded the gray walls, and heavy green shutters shielded the windows.

Seth gaped at the manor, taking in a ghastly difference since his previous visit. Now, hundreds of slender black cords converged on the mansion from all directions, entering through the walls, a few of them fairly thick, most slender and hard to see. The shadowy cords snaked away from the estate in all directions, many disappearing into the ground, some winding through the surrounding vegetation.

"What's with all the wires?" Seth asked.

"Wires?" Grandpa questioned.

"Ropes, strings, whatever," Seth clarified. "They're everywhere."

The others regarded him with concern.

"You don't see them?" Seth already knew the response.

"No wires," Warren confirmed.

"I've noticed cords like this before," Seth said. "Connected to the dark creatures. It looks like all the cords lead to the manor."

Grandpa puckered his lips and exhaled noisily. "We've uncovered hints that the culprit was a creature who had somehow merged with Kurisock. And we had information

that the apparition who haunts this property has some relation to the demon."

"What could the creature be?" Warren asked.

"Anything," Grandpa said. "When it merged with
Kurisock, it became a new entity."

"But if it merged with the demon, how can it be here?"
Dale asked. "Kurisock must remain in his domain."

Grandpa shrugged. "Best guess? Some sort of distant
connection. Something like the dark cords that apparently
unite the monster in the manor to the darkened creatures
all over the preserve."

"Do we still go after the artifact?" Warren asked.

"I see no alternative," Grandpa said. "Fablehaven may
not survive another week. This could be our only shot.
Besides, we can't plan to defeat whatever dwells here until
we confirm what it is."

"I agree," Grandma said.

Dale and Warren nodded.

Grandpa glanced at his wristwatch. "We'd better get
moving or the opportunity will pass us by."

Leaving Hugo behind, Grandpa led them to the front
steps of the manor. Seth remained on high alert, watching
for suspicious animals, but saw no signs of life. No birds, no
squirrels, no insects.

"Quiet," Dale murmured suspiciously.

Grandpa raised his hand and twirled a finger, suggest-
ing they do a lap around the manor. So near the building,
Seth could not avoid touching some of the dark cords. He
was relieved to find them as intangible as a shadow. As they

progressed, Seth stayed ready for an attack at any instant, especially as they rounded each new corner, but they finished a complete circuit around the manor without encountering any interference. They identified a few windows low enough to grant them access, as well as a back door.

"Last time the front door was unlocked?" Grandpa whispered to Seth.

"Yes."

"Ruth and I will enter through the front," Grandpa said. "Warren will take the back door. Dale, choose a side window. Seth, you wait outside. Should we fail, unless there is a monumentally compelling reason to do otherwise, return immediately to Hugo and take word to your sister and the other creatures. If we become shadows ourselves, we'll try to contact you. Remember, everyone, we want the northernmost room on the third floor." He gestured to show which was the northern side of the manor. "Probably at the end of a hall. The combination is 33–22–31." He checked his wristwatch. "We have about seven minutes."

"What's the go signal?" Warren asked.

"I'll whistle," Grandpa said, raising a pair of fingers to his lips.

"Let's get this over with," Dale said.

Warren and Dale jogged around the manor out of sight while Grandpa and Grandma mounted the steps. Grandpa tried the front door, found it unlocked, and stepped back, eyes on his watch. Seth's hands were clenched into such tight fists that when he uncurled his fingers, he found that his nails had printed tiny crescents in his palms.

Eyes on his wristwatch, Grandpa slowly raised his fingers to his lips. A piercing whistle shattered the silence. Clutching her crossbow in one hand and flash powder in the other, Grandma followed Grandpa through the front door. Grandpa closed the door behind them.

From the side of the house, Seth heard wood splintering and glass breaking. He figured it was Dale gaining access through a window. Silence returned.

Seth flexed his fingers and tapped his toes. He could feel his heart beating in his hands. Staring at the quiet house was torture. He needed to see what was happening inside. How could he judge whether there was a monumentally compelling reason to enter and help if he didn't know what was going on?

Seth climbed the steps to the front porch, nudged the front door open, and peered through the resulting crack. The house was much as he remembered—well furnished but heavily powdered with dust and festooned with cobwebs. Grandma and Grandpa stood frozen at the foot of a sweeping staircase. At the top of the stairs, dust swirled in a vortex from floor to ceiling. All of the wires and cords of varying thickness converged on the whirlwind in a clot of shadow vaguely shaped like a human figure.

Seth took a step through the doorway. The air felt severely chilled. His breath plumed white in front of him. Grandma's hand with the crossbow trembled as if she were striving to lift it under tremendous duress.

The spinning column of dust glided down the stairs. Seth's petrified grandparents made no move to get out of the way. Although he did not experience the same paralyzing terror that gripped Grandma and Grandpa, the cold was real, and the sight horrifying. If he failed to act, his grandparents were doomed—the black hub of the shadow plague was bearing down on them.

He pulled the walrus butter from his pocket, tore the plastic, smeared a fingertip in the paste, and stuck the finger into his mouth. As he swallowed, the scene resolved itself more clearly. The pillar of dust vanished, replaced by a spectral woman swathed in flowing black garments, her bare feet hovering several inches above the stairs.

Seth recognized her! She was the same apparition who had appeared outside the attic window on Midsummer Eve the previous year! She had fought alongside Muriel and Bahumat in the battle at the Forgotten Chapel!

All of the dark threads converged on her. Her clothes and skin were drenched in shadow. Her eyes were black voids. Undulating ribbons of material stretched from the apparition toward his grandparents, moving as if coaxed by a slow breeze.

"Grandpa! Grandma!" Seth yelled. They did not budge. "Stan! Ruth! Run!" Seth screamed the words, his voice cracking. Neither of his grandparents flinched. The apparition paused. Her soulless pits gazed at Seth for a heartbeat. Seth ran toward his grandparents, moving quicker than the fabric, but with more ground to cover. The tendrils of black fabric arrived first, seizing Grandpa and Grandma Sorenson like tentacles. Seth skidded to a stop, staring in shock as shadow overcame them.

Seth turned and ran out of the front door. His grandparents were shadows. He had to hurry. Maybe he could still rescue Dale or Warren.

While racing around the house, Seth struggled to convince himself that he would find a way to restore his grandparents to normal. And Tanu. And Coulter. He wondered how much time remained before the safe was scheduled to appear. Even if everyone else failed, he had to make it to that upper room and claim the artifact.

It was apparent which window Dale had entered, courtesy of the unhinged shutters and broken glass. With a hop, Seth grabbed the windowsill and boosted himself up. Dale stood in a dusty parlor, unmoving, his back to the window.

"Dale, back up," Seth hissed. "You have to get out."

Dale gave no indication of having heard the warning. He did not twitch. Beyond him, through a doorway, Seth saw the apparition gliding in their direction.

Seth dropped from the window and dashed to the back of the house. Maybe while the shadow lady claimed Dale, he could bolt up the stairs.

He flung open the back door and found Warren sprawled on the far side of the kitchen floor, positioned as if he had been trying to crawl forward.

How long would it take to lug Warren outside? Would the time spent dragging Warren cause him to miss his window of opportunity for slipping up the stairs? Maybe, but he couldn't just leave him there! Crouching, Seth looped his arms under Warren's and began hauling the larger man backward across the tile floor toward the door.

"Seth," Warren breathed.

"You with me?" Seth asked, surprised.

Warren tucked his feet beneath himself, and Seth helped him stand. "So cold . . . like the grove," Warren mumbled.

"We have to hurry," Seth exclaimed. He started across the kitchen, but Warren did not follow. Once again, he appeared paralyzed.

Seth returned to Warren and grabbed his hands. Life rekindled in his eyes.

"Your touch," Warren murmured.

"Run," Seth said, leading his friend by the hand through the house toward the entry hall. Staggering along with stilted strides, Warren managed a respectable pace. They reached the bottom of the stairs and started up. Breathing hard, Warren stumbled, fighting his way up the steps with his free arm and both legs. Seth tried his best to pull the struggling man forward.

Glancing down the steps, Seth saw the shadowy apparition return to the entry hall. Garments unfurling and billowing with dreamlike slowness, she drifted toward them, levitating forward and upward.

Seth and Warren reached the second-story hall, passing a photograph of Patton and Lena hanging on the wall. Seth held Warren with both hands—the added contact seemed to invigorate him. Shambling forward, they arrived at the foot of a staircase to the third level just as the spectral woman reached the second floor and came floating down the hall.

They were most of the way up the stairs when Warren stumbled badly. Seth lost his grip and Warren tumbled down several steps, coming to rest in a motionless heap. Seth leaped down to him, clasping one of Warren's hands in both of his.

Warren stared at him, pupils unevenly dilated, blood trickling from the corner of his lips. "Go," Warren mouthed. He dug a hand into a pouch at his waist, pulling out a fistful of flash powder.

The shadowy apparition appeared at the base of the stairs, dragging her numberless dark wires. Warren flung the powder at her. There was no crackle or flash. Her fluttering garments flowed toward them.

Seth released his friend and charged up the stairs two at a time. If he failed to claim the artifact, all these sacrifices would be in vain. He dashed down the third-story corridor to the north end of the manor, relieved at how fast he could run without towing Warren, eyes fixed on the door at the end of the hall. His legs and arms pumped hard until he rammed the door with his shoulder, clawing at the knob.

It was locked.

Seth stepped back and kicked the door. It shuddered but did not open. The shock of the impact hurt his shin. He kicked the door a second time to no avail. Taking a few steps back he crouched and charged, shoulder lowered, transforming himself into a projectile, aiming not at the door but beyond it. Wood cracked and split, the door flew open, and Seth tumbled through to land on his hands and knees.

Rising, he shut the splintered door as best he could. The

room he had broken into was broad, with two shuttered windows. A huge oriental rug covered the hardwood floor. Bookshelves lined one wall. There were a couple of chairs in a sitting area beside a canopied bed. He saw no safe.

Had they been correct to account for daylight saving time? Had the safe come and gone? Or was it yet to arrive? Perhaps the safe was currently there, but hidden. Whatever the answer, Seth had only seconds before he joined the others as a shadow.

He raced to the bookshelf, frantically scooping armfuls of volumes out of place, hoping to find a hidden safe in the wall. When that yielded no result, he turned, eyes darting around the room, and there it was, standing in a corner where it had not been a moment before—a heavy, black safe, almost as tall as Seth, with a silver combination dial in the center.

Bounding across the room to the safe, he began turning the dial. It rotated smoothly, unlike the dial on his locker, which was jerky and clicked a little when you reached the correct number. He spun the dial right twice to 33, left once to 22, then directly back to 31. When he pulled the handle, the door swung open silently.

A single object rested on the floor of the safe, a golden sphere approximately a foot in diameter, its polished surface interrupted by several dials and buttons. Seth could not imagine what the peculiar device did.

He pulled the sphere from the safe, finding it somewhat heavier than it looked. The room had been cold when he

entered, but the temperature was now dropping rapidly. How near was the shadow lady? Perhaps just outside the door.

Seth dashed to a window and threw open the shutters. There was no roof outside this window, just a three-story drop to the yard. Desperate, he began pressing the sphere's buttons.

And suddenly he was not alone in the room.

A tall man with a mustache appeared in front of him. He wore a white shirt with the sleeves rolled back, gray trousers with suspenders, and black boots. He was fairly young, with a solid build. Seth instantly recognized the mustached man from his photographs. It was Patton Burgess.

"You must be the youngest safecracker I have ever seen," Patton said amiably. His expression changed. "What is going on?"

The door to the room blew open. The shadowy apparition hovered at the threshold. Sweat beaded on Patton's brow, and he stiffly tried to turn, his body jerking weakly. Seth took his hand, and Patton swiveled to face the apparition. "Hello, Ephira."

The apparition recoiled.

"What has happened to you?" Patton backed toward the window, keeping hold of Seth's hand. "I suppose darkness always was a downward spiral."

"No roof," Seth warned quietly.

Turning, Patton leaped onto the windowsill. Releasing Seth's hand, he jumped, not down, but up, twisting to catch hold of the eaves of the roof above. His legs scissored as he hoisted himself up. Then he reached a hand down. "Come on."

Ephira glided into the room, face enraged, fabric unwinding, rippling toward Seth. Clutching the sphere in one arm and blindly trusting Patton, he climbed onto the windowsill, stretched out his free hand, and pushed off. Patton's hand closed tightly around his wrist and swung him onto the roof.

"We need to get out of here," Seth said.

"Who are you?"

"The caretaker's grandson. Fablehaven is at the brink of destruction."

Patton rushed along the roof, shingles groaning and splitting beneath his boots. Seth followed. Patton ran toward the corner of the roof near where a tall tree grew. Surely he wasn't going to jump!

Without hesitation, Patton sailed off the roof, catching hold of a limb that sagged and broke. Releasing it, he caught hold of a lower limb. Hand over hand, Patton made his way toward the trunk. When he got there, he swung up, straddling the bough. "Toss me the Chronometer."

"You expect me to jump?"

"When jumping is the sole option, you jump, and try to make it work. Toss it."

Seth threw the sphere to Patton, who deftly caught it in one hand. "What branch should I aim for?"

"Go left of where I went," Patton said. "See it? I left the best branch for you."

The branch was at least ten feet from the roof, and five

or six feet lower. It would be easy to miss it. He pictured his hands slapping against the limb, failing to grasp it securely.

"Do not think," Patton ordered. "Back up a few steps and take the leap. Looks worse than it is. Anyone could do it."

Seth stared at the distant ground. To fall from this height was almost certain death. He backed up, the shingles creaking underfoot.

Peering over his shoulder, Seth saw the apparition floating toward him along the roof. That was the extra incentive he needed. He took three steps and flung himself off the roof. As he fell, the branch rose to meet his outstretched hands. The impact was jarring, but he held on. The limb drooped and bobbed, but it did not break.

Like Patton had done, Seth advanced hand over hand toward the trunk of the tree. Patton was already climbing down below him. Seth descended recklessly, concerned about the shadow lady above. There were no limbs for the last ten feet. He hung and dropped. Patton caught him.

"You have a way out of here?" Patton asked.

"Hugo," Seth said. "The golem."

"Lead on."

They dashed across the yard. When Seth looked back, he could no longer see Ephira. "Where'd she go?"

"Ephira detests sunlight," Patton said. "Coming out on the roof like that pained her. She never was very fast, and she looks more weighed down than ever. She knows she won't catch us, at least not by giving chase. Any notion what happened to her?"

"You know the revenant in the grove in the valley between four hills?"

Patton shot him a surprised glance. "Matter of fact, I do."

"We think Kurisock got hold of the nail that gave the revenant his power."

"How did the revenant lose the nail?"

They reached the cart and clambered into the bed. "Go, Hugo," Seth panted, "fast as you can, run to the pond." The cart began rattling over the unkempt road. Seth located the spare flash powder and shared some with Patton. "Actually, I pulled the nail out."

"You did?" Patton looked astonished. "How?"

"Pair of pliers and some courage potion."

Patton regarded Seth with a broad grin. "I think the two of us are going to get along just fine."

"Keep an eye out for dark creatures," Seth said. "Somehow between Kurisock, the shadow lady, and the nail, a plague has spread through Fablehaven turning the light creatures dark. Dark fairies, dwarfs, satyrs, dryads, centaurs, brownies—you name it. If the darkness spreads to humans, they turn into shadow people."

Patton smirked. "Looks like I landed in hotter water than I planned on."

"Which reminds me," Seth said, "how are you here? You're not even old."

"The Chronometer is one of the artifacts. It has power over time. Nobody knows all it can do. I've learned a few tricks. I pressed a certain button on the Chronometer, knowing that when the button was pressed again, I would leap forward to that point in time and remain there for three days. You must have pushed the button and called me here."

"No kidding," Seth said.

"I only hit the button as an additional precaution to protect the artifact. I figured if a thief ever got hold of it, the culprit would eventually push the button, and then I could steal it back. I never dreamed I would land myself in a predicament like this."

"My Grandpa Sorenson is a shadow. So is my Grandma. Everyone but my sister, Kendra."

"Why are we going to the pond?"

"Dark brownies took over the house. The pond repels the dark creatures."

"Right. The shrine." Patton looked thoughtful. He spoke hesitantly. "What about Lena? Has she passed yet?"

"No, actually, she's a naiad again."

"What? That is not possible."

"Lots of impossible things have been happening lately," Seth said. "It's a long story. Lena was the person who told us about the safe. We should probably get under the tent." Seth started pulling the tent up.

"Why?"

"The dark creatures are everywhere. When we came to the manor, none of us drank the milk. We hid under the tent, and no dark creatures bothered us."

Patton stroked his mustache. "I don't have to drink milk to see the creatures here."

"I just ate some walrus butter, so I can see them now too. Hiding may not do as much good."

"After what happened at the manor, I wager we can expect a serious ambush. We ought to avoid the paths. Have Hugo abandon the cart and carry us to the pond cross country."

Seth considered the idea. "That might work."

"Of course it will." Patton winked.

"Hugo, stop," Seth ordered. The golem complied. "We're leaving the cart here, and you're going to carry us as quickly as you can through the woods back to the pond. Try not to let any creatures see us. And grab that tent; we'll need it back at the refuge."

The golem slung the tent over his shoulder, cradled Seth in one arm and Patton in the other, and then tromped off the road into the trees.

Duel

Hooves clomping over the whitewashed planks, Doren sprinted along the boardwalk after Rondus, a portly satyr with butterscotch fur and horns that curved away from each other. Puffing hard, Rondus cut through a gazebo and started down the stairs to the field. Only a few steps behind, Doren went airborne and slammed into the heavyset satyr. Together they pitched violently forward into the grass, staining their skin green.

Doren rose swiftly and started after a petite hamadryad with short, feathery hair. Rondus lunged at a small, thin satyr, wrapping his legs together in a savage embrace. The small satyr toppled with a yelp.

Kendra sat on a wicker chair in a nearby gazebo watching the game of tackle tag. Each new individual tackled became a tackler until the last participant was brought down. The last person tackled became the first tackler of the next round.

The agile hamadryad twirled away from Doren several times, but he stayed doggedly after her until he finally got a hand on her waist, scooped her into his arms, and set her on the grass. The satyrs tackled each other as if causing injuries were the point of the game, but they treated the hamadryads more gently. The hamadryads quietly returned the favor by allowing themselves to be caught. Having seen the hamadryads in action earlier that day, Kendra knew that the satyrs would never have been able to lay a hand on them unless the nymphs only evaded them halfheartedly.

Kendra most enjoyed watching the hamadryads take down the satyrs. The nymphs never dove at them or wrapped them up. They knocked satyrs to the turf with perfectly timed shoves and nudges, or else by tripping them. What the satyrs made look hard, the hamadryads made look effortless.

The frenetic game helped distract Kendra from her worries. What if nobody returned from the excursion to the manor? What if her friends and family had all been transformed into shadows that she lacked the ability to see? How long would it be before she followed?

"Why not join in this round?" Doren asked, calling up to the gazebo from the grass below.

"I'm not big on tackling," Kendra said. "I prefer watching."

"It isn't as rough as it looks," Doren said. "At least it wouldn't be for you."

At that moment, Hugo loped through the gap in the hedge across the field, ramming dark satyrs aside, holding Seth high in one hand and a stranger in the other. Once inside the field, Hugo slowed.

"Well, pluck out my horns and call me a lamb," Doren murmured. "Patton Burgess."

"Patton Burgess?" Kendra asked.

"Come on," the satyr said, already running across the grass.

Kendra vaulted the gazebo railing and took off after Doren. Where was the cart? Where were Grandma and Grandpa? Warren and Dale? How was it possible that Patton Burgess was with Hugo and Seth?

The golem set Patton and Seth on the ground. Patton smoothed his suspenders and adjusted his sleeves.

"Patton Burgess!" Doren exclaimed. "Back from the grave! Should have known you'd turn up again sooner or later."

"Glad to see you aren't mangy and snarling," Patton said with a smile. "I was grieved to hear about Newel. And you must be Kendra."

Kendra stopped in front of him, a little winded by her run. He looked familiar because of his photographs, but they did not quite do him justice. "It's really you. I've read your journals."

"Then you have an advantage over me," Patton said. "I look forward to getting acquainted."

Kendra looked to Seth. "What about the others?"

"Shadows," Seth answered.

Kendra hid her eyes in her hands. The last thing she wanted to do was burst into tears in front of Patton.

"The creature at the manor was the lady outside our window on Midsummer Eve," Seth continued. "The shadow lady who helped Muriel and Bahumat. She's the source of the plague."

"There is no shame in sorrow, Kendra," Patton said.

Kendra lifted her damp eyes. "Where did you come from?"

Glancing at Doren, Patton hefted the golden sphere. "The object at the manor let me travel here temporarily."

Kendra nodded, realizing that he didn't want to elaborate about the artifact in front of the satyr.

Approaching hoofbeats made all of them turn. Cloudwing cantered over to them, pounding to a stop in front of Seth. The centaur stared at Patton, then inclined his head slightly. "Patton Burgess. How have you exceeded your life span?"

"We all have our little secrets," Patton said.

Cloudwing shifted his gaze to Seth. "Broadhoof sends congratulations on your safe return. He wishes to remind you of your engagement on the morrow."

"I remember," Seth said.

"What engagement?" Patton interjected.

"Seth must answer for his egregious insults," Cloudwing said.

"A duel?" Patton exclaimed. "A centaur against a child! This is low, even for Broadhoof."

"I witnessed the exchange," Cloudwing said. "Broadhoof provided the young human several opportunities for clemency."

"I insist upon having words with Broadhoof," Patton said.

"I am sure he will oblige," Cloudwing answered. The centaur cantered away.

"He treated you politely," Seth marveled.

"He has good reason to do so," Patton replied. "I recently gave the centaurs of Fablehaven their most prized possession. Well, recently for me—a long time ago for you. Tell me about this duel."

Seth glanced at Kendra. "When we left for the manor this morning, a bunch of the creatures here ran out past the hedge as a distraction, so Hugo could get away with us in the cart. We wanted the centaurs to lead the charge, so Kendra and I begged them. When they turned us down, I basically called them cowards."

Patton winced. "The only words a centaur hears are insults. Go on."

"They tried to get him to take it back but he kept antagonizing them," Kendra said.

"Finally I agreed to a duel if they would lead the charge," Seth said.

"And they led the charge?" Patton asked.

"They did a good job," Kendra confirmed.

Broadhoof and Cloudwing were galloping toward them.

Patton whistled softly. "You deliberately insulted Broadhoof, he challenged you, you agreed on conditions, and he met the conditions."

"Right," Seth said.

"Then Cloudwing has it right. You owe Broadhoof a fight."

The centaurs halted in front of Patton. "Greetings, Patton Burgess," Broadhoof said, dipping his head.

"I understand you intend to seek satisfaction against a youngster," Patton said.

"His impudence was flagrant," Broadhoof replied. "We covenanted to resolve the matter tomorrow at dawn."

"The boy filled in the particulars," Patton said. "I can imagine how your reluctance to assist with their diversion would have appeared an act of cowardice to such youthful eyes."

"With respect, you have no cause to intervene here," Broadhoof said.

"I am asking you to pardon the boy," Patton said. "He may have been mistaken about your motives, perceiving indifference as cowardice, but his intentions were laudable. I fail to see what shedding his blood will resolve."

"We helped with the charade as requested in tribute to his courageous intentions," Cloudwing replied. "In so doing, we fulfilled our portion of the compact. The injuries to Broadhoof must not go unavenged."

"Injuries?" Patton asked Broadhoof. "Is your self-worth so fragile? Was the humiliation public?"

"I was present," Cloudwing said, "as was the sister."

"We have a binding arrangement," Broadhoof declared with finality.

"Then I suppose we will require an arrangement of our own," Patton said. "From where I stand, Broadhoof, your willingness to engage a child in a duel, whatever the provocation, is a sure mark of cowardice. So now a grown man is calling you a coward in front of your friend, a boy, a girl, and a satyr. Furthermore, I perceive your indifference as a greater fault than your cowardice, and condemn your entire race as a tragic waste of potential." Patton folded his arms.

"Recant your words," Broadhoof warned grimly. "My quarrel is not with you."

"Wrong. Your quarrel is with me. Not tomorrow, or the day after, but now. I personally assume whatever blame you assigned to this boy, I support and restate every insult he uttered, and I offer the following terms. We duel. Now. If you kill me, the matter of the boy is settled. If I best you, the matter of the boy is settled. Either way, all debts end up paid. And you get the opportunity to resolve this with a man instead of through a senseless mockery."

"A mockery?" Seth asked, sounding offended.

"Not now," Patton muttered out of the side of his mouth.

"Very well," Broadhoof said. "Without forgetting the good you have done for my kind, I acknowledge your challenge, Patton Burgess. Slaying you will bring me no joy, but I will consider all debts to my honor paid."

"I requested the duel," Patton said. "Choose your weapon."

Broadhoof hesitated. He consulted briefly with Cloudwing. "No weapons."

Patton nodded. "Boundaries?"

"Within the hedge," Broadhoof said. "Excluding the woodwork and the pond."

Patton surveyed the area. "You want some room to run. I can live with that. I am sure you will forgive me if I fail to make use of all the space provided."

"We must clear the field," Cloudwing said.

Patton looked at Doren. "Get the dwarfs to move up onto the boardwalk. And strike these tents."

"You got it, Patton." Doren ran off.

"When the field is clear," Cloudwing said, "I will signal the commencement of combat."

Broadhoof and Cloudwing cantered away.

"Can you take him?" Seth asked.

"I've never tested myself against a centaur in mortal combat," Patton admitted. "But I was unwilling to discover whether you would have survived. In this predicament, we had a single certitude—mercy would not have come to your rescue. Centaurs have let important wars pass them by without lending a hand, but insult their honor, and they fight to the death."

"But if you die, you won't be able to return to your own time!" Seth exclaimed. "History will be changed!"

"I'm not aiming to lose," Patton said. "And if I do, at this point in time, my life is over and done with—I don't see how what happens now can change what already happened."

"Because if you don't return, what already happened will never happen!" Seth cried.

Patton shrugged. "Maybe. Too late to back out now. Guess I better focus on winning. When jumping is the sole option . . ."

" . . . you jump," Seth finished.

"Kendra," Patton said, "I suppose you have been told that you shine like an angel."

"By fairies," Kendra said.

"Does your brother know?"

"Yes."

"You are more than fairystruck. Could you be fairykind?"

"It's supposed to be a secret," she said.

"Would be for most eyes," Patton said. "And I thought being fairystruck was an accomplishment! Seth, never let your opinion of yourself get inflated. There is always somebody out there to humble you!"

"You were fairystruck?" Kendra asked.

"One of my little secrets," Patton said. "We will have much to catch up on if I live through this."

A group of satyrs had already struck Kendra's tent. Another was tearing down the big one. A huge team of them had invaded the dwarfish encampment.

"I've never seen the satyrs work so hard," Kendra remarked.

"They will do almost anything for sport," Patton said. "The field will be clear in no time. You had better go find a place to watch."

"Why didn't Broadhoof want to use his sword?" Seth asked.

Patton grinned. "He knows how much I like using swords."

"It isn't fair," Kendra complained. "He has hooves."

Patton patted her shoulder. "Pray for me."

"Good luck," Seth said. "Thanks."

"My pleasure," Patton said. "I can always use an extra feather in my cap. I just regret missing the original exchange! A boy your age criticizing a centaur would be a sight worth seeing!"

Kendra and Seth set off toward the boardwalk.

"If you get Patton killed, I'll never forgive you," she seethed.

"He knows how to handle himself," Seth replied.

"You haven't seen the centaurs in action," Kendra said. "I don't want to watch this."

As Kendra and Seth took up positions on the boardwalk, the satyrs cleared the last of the tents from the field. Kendra noticed one satyr toting a reluctant dwarf under one arm. She glanced back at the pond, but no naiads had surfaced. What would Lena think if she knew Patton was here, not a photograph, but the actual man in his prime?

Walking toward the boardwalk, Patton waved at the onlookers. Cheering satyrs and dryads returned the gesture. He seemed to be positioning himself in order to give everyone a good view of the fight.

Cloudwing trotted toward the boardwalk with a regal bearing. He raised a muscular arm. "The contest between

Patton Burgess and (he made a strange, braying sound) will commence on my mark. Stand ready. Go." He dropped his arm.

Broadhoof came loping across the field, face stern, massive muscles rippling. Patton stood his ground, hands at his sides. Broadhoof increased his speed to a furious gallop. "Prepare to defend yourself, human!" Broadhoof roared.

Kendra fought the urge to turn away. Patton looked small and defenseless as the raging centaur bore down on him. He was going to be flattened! At the last second, Patton skipped to the side with the nonchalance of a matador and the centaur raced past him.

Broadhoof wheeled around for a second charge. "I am not here to dance," the centaur declared. If anything, Broadhoof came at Patton even faster the second time. Patton feinted to the left. When Broadhoof swerved, Patton stepped in the other direction. As Broadhoof thundered past him, Patton swiveled and punched the centaur squarely in the flank.

The blow knocked the centaur crooked. With pain etched on his features, Broadhoof stumbled badly, narrowly avoiding a fall. The spectators groaned empathetically, then applauded, the satyrs in particular hooting their approval.

Broadhoof slowed and turned. Fixing Patton with a murderous glare, the centaur walked toward him. Straightening his shirt, Patton calmly awaited his arrival. When Broadhoof drew near to Patton, he reared, lashing out with his sharp hooves. Patton backed away just enough to stay out of range.

Advancing patiently, Broadhoof reared again and again,

front hooves flailing. Each time Patton kept just out of reach. "I am not here to dance," Patton mimicked with a smirk.

The spectators chuckled.

Angered, Broadhoof curveted recklessly forward, stamping and bucking and swinging his fists. Dancing nimbly, ducking and twisting, Patton ended up at the side of the wild centaur and vaulted onto his back, clamping Broadhoof in a headlock while riding him like a rodeo cowboy. Leaping and plunging, Broadhoof reached back for Patton. Taking the opportunity to release the headlock and seize one of Broadhoof's hands, Patton slid off his back and abruptly wrenched the centaur to the ground.

With one palm braced against Broadhoof's meaty forearm, Patton bent the centaur's hand to an unnatural angle. He also appeared to have one of his fingers in a painful lock. The centaur's face contorted in agony. When Broadhoof endeavored to rise, Kendra heard a sharp crack. The centaur quit struggling, and Patton shifted his grip.

"I have the upper hand here," Patton warned loudly. "Yield, or I'll break your bones one by one."

"Never," Broadhoof gasped venomously.

Cupping one hand, Patton momentarily relinquished his hold in order to clap the centaur on the ear. Broadhoof howled. Patton quickly reestablished the hold, levering the centaur's arm to a more vicious angle.

"This contest is over, Broadhoof," Patton said. "I don't want to leave you permanently maimed, or to deprive you of your senses. Yield."

Sweat shined on Broadhoof's flushed face. "Never."

The crowd was now silent.

Patton added pressure to the trembling arm. "Which is worse? To yield, or to lie before an audience while a human humiliates you with his bare hands?"

"Slay me," Broadhoof pleaded.

"Centaurs are nearly immortal," Patton said. "My intent is not to prove why we say 'nearly.' I vowed to best you, not to dispatch you. If I must, I'll simply leave you incapacitated for whatever time remains to you, an irrefutable monument to human superiority."

Cloudwing walked forward. "You are at his mercy, Broadhoof. If Patton refuses to end your life, you must yield."

"I yield," Broadhoof relented.

The crowd roared. Kendra stared in shocked relief, hardly noticing as the enthusiastic satyrs jostled against her. She saw Patton help Broadhoof to his feet, but could not hear the words they exchanged over the clamor around her. Kendra began shouldering through the crowd to get to the lawn. She had not fully appreciated how much the satyrs disliked the centaurs until she witnessed the exultant tears they shed as they embraced one another.

As Broadhoof plodded away with Cloudwing, Kendra and Seth ran to Patton. None of the satyrs or naiads were thronging him. They apparently preferred celebrating at a distance.

"That was incredible," Seth said. "I heard something snap . . ."

"A finger," Patton said. "Remember this day, Seth, and

take great care before you offend a centaur. I despise injuring a vanquished opponent. Curse Broadhoof for his stubborn pride!" Patton clenched his jaw. Were his eyes misty?

"He forced the situation," Kendra reminded him.

"I fought him because the brute would have it no other way," Patton said. "I hurt him for the same reason. Yet I cannot help admiring his resistance to yield. Breaking him was not pleasurable, even knowing that he would have killed me had our roles been reversed."

"I'm so sorry it happened," Seth said. "Thank you."

"You're welcome. One moment." Patton cupped his hands around his mouth and raised his voice. "Satyrs, dryads, and other spectators—but most especially satyrs. The price of these festivities is that you return the field to how it looked before. I want every tent stake where it belongs. Do we have an understanding?"

With no direct response, the satyrs moved to carry out his orders.

Patton turned back to Kendra and Seth. "Now, if I comprehend the situation correctly, Lena is over yonder in the pond?"

"Right," Kendra said. "She's a naiad again."

Patton placed his hands on his hips and sniffed. "Then I expect I had better go say hello to the missus."

CHAPTER TWENTY

History

E ven though Lena went back into the water against her will, she has voluntarily remained there," Patton recapped as he, Seth, and Kendra overlooked the pier from a gazebo. Although he had set off full of confidence to converse with Lena, he now seemed nervous about her potential reaction.

"Right," Kendra said. "But she has always been very responsive to any mention of you. I think she'll come when you call."

"Naiads are peculiar creatures," Patton said. "Of all the beings at Fablehaven, I consider them the most selfish. Fairies take notice if you flatter them. Centaurs get riled if you insult them. It is difficult to win the attention of a naiad. Their only preoccupation is their next diversion."

"Then why do they bother drowning people?" Seth asked.

"For sport," Patton said. "Why else? There is little deliberate malice in it. Swimming is all they know. They find the idea of water killing somebody hilarious. They can never get enough of it. Plus, naiads are avid collectors. Lena once mentioned they have a chamber full of prized trinkets and skeletons."

"But Lena is different from other naiads," Kendra said. "She cares about you."

"A victory years in the making," Patton sighed, "hopefully not undone by her return to the water. Her interest in me was what eventually separated Lena from the other naiads. Little by little, she began to care for someone other than herself. She began to enjoy my company. The others loathed her for it. They despised having a reason to wonder whether there might be more to existence than wallowing in fruitless self-absorption. But now I worry that her mind may have reverted. You say Lena remembers our marriage fondly?"

"After you died, I don't think she ever really found her place," Kendra said. "She went out to experience the world, but ended up back here. I know she hated growing old."

"She would," Patton smiled. "Lena dislikes many aspects of mortality. We've been married five years—from my point of view, I mean—and our relationship has not been easy. We had a very stormy argument not long before I came here. We have yet to make up. Back in my time, if Lena received an offer to return to the water, I suspect she might gladly accept it. I'm encouraged to hear that our marriage survives in the end. Shall we find out if she still wants me?" He studied the water with trepidation.

"We need her to grab the bowl," Kendra said. "At least to try." As they had conversed in the gazebo, Kendra had explained how she became fairykind, and how she hoped to use the bowl to approach the Fairy Queen a second time.

"I wish I had my violin," Patton lamented. "I know just the melody I would use. Wooing Lena the first time around was hard enough, but at least I had time and resources. I hope she responds favorably. I would prefer wrestling another centaur to learning that her affection for me has cooled."

"Only one way to find out," Seth said.

Patton descended the stairs from the gazebo to the pier, tugging on his sleeves and smoothing his shirt. Seth moved to follow him but Kendra held him back. "We should watch from here."

Patton strode along the pier. "I'm looking for Lena Burgess!" he called. "My wife."

Numerous overlapping voices responded.

"It couldn't be."

"He's dead."

"They were chanting his name earlier."

"Must be a trick."

"It sounds just like him."

Several heads surfaced as he reached the end of the pier.

"He's back!"

"Oh, no!"

"The devil himself!"

"Don't let her see!"

The water near the end of the pier became turbulent. Lena poked her head up, eyes wide, and was promptly dragged under. After a moment she resurfaced. "Patton?"

"I'm here, Lena," he said. "What are you doing in the water?" He kept his voice conversational with a hint of curiosity.

Lena's head disappeared again. The water churned. Voices resumed.

"She saw him!"

"What do we do?"

"She's too wriggly!"

Lena yelled, "Unhand me or I'll leave the pond this instant!"

A moment later her head rose above the water again. She gazed raptly at Patton. "How are you here?"

"I came forward in time," he said. "I am only visiting for three days. We could use some assistance—"

Lena held up a hand to silence him. "Say no more, human," she demanded sternly. "After much travail, I have reclaimed my true life. Do not attempt to befuddle me. I need time alone to realign my thoughts." With a wink, she disappeared beneath the water.

Kendra heard the naiads murmuring in surprised approval. Patton did not move.

"You heard her," a snide voice called to him. "Why don't you crawl back into your grave!"

A few nervous titters followed the comment. Then Kendra heard other voices, desperate ones.

"Stop her!"

"Grab her!"

"Thief!"

"Traitor!"

Lena burst from the water at the end of the pier, leaping into the air like a dolphin. Patton caught her in a strong embrace, dousing his shirt and trousers in the process. She wore a shimmering green slip. Her long, glossy hair hung heavy and wet, draped over her shoulders like a shawl. In one webbed hand, she gripped the silver bowl from the Fairy Queen's shrine. Lena leaned her forehead against Patton's, then her lips found his. As they kissed, the webbing between her fingers dissolved.

All around the pier, naiads wailed and cursed.

Cradling Lena in his arms, Patton walked back toward the gazebo. Kendra and Seth descended the stairs to the pier. Patton deposited Lena on her feet.

"Hi, Kendra," Lena said with a warm smile. She was familiar—her eyes, her face, her voice—and yet so different. She stood a couple of inches taller than before, her skin smooth and unblemished, her body curvy and fit.

"You're beautiful," Kendra said, reaching to give her a hug.

Lena stepped back, grasping Kendra's hands instead. "I'll get you soaked. You've grown so tall, dear. And Seth! You're a giant!"

"Only compared to tiny naiads," Seth said, looking

pleased. Standing straighter, he was more than half a head taller than her.

"You'll only have Patton for three days," Kendra reminded her friend, concerned that Lena would end up regretting her decision.

Lena handed Kendra the untarnished bowl, then gazed adoringly at her husband, caressing his face. "I would have left the pond for three minutes."

Tilting his head down, Patton rubbed his nose against hers.

"I think they need some alone time," Seth said disgustedly, tugging on Kendra.

Patton locked eyes with Seth. "Don't go. We have much to discuss."

"The yellow and purple tent is soundproof," Seth said.

"Sounds perfect." Holding Lena's hand, Patton led her up the stairs and into the gazebo.

"Not long before you died," Lena said, "you told me we would be together again someday, young and healthy. At the time I assumed you meant heaven."

Patton gave her a wry smile. "I probably meant this. But heaven will be nice too."

"I can't tell you how thrilling it feels to be young again," Lena gushed. "You look fairly boyish yourself. You're what, thirty-six?"

"That's not far off."

Stopping, Lena pulled her hand from his and folded her arms. "Wait a minute. Early in our marriage, you came forward in time to visit me, and you never told me."

"Evidently not."

"You and your secrets." She returned her hand to his. They continued across the field toward the striped tent. "What were you doing before you came here?"

"Last thing I did was press a button on the Chronometer," Patton said in a confidential tone, nodding to the sphere Seth was carrying. "I was hiding it in the manor. Before I locked it up, I pushed a button that would send me forward in time to the next instance when the button was pressed."

"I pressed it," Seth announced.

"You didn't tell me about the artifact until you were in your sixties," Lena scolded. "I rarely knew what you were up to."

"We just had a fight," Patton said. "About the drapes in our bedroom. Remember? It started about the drapes, and ended up being about how I wasn't living up to my promises—"

"I remember that spat!" Lena said nostalgically. "In fact, that may have been the last time you ever raised your voice at me. That was a hard period for both of us. Take heart. Not long afterward, we hit our stride. We had a beautiful marriage, Patton. You made me feel like a queen, and reciprocating was effortless."

"Resist telling me too much," Patton said, covering his ears. "I would rather watch it unfold."

They reached the tent and entered. Patton dropped the flap to shield the door. They sat down on the floor, facing one another.

"I can't believe you left the pond so eagerly," Kendra said to Lena. "I've wanted you out of there ever since you entered."

"You were sweet to come for me," Lena replied. "I remember when you first tried to talk me out of it. My mind was cloudy. It functioned differently. I had lost much of who I became in mortality. Not enough to really fit in, but enough to stay put. Life in the pond is indescribably easy. Virtually meaningless, but devoid of pain, almost devoid of thought. There were many things I did not miss about mortality. In a way, returning to the water was like dying. I no longer had to cope with living. Until I saw Patton, I wanted to stay dead."

"You feel lucid now?" Patton asked.

"Like my old self," Lena said. "Or I guess I should say like my young self. With my present mind, with or without you, Patton, I would never choose the numbness of the pond. That spell grips me only when I'm in there. Tell me about this plague."

Kendra and Seth related all the details about the plague. Seth told about his meeting with Graulas and the cords he had seen connected to Ephira at the manor. Lena was saddened to hear that Grandma, Grandpa, and the others had become shadows. Patton expressed surprise at the mention of Navarog.

"If Navarog has truly emerged from captivity, you have not heard the last from him. In lore, Navarog is widely acknowledged as the most corrupt and dangerous of all dragons. Recognized as a prince among demons, he will stop at nothing to liberate the monstrosities confined in Zzyzx."

Next the conversation shifted to the artifacts. Kendra and Seth shared all they knew about the five artifacts, and recounted how they had recovered the healing artifact from the inverted tower. Kendra went on to outline her exploits at Lost Mesa, and told how the Knights of the Dawn lacked information about one of the secret preserves.

"So the inverted tower held the Sands of Sanctity," Patton said. "I never checked. I wanted to leave the traps armed and undisturbed."

"Why did you take the Chronometer from Lost Mesa?" Kendra asked.

Patton scratched his mustache. "The more I thought about the potential of those artifacts to open the gates of the great demon prison, the less I liked how many people knew where they were hidden. The Knights of the Dawn mean well, but organizations like that have a way of keeping secrets alive and helping them spread. I knew only one person in the world I would trust with such vital information. Me. So I took it upon myself to uncover all I could about the artifacts, in order to make them harder to find. The only artifact I ever actually removed was the one at Lost Mesa."

"How did you get by the dragon?" Kendra asked.

Patton shrugged. "I have my share of talents, among them taming dragons. I am far from the most accomplished dragon tamer you will meet—barely passable, in fact—but I can normally conduct a conversation without losing control of my faculties. The artifact at Lost Mesa was protected by a wicked dragon named Ranticus, rotten to the core."

"Ranticus was the name of the dragon in the museum," Kendra recalled.

"Correct. Vast networks of caverns lurk below Lost Mesa. After much exploration, I learned of a band of goblins with access to the lair where Ranticus dwelled. The goblins worshipped him, using their secret entrance to bring him tributes—food, mostly. Slaying a dragon is no small feat, a task more for wizards than for warriors. But there is a rare weed called daughter-of-despair from which you can derive a toxin known as dragonsbane, the only venom capable of poisoning a dragon. Finding the weed and formulating the poison was a quest all its own. Once I had the toxin, disguised as a goblin, I brought Ranticus a dead ox saturated with the poison."

"Couldn't Ranticus smell it?" Seth wondered.

"Dragonsbane is imperceptible. If not, it would never work against a dragon. And I was heavily disguised, down to wearing goblin skin over my own."

"You poisoned him?" Seth exclaimed. "It worked? Then you really were a dragon slayer!"

"I suppose I can own up to it now. During my lifetime I did not want word getting around."

"You started a few of those rumors yourself," Lena chided.

Patton cocked his head and tugged at his collar. "Vainglory aside, after disposing of Ranticus, I defeated the guardians of the artifact, a troop of ghostly knights, in a battle

I would rather forget. Then, in order to avoid suspicions that I had removed the Chronometer, I needed to restore a guardian to the caves. When other business took me to Wyrmroost, one of the dragon sanctuaries, I swiped an egg and hatched it at Lost Mesa. I named the dragon Chalize and kept an eye on her during her infancy. Before long, the goblins took to her, and my assistance was no longer required. Some years later, I donated the bones of Ranticus to the museum."

"Have you killed other dragons?" Seth asked eagerly.

"Killing a dragon is not always a good thing," Patton said earnestly. "Dragons are more humanlike than most magical creatures. They have a great deal of self-possession. Some are good, some are evil, many are in between. No two dragons are identical, and few are very much alike."

"And no dragons appreciate it when somebody outside their community slays one of their kind," Lena said. "Most consider it an unpardonable crime. Which is why I insisted that Patton keep his dragon slayings unconfirmed."

Seth stabbed a finger at Lena. "You said 'slayings.' As in multiple dragons."

"Now would be a poor time to relive past adventures unrelated to our present predicament," Patton said. "I can fill in some of your other missing connections. I know a lot about Ephira. Much more than I would like." He lowered his eyes, the muscles tensing in his jaw. "Hers is a tragic story I have never shared. But I think the time has come."

"You used to tell me I would hear this story one day," Lena said. "Is this what you meant?"

"I expect so," Patton replied, folding his hands. "Long ago, my uncle Marshal Burgess ran Fablehaven. He was never officially the caretaker—my proud grandfather retained the title but delegated all responsibility to Marshal, who managed the preserve admirably. Although not the best in a fight, Marshal was a skillful diplomat and a wonderful mentor. Women were his big weakness. He had an undeniable knack for attracting them, but he could never settle on one. Marshal weathered numerous scandals and three failed marriages before becoming infatuated with a certain hamadryad.

"Of all the tree nymphs at Fablehaven, she was the brightest, the bubbliest, the most flirtatious, always laughing, always leading a game or a song. Once she caught his fancy, Marshal became obsessed. When Marshal gave chase, I never knew of a woman who could resist him, and this vivacious hamadryad was no exception. Their courtship was brief and passionate. Amid ardent promises of everlasting fidelity, she renounced the trees and married him.

"I do not believe Marshal planned to betray her. I am convinced that he sincerely believed he would finally settle down, that winning a hamadryad would allow him at long last to conquer his wandering heart. But his behavioral patterns were deeply ingrained, and before long, the infatuation began to wither.

"The hamadryad truly was a remarkable woman worthy of a loving mate. She quickly became my favorite relative. In fact, it was through her guidance that I became fairy-struck. Tragically, our relationship was short-lived.

"Within months, the marriage unraveled. The hamadryad was crushed. She had forsaken immortality under false pretenses. The betrayal cut her to the core. It poisoned her reason. She abandoned Marshal and disappeared. I searched, but failed to find her. It was years before finally I pieced together what happened to Ephira."

"Your aunt is the shadow lady!" Seth exclaimed.

"I'm beginning to see why you withheld this story," Lena remarked sadly.

"Ephira became obsessed with regaining her status as a hamadryad," Patton continued. "She did not care that such a feat was impossible. She saw it as the only possible compensation for her unjust treatment. As part of her desperate pursuit, she loosed one of Muriel Taggert's knots. She later visited the swamp hag, who directed her to Kurisock. It was finally the demon who struck a bargain with Ephira that would enable her to return to a nonmortal life.

"To understand what comes next, you must realize that the life of a hamadryad is inextricably connected to a particular tree. When the tree dies, she dies with it, unless the connection is passed through a seed of the original tree to a new one. Because their trees can be reborn as seedlings, hamadryads are virtually immortal. But the tree also constitutes a weakness, a secret that must be zealously guarded.

"When Ephira fell to mortality, she lost the connection with her tree. But any magic that can be done can also be undone. Ephira still knew where her tree was located. Under orders from Kurisock, she cut it down with her own hands, burned it, and brought the last seed to the demon.

"The bond between Ephira and her tree may have been sundered, but like all broken magic, it was mendable. Using his unusual gifts, Kurisock bound himself to the seed, and through the seed to Ephira, reforging her connection."

"But she didn't turn back into a hamadryad," Kendra realized, chills racing down her back. "She became something else."

"Something new," Patton agreed. "She became dark and spectral, tainted by demonic power, a negative of her former self. Merging with Kurisock magnified her vengeful feelings. Still within her rights to enter the manor, she returned and destroyed Marshal and some others who lived there. I managed to swipe the key pages of the treaty from the register and flee."

"How did you piece all this together?" Kendra asked.

"I became preoccupied with knowing. Many of the details are inferences, but I am convinced they are correct. I interviewed Muriel and the swamp hag. I found the tree Ephira cut and burned. And finally I visited the tar pit and beheld the dark sapling. I wish I had hazarded to hack it down at the time. Now, presumably, the nail from the revenant has been added to the accursed tree, heightening Kurisock's might and Ephira's power, making the darkness that cankered her soul contagious. The same way Kurisock transformed her by inhabiting the tree, he can now reach out through her and transform others."

"Did you ever visit Ephira?" Kendra asked.

"I rarely approached the manor," Patton said. "I left her notes, and a picture of me and Lena after we were married.

She never responded. The only time I reentered the manor was to hide the Chronometer in the safe."

"How did you get the safe in there?" Seth asked.

"I went during the night of the vernal equinox," Patton said. "I had noted on a previous festival night that Ephira roams the preserve on those boisterous evenings. It was risky, but to me the danger was worth hiding the artifact in a secure place."

"Patton," Lena said tenderly. "What a burden this tale must have been! What a source of worry throughout our courtship and marriage! How did you ever fall in love with me?"

"You can see why I hesitated to share the story," Patton said. "After I allowed myself to be drawn to you, I vowed our relationship would be different, that you would have all Ephira had lacked. But the story haunted me. Haunts me. Those who knew the tale of Ephira and Marshal questioned my judgment when I led you from the water. I sent away those who could not keep quiet. Despite my determination to make our relationship flourish, there have been times when doubt has tormented me. I could not imagine what the tale might have done to you, with so much more at risk."

"I'm glad I didn't hear the account during the early years of our marriage," Lena admitted. "It would have made a difficult period harder. But know this now: Ephira understood the risks before she made her leap. We all do. She did not have to ruin her existence, betrayal or no. And even though you may not want me to spoil the secrets of our years together, know this much: I made the right choice. I proved that, didn't I, by choosing you again?"

Patton struggled with emotion. Veins stood out on the back of his fists. All he could manage was a nod.

"What an unfair situation for you, Patton, speaking to me after I've experienced our entire mortal relationship. You are not yet fully the man you will become. In your life, our relationship has not yet arrived at full fruition. I don't mean to overwhelm you with implications about what our marriage will be, or make you feel obligated to take it there. Don't worry, just let it happen. As I look back, I loved all of it, the man you were at first, as well as the man you became."

"Thank you," Patton said. "The situation is extraordinary. I must say, it is a relief to come here and find my best friend waiting."

"We should save some of these words for later," Lena said, glancing at Kendra and Seth.

"Right," Patton said. "You all now know the secrets I have carried about Kurisock and Ephira."

"Now the big question," Seth said. "How do we stop them?"

The tent was silent.

"The situation is dire," Patton said. "I am going to level with you. I have no idea."

CHAPTER TWENTY-ONE

Fairykind

A heavy atmosphere pervaded the tent. The house-fly performing acrobatics above Patton and Lena sounded unusually noisy. Kendra smoothed her hands over the fabric floor, feeling the contours of the ground underneath. She exchanged a concerned glance with Seth.

"What about this thing?" Seth asked, hefting the Chronometer. "Maybe we could travel back in time and stop the plague before it starts."

Patton shook his head. "I spent months trying to unravel the secrets of the Chronometer. It has the reputation as the most difficult of the artifacts to use. Although the artifact allegedly has many functions, I managed to discover only a few."

"Anything useful?" Seth asked, fingering a slightly raised dial on the sphere.

"Careful," Patton warned sharply. Seth stopped fiddling with the dial. "I know the button to use in order to travel forward in time to the next moment that same button is pressed. I figured out how to set the Chronometer in order to make the safe appear once per week for a minute. And I can temporarily slow down time, making the rest of the world move faster than the person in possession of the Chronometer. I can't foresee how any of those functions will help resolve our present concerns."

"If we're out of ideas," Kendra said, "the Fairy Queen might be our best chance. I could return the bowl to the island and explain the situation. Maybe she can help."

Patton picked at a frayed gap where his sleeve had torn near the elbow. "I do not fully comprehend what it means to be fairykind, but I am well informed about the shrine. Are you certain returning a bowl will be sufficient excuse to tread on forbidden soil? Before you, Kendra, none have set foot on that island and lived."

"A fairy named Shiara suggested I could," Kendra said. "In a way I can't explain, it feels true. Normally I can't think of returning to the island without a feeling of dread. My instincts agree with what the fairy told me. The bowl belongs there. Replacing it should allow me access."

"Shiara?" Patton said. "I know Shiara—silver wings, blue hair. I consider her the most reliable fairy at Fablehaven. She used to have a close friendship with Ephira. After I was fairystruck and Ephira vanished, Shiara became my closest confidante in matters pertaining to the fairy world. If I were ever to heed advice from a fairy, it would be hers."

"You can talk to fairies too?" Seth asked.

"One of the advantages of being fairystruck," Patton said. "Their language, Silvian, is otherwise quite difficult to master, although some have learned it through study. I can also read and speak their secret language. So can Kendra. That was how she deciphered the inscription I left in the vault at Lost Mesa."

"That was in a secret fairy language?" Kendra asked. "I can never tell what language I'm hearing or speaking or reading. Everything seems like English."

"It takes time," Patton said. "When a fairy speaks, you hear English, but with practice you can also perceive the actual language the fairy is using. At first, the different languages are difficult to distinguish, probably because the translation is so effortless. With some effort, you will grow more conscious of the words you hear and say."

"Why did you leave a message in the vault in the first place?" Kendra wondered.

"The unteachable fairy tongue is a well-kept secret," Patton said. "The language is inherently incomprehensible to all creatures of darkness. I felt I needed to leave a clue regarding what I had done in order to prevent a panic if the Knights found the artifact missing, so I inscribed a message in an arcane language that only a friend of light would be able to comprehend."

"Since you trust Shiara, are you okay with me going to the island?" Kendra asked.

"In this matter, you know better than I do," Patton admitted. "Under less dire circumstances, I would implore you not to undertake such a risky venture. But this predicament is calamitous. Do I believe the Fairy Queen will be able to help us resist the plague? Hard to say, but she helped you once before, and some hope is better than none."

"Then I'm going to try it," Kendra said firmly.

"When you have to jump, you jump," Seth agreed.

"Crossing the pond will be dangerous," Lena cautioned. "The naiads are riled. They'll want the bowl back. They'll want vengeance for my departure. Patton had better ferry you across."

"I would have it no other way," Patton said. "I have some experience navigating those hazards." He winked at Lena.

The former naiad raised her eyebrows. "And getting dragged into the pond by those hazards, if memory serves."

"You're sounding more and more like the Lena I know," Patton said with a grin.

"As soon as the sun goes down, I'll watch for Grandpa and Grandma," Seth said. "They'll probably drop by as shadows. Maybe they can still help us."

"In the meantime, should we go to the pond?" Kendra asked.

"We ought to strike while daylight persists," Patton said.

Seth stowed the Chronometer in a backpack that had formerly held camping gear. He hooked his arms through the straps, and they exited the tent together. Curious satyrs, dwarfs, and dryads had congregated outside. They began eagerly whispering to one another and gesturing at Patton.

Doren trotted up to Patton. "Show me the hold you put on Broadhoof!"

"To prevent an epidemic of crippled satyrs, I had best refrain," Patton said. He held up both hands, raising his voice. "I have only returned for a short while. I journeyed forward through time, and mean to reverse this plague before I depart." Several of the bystanders applauded and whistled. "I hope I can rely on your assistance as needed."

"Anything for you, Patton!" a hamadryad cried in a breathy tone that earned a glare from Lena.

"We will want some privacy at the pond as we approach the shrine," Patton said. "Your cooperation will be appreciated."

Patton escorted Kendra toward the nearest gazebo. She felt tense as Patton led her up the steps and along the boardwalk. The last time she had crossed the pond to the island was among her scariest memories. The naiads had fought hard to capsize her little paddleboat. At least this time the sun was out, and she would not be alone.

Patton strode down the steps to the pier beside the boathouse. He walked over to the floating shed and smashed open the locked door with a single, measured kick.

"Patton is entering the boathouse!" shouted an exultant voice from below the water.

"We'll have his bones in our collection after all!" raved a second naiad.

"Look who's with him!" the first voice gasped.

"The viviblix who raised him from the grave!" a new voice mocked.

"Beware her zombie magic," sang the second naiad.

"They have the bowl!" an outraged naiad noticed.

The voices became lower and more urgent.

"Hurry!"

"Gather everyone!"

"Not a moment to lose!"

The voices trailed off as Patton and Kendra entered the boathouse. The inside looked much as Kendra recalled. Two rowboats floated on the water, one broader than the other, alongside a small paddleboat outfitted with pedals. Patton tromped across the boathouse, selected the largest pair of oars, and placed them in the broad rowboat. Then he laid one of the next largest oars in the boat as well.

"Sounds as though our underwater antagonists mean to give us a rough time," Patton said. "Are you sure you want to do this?"

"Do you think you can get me to the island?" Kendra asked.

"I am confident that I can," Patton said.

"In that case, I have to try."

"Do you mind retaining the bowl?"

Kendra held it up. "I've got it. I'm sure you'll have your hands full."

Patton pulled a lever beside the damaged door, and then started turning a crank. A sliding door on the far side of the boathouse gradually opened, granting direct access to the pond. Patton untied the rowboat and climbed inside. He held out a hand for Kendra and helped her into the craft. The boat wobbled as she stepped into it.

"You made it to the island in that little dinghy?" Patton asked, nodding at the paddleboat.

"Yes."

"You're even braver than I thought," Patton said with a smile.

"I didn't really know how to use oars, but I knew how to pedal."

Patton nodded. "Remember, lean opposite from the direction they try to tip us. But not too far, or they might reverse tactics and tip you out of the boat the other way."

"Gotcha," Kendra said, glancing over the side, expecting naiads to accost them at any second.

"They can't bother us while we're in the boathouse," Patton said. "Only once we pass beyond these walls." He slid the oars into the oarlocks and held them poised to stroke. "Ready?"

Kendra nodded. She did not trust her voice.

Beneath the water just ahead of them, Kendra heard a giggle. Several voices shushed the laughter.

Dipping the blades of the oars into the water, Patton propelled the craft out of the boathouse. The instant the rowboat passed through the door, it began to pitch and rock. Grimacing, Patton wielded the oars aggressively, fighting to keep the boat steady. Bucking and tilting, the rowboat spun in tight circles. Kendra tried to position herself toward the center of the small vessel, but the violent jostling kept her lurching from side to side, clinging to the bowl with one hand while attempting to steady herself with the other.

"I've never seen an effort like this," Patton growled, jerking one of his oars out of a naiad's grasp.

The right side of the boat tipped alarmingly high, as if many hands were pushing it up. Patton lunged to the right, jabbing at the water with an oar. The right side dropped and the left tipped high, nearly rocking Kendra overboard. Patton flung himself in the other direction, steadying the boat.

The battle raged on for several minutes, the naiads tirelessly striving to capsize the rowboat and simultaneously towing them away from the island. The oars were instantly seized whenever Patton dipped them in the water, so he spent much of his time wrestling one or the other from an unseen grasp. Meanwhile, the boat twirled and swayed like a carnival ride.

As time passed, instead of dwindling, the attack became more brazen. Webbed hands reached up out of the water to grip the gunwale. During a particularly bad bout of tilting, Kendra toppled against the side of the boat and found herself staring into a pair of violet eyes. The pallid naiad had boosted herself out of the water with one hand and grasped at the silver bowl with the other.

"Back, Narinda!" Patton barked, brandishing an oar.

Baring her teeth, the determined naiad hauled herself farther out of the water. Kendra held the bowl away from Narinda, but the naiad caught hold of her sleeve and began pulling her overboard.

Patton brought the oar down sharply, slapping the naiad on top of her head with the flat of the blade. Shrieking, the frenzied naiad released Kendra and vanished with a splash. Another hand grabbed the gunwale and Patton instantly brought the oar down on the webbed fingers.

"Stay in the water, ladies," Patton warned.

"You'll pay for your audacity," snarled an unseen naiad.

"All you have felt is the flat side of the oar," Patton laughed. "I'm spanking, not wounding. Keep this up and I'll deal out more lasting injuries."

The naiads continued to hinder the progress of the rowboat, but they no longer reached up out of the water. Patton began using quick strokes that skimmed the surface of the water, throwing a great deal of spray with each pull. The rapid, shallow strokes were harder for the naiads to grab, and the rowboat began to make progress toward the island.

"Chiatra, Narinda, Ulline, Hyree, Pina, Zolie, Frindle, Jayka!" Lena called. "The water has never felt finer."

Kendra turned and saw Lena sitting at the edge of the pier, smiling serenely, feet dangling in the water. Seth stood behind her, an eager look on his face.

"Lena, no!" Patton called.

Lena began humming a lazy melody. She kicked her bare feet gently, making small splashes. Suddenly, Lena yanked her feet out of the water and danced a step back from the edge of the pier. Groping webbed hands broke the surface of the pond nearby.

"So close," Lena lamented. "You almost had me!" She skipped a few steps back along the quay and dipped her toe in, again hopping away just in time to avoid another grasping hand.

"The naiads have never made such a unified, persistent effort," Patton muttered. "Lena is trying to distract them. Chop at the water with the spare oar."

Kendra set the bowl in her lap and picked up the extra oar Patton had brought. Gripping it at the middle of the handle, she began stabbing the blade briskly into the water at either side of the boat. Occasionally the tip of the oar struck something. Kendra began hearing grunts and complaints.

Patton began dipping his oars deeper, and the boat surged toward the island. Encouraged, Kendra jabbed the water more frantically, breathing hard with the effort. She became so intent on hacking at naiads that she was caught off guard when the rowboat ran aground on the island.

"Get out," Patton ordered.

Laying down the oar and picking up the bowl, Kendra stepped to the prow. She hesitated for a moment. Having survived the island once was no guarantee she would survive again. What if her confidence was misplaced? Others who had dared to tread on the island had been instantly transfigured into dandelion fluff. The moment her foot came into contact with the muddy bank, she might dissolve into a downy cloud of dandelion seeds and drift away on the breeze.

Then again, if she opted not to take this risk, her apparent destiny was to become a shadow person on a fallen preserve ruled by a demon and a wicked hamadryad. In a way, an exit as dandelion seeds might be preferable.

All considerations aside, she had made the decision already, and now just needed the courage to carry it out. The naiads could drag the boat back into the water at any moment!

Braced for the worst, she leaped out of the rowboat and onto the firm mud of the island. As on her previous excursion to the shrine, the moment was anticlimactic. She did not transform into seeds. There was no signal to indicate she had done anything out of the ordinary.

Kendra glanced back at Patton, giving him a thumbs-up. He touched his forehead in a casual salute. A moment later, the boat was dragged back into the water and began to twirl.

"Don't fret about me," Patton instructed lightheartedly, skimming an oar across the surface of the water with a ferocious swing. "Go commune with the queen."

On her prior visit to the island, Kendra had not known the location of the tiny shrine, and it had proven difficult to find. This time, bowl in hand, Kendra traipsed diagonally across the island, shoving between shrubs on an undeviating path to her destination. She found the gentle spring burbling out of the ground at the center of the island, trickling down a mild slope into the pond. At the source of the spring stood a finely carved statue of a fairy about two inches tall.

Crouching, Kendra placed the bowl in front of the miniature pedestal supporting the fairy figurine. At the same moment, Kendra inhaled an aroma like young blossoms blooming in rich soil near the sea.

Thank you, Kendra. The words were distinct in her mind, arriving with as much clarity as hearing could have provided.

"Is that you?" Kendra whispered, thrilled to have achieved contact so quickly.

Yes.

"I can hear you more clearly than last time."

You are now fairykind. I can reach your mind with much less effort.

"If you can reach me so easily, why haven't you spoken with me before now?"

I do not inhabit your world. I dwell elsewhere. My shrines mark the locations where my direct influence can be perceived. They are my contact points to your world.

The thoughts were accompanied by mirthful feelings. The combination of thoughts and emotions made Kendra feel as though she had never truly communicated with anyone before. "You're called the Fairy Queen," Kendra said. "But who are you really?"

I am molea. *There is no word to aptly describe me in your language. I am not a fairy. I am the fairy. The mother, the eldest sister, the protector, the first. For the good of my sisters, I reside beyond your world, in a kingdom untouched by darkness.*

"Fablehaven is in danger," Kendra said.

Although I can rarely speak to their minds, I see through the eyes of my sisters in all the spheres they inhabit. Many of my sisters in your vicinity have been tainted by a terrible darkness. If such darkness were to pollute me, all would be lost.

For a moment Kendra could not speak, as a forlorn

feeling overwhelmed her. She realized the bleak emotion had flowed from the Fairy Queen as part of her communication. When the emotion subsided, Kendra spoke again. "What can I do to stop the darkness?"

The darkness emanates from an object endowed with tremendous black power. The object must be destroyed.

"The nail Seth pulled from the revenant," Kendra said.

The object inflames the anguish of a corrupt hamadryad and enhances the strength of a demon. The profane object is embedded in a tree.

For a moment, Kendra beheld a gnarled, black tree beside a fuming pool of tar. A nail projected from the tortured trunk. The image made Kendra's eyes burn, and engendered a feeling of deep regret. Without accompanying words to explain the scene, Kendra felt certain she was witnessing the tree through the eyes of a dark fairy as perceived by the Fairy Queen.

"How can I destroy the nail?" Kendra asked.

A lengthy pause followed. She heard Patton's oars sloshing as he continued to resist the attacking naiads.

"What if we make the fairies big again?" Kendra tried.

An image of giant dark fairies flashed vividly into view. Terrible and beautiful, they shriveled trees and oozed shadows. *Aside from the other potential drawbacks, I am still recovering from the energy it required to transform the fairies and initiate you as fairykind.*

"What did you do to me?" Kendra asked. "Some fairies called me your handmaiden."

When I looked into your heart and mind, and witnessed the

purity of your devotion to your loved ones, I chose you to serve as my agent in the world during these turbulent times. You are indeed my handmaiden, my steward. You and I draw energy from the same source. With the office comes great authority. Command the fairies in my name, and they will hearken to you.

"The fairies will obey me?" Kendra asked.

If you issue orders in my name, and do not abuse the privilege.

"What is your name?"

Kendra felt a response like melodic laughter. *My* true *name must remain secret. Issuing commands in the name of the queen will suffice.*

Kendra suddenly remembered when the fairy at the mansion where the Knights of the Dawn met had suggested she issue a command in the name of the Queen. "Can the fairies help me destroy the nail?"

No. The fairies lack sufficient power. Only a talisman imbued with tremendous light energy could unmake the dark object.

"Do you know where I can find a talisman full of light?"

Another long pause followed. *I could make one, but such an action would require destroying this shrine.*

Kendra waited. A vision unfolded to her mind. As if gazing down from high above, she beheld the island and the shrine shining in the midst of darkness. The water of the lake had turned black, and teemed with foul, misshapen naiads. The boardwalk and gazebos had crumbled; dark fairies flitted among the rotting debris. Darkened dwarfs, satyrs, and dryads roamed among withered trees and parched fields.

Preserving the shrine is not worth so much devastation. I would rather lose one of my precious points of contact with your world than see my sisters condemned to benighted slavery. I will concentrate the energy protecting this shrine into a single object. After I forge the talisman, my influence will no longer persist here.

"I won't be able to contact you anymore?" Kendra asked.

Not from this place. As soon as the talisman passes beyond the hedge, the pond and the island will be stripped of all defenses.

"What do I do with the talisman?" Kendra asked.

Retain possession of the talisman. The energy inside of you will help keep it stable and fully energized. While in your possession, the talisman will cast an umbrella of energy that will help protect those around you. If you bring the talisman into contact with the dark object, both will be destroyed. Be forewarned. Whoever connects the objects will perish.

Kendra swallowed. Her mouth felt dry. "Do I need to be the person who touches them together?"

Not necessarily. I would prefer that you survive the endeavor. But whether you or another will complete the task, if the light and dark objects can be joined, the sacrifice will be worthwhile. Much that has darkened will be restored.

"Can we fix your shrine afterward?" Kendra asked hopefully.

This shrine will be beyond repair.

"I won't hear from you again?"

Not here.

"I'd have to find another shrine. Could I approach it if I find it?"

Kendra sensed laughter mingled with affection. *You wonder why my shrines are so heavily protected. Having points of contact to your world makes me vulnerable. If evil finds my kingdom, all creatures of light will suffer. For their welfare, I must keep my realm unspoiled, and so I zealously guard my shrines. As a rule, all trespassers must perish. I rarely grant exceptions.*

"Does being fairykind allow me access?" Kendra asked.

Not inherently. If you ever find another shrine, search your feelings for the answer. You have sufficient light to guide you.

"I'm afraid to try to destroy the nail," Kendra confessed. She did not want the conversation with the Fairy Queen to end.

I am reluctant to destroy this shrine. Kendra could feel her deep sadness. The emotion brought tears to her eyes. *Sometimes we do what we must.*

"Okay," Kendra said. "I'll do my best. One last question. If I survive this, what am I supposed to do? As fairykind, I mean."

Live a fruitful life. Resist evil. Give more than you take. Help others do likewise. The rest will take care of itself. Step away from the shrine.

Kendra backed away from the miniature statue on the tiny plinth. Her vision blurred, and a flood of sensations overwhelmed her. She tasted sweet honey, crisp apples, fleshy mushrooms, and pure water. She smelled plowed fields, damp grass, ripe grapes, and pungent herbs. She heard the rush of wind, the crash of waves, the roar of thunder, and the faint crackle of a duckling punching through an eggshell. She felt sunlight warming her skin and a light mist cooling her. Sight was temporarily unavailable, but she simultaneously tasted, smelled, heard, and felt a thousand other sensations, all distinct and unmistakable.

When her vision returned, Kendra found the tiny fairy statue shining intensely. She instinctively squinted and shielded her eyes, worried that the brilliant light might cause lasting damage. When she peeked, the radiance did not inflict any pain. Hoping the brightness was benign, she gazed openly at the statue. By contrast, the rest of the world became dull, drained, dreary. All color, all light, had converged on the thumb-sized figurine.

And then the statue shattered, stone flakes chiming as they dispersed. Upon the small pedestal remained a dazzling, egg-shaped pebble. For an instant, the pebble flashed brighter than the statue had gleamed. Then the light diminished, absorbed into the stone, until the ovoid pebble became rather unremarkable, except for being so white and smooth.

Color returned to the world. The late afternoon sun shone brightly again. Kendra could no longer sense the presence of the Fairy Queen.

Kneeling, she picked up the smooth pebble. It felt ordinary, weighing no more or less than she expected. Although it no longer glowed, she felt certain the pebble was the talisman. How could all the power protecting the shrine fit inside such a small, nondescript object?

Looking around, Kendra saw that Patton had the

rowboat back on the shore. She hurried over to him, worried that the naiads would haul the boat away before she got there.

"No rush," Patton said. "They're under orders."

"Reluctantly," a voice muttered from under the water.

"Hush," a different naiad scolded. "We're not supposed to talk."

"I got a free ride back last time as well," Kendra said, stepping into the boat.

"Good news?" he asked.

"Generally," Kendra said. "I'd better wait until we're back at the tent."

"Fair enough," Patton agreed. "One thing I'll say—that stone shines almost as brightly as you do."

Kendra glanced at the stone. It was flawlessly white and smooth, but did not seem to her to emit any light. She sat down. Patton rested the oars across his lap. Guided by unseen hands, the rowboat coasted away from the island and drifted toward the boathouse. Glancing up, Kendra saw a golden owl with a human face gazing down at her from a high limb, a tear sliding from one eye.

CHAPTER TWENTY-TWO

Light

Seth waited beside Lena in the gazebo above the pier. None of the satyrs, dryads, or dwarfs lingered on the boardwalk or in any of the other pavilions. As Patton had asked, they remained out of sight.

Kendra and Patton reclined in the rowboat, returning placidly toward the boathouse, apparently towed by the same naiads who had recently been attacking them. Seth wished he could have seen what Kendra was doing out on the island, but she spent most of the time screened by bushes. Lena had described a blinding light, but Seth had failed to see it.

"You were awesome at dodging those naiads," Seth said.

"Anything to distract them from drowning my husband," Lena replied. "Part of me will always love my sisters,

[415]

but they can be such pests! I was glad for an excuse to bait them."

"Do you think Kendra succeeded?"

"She must have made contact. Only the queen could have ordered the naiads to conduct them safely back to shore." Lena narrowed her eyes. "Something has changed about the island. I can't quite put my finger on it. After the flash, there is a new feeling permeating this whole area." Lips pursed, Lena thoughtfully watched the rowboat glide into the boathouse.

Seth bounded down the steps to the pier, arriving at the boathouse door as Kendra and Patton exited. "Anything good happen?" Seth asked.

"Pretty good," Kendra said.

"What's with the egg?" Seth inquired.

"It's a pebble," Kendra corrected, closing her fingers around it tightly. "I'll fill you guys in, but we should do it back at the tent."

Patton embraced Lena. "You were wonderful," he said, pecking her on the lips. "However, I don't enjoy seeing you so near those naiads. I can think of few people they would rather drag to the bottom of the pond."

"I can think of few people they would have a harder time catching," Lena responded smugly.

They mounted the stairs to the gazebo and then descended a few steps into the grassy field. Three towering dryads strode briskly toward them, obstructing their route to the tent. In the middle, tallest of the three, walked the dryad Seth had seen consulting with Grandpa and Grandma, her auburn hair flowing past her waist. The dryad to her left looked Native American and wore earthy robes. The dryad on the right was a platinum blonde with a gown like a frozen waterfall. All of the graceful women stood at least a head taller than Patton.

"Hello, Lizette," Patton said amiably to the dryad in the middle.

"Don't 'hello' me, Patton Burgess," she said, scowling down at him, her voice melodious but hard. "What have you done to the shrine?"

"The shrine?" Patton asked, checking quizzically over his shoulder. "Is something amiss?"

"It has been destroyed," the blond dryad announced firmly.

"After you sent us away," the Native American added.

Lizette gazed at Kendra, her eyes narrow. "And your friend is outshining the sun."

"I hope you aren't insinuating that we overthrew the monument!" Patton objected scornfully. "Not only do we lack the desire—we lack the means! The Fairy Queen dismantled the shrine for reasons of her own."

"You realize the preserve has permanently lost contact with her highness," Lizette said. "We find this unacceptable." She and the other two leaned forward menacingly.

"Less acceptable than Fablehaven and all who dwell here descending into irredeemable darkness?" Patton asked.

The dryads relaxed slightly.

"Do you have a plan?" Lizette asked.

"Has Kendra ever gleamed any brighter?" Patton

exclaimed. "Her glow is a token of good things to come. Lend us a few minutes to confer in private, and we will announce our plot to reclaim Fablehaven, a strategy formulated by the Fairy Queen herself." Patton glanced at Kendra as if hoping his words were true. Kendra gave a slight nod.

"There had best be a satisfactory explanation for this desecration," Lizette threatened darkly. "This day will be mourned until the end of leaf and stream."

Reaching up, Patton patted Lizette on the shoulder. "Losing the shrine is a grievous blow to all who love light. We will avenge this tragedy."

Lizette stepped aside, and Patton led the others between the somber dryads. Although temporarily appeased, the towering women clearly remained unsatisfied.

When Seth, Kendra, and Lena reached the tent, Patton followed the others inside, dropping the flap to cover the opening.

"What happened?" Seth asked.

"The Fairy Queen destroyed the shrine in order to make this." Kendra held up the pebble.

Patton squinted. "No wonder you have been gleaming so much brighter."

"I don't see any light," Seth complained.

"Only some eyes can see it," Lena said, eyes narrowed.

"Why can't I?" Kendra asked. "The pebble only looked bright while the Fairy Queen was making it."

"The light of the stone must have united with your inner light," Patton said. "Your own light can be difficult to distinguish. I imagine you can see in the dark."

"I can," Kendra said.

"Whether or not you recognize it, Kendra, you carry much light within you," Patton said. "With the stone, your radiance has grown even more brilliant. To those who can perceive such light, you glare like a beacon."

Kendra curled her fingers around the stone. "The Fairy Queen filled the stone with all of the power protecting the shrine. When I remove the stone from this area, dark creatures will be able to enter. If we touch the pebble to the nail in the tree, the objects will destroy each other."

"All right!" Seth exclaimed.

"There's a catch," Kendra said. "The Fairy Queen said that whoever connects the objects will die."

"Not a problem." Patton dismissed the concern with a wave of one hand. "I will personally resolve this dilemma."

"No you won't," Lena said anxiously. "You have to return to me. Your life can't end here."

"What we shared already happened," Patton said. "Nothing I do here can change that."

"Don't you try to con me, Patton Burgess," Lena growled. "I've put up with your pacifications for decades. I know you better than you know yourself. You're always stretching for an excuse to protect others at your expense—partly out of a noble sense of duty, mostly for the thrill. You're well aware that if you fail to return to the past, you may wipe out the majority of our relationship. My whole history could change. I refuse to lose our life together."

Patton looked guilty. "There are many uncertainties with time travel. To my knowledge, the Chronometer is the only successful time travel device ever created. Most practicalities remain untested. Keep in mind, in your past, I returned after I traveled through time. Some would argue that nothing I do now can possibly contradict that reality. If I die during my visit here, somewhere else, along some alternate timeline, there might be a Lena I won't see again. But your history is secure. Regardless of what happens to me, you will very likely persist here as if nothing in your past has changed."

"Sounds like a flimsy theory," Lena refuted. "If you're wrong, and you fail to return, you could completely alter history. You have to go back. You have important duties to perform. Not only for my sake, for the good of countless others. Patton, I've lived a full life. If any of us must expire, it should be me. I could move on with no complaints. Seeing you again is the perfect culmination of my mortality." She gazed at Patton with such undisguised adoration that Seth averted his eyes.

"Why does anybody have to die?" Seth asked. "Why not throw the stone at the nail? Then nobody would actually connect the objects."

"We could try," Patton said. "It introduces an additional element of risk. Merely getting close enough to the tree will be a challenge."

"I could do it," Seth said.

Lena rolled her eyes. "As candidates for uniting the talismans, you and Kendra are out of the question."

"Am I?" Seth asked. "What if we get there and everyone but me ends up paralyzed by fear?"

"Ephira may not be able to radiate magical fear as readily as she could inside of her lair," Patton said. "She may not even be able to reach Kurisock's domain. Besides, as a dragon tamer, I'm fairly resistant to magical fear."

"You froze back at the house," Seth reminded him.

Tilting his head, Patton gave half a nod. "If needed, you can hold my hand and get me close, then I'll take the stone the rest of the way."

"I'm supposed to hold the pebble as long as I can, to keep it stable and fully charged," Kendra said. "Maybe I should do it."

"No, kids," Patton emphasized. "My newest goal is to go my entire life without any children sacrificing themselves on my behalf."

"As part of being fairykind, I can command fairies," Kendra said. "Is there something they could do?"

"Since when can you command fairies?" Seth blurted.

"I just found out," Kendra said.

"Then have a fairy connect the pebble and the nail!" Seth said enthusiastically. "The fairies have always hated me. Maybe you could have all of them destroy the nail together!"

"Seth!" Kendra exclaimed chidingly. "That isn't funny!"

"Forcing a fairy to undertake a suicide mission could have serious repercussions," Patton cautioned. "I don't like it."

"I love it!" Seth reaffirmed, grinning.

"Maybe I could ask for volunteers," Kendra suggested. "You know, so it won't be me compelling anyone."

"This line of thinking is futile," Lena said. "No creatures of light will be able to enter Kurisock's domain."

Kendra held up the egg-shaped pebble. "The Fairy Queen said that as long as I hold the stone, an umbrella of light will help protect those near me."

"Now, that is useful information," Patton mused. "If the power that keeps this area a sanctuary of light were to enter a stronghold of darkness, the influx of positive energy might allow light creatures to enter."

"Let's recruit some fairies," Seth said, clapping his hands together eagerly. "Better them than us."

"We can try the fairies as a backup," Patton replied. "But be forewarned—fairies are notoriously unreliable. And we should leave intentionally compelling a fairy to die on our behalf out of the question. I am more excited that we might be able to cajole some more responsible allies into joining us and helping us win through to the tree."

"If all else fails, I'll finish the task," Lena vowed. "I'm young, I'm agile, I'm strong. I can do it."

Patton crossed his arms. "Permit me to revise my latest goal—I also want to go my whole life without my wife dying on my behalf. If a fairy fails to voluntarily destroy the talismans, I'll throw the stone. I have excellent aim. Then nobody will be touching the objects when they connect."

"And if you miss?" Lena asked.

"We'll worry about that if it happens."

"Which is Pattonese for you will unite the objects yourself," Lena huffed.

Patton shrugged innocently.

"Have you ever considered that you might be worth more to the world alive than dead?" Lena groused.

"If I were going to die doing something dangerous, it would have happened a long time ago."

Lena swatted at him. "I hope I'm not there the day all your cocky words return to humble you."

"You'll be there," Patton said, "scoffing and pointing."

"Not if you're in a coffin," Lena grumbled.

"When should we do this?" Seth asked.

"Daylight is failing," Patton said. "We'll want the sun with us when we embark on this murky venture. I recommend we sally forth in the morning, with as many companions as will join us."

"And I get to come, right?" Seth confirmed.

"We can't leave you behind unprotected from dark influences," Patton said. "This final gamble is all or nothing. Whether we triumph or fail, we will do it together, pooling our talents and resources."

"Speaking of talents," Lena said, "Seth had better get to the gap in the hedge, so he can see if any shadow people come to us with information."

Only then did Seth notice how much the glow of the yellow and purple tent walls had reddened with the setting sun. "I'll go right now," he said.

"I'll join you," Kendra offered.

"Lena and I will go rally support among the other citizens of Fablehaven," Patton said. "Our story will be that the Fairy Queen has given us the power to attack Kurisock and reverse the plague. We do not want to be any more specific, in case the information reaches unfriendly ears."

"Got it," Seth said, stepping out of the tent. The others followed. While Patton was mobbed by satyrs, dryads, dwarfs, and fairies, Kendra and Seth slipped through the crowd and headed for the main entrance. A few fairies flitted along behind Kendra, as if hoping to approach her, but when Patton began explaining the situation, they zipped away in his direction.

When Kendra and Seth reached the opening in the hedge, the dark satyrs stationed there backed away a good distance, a couple of them bleating angrily. They squinted at Kendra, fuzzy hands raised to shield their feral eyes.

"Looks like you're blinding the freaky satyrs," Seth said. "Do you think your rock will keep Grandma and Grandpa away?"

"Maybe my shininess will help them find us," Kendra said.

Seth plopped down in the grass. The sun hung just above the treetops west of the field. "They'll be able to come soon."

"Who do you think will show up?"

"Hopefully all six of them."

Kendra nodded. "Too bad I won't be able to see them."

"Well, I guess one person can't have every single magical ability the universe has to offer. You aren't missing much. You can't really recognize them except by their outlines."

Seth started plucking at the tiny blue flowers in the grass. Kendra sat with her knees scrunched up to her chest, hugging her folded legs. Shadows crept across the field until the sun went down and twilight engulfed the clearing.

Kendra appeared content with silence, and Seth could not muster the effort to spark a conversation. He stared through the gap in the hedge, hoping to see a familiar shadow join the dark satyrs lurking beyond the opening. As the vivid sunset dimmed, the temperature faded from hot to warm.

Finally a single black form emerged from among the restless satyrs. The silhouette plodded toward the gap in the hedge as if resisting a mighty wind. Seth sat up. "Here we go."

"Who do you see?" Kendra asked.

"He's short and thin. Might be Coulter." Seth raised his voice. "That you, Coulter?"

With apparent effort, the figure raised a hand to display the missing fingers. He kept trudging forward, each step seeming to demand greater effort than the last.

"He's struggling," Seth said. "Must be your light."

"Should I back away?"

"Maybe."

Kendra rose and walked away from the gap in the hedge.

"Wait!" Seth cried. "He's waving his arms. He's motioning for you to come back. No, not just back, he wants you to come toward him."

"What if it isn't Coulter?" Kendra worried.

"He can't pass through the gap," Seth said. "Just don't get within grabbing distance."

Seth and Kendra walked toward the gap, stopping two

paces from the entrance. Coulter hunched forward, trembling with the effort of each arduous step, but managed to keep his feet moving.

"Where is he?" Kendra asked.

"Almost to the gap," Seth said. "He looks like he's about to pass out."

Coulter slogged forward another few steps. Pausing, he leaned forward, bracing one hand against his thigh. Quivering, he strained to lift the other arm, but failed to hoist it very high.

"He's reaching for us," Seth said. "Step a little closer."

"I can't let him touch me!" Kendra exclaimed.

"Just a step," Seth said. "I think he's come as far as he can."

"Why don't I back away?"

"He wants you near him."

Kendra took a cautious half-step forward, and suddenly Seth glimpsed flesh flickering beneath the shadow.

"I see him!" Kendra shrieked, lifting her hands to her lips. "Part of him, anyway, faintly."

"Me too," Seth said. "I've never seen any of the shadow people do that. I think you might be healing him. Yes! He's nodding. Get closer!"

"What if he contaminates me?"

"Just a little closer. He still won't be able to reach you."

"What if he's faking how far he can reach?"

"He fell to his knees!" Seth cried.

"I can see," Kendra said, taking another half-step toward the gap in the hedge. Coulter flashed into clearer view, slumped forward, both hands buttressed against his thighs. His face looked anguished, contorted by tremendous effort. He tried to keep his head up, but it was slowly bowing.

"Help him!" Seth yelped.

Kendra stepped into the gap between the hedges and seized Coulter's shoulder. Instantly he came into full view and flopped through the gap in the hedge to lie panting on the path.

"Coulter!" Seth exclaimed. "You're back!"

"Barely," he wheezed, face ruddy from the recent exertion. "Just barely. Give me . . . a minute."

"We're so happy you're alive!" Kendra gushed, tears blurring her vision.

"We should . . . stay back . . . from the entrance," he gasped, crawling away from the gap in the hedge.

"A pair of satyrs just took off running," Seth reported.

"They'll want to . . . spread the word . . . that Kendra can overcome the darkness," Coulter panted. He sat up, taking deep breaths. Gradually he appeared to relax.

"Did you see my light?" Kendra asked.

Coulter chuckled. "Did I see it? I was scalded by your light, Kendra, blinded by it. I thought it might consume me. It scorched me differently than sunlight. Sunlight only inflicted pain. Cold pain. Your light beckoned as well as burned. It gave me warmth along with the pain, the first warmth I've felt since the shadow fairies transformed me. I could feel the darkness that possessed me cringing away from your light, and that gave me hope. I thought if I could just get close enough to your light, I would either perish or be cleansed. Either way, my frigid existence would end."

"What was it like as a shadow?" Seth asked.

Coulter shivered. "Colder than I could ever describe. A normal human body would go numb long before it could experience the cold I felt. Sunlight intensified the cold into agony. As a shadow, it was tough to focus. My emotions became confused. I felt desolate. Utterly empty. My mind wanted to shut down. I was constantly tempted to collapse and wallow in my emptiness. But I knew I had to fight those inclinations. Tanu helped me keep my mind whole after he was changed."

"Where is Tanu?" Kendra asked. "And what about the others? Have you seen Grandma or Grandpa?"

Coulter shook his head. "Gone, all of them. I met up with Warren and Dale briefly. As fellow shades, we could communicate, more like telepathy than speaking. They warned me she was after them, that she had already taken Stan and Ruth away. We split up, with plans to reunite at a rendezvous. None of the others ever arrived. I came here, hoping to warn you what had happened to the others. You were shining, I approached, and here we are."

"What did Ephira do to them?" Kendra asked.

"Is that her name?" Coulter asked. "Warren and Dale suspected she was imprisoning them somewhere. Stashing them away. Hard to say for sure. Tell me, Kendra, why you were shining so brightly."

"I'm not shining anymore?" she asked.

Coulter scrutinized her. "I expect you are, but not to my eyes."

She eyed the dark satyrs, who had retreated even farther from the gap in the hedge. "We'll give you all the details later, in a place where we won't be overheard. The Fairy Queen gave me a gift full of light energy." She lowered her voice to a whisper. "It might help us stop the plague."

"It certainly cured me," Coulter said. "Hurt plenty, though. I expect it will rank right up there with my least favorite memories." He stretched his arms. "I guess it's up to the three of us to rescue the others."

"We also have Patton Burgess helping us," Seth said.

Coulter snickered. "Right, and I expect Paul Bunyan will also be lending a hand. We should check if Pecos Bill is available."

"He's serious," Kendra confirmed. "Patton came forward through time. He's here. When Lena saw him, she abandoned the pond again, so we have her too."

Coulter failed to resist a broad grin. "You're pulling my leg."

"Would we kid around during such a dangerous time?" Seth asked.

"I was raised on stories about Patton Burgess," Coulter said, eagerness entering his voice. "I've always dreamed of meeting him. He died not long before I was born."

"I don't think you'll be disappointed," Seth assured him.

"Can you walk?" Kendra asked. "We could bring him here."

Grunting, Coulter tottered to his feet. Seth steadied him

as he swayed. "Now, don't start coddling me," Coulter griped. "I just need half a second to get my bearings."

Coulter started walking toward the tent, his measured steps a bit wobbly. Seth stayed near him, ready to catch the older man if he stumbled. Coulter's paces grew more confident, and his posture became more natural.

"Here they come," Kendra said, pointing across the field. Holding hands, Patton and Lena were swiftly approaching.

"What do you know," Coulter murmured. "Who could have guessed I would meet Patton Burgess in the flesh?"

"You found a friend," Patton called to Kendra and Seth.

"Coulter!" Lena cried. "It has been far too long!" She danced forward and took his hands, sizing him up.

"You look young," Coulter marveled.

"Patton Burgess," Patton said, extending a hand. In a daze, Coulter gripped the hand and shook it.

"Coulter Dixon," Coulter managed, his mannerisms unabashedly starstruck.

"I take it you were a shadow?" Patton asked.

"I staggered as close as I could to the space between the hedges, drawn by Kendra's light. When she reached out and touched me, her radiance purged the darkness from me."

Patton assessed Kendra. "I suppose a risk that paid off was a risk worth taking. Then again, had you become infected yourself, we could have been finished before we began."

"How did it go with the others?" Seth asked.

"We can expect considerable assistance tomorrow," Patton forecasted. "You willing to join us, Coulter?"

"Absolutely," he said, nervously running a hand over his mostly bald pate, smoothing down the wispy tuft of hair in the middle. "I'm relieved you're here."

"Glad if I can help," Patton said, "but our hope resides in Kendra. We should adjourn to the tent so we can fill you in on the details. Tomorrow we will decide the fate of Fablehaven."

Darkness

The morning was already hot when Kendra awoke alone in her tent. She felt bleary, having slept late. Patton and Lena had spent the night in the big tent, Seth and Coulter in the other. Lying on her back with a sleeping bag tangled around her legs, Kendra felt sticky with sweat. How had she remained asleep when her tent was this stifling?

The egg-shaped pebble remained in her palm, held the same way as when she had fallen asleep. She fingered the smooth stone, which gave off no heat or light that she could perceive, but had empowered her to restore Coulter from his shadowy state with a brief touch. Would her touch retrieve any creature from the darkened state? The others seemed optimistic.

The task awaiting Kendra made her wish she could

return to her dreamless slumber. If the Fairy Queen was right, whoever connected the light pebble with the dark nail would die today. She hoped that Seth and Patton had found a loophole, that throwing the stone or some similar trick would resolve the problem without a fatality. But if all other attempts failed, if nobody else could accomplish the feat, Kendra wondered whether she would have the courage to sacrifice herself. Losing her life would be worth it to save her friends and family. She hoped she would be brave enough to take the necessary action if the decisive moment arrived.

Slipping the pebble into her pocket, Kendra pulled on her shoes and tied them. She crawled to the door of her tent, unzipped it, and stepped outside. The fresh air, though hot, was a relief after the stale confines of the tent. Kendra tried her best to blindly arrange her hair with her finger-tips. Sleeping in her clothes had left her feeling in desperate need of a shower.

"She's up!" Seth hollered, jogging toward her, wearing the backpack with the Chronometer. "Looks like we can do it today after all."

"Why didn't you wake me?" Kendra accused.

"Patton wouldn't let us," Seth said. "He wanted you rested. We're all ready."

Turning, Kendra beheld an impressive crowd of satyrs, dryads, dwarfs, and fairies occupying the field between the tents and the gap in the hedge wall. They were all staring at her. Her eyes swept across the gathering. She was keenly aware that she had just emerged from a hot tent dressed in the same clothes she had worn yesterday.

Hugo approached from a distance pulling the cart, flanked by Cloudwing and Broadhoof. Patton, Lena, and Coulter rode in the cart.

"Where did Hugo get the cart?" Kendra asked.

"Patton sent him to retrieve it at dawn," Seth replied.

"The centaurs are joining us?" she asked.

"Almost all of the creatures are coming," Seth enthused. "For one thing, Patton told them how the defenses protecting this area will collapse after we pass beyond the hedge. For another, they all respect him, even Broadhoof."

"Good morning, Kendra," Patton boomed joyfully as Hugo came to a stop near the kids. He looked dashing standing with one foot on the side of the cart. Had his clothes been laundered and mended? "Are you rested and ready for our outing?"

Kendra and Seth walked around Hugo to the side of the cart. "I guess so," she said.

"I found a trio of volunteers willing to help us join the talismans should the need arise," Patton said, gesturing at three fairies hovering nearby.

Kendra recognized Shiara with her blue hair and silver wings. She also recognized the slender albino fairy with black eyes who had helped carry her into battle against Bahumat. The third was tiny even for a fairy, with fiery wings shaped like flower petals.

"Greetings, Kendra," Shiara said. "We are willing to give all we have to carry out the final wish our Queen imparted through this hallowed shrine."

"We'll be holding you in reserve," Patton reminded

them. "You three must remain hidden throughout the battle. We won't ask for your assistance unless it becomes absolutely necessary."

"We will not fail our Queen," squeaked the red fairy in the tiniest voice Kendra had ever heard.

Patton jumped down from the cart. "Hungry?" he asked, holding out a napkin piled with nuts and berries.

"I don't have much appetite," Kendra admitted.

"You'd better eat something," Coulter encouraged. "You'll need your energy."

"Okay," Kendra relented.

Patton handed her the napkin. "You know, if sufficiently motivated, the fairies could outfit Hugo for battle."

Kendra chewed on a crunchy mouthful of nuts and berries. The nuts tasted bitter. "You sure these are safe to eat?"

"They're nutritious," Patton assured her. "I asked the fairies to assist with equipping Hugo, but most were unwilling."

"I offered to help," chirped the albino fairy.

"We need you three to save your strength. Kendra, the majority of the other fairies would need to participate in order to get the golem soundly outfitted."

"You want me to issue a command?" Kendra asked around a second unpleasant mouthful.

Patton cocked his head and touched his mustache. "The effort will tire them, but having Hugo in top form would be very useful."

Kendra spit out the nuts she had been chewing. "I'm sorry, these are making me gag. Do you have any water?"

Lena tossed a canteen to Patton from the cart. He unstopped it and passed it to Kendra. She guzzled several swallows. The warm water had a metallic tang. She wiped her lips with her sleeve.

"Well?" Seth asked, glancing over at Hugo.

Would the fairies really respond to her demand? She supposed there was only one way to find out. "This command does not apply to you three," Kendra told the reliable trio of fairies hovering nearby.

"Understood," Shiara responded.

"Fairies of Fablehaven," Kendra called out, using her best authoritative voice. "For the good of the preserve, and in the name of your Queen, I command you to outfit Hugo the golem for battle."

Fairies streaked toward them from all directions. They swirled around Hugo, forming a scintillating, multicolored tornado. Some fairies flew clockwise, others counterclockwise, weaving past each other without colliding. Vivid bursts of light began zapping the golem. Scores of fairies detached from the twirling vortex to form wider rings. While some fairies continued to frantically orbit the golem, the stationary halos of hovering fairies twittered in dozens of overlapping melodies.

The ground rumbled. Jagged stones erupted through the turf at Hugo's feet. The golem staggered as the earth beneath him began to churn. Ropelike vines snaked up his body.

Upturned soil flowed up his sturdy legs and Hugo swelled, becoming broader and thicker and taller.

The whirling column of fairies began to disperse and the chanting diminished. Numerous fairies fluttered slowly to the ground, clearly spent. The patch of soil where Hugo stood grew more stable.

Hugo let out a fearsome roar. He had grown a few feet taller, and considerably more massive. Brown vines with long thorns crisscrossed his torso and limbs. Rocks shaped like spearheads jutted from his shoulders, legs, and arms. Serrated plates of stone projected from his back. A group of fairies presented the golem with an enormous club made from a sturdy length of wood and a boulder the size of an anvil.

After delivering the club, more exhausted fairies spiraled to the ground. The fairies who retained sufficient vigor to fly coasted about languidly. A few of the earthbound fairies lapsed into unconsciousness.

"How do you feel, Hugo?" Seth yelled.

The golem's gravelly mouth formed a gaping grin. "Big." His voice sounded deeper and rougher than ever.

"All fairies who wish to move out with us should pile in the wagon," Patton called. "I encourage those capable of movement to assist those who have fainted." Removing a small ivory box from a pocket, he beckoned Shiara and the other two emergency fairies. "You three belong in here." The fairies compliantly flitted into the box.

Lena hopped down lightly from the wagon and began gently scooping up unconscious fairies. Coulter, Patton, and

Seth assisted as well. Many fairies alighted on the wagon under their own power.

At first, Kendra watched the others in silence. At her behest, the fairies had expended their energy until they were exhausted. Their weakened state could lead to hundreds of them being converted into dark fairies in the upcoming conflict, and yet none had resisted the order. The power to compel others to obey her commands was sobering, even frightening.

Kendra knelt and began gathering fallen fairies, carefully arranging the limp, fragile bodies on her palm. The handful of unconscious fairies seemed almost weightless. Their translucent wings felt sticky against her skin, like gummy scraps of tissue paper. The fairies in her hand began to glow brightly, although none awakened. Placing the delicate bodies in the cart illustrated why she would have to be very careful with her new ability. She did not want to inadvertently harm these tiny, beautiful creatures.

Patton climbed onto the cart and waved his arms. Movement in the field ceased as all eyes regarded him. "As you know, I supervised this preserve for decades," he began in a strong voice. "I have a profound love for Fablehaven and for all of the creatures who dwell here. The threat we now face is unlike any I have experienced. Fablehaven has never been closer to obliteration. Today we march on a stronghold of darkness. Some of us may not be able to enter, but I will be forever grateful to all who were willing to try. If you can help us win through to the tree beside the lake of tar, we will bring an end to the shadow plague. Shall we get under way?"

A resounding cheer answered his inquiry. Kendra watched as satyrs waved clubs, dryads brandished staffs, and dwarfs shook war hammers. The centaurs reared majestically, Broadhoof holding his sword aloft, Cloudwing shaking his tremendous bow. It was an impressive sight, until Kendra remembered that all those allies could be changed into enemies with a bite.

"Ready, Kendra?" Patton asked, reaching down for her.

Kendra realized that Seth, Lena, and Coulter had already joined Patton in the cart. The exhausted fairies were safely stowed. It was time to move out.

"I think so," Kendra said, accepting his hand. He swung her up easily.

"Hugo," Patton said, "protecting us as needed, please deliver us to the tree beside the lake of tar at the heart of Kurisock's domain. Move swiftly, but do not outdistance those who have elected to accompany us unless I issue a special command."

At his new height, Hugo had to hunch awkwardly in order to pull the cart without tilting the front too high. As the cart wheeled forward, Kendra stared at the golem's jutting stones and prickly thorns. It looked like Hugo had joined a biker gang.

Satyrs, dwarfs, and dryads parted to let the cart pass, and then fell into step alongside and behind. As the cart approached the gap in the hedge, the dark satyrs stationed there fell back. When the cart passed beyond the hedge,

Kendra discerned no particular sensation. She glanced back; the pond and the gazebos looked no different.

The dark satyrs fled before them, scattering into the forest. Hugo turned down the road toward the hill where the Forgotten Chapel once stood. Hamadryads skipped alongside the cart, a few of them holding hands with satyrs. The tall dryads paralleled them at a greater distance, gliding through the trees, unhindered by the undergrowth. The two centaurs made their way through the woods as well, out of sight most of the time. The dwarfs jogged behind the cart, moving without grace and breathing hard, but never lagging.

"I can see your light around us like a dome," Patton remarked to Kendra.

"I can't see it," Kendra replied.

"It didn't take shape until we passed beyond the hedge," Lena said. "Then it became distinct, a bright hemisphere with us at the center."

"Is it covering everyone?" Kendra wondered.

"The dome reaches a fair distance beyond the farthest dryads," Patton said. "I will be interested to see how effectively it repels our foes." He pointed down the road.

Up ahead, a group of enemies awaited in an undisguised trap. Logs and brambles had been stacked across the road to form an impressive barricade. At either side of the barrier crouched dark dwarfs and evil satyrs. Kendra spotted two tall women with dull gray skin and white hair peering over the top of the blockade. The dark dryads had hard, lovely features and sunken eyes. Above the barrier fluttered shadowy fairies.

Hugo strode forward, neither hurrying nor slowing. Kendra squeezed the stone in her fist. The satyrs and hamadryads held firm at either side of the cart, and the dryads whispered through the woods beyond the path. The dwarfs clomped noisily at the rear.

When the cart came within seventy yards of the barricade, the dark dryads shielded their eyes. At sixty yards, the dark dryads, sinister satyrs, and creepy dwarfs began to fall back. The dark fairies dispersed. By the time the cart was within fifty yards of the barricade, the darkened creatures were in full retreat, most of them abandoning the path to take flight through the woods.

The hamadryads, satyrs, and dwarfs surrounding the cart gave a victorious shout.

"Hugo, clear the path," Patton ordered.

Setting his club aside, the golem released the cart and began fluidly hurling logs and boulders out of the road. The heavy objects thumped heavily as they crashed into the woods.

"It appears our protection is sound," Patton told Kendra. "Your luminance did not even need to touch them. I wonder what would have happened had the light overtaken them."

Hugo finished clearing the path and started pulling the cart again without any prodding from Patton. They passed the site where the Forgotten Chapel once stood and soon journeyed down paths Kendra did not know. They encountered two unmanned barriers but saw no further signs of any dark creatures. Evidently word had spread.

They traversed an unfamiliar bridge and advanced along a path barely wide enough to accommodate the cart. Kendra had never traveled so far from the main house at Fablehaven. The satyrs and hamadryads remained merry as they jogged alongside the cart. Only the sweaty dwarfs huffing and puffing at the rear seemed tired.

"I see a black wall," Seth announced as they topped a gentle rise in the road. "Everything beyond it looks dim."

"Where?" Patton asked, brow furrowed.

"Up ahead, near that tall stump."

Patton scratched his mustache. "That is where Kurisock's realm begins, but I cannot discern the darkness."

"Me neither," Coulter said.

"I see only that the trees beyond the stump have less vigor," Lena said.

Seth grinned proudly. "It looks like a wall made of shadow."

"This will be the test," Patton said. "My hope is that all who stay near us will be able to cross this border. If not, the five of us will proceed on foot."

Broadhoof and Cloudwing trotted over to the cart. Cloudwing held an arrow nocked; Broadhoof gripped his sword. Kendra noticed that one of Broadhoof's fingers on his free hand was discolored and swollen. "We have reached the fell province," Cloudwing confirmed.

"If we are unable to enter, we will harass the enemies and attempt to draw some away," Broadhoof declared.

Patton raised his voice. "Stay near the cart. If any are unable to pass into this dark realm, Broadhoof will escort you to the final refuge at Fablehaven, a sanctuary frequented by his kind. If we manage to penetrate the darkness, stay near us, and protect the children at all costs."

Hugo had not paused during the exchange. The huge stump beside the path was drawing closer. All the creatures, dryads included, huddled near to the cart.

"The wall is falling back," Seth announced.

"The light ahead is fading," Patton reported a moment later.

"The light and dark seem to be canceling each other, creating neutral territory," Lena guessed. "Make ready for trouble."

Hugo never paused as he plodded past the stump. All of the other creatures remained with them.

"I never imagined my hooves would tread this profane ground," Cloudwing murmured disdainfully.

"I don't see our dome anymore," Patton warned in a low voice. "Only a glimmer around Kendra."

"The darkness is holding back in a wide circle around us," Seth said.

Kendra observed no abnormal light or darkness, only the path winding ahead into a thick stand of trees. From the trees emerged a grotesque centaur. His fur was black, his skin maroon. In one hand he clutched a heavy mace. A bushy mane went from the top of his head down the center of his broad back. He stood considerably taller than Broadhoof or Cloudwing.

"Intruders, beware," the dark centaur called in a deep snarl. "Turn back now or face destruction."

A bowstring thrummed as Cloudwing let an arrow fly. The dark centaur shifted his mace, deflecting the slender projectile.

"You are a traitor to our kind, Stormbrow," Broadhoof accused. "Stand down."

The dark centaur bared his grimy teeth. "Hand over the girl and depart in peace."

Cloudwing pulled a second arrow. As he adjusted his aim, the dark centaur altered the position of his mace. "I have no shot," Cloudwing muttered.

"Requesting permission to engage," Broadhoof growled with a sidelong glance at Patton.

"Forward!" Patton roared, pulling out a sword. Kendra recognized it as the sword Warren had recovered from the vault at Lost Mesa. Warren must have brought the weapon when they had gathered the tents. "Charge!"

The cart lurched as Hugo rushed toward the centaur. Kendra grabbed the railing at the side of the cart to avoid toppling backward and dropped her eyes to avoid stepping on unconscious fairies as she shifted her position. She heard the centaurs' hooves pounding. Looking up, she saw the dark centaur twirling his mace above his head, the muscles of his maroon arm bunching powerfully.

From the trees emerged a second dark centaur, not quite as large as the first. Behind the centaur came four dark dryads, several dark satyrs, and two dozen minotaurs. Most of the minotaurs looked shaggy and disheveled. A few had broken horns. Some were black, some red-brown, some gray, a few almost blond. Looming over all the other creatures strode three titanic men dressed in mucky furs. They had long, bedraggled hair and thick beards tangled in tar. Even at his new height, Hugo barely came to their waists.

"Fog giants!" Seth cried.

"Keep us away from the giants, Hugo," Patton instructed.

The cart veered away from the colossal threesome. Broadhoof and Stormbrow charged one another at full gallop. The giants hustled to intercept the cart. Satyrs, hamadryads, and dryads closed on the dark satyrs, dark dryads, and minotaurs. The winded dwarfs ran along behind, struggling to keep up.

Broadhoof and Stormbrow were the first combatants to meet. Stormbrow used his mace to deflect Broadhoof's sword, and the centaurs collided, tumbling wildly to the earth. An arrow from Cloudwing pierced the arm of the other dark centaur. Twirling their staffs, the dryads fell upon the minotaurs, gracefully whirling and leaping and dodging, landing fierce blows at will, effortlessly outclassing the shaggy brutes. But when the dark dryads joined the fray, two light dryads were quickly bitten and transformed, forcing the other light dryads to drop back and regroup.

As the fog giants came at them with enormous strides, it became clear that Hugo had no hope of avoiding them. "Engage the giants, Hugo!" Patton ordered.

Moving in loping leaps, Hugo released the cart and charged the giants, huge club raised high. The lead giant swung a cudgel at Hugo, who ducked the blow and bashed the giant on the kneecap. Howling, the giant crashed to the ground. The other two giants swerved away from Hugo. The golem dove at one of the giants, but, fervent eyes intent on Kendra, the giant smoothly hurdled him.

Lizette, tallest of the dryads, dashed alongside one of the giants, her head not much higher than his knee, jabbing at his shin with her wooden rod. Infuriated by the needling, the giant turned and began stomping at her. Narrowly avoiding each increasingly frustrated stamp, she baited the oaf away from the cart.

Patton, Lena, and Coulter jumped down from the cart as it coasted to a stop, looking tiny as they faced the final oncoming giant. The tremendous brute kicked at Patton, who spun to one side, barely avoiding the blow. The giant reached to grab him, but Patton sliced open his palm.

"Patton!" Lena called, having maneuvered behind the giant.

Patton tossed the sword to his wife. She caught it by the hilt and slashed the back of the giant's heel. He crumpled, clutching where his tendon had been severed.

Wearing a savage grimace, the giant Hugo had toppled scooted forward. Hugo returned and hobbled him with a pair of precise blows.

The giant stomping at Lizette noticed his fallen comrades, and then locked eyes with Kendra. Scowling, he abandoned Lizette and charged the cart. Hugo flung his oversized club, and the anvil-sized stone struck the giant in the back of the skull. The giant dove forward, his outspread arms landing a few feet shy of the cart. He briefly raised his head, eyes unfocused, and then his face drooped to the dirt.

Roaring, the giant Lena had slashed sat up, struggled forward, and kicked the cart, splitting it and flipping it over. Kendra went flying, the pebble still gripped in her hand. She landed sharply on her back, suddenly finding that she could get no breath into her lungs. Her mouth hung open, the muscles in her torso tensing repeatedly. No air would enter or exit. Panic overwhelmed her. Was her back broken? Was she paralyzed?

Finally, after a desperate gasp, she was breathing again. Kendra noticed fairies fluttering weakly around her, searching for a refuge besides the overturned cart. Hugo had caught up to the giant Lena had slashed. The giant punched the unarmed golem, sending Hugo tumbling, then growled, squinting at where sharp rocks and thorns had maimed his knuckles.

Seth knelt at Kendra's side. "You all right?"

She nodded. "I just had the wind knocked out of me."

Rising, Seth dragged his sister to her feet. "Do you still have it?"

"Yes."

Peering over Kendra's shoulder, Seth's eyes widened. "Here come reinforcements!"

Kendra whirled. Six dark dryads raced toward them from a different direction than the other dark creatures had come from. Above them soared a menacing swarm of shadowy fairies.

Kendra peered over her shoulder. Patton, Lena, and Coulter were contending with a quintet of minotaurs. Cloudwing was wrestling a dark centaur that had to be an altered version of Broadhoof. Stormbrow and the injured dark centaur were wreaking havoc among the satyrs and hamadryads, transforming them into creatures of darkness. Despite his injuries, the giant Lena had hamstrung continued to fend off Hugo.

With a meaningful glance, Seth and Kendra communicated what they both realized. Nobody was coming to help them.

The six dark dryads approached at superhuman speed, low and swift like jungle cats. Beams of blackness rained down from the oncoming dark fairies. The shadowy streaks did not affect Kendra, but Seth yelped as they struck him, darkening his clothes and turning his flesh invisible wherever they struck. Some light fairies feebly rose to intercept the dark ones, but most were swiftly transformed.

"Run, Kendra," Seth urged, an invisible patch spreading across the side of his jaw.

"Not this time," Kendra said. The dark dryads were too quick for her to have any hope of escape.

The dark dryads closed in fast, reddened eyes glinting, thin lips parted to reveal hideous fangs. A dark dryad snatched Seth, hoisting him into the air with a single arm and plunging her teeth into his neck. He thrashed, but the gray dryad held him firmly, and a moment later he was invisible.

The six dryads formed a ring around Kendra, seeming somewhat hesitant to engage her. Kendra held up the pebble threateningly. Wincing, they fell back a couple of paces. Face scrunched into a mask of determination, one of the dark dryads sprang forward, grasping at Kendra. As soon as her gray fingers closed around Kendra's wrist, her entire aspect transformed. Pale, lank hair became curly and dark. Gray flesh bloomed to full health. Looking startled, a tall, beautiful woman staggered away from Kendra, turning to face the dark dryads.

Kendra lunged at another dark dryad, swatting her surprised target on the arm as the dryad stumbled uncertainly backward. Instantly the dryad had fiery red hair, a creamy countenance, and flowing robes. The gorgeous dryad Kendra had first restored tackled a dark dryad, pinning her to the ground. Kendra raced over and patted the dark dryad on the cheek. Suddenly the dark dryad became a tall Asian woman.

Invisible fingers closed around Kendra's wrist, and Seth reappeared. "I could have done that faster if you would hold still," he panted, looking unsteady.

"No time," Kendra said, charging after a fourth dark dryad, feeling almost like she was on a playground. She was It, and this was a high-stakes game of tag. The other three dark dryads were now in full retreat. Seth staggered along behind Kendra.

The dryad Kendra was chasing kept stretching her lead, so Kendra paused to consider a better move. All around the cart, shadowy fairies were turning huge quantities of fairies dark. Kendra turned her attention elsewhere—fairies were too small and quick for her to lose time trying to touch them. The good dwarfs had caught up to the skirmish and were using their hammers to drop minotaurs. The dark side had reinforcements as well—goblins and dark dwarfs.

Increasingly, dark fairies were joining the battle to transform satyrs and hamadryads.

Seth grabbed Kendra's arm. "Trouble."

She saw the problem a moment after he said it. The fog giant who had been knocked unconscious had reawakened and was drowsily crawling toward them. Kendra had no idea how her light talisman would affect him since he was not in a darkened state—as with a goblin or a minotaur, darkness was simply part of his nature.

As Kendra started backing away, the giant sprang, diving at her with unavoidable quickness, his huge hand closing around her waist. Blinding light flared for an instant, and the giant flopped away from her, convulsing, unconscious once more, his smoking palm seared and blistered.

The flash of light left the surrounding dark creatures temporarily dazzled. Kendra dashed to where the darkened version of Broadhoof was trying to sink his teeth into Cloudwing. With a valiant effort, Cloudwing wrenched Broadhoof toward Kendra, and she slapped him on the flank. Instantly Broadhoof was restored.

Cloudwing showed Kendra a rapidly spreading maroon wound on his arm, and she healed it with a touch. "Remarkable," he approved.

The fighting continued, but the dark creatures were now doing their best to remain far from Kendra as they relentlessly transformed satyrs, dwarfs, and dryads. Hugo had the giant he had been brawling in a chokehold, and the tremendous brute finally collapsed. The three dryads Kendra had transformed were helping Patton, Lena, Coulter, and

Lizette fight off a group of dark hamadryads. Half of Patton's face was invisible, along with one hand.

Kendra and Seth raced to help, and the dark hamadryads withdrew, shifting their attention to easier prey.

Patton embraced Kendra, instantaneously becoming fully visible. "You're doing well, my dear, but the dark creatures are changing too many of our allies too quickly. We have to get to the tree before no allies remain."

"I know the way," offered the first dark dryad Kendra had transformed. "My name is Rhea."

"Hugo, Broadhoof, Cloudwing!" Patton called. The golem and the centaurs hurried to them. "Take us to the tree. We'll be following Rhea."

The two other dryads Kendra had transformed resolved to stay behind and help with the battle. Lizette, her autumnal robes torn, opted to accompany Rhea.

Broadhoof swung Kendra and Seth onto his back. Cloudwing bore Patton. Hugo picked up Coulter and Lena.

"Lead on," Cloudwing proposed.

Rhea and Lizette ran in front, with Broadhoof behind them, Hugo on one side, and Cloudwing on the other. Broadhoof cantered so smoothly that Kendra had no fear of falling. She held her pebble high, and dark creatures lunged out of the way to let them pass. Glancing back, Kendra saw the two dark centaurs and several dark dryads following them at a distance.

Moving with astonishing speed, Rhea dashed into the woods from which the dark creatures had emerged. The trees were dense, but there was little undergrowth. Kendra held tightly to the pebble as tall trunks sped by on either side.

Before long, they halted abruptly at the rim of a bowl-shaped valley. To Kendra, it looked like they were peering into a crater. A pool of sludge simmered in the middle of the deep depression, the steaming black surface occasionally disturbed by slow bubbles. The only plant in the rocky valley was a gnarled tree beside the lake of tar. Leafless and contorted, the tortured tree was even darker than the seething sludge.

The dryads jumped down the steep side of the valley, and the centaurs followed. Kendra leaned back, squeezing with her legs, her stomach in her throat, as Broadhoof plunged down the sheer slope, his hooves guiding their fall more than propelling them forward. The slope leveled out, and miraculously she and Seth remained astride the centaur, whose hooves now clopped noisily over the rocky ground.

From hiding places among boulders and cavities in the ground emerged three dark centaurs, four dark dryads, several armor-clad hobgoblins, and an obese cyclops wielding a poleax. The black tree was not far ahead—maybe fifty yards. But many dark creatures barred the way.

"Huddle close to Kendra!" Patton urged.

Cloudwing, Broadhoof, Rhea, Lizette, and Hugo skidded to a stop.

Hoofbeats sounded behind them as two dark centaurs plunged down the valley wall, accompanied by more dark dryads. "Her touch will undo your darkness," Stormbrow warned the others.

"Not mine," the fat cyclops bellowed.

"She'll burn you," Stormbrow cautioned. "Her touch overcame a giant."

The dark creatures stirred uncomfortably. The cyclops appeared uncertain.

"Have no fear," a cold, penetrating voice rang across the valley.

All eyes turned to the lip of the valley beyond the tormented tree, where a spectral woman bundled in shadow floated down from the rim, her robes flowing strangely, as if underwater.

"Oh, no," Seth breathed behind Kendra.

"The girl can do no lasting harm here," Ephira continued. "This is our domain. My darkness will quench her spark."

"Come no closer, Ephira," Patton shouted. "Do not interfere. We bring release from the bleak prison to which you have been confined."

Ephira gave a chilling, joyless laugh. "You should not have meddled here, Patton Burgess. I am not in need of rescue."

"That will not stop us," he replied in a softer voice.

"You cannot possibly imagine the depth of my power," she purred, gliding ever closer.

"Too much darkness can be blinding," Patton cautioned.

"As can too much light," she replied. She now floated protectively in front of the black tree.

"A fact you will soon appreciate as never before." Patton

nudged Cloudwing with his heels. "Onward! Hugo, flatten our opponents!"

Hugo set down Lena and Coulter and rushed the blubbery cyclops. The oaf embedded his poleax in Hugo's side before the golem seized him and hurled him into the lake of tar. Rhea and Lizette began battling dark dryads, driving them away from the centaurs. Hooves hammering the stony ground, Cloudwing and Broadhoof galloped forward, ramming enemies aside. Patton motioned for Broadhoof to loop around while he charged Ephira.

In order to impede both centaurs, the spectral woman glided sideways, dark tendrils of fabric flowing out in either direction. As soon as the fabric reached Cloudwing, his legs buckled and he crashed to the rocky ground, snapping his right foreleg and his right arm. Patton sprang free, rolling deftly to his feet. An instant later, limping awkwardly, Cloudwing arose, taller, thicker, his flesh maroon.

Another grasping fabric tentacle tangled around one of Broadhoof's front legs. Grunting, the centaur clattered to an abrupt stop. Sweating and groaning, Broadhoof swayed, but remained standing. He began to transform as Cloudwing had, but then the effect faded. Kendra felt the pebble warming her palm. Beneath her, Broadhoof felt warmer as well. Her hand glowed red. Brilliant beams of light escaped between her fingers. The creatures of darkness fell back. Broadhoof quivered beneath her, temporarily darkening and then returning to normal.

"Ephira can't change him," Seth whispered.

More tendrils of dark fabric snaked forward to entangle

the centaur. The stone was becoming uncomfortably hot. Ephira looked grimly focused. Broadhoof's breathing became increasingly rapid. He trembled, muscles clenched in anguish. Dimly Kendra was aware of Hugo wrestling with the dark creature Cloudwing had become.

Aware of the brightening pebble, Kendra opened her hand, flooding the area with harsh white luminance. The dark creatures retreated further, yowling, hands raised to their eyes. Ephira hissed, grasping Broadhoof with even more shadowy tentacles.

Hands balled into fists, tendons standing out on his thick neck, Broadhoof released a full-throated cry of agony. The centaur folded his legs and collapsed, slumping life-lessly to the earth. The stone no longer glowed. Broadhoof no longer breathed.

Ephira's flowing fabric slithered free from Broadhoof and reached for Kendra. Pushing away from the dead cen-taur, Kendra tried to avoid the fabric, but one serpentine ribbon brushed against her. The instant the fabric touched her, the stone flared brightly, and the length of fabric van-ished in a blaze of white flame.

Ephira shrieked and reeled as if she had been physically struck. The other tendrils of fabric retreated from Kendra and Seth.

"Kendra!" Patton called adamantly. "The stone!"

Patton stood not far from Ephira, considerably closer to the black tree than Kendra. Trusting his judgment, she tossed the stone to him and he caught it with both hands. Coulter and Lena were rushing to catch up to Patton. Hugo heaved the crippled, darkened Cloudwing into the lake of tar.

Scowling, Ephira raised a hand palm outward. Kendra felt a wave of fear wash over her, and noticed that both her skin and the stone that Patton held began to glow. She could feel the fear trying to take hold, but the emotion kept burning away before it could really penetrate. Lena and Coulter were no longer running. They stood immobilized, trembling. Coulter dropped to his knees.

Patton was also trembling. He took a few stiff steps. Flowing lengths of fabric reached out for him. Seth ran to him. Arriving an instant before the fabric, Seth seized Patton's hand.

Pinching the pebble between his thumb and forefinger, Patton touched the stone to the nearest fabric tentacle. With a fiery flash, the fabric disappeared.

Ephira screeched, once again retracting the other long strips of fabric. Coulter arose and Lena once again dashed forward toward Patton. Holding the pebble up menacingly, and keeping hold of Seth, Patton raced around Ephira. The shadowy woman glared at Patton with impotent rage, pivoting to follow him with her eyes.

Patton released Seth and gestured for him to return to Kendra. Seth hesitantly retreated. Ephira closed her eyes and raised both palms. Lena came to a stop again, and Kendra glowed brightly. Patton advanced as if weighed down. Paralysis seemed to be setting in, but he kept his legs plodding toward the tree. When he was within ten feet of the black tree he raised the hand with the pebble as if aiming a dart.

That was the first time Kendra noticed the nail near the base of the trunk. Ephira opened her eyes and howled. With a gentle motion, Patton tossed the pebble. It spun through the air on a perfect trajectory to ping against the nail. As the glowing pebble drew near, it abruptly changed course, soaring away sideways and bouncing over the rocky ground toward the lake of tar.

"What happened?" Seth yelled in disbelief.

"They repelled each other," Kendra moaned.

Dark fabric stretched from Ephira toward where Patton knelt hunched near the dark tree. Arms moving jerkily, Patton removed a small box from a pocket and opened it. Three fairies zipped out. A moment later the tendrils of fabric twined around Patton and he vanished.

Dark dryads and hobgoblins mobbed Hugo, hacking at him with swords and beating at him with cudgels, attempting to drive him into the tar. Hugo resisted them staunchly, occasionally landing a blow of his own.

The dark centaur Stormbrow galloped along the edge of the asphalt lake, clearly heading for the pebble. Shiara reached the stone first. When she touched it, her natural glow increased a hundredfold. Gleaming blindingly, she fell to the ground, apparently having fainted. The other two fairies attempted to lift the pebble and also passed out, shining with eye-watering brilliance.

Kendra and Seth ran toward the stone, even though they could see that the centaur would obviously beat them to it and that Ephira was blocking their way. Stormbrow lowered an arm and scooped up the pebble. He instantly shrank slightly, and his maroon flesh changed to a healthy, natural color. His horse fur became white dappled with gray.

Stormbrow immediately dropped the flashing stone as if he had picked up a hot ember.

"Stormbrow!" Kendra called, skidding to a stop near Lena. "We need the stone!"

Ephira glided toward the rejuvenated centaur, all her fabric tentacles groping for him. Wincing, he picked up the stone and tossed it a moment before the black tendrils seized him and made him dark again.

He threw the stone much too far. It flew over Kendra and Seth, skipping across the hard ground until it stopped near Coulter. Crawling as if carrying a great weight on his back, Coulter approached the egg-shaped stone. Ephira whirled and raised a palm. Coulter froze momentarily. Sweat beading on his brow, his face contorted with effort, he crawled forward unsteadily. When he could crawl no longer, he slithered on his belly. His arm inched forward until he finally grasped the stone. Trembling, he shifted his grip, cradling the pebble on his forefinger in front of his thumb, as if preparing to shoot it like a marble.

"Here!" Kendra called, waving her arms.

"Seth," Lena hissed, standing immobilized.

Seth took her hand. Freed to move, she ran with him toward the tree, sprinting so swiftly that he could hardly keep his feet on the ground.

With a hard flick of his thumb, Coulter shot the pebble.

The egg-shaped stone rattled across the ground, stopping a few yards short of Kendra. Cold eyes burning, Ephira floated toward the fallen stone. Kendra pounced on the pebble, picked it up, and turned to face the oncoming apparition.

Ephira spread her shadowy wrappings wide and extended her palms at Kendra. Kendra and the stone shone brightly. She felt the fear skimming across the surface of her body, but none of it could truly reach her. The sight of Ephira was horrific, everything Kendra had feared on that first night when she had seen the apparition through the attic window, but all Kendra cared about was getting the pebble to the nail.

Ephira drew closer, arms groping, fingers splayed. She would not use her fabric this time—she wanted direct physical contact.

Kendra felt fingers close around her ankle. Looking down, she saw Patton on his hands and knees, having invisibly crawled to her. His face looked drawn, as if all vitality had been sapped away. He held up a hand, silently offering to take the stone.

"Kendra!" Lena's clear voice called from behind Ephira. "Throw the pebble!"

Kendra could barely make out the former naiad beyond Ephira, glimpsed through rippling swaths of dark fabric, holding hands with Seth. There was no time to make a calm, reasoned choice. A few thoughts flashed through Kendra's mind at once. If Ephira touched her, the spectral woman might destroy the stone, leaving the matter of the nail and Kurisock irresolvable. Patton did not appear to be in any shape to reach the tree again, especially with Ephira in the way. He looked exhausted.

Kendra threw the pebble.

The toss was imperfect, but, lunging, Lena made the catch.

Ephira turned, intent on a new target.

Lena and Seth neared the black tree. As if sensing danger, the tree began to shudder. The branches creaked and swayed. A root lifted as if the tree hoped to run away.

Patton extended a feeble hand toward his wife. "No," he whispered. Kendra had never heard a word sound more forlorn, more defeated.

A few yards from the trunk, Lena shoved Seth away. She met Patton's gaze for a moment, her eyes tender, a half-smile on her lips, and sprang. Landing just shy of the nail, she scrambled forward jerkily, moving like a puppet with half of her strings cut. The trunk of the hideous tree bent slightly. Branches arched down to block her. Slowly, arduously, Lena's outstretched hand strained toward the trunk until the stone came into contact with the nail.

For an instant, all light and all shadow seemed drawn into those two objects, as if the world had imploded to a single point. And then a shock wave radiated outward, light and dark, hot and cold. The shock wave did not strike Kendra; it passed through her, momentarily stripping away all thought. Every particle of her body vibrated, especially her teeth and bones.

Silence followed.

Dimly, Kendra recovered her senses. Ephira crouched

before her, no longer spectral and inhuman, a frightened woman draped in black rags. Her lips parted as if to speak, but she uttered no sound. Her wide eyes blinked twice. Then the remnants of her black robes deteriorated, and her body aged until she dissolved into a cloud of dust and ash.

Beyond where Ephira had perished, the tree lay torn asunder, no longer unnaturally black, but rotten to the center. Near the tree, inert, lay a slimy, shadowy lump of mush. Only when she noticed teeth and claws did Kendra realize it must be what remained of Kurisock. Not far from the tree, Seth was sprawled on his back, stirring slightly. Lena lay facedown and motionless at the base of the trunk.

Behind Kendra, a restored Cloudwing clambered out of the lake of tar, hobbling on his injured leg, his body gooey with steaming sludge. Some distance away, the hobgoblins fled from the restored centaurs and dryads. Seth sat up, rubbing his eyes. Broadhoof remained lifeless where he had fallen.

Patton surged to his feet and staggered a few steps before tumbling to the stony ground. He rose again and fell again. Finally, clothes torn and smudged, he proceeded on hands and knees until he reached Lena, pulling her to him and cradling her in his arms, rocking her limp body as he clung to her, shoulders heaving.

CHAPTER TWENTY-FOUR

Good-byes

Two days later, Kendra reclined on her back behind a hedge in the yard, overhearing snatches of conversation from fairies. Around her, the garden was in full bloom, more splendid than ever, as if the fairies were attempting to apologize. She had overheard a few fairies lamenting the loss of their darkened state. From what Kendra had observed, only those creatures who had enjoyed being dark retained any memory of the experience.

Kendra heard the back door of the house open. Somebody else was coming to cheer her up. Why couldn't they leave her alone! They had all tried—Grandpa, Grandma, Seth, Warren, Tanu, Dale, even Coulter. Nothing anyone could say was going to erase her guilt for killing Lena. Sure, it had been a desperate situation, and yes, it may have been their best hope for success, but still, if she had not tossed Lena the stone, Lena would not have died.

Nobody called for her. She heard footsteps on the deck.

Why couldn't they treat her like Patton? He had wordlessly made it clear that he required time to grieve, and so nobody pestered him. He had taken Lena's body to the pond, arranged it tenderly inside a rowboat, set the craft ablaze, and watched it burn. That night he had slept under the stars. The next day, after they had discovered that the restored brownies had removed all the traps and repaired the house, Patton had spent most of his time alone in a bedroom. When he chose to mingle with the others, he was subdued. He did not bring up Lena, nor did anyone else.

Kendra was not entirely unhappy. She was immeasurably glad that some dryads had found Grandma, Grandpa, Warren, Dale, and Tanu caged deep in the woods, unharmed, beside an old stump. She was pleased that all the darkened creatures had been restored, that satyrs and dryads once again frolicked in the woods, and that the nipsies were back inside their hollow hill rebuilding their kingdoms. She felt relieved that Ephira was no longer a threat, that the plague had been vanquished, and that Kurisock had met his demise. She found it fitting that the demon should end up as an unrecognizable clump of shadowy pudding.

The cost of victory, along with the part she had played, was what prevented Kendra from actually rejoicing. Not only did she grieve for Lena and Broadhoof, she could not silence certain nagging questions. What if she had jumped off of Broadhoof before he had died, allowing him to be changed to darkness instead of trapping him between light and dark until the struggle killed him? What if she had courageously used the stone to drive Ephira back, and had gone on to destroy the nail herself?

"Kendra," said a slightly hoarse voice.

She sat up. It was Patton. His clothes remained torn, but he had washed them. "I didn't think I'd see you again."

He clasped his hands behind his back. "My three days are almost spent. I'll soon be whisked back to my proper time. I wanted to have words with you first."

That was right! He was leaving soon. Kendra suddenly remembered what she had meant to discuss with him before his departure. "The Sphinx," Kendra said hastily. "You might be able to prevent a lot of trouble, he's probably—"

He held up a finger. "I have already spoken with your grandfather on the subject. Not many minutes ago, in fact. I never did really trust the Sphinx, although if you think he is elusive now, you should try tracking him down in my day. I have met him only once, and it was no minor feat. In my time, many believe the Society of the Evening Star is gone for good. From afar, the Sphinx has been very kind to us caretakers. It would be difficult to find him, and harder still to rally support against him. I'll see what I can do."

Kendra nodded. She stared at the grass, mustering courage. She looked up, tears making her vision shimmer. "Patton, I'm so sorry—"

Again he held up a finger to silence her. "Say no more. You were magnificent."

"But if I—"

He wagged his finger. "No, Kendra, you had no other choice."

"And Broadhoof," Kendra muttered.

"None of us could have seen that coming," Patton said. "We were contending with unexplored powers."

"People around me keep dying," Kendra whispered.

"You're thinking about it all backwards," Patton said firmly. "Around you, people who should have died live on. Shadows return to light. You and Lena saved us all. I would rather it had been me, I would give anything, anything, but such wishing is futile."

"Are you okay?"

He exhaled sharply, half-laugh, half-sob. He brushed a finger across his mustache. "I try not to relive how I might have destroyed the nail myself instead of throwing the pebble. I try not to obsess about failing my bride." He paused, muscles pulsing in his jaw. "I must go forward. I have a new errand. A fresh quest. To love Lena for the rest of her life as much as she deserves. To never again doubt her love or mine. To give her my whole self, every day, without fail. To keep secret how her life will end, while forever honoring her sacrifice. I am in a unique position, to have lost her, and yet to have her still."

Kendra nodded, trying to restrain her tears for his sake. "You'll have a long, happy life together."

"I expect we will," Patton said. Smiling warmly, he reached out a hand to pull her up. "If I am done grieving, it is time for you to quit as well. It was a deadly predicament.

We all should have perished. You made the necessary decision."

Others had assured Kendra of that very thing. Only as she heard the words from Patton did she sincerely believe it might be true.

He pulled her to her feet. "Your ride is here."

"My ride?" Kendra asked. "Already?" They walked toward the deck.

"It will be noon before long," Patton said. "I overheard him saying he bears news. I did not let him see me."

"You think I should go home?" Kendra asked.

"Your grandparents are right," he assured her. "It is the best option. You cannot be kept from your parents any longer. You will be under constant watch by concerned friends—at home, at school, wherever you go."

Kendra nodded vaguely. Patton stopped at the steps to the deck. "Won't you come inside?" Kendra urged.

"I'm returning to the pond one last time," Patton said. "I already said my farewells to the others."

"Then this is it."

"Not entirely," Patton said. "I had a private conversation with Vanessa this morning. I temporarily put one of the goblins into the Quiet Box. She is a hard woman—I failed to break her. I believe she has useful information. At some point, if all else fails, you might consider bargaining with her. But do not trust her. I told Stan the same."

"Okay."

"I understand you discovered my Journal of Secrets," Patton said.

"That was yours? Not much in it."

Patton smiled. "Kendra, I'm disappointed. You know, it was your grandfather who wrote 'Drink the Milk,' not me. All of my words in the journal are written in the secret fairy language, in umite wax."

"Umite wax?" Kendra thumped her palm against her forehead. "I never thought to try that. I learned about the wax a year after I stopped paying attention to the journal."

"Well, pay attention to the journal. Not all of my secrets are in there, but you will find some that may prove useful. And I'll be sure to keep adding to it. The troubled times are far from over for you and your family. I'll do what I can from my own era."

"Thanks, Patton." It was comforting to think she would hear from him again through the journal, and to know he might find ways to help her.

"I'm glad we met, Kendra." He gave her a tight hug. "You are truly extraordinary—it goes far beyond anything fairies could bestow. Keep an eye on that brother of yours. If he doesn't get himself killed, he might save the world one day."

"I will. I'm glad we met too. 'Bye, Patton."

He turned and jogged away, glancing back once to wave. Kendra watched him until he disappeared into the woods.

Taking a deep breath, Kendra crossed the deck and entered through the back door. "Happy birthday!" numerous voices shouted.

It took Kendra a moment to make sense of the huge

cake with fifteen candles. Her birthday was still more than a month away.

Grandpa, Grandma, Seth, Dale, Tanu, and Coulter all broke into song. Newel and Doren were there as well, adding boisterous harmonies. Dougan was also present, singing softly. So he would be their escort home. At the end of the song, Kendra blew out the tiny flames. Grandma snapped a photograph.

"It won't be my birthday for weeks!" Kendra scolded.

"That's what I told them," Seth laughed. "But they wanted to do it now since they won't be around for the actual day."

Kendra smiled at her friends and family. She suspected the celebration had more to do with her recent moodiness than it did with marking the day she was born. She smiled. "That is one advantage of holding a birthday party more than a month early—you totally surprised me! Thanks."

Seth leaned close. "Did Patton cheer you up?" he whispered. "He promised he would."

"He did."

Seth shook his head. "That guy can do anything!"

"I heard Dougan has news," Kendra said.

"It can wait," Dougan said. "I hate to interrupt the happy occasion. Gavin sends his best, by the way. He's out on assignment, or he would have joined me to escort you home."

"If you make me wait for the news I'll just be wondering about it the whole time," Kendra maintained.

"I agree," Seth seconded.

Dougan shrugged. "Stan knows some of this already, but given your level of involvement, I may as well inform all of you. Or perhaps I should say most of you." He paused, eying Newel and Doren.

"My finely tuned social weather vane is detecting a hint," Newel said.

"Maybe we should remove ourselves for a few minutes," Doren suggested. "Discuss a few secrets of our own."

The two satyrs headed out of the room.

"Big secrets," Newel emphasized. "The kind of secrets that keep you up late at night gnawing at your fingernails."

"Secrets that would curl your hair," Doren agreed.

Dougan waited until the satyrs were well out of the room, then proceeded in a low tone. "The Sphinx is a traitor. I'm sorry, Warren, when I lied to you about him not being Captain of the Knights of the Dawn. I had vowed to guard that secret. At the time I still thought it was worth protecting."

"How did you confirm his treachery?" Warren asked.

"I conferred with my fellow Lieutenants about the artifact recovered from Fablehaven. None had heard of the incident—a severe breech of protocol. The four of us confronted the Sphinx, prepared to apprehend him. He made no protest as we named the suspicious circumstances, then arose slowly and told us he was disappointed it had taken us so long to suspect him. He picked up a copper rod from his desk and vanished, replaced by a burly man who instantly threw the rod out the window, transformed into a massive grizzly bear, and attacked. Fighting the werebear in such close quarters was dicey. Travis Wright was seriously wounded. Rather than try to take our enemy captive, we were forced to slay the beast. By the time we started hunting for the Sphinx, he was nowhere to be found."

"Then it's true," Coulter murmured, sounding crestfallen. "The Sphinx is our great enemy."

"And it's my fault he escaped!" Kendra exclaimed. "I restored the power of that rod he used to teleport away!"

Grandpa shook his head. "If he had not had the rod, the Sphinx would have had other exit strategies."

"What about Mr. Lich, his bodyguard?" Seth wondered.

"Mr. Lich had not been seen for days, and has not yet resurfaced," Dougan reported.

"Now that the Sphinx has made his true allegiance known, he may hasten his plans," Grandma said. "We'll have to be ready for anything."

"There is additional worrisome news," Grandpa prompted.

Dougan frowned. "Lost Mesa has fallen. So far as we know, only Hal and his daughter, Mara, survived."

"What happened?" Kendra gasped.

"Hal related the tale," Dougan said. "First, a young coppery dragon got free from the labyrinth inside the mesa and used lightning attacks on the main house. Then, several of the skeletons inside the museum on the property came to life and launched their own assault. An enormous dragon skeleton caused the most notable harm—most likely reanimated by a powerful viviblix. A few dozen zombies got loose as well. Like here at Fablehaven, somebody wanted to close the preserve permanently. At Lost Mesa, the plot succeeded."

"Like Vanessa told us," Kendra murmured, "when the Sphinx commits a crime, he burns down the neighborhood to cover his tracks."

"We left that dragon trapped inside the mesa," Warren said. "We locked it ourselves."

"I know," Dougan said. "Sabotage."

"Is there reason to suspect Hal or Mara?" Warren asked.

"Some suspicion must fall on the survivors of any such calamity," Dougan said. "But they made contact with us voluntarily, and their grief over Rosa and the others seemed sincere. If you ask me, the culprit remains nameless."

"Or he's named after an Egyptian monument," Seth said bitterly.

Dougan dipped his chin. "True, the Sphinx probably masterminded the assault, but we remain uncertain who executed his orders."

"After taking what he wanted from Fablehaven and Lost Mesa, he tried to wipe out both preserves," Kendra said numbly.

"He failed here," Grandma said, "as he is destined to fail in the end."

Kendra wished the words sounded less hollow.

"We are doing what we can," Dougan said. "Keeping two pairs of eyes on Kendra and Seth through the coming months will be a major priority. Oh, Kendra, before I forget, Gavin asked me to give you this letter." He held out a gray, speckled envelope.

"Happy birthday to you!" Seth exclaimed, his voice full of implications.

Kendra tried not to blush as she tucked the envelope away.

"Dear Kendra," Seth improvised, "you're the only girl who really gets me, you know, and I think you're very mature for your age—"

"What about some cake?" Grandma interrupted, holding the first piece out to Kendra and glaring at Seth.

Kendra accepted the cake and sat down at the table, grateful for the opportunity to compose herself. She discovered that the cake had been prepared by brownies. Cutting into it she found creamy layers of vanilla filling, moist patches of chocolate mousse, gooey pockets of caramel, and an occasional clump of raspberry jam. Somehow the flavors never conflicted disagreeably. She could not recall a more delicious birthday cake.

Afterwards, Grandpa escorted Kendra up to the attic. She found her bags packed and ready.

"Your parents are expecting Dougan to deliver you this evening," he said. "They'll be happy to see you. I think they were on the verge of calling the FBI."

"Okay."

"Patton said good-bye?" he asked.

"Yes," Kendra said. "He told me something important about the Journal of Secrets."

"He mentioned I was to entrust it to you. You'll find the journal in your bags, along with a few other birthday presents. Kendra, we're going to keep the discovery of the

Chronometer a secret for now, even from Dougan, until we become more certain whom we can trust."

"I like that idea," Kendra said. She stared into Grandpa's eyes. "I'm scared to go home."

"After all that has happened, I would think you would be more scared to stay here."

"I'm not sure I want the Knights of the Dawn looking after me. They all might be working for our enemies!"

"Either Warren, Coulter, or Tanu will always be one of your guardians. I will only allow the most trustworthy eyes to watch over you."

"I guess that makes me feel better."

Seth burst into the room, followed by Dale. "Dougan says he's all set. Warren is coming with us. You ready, Kendra?"

She did not feel ready. After a great loss, after a difficult victory, after suffering extreme trauma, she wished she could have some time to hibernate. Not two days. Two years. Some serious time to pull herself together. Why did life always have to roll relentlessly forward? Why was every victory or defeat followed by new worries and new problems? Adjusting to high school would be hard enough, let alone worrying about what new plots the Sphinx might be hatching and how Navarog, the demon prince, might factor into them.

Despite her uncertainties, Kendra nodded. Grandpa and Dale grabbed her luggage, and she followed them down the attic stairs. In the hallway, Coulter motioned for her to come inside his room. He shut the door behind her.

"What is it?" Kendra asked.

He held up the staff with the rattles she had brought back from Lost Mesa. "Kendra, have you any idea what this can do?"

"It seemed to make the storm worse on Painted Mesa."

He shook his head. "Magical artifacts are my specialty, but in all my years, I have encountered few that could match the power of this staff. I experimented with it yesterday. After shaking it outdoors for less than fifteen minutes, I summoned clouds into what had been a clear sky. The more I shook the rattles, the more the weather intensified."

"Wow."

"You brought home an authentic, functional rain stick from Lost Mesa."

Kendra smiled. "Gavin called it my souvenir."

"Gavin must be a very generous person. An item of this magnitude is absolutely priceless. Take good care of it."

"I will," Kendra said, accepting the staff. "Should I leave it here?"

"It's yours; keep it with you. Who knows when it might be useful? There is plenty of trouble on the horizon."

"Thanks, Coulter. See you soon."

"Count on it. I'll be taking a shift to watch over you and Seth before long."

Kendra exited the room and went down the stairs to the entry hall. Grandpa and Dale had already lugged the bags outside. In the doorway, Seth dropped his emergency kit. It seemed to land with an unusually heavy clunk. Looking guilty, he picked up the box hurriedly and went out the door.

Finding herself alone for a moment, Kendra pulled out the envelope, tore it open, and removed the letter from Gavin. She unfolded the single sheet of paper, trying not to feel eager, trying to forget the stupid things Seth had guessed it might contain.

> *Dear Kendra,*
>
> *I'm very sorry I can't be there to escort you home. Crazy news from Dougan, huh? I can hardly believe how upside down everything has become! I knew there was something shady about good guys wearing masks . . . they've done away with them now.*
>
> *I'm off on another mission. Nothing as dangerous as what we went through together, but another chance for me to prove myself useful. I'll fill you in later.*
>
> *Guess why I like letters? No stuttering!*
>
> *You're an amazing person, Kendra. I want you to know how much I have appreciated getting to know you. Hopefully I'll get a turn standing guard over you and your brother in the fall. I hope someday soon we'll get to know each other better.*
>
> *Your friend and admirer,*
> *Gavin*

Kendra reread the letter, then triple-checked the part about her being amazing and him wanting to get to know her better. He didn't just sign it "your friend." It was "your friend *and admirer*."

With a smile tugging at the corners of her mouth, Kendra folded up the letter, slipped it into her pocket, and walked out the front door, marveling at how fine a line divided dreading the future from looking forward to it.

The world's greatest
adventurer was here!

THE ADVENTURE WILL
CONTINUE IN BOOK FOUR

Secrets of the Dragon Sanctuary

Acknowledgments

I love writing the final words of a novel. It feels like a miracle when a story that resided abstractly in my mind finally takes concrete form. The months required to translate ideas into words culminate in a huge rush of satisfaction as I finish the initial writing phase and can then transition to polishing the narrative. Regardless of the imperfections in the first draft, I find it a vast relief to know that the story exists outside of my imagination.

Many people have contributed to making the third Fablehaven novel a reality. My understanding wife and children not only help me find time to write and promote my novels—they make the rest of my life worth living. The initial feedback I get from my wife routinely helps shape my ideas and my writing for the better.

Early readers who provided feedback include my wife, Mary, Chris Schoebinger, Emily Watts, Tucker Davis, Pamela and Gary Mull, Summer Mull, Bryson and Cherie Mull, Nancy Fleming, Randy and Liz Saban, Mike Walton, Wesley Saban, Jason and Natalie Conforto, and the Freeman family. Ty Mull had every intention of helping, but high school and video games interfered. My sister Tiffany was excused from contributing, since she is busy in Brazil.

Once again, Brandon Dorman created awesome art. The sweet centaur he drew for the cover had my inner ten-year-old high-fiving himself. Richard Erickson oversaw the design elements, Emily Watts kept me honest as editor, and Laurie Cook was the typographer. I'm grateful for their valuable contributions!

I owe much appreciation to the marketing team at Shadow Mountain, led by Chris Schoebinger, along with Gail Halladay, Patrick Muir, Angie Godfrey, Tiffany Williams, MaryAnn Jones, Bob Grove, and Roberta Stout. Once again, my sister Summer Mull coordinated my tour and traveled with me as I visited schools to do assemblies about reading and creating. I am deeply grateful for her help and companionship. I also want to thank Boyd Ware and the sales team, Lee Broadhead, John Rose, and Lonnie Lockhart, along with all the folks at Shadow Mountain who work so effectively to get my books into the readers' hands.

As I've traveled the country visiting schools, libraries, and bookstores, many kind people have opened their homes to me. Thanks go out to the Bagby family in California, the McCalebs in Idaho, the Goodfellows in Oregon, the Adams family in Maryland, the Novicks in California, Colleen and John in Missouri, the Flemings in Arizona, the Panos clan in California, the MacDonalds in Nevada, the Browns in Montana, the Millers in Virginia, the Wirigs in Ohio, the folks at Monmouth College, and Gary Mull in Connecticut. Special thanks go to Robert Marston Fanney, author of *Luthiel's Song,* who helped spread the word online.

I haven't thanked Nick Jacob in an acknowledgment. He was one of my best friends in high school, and often took the time to read the junk I was writing back then. His feedback and encouragement were important to my formative years as a writer.

Thank you, dear reader, for continuing to digest the *Fablehaven* series. I'm already working on the fourth book. If you're enjoying the story, please tell others about it. Your personal recommendations make a big difference!

Swing by BrandonMull.com to find out more about me and my books.

Reading Guide

1. Throughout the *Fablehaven* series, obedience has been an issue for Seth. What do you think Seth has learned about obedience since the first book? How is he more obedient in this book? How is he disobedient?

2. The Knights of the Dawn value members with special abilities. What abilities set you apart from others?

3. At Lost Mesa, Hal wants to protect the zombies even though they are disgusting and freaky. Do you agree with him? Why or why not? We have many types of dangerous, unsightly, and annoying animals in our world. Do you think it's important to protect even creepy animals from extinction? Why or why not?

4. For most of the book, an infectious shadow plague affected the creatures of Fablehaven. Have you ever seen evidence that evil can be contagious? Explain.

5. Grandpa Sorenson did not hold the creatures of Fablehaven responsible for their behavior while under the influence of the plague, nor did he fully blame dark creatures for their actions. What thinking led to those conclusions? Why did Warren disagree? What evidence is there to support both positions?

6. Do you agree with Grandpa that all humans have potential for good and evil? How do our choices define who we are?

7. Many characters have assisted Kendra and Seth during risky situations (including Grandpa, Grandma, Dale, Lena, Tanu, Coulter, Warren, Gavin, Dougan, and Patton). If you were in trouble, which of those characters would you most want on your side? Why?

8. On the roof of the old manor, Patton told Seth, "When jumping is the sole option, you jump." What did he mean? How does Patton exemplify this idea? Can you think of a time when you did something difficult because it was necessary?

9. Why was Lena willing to sacrifice herself at the end of the story? What did that sacrifice do for her relationship with Patton? How can selfless sacrifice strengthen any relationship?

10. Unbelief prevents Kendra's parents from perceiving the creatures at Fablehaven. In what ways can unbelief blind us to the possibilities around us?

11. If you could see in the dark like Kendra, smell any scent like a goblin, or maneuver as swiftly as a dryad, which

would you choose? Why? How would you use this gift to your advantage?

12. If you were forty years old and were confined to the Quiet Box for fifty years and then released, you would still be forty years old. Suppose you had a child who was ten years old when you entered the Quiet Box. How old would that child be when you came out? Would you treat your child differently? How? How do you think your child would treat you? Why?

13. If you could spend a day at Fablehaven with Kendra and Seth, what is the first thing you would want to see? Who is the first person or creature you'd like to meet?

14. What would you do if Seth tried to coax you into the woods without Grandpa's permission?

15. As far as personality goes, how would you describe the centaurs? The dryads? The fairies? What are their strengths? What are their weaknesses? Which of those strengths and weaknesses do you have?